Erin Kaye was born in 1966 in Larne, Co Antrim to a Polish-American father and an Anglo-Irish mother. She pursued a successful career in finance before becoming a writer. Her previous bestselling novels include *Mothers and Daughters* (2003), *Choices* (2004), *Second Chances* (2005) and *Closer to Home* (2006) – all published by Poolbeg Press. She lives in North Berwick on the east coast of Scotland with her husband Mervyn, two young sons and Murphy the dog.

You can find out more about Erin Kaye and her books at **www.erinkaye.com**

Also by Erin Kaye

Closer to Home
Second Chances
Choices
Mother's and Daughters

All published by Poolbeg

For Liz and Tom

One

"I'm warning you, Chris, that Bernie Sweeney's up to something," said Karen Magill, throwing the comment down on the distressed oak table in her sister's kitchen like a gauntlet. She put the rim of a large wine glass to her red lips, wet them with the honey-coloured liquid and stared at her younger sister, waiting for a reaction.

"Oh Karen, don't be so dramatic," said Chris, trying not to rise to the bait. "She's only coming to Ireland for a long holiday. What's so sinister about that?"

"I'll tell you what's sinister," said Karen, lifting her right arm to stab the air, the silver charms on her bracelet jangling like bells. She wore a fashionable slit-sleeve top in a rich royal blue that did not flatter her rather plump upper arms, but nevertheless she cut a glamorous figure with her long black suede skirt, wide studded belt and tasteful costume jewellery. Her hair was expertly highlighted and her face well made up.

"You've hardly heard from her since you both left school nearly twenty years ago," continued Karen, "and suddenly she's on the phone and e-mailing you like you're long-lost buddies. And the next thing she's inviting herself to stay in your home for a month."

1

"So what? She's coming all the way from Australia and she needs somewhere to stay," said Chris defensively, as the thought crept into her mind that maybe, just maybe, Karen was right. Maybe Bernie was just using her. "Anyway, she didn't invite herself. I asked her," she added firmly, deciding to dismiss her sister's concerns.

She preferred to think that Bernie was looking up her old school pal for all the right reasons – like wanting to rekindle their friendship, to reminisce about their shared past growing up in Ballyfergus, their first clumsy forays into drink and discovering the opposite sex. Always the Plain Jane at school, the clever swot few noticed, Chris wanted to believe that Bernie had got in touch because she actually liked her ...

Suddenly from upstairs came the pounding of music – the Arctic Monkeys probably. Not that Chris would know their music from any other racket but, according to sixteen-year-old Finn, they were the coolest band on earth. His room was directly above the kitchen and, in spite of Castlerock's thick one-hundred-year-old walls, the music still penetrated every room in the house. Chris felt a headache coming on and briefly pressed the middle of her brow with the index finger on her right hand.

"If he doesn't turn off that flippin' music ..." she began, and placed both palms on the table as she prepared to rise from her seat.

Just then the kitchen door burst open and Chris's eldest child, Hannah, came in. She was wearing tiny earphones in her ears, connected to an iPod clipped to her low-slung slouch jeans. She wore several messy layers of clothes and Chris wished she would make more of her slim figure and pretty oval-shaped face which was encased in a thick layer of heavy make-up, her eyes blackened with kohl. It was hard to believe that, underneath all that muck, they were practically mirror images of each other. Hannah's curly auburn hair – which she inherited from her mother along with her green eyes – was scrunched up into a fuzzy bush at the top of her head and a diamond stud glistened menacingly in her delicate right nostril.

She opened the fridge without so much as a glance in the direction of the two women and Chris said, "Hannah."

No reaction.

"Hannah!" she said again in a loud voice.

"Uhh?" said Hannah, removing the plug from her right ear and frowning a little at her mother.

"It would be polite to say hello to your Auntie Karen," said Chris, more sarcastically than she'd intended. As soon as she'd said it she hated herself. She sounded just like her own mum and she'd always sworn she would never turn into her mother. Nowadays, it seemed, she was doing just that.

"Oh, hi, Karen," said Hannah, sounding like the act of opening her mouth to speak required enormous effort.

"Hi, Han," said Karen, apparently not in the least put out by the omission of 'Auntie' and the lack of respect this implied to Chris. "What're you up to?"

"Oh, just chilling with the girls. Watching TV," said Hannah, with a nonchalant toss of her head in the direction of the doorway. The sound of the TV could be heard from the family room along the hall.

"Hannah, could you do me a favour, please?" said Chris. "Could you tell that brother of yours to turn down the music or I'll come up and turn it off."

"I'll tell him," sighed Hannah, "but it won't do any good. He's showing off in front of his mates. Anyway, he never listens to me."

Hannah left the room with a clutch of probiotic drinks in one hand and a multipack of cheese and onion crisps in the other – the good thereby cancelling out the bad – at least that was Hannah's skewed philosophy on healthy eating.

Chris slumped back in her chair. "I don't know which is worse – him," she said, raising her eyes to the ceiling, "or her," she glanced at the door through which Hannah had just exited. She fingered the stem of the wine glass in front of her and thought fleetingly of how, in spite of three comfortable reception rooms to choose from, she always ended up sitting around the kitchen table drinking tea or more often, given her husband Paul's extensive and discerning cellar, very good wine. And the comfortably furnished lounge, family room and snug were, more often than not, occupied by gangly teenagers.

But the welcoming kitchen with its burr oak units, retro Smeg fridge-freezer and cream Britannia range cooker really was the heart of this home and the place where Chris felt most comfortable. In the corner by the bay window was an old squishy armchair in which she liked to curl up with a favourite book – when she got the chance – for Murphy the Border Terrier puppy had claimed it as his own and Chris usually didn't have the heart to oust him. He was in it now on his back fast asleep, exhausted from tearing round the garden all afternoon. His little fat belly, pink under straw-coloured hair, rose and fell gently with every breath.

The sound of the music miraculously quietened and Chris looked at the ceiling.

Karen put her hand, two fingers of which sported over-sized sparkly rings, on Chris's arm. "The day'll come when they've both left home and the house'll be as quiet as a morgue," she observed, sounding like a sage – a role, as the elder sister, she often played.

"I wish."

"And," Karen went on, ignoring the interruption, "you'll remember these days and wish them back again."

Chris took a long drink from the glass in front of her and said crisply, "I find that hard to believe."

Karen tutted, almost inaudibly, and said, "What is wrong with you, Chris? Did you get out the wrong side of bed this morning?"

"I'm sorry," said Chris, letting go of a little of the tension that had been building up all day. "I just feel a little bit stressed out at the moment. I didn't appreciate how involved and time-consuming this campaign against Tesda supermarket was going to be, and work's crazy with Bob's retirement coming up and the new management team in place from Monday. I don't know what to expect. And there's Murphy, of course," she added, glancing at the grizzly little body in the corner and smiling involuntarily. "I love him to bits but he's still a fair bit of work. I can't leave him alone for a minute or he's chewing everything."

"And now you've got Bernie Sweeney arriving in just a few days."

"Well, much as I'm looking forward to seeing her, yes, I suppose that is added pressure."

"Your problem, Chris," said Karen, leaning her plump arm on the table while she took a deep slug of wine, "is that you don't know how to say 'no'."

"But how could I?" said Chris, knowing full well that Karen was right but not willing to admit it. She was constantly under pressure, most of it self-imposed as the result of taking on board more than she could reasonably handle. She wasn't very good at putting herself first. But it was more, much more, than that. She kept herself busy to keep the melancholy that nipped at her well-shod heels like an untrained puppy, at bay. It had been with her for a long time, years rather than months, and sometimes it threatened to consume her. And because she wasn't entirely sure what the cause of that unhappiness was, she preferred not to dwell on it.

So now she did as she always did, she pushed those gloomy thoughts to the back of her mind and said, "The woman's only coming halfway round the world to see me. I couldn't just put her out on the street, now could I?"

"Hmm, I suppose not," said Karen, and she pursed her lips and stared at Chris for a few moments. "But what I can't understand is why she can't stay with one of her brothers?"

"I'm not sure. She hinted in an e-mail that they weren't on good terms and I didn't like to pry. She said that if it was okay and it wasn't too much bother, she'd rather stay with me."

"And what's wrong with the Marine Hotel?"

"Oh, I don't know, Karen. I imagine it would be too expensive to stay in a hotel for a month." She paused then and added, "You never did like Bernie Sweeney, did you?"

"Well, you can hardly blame me. She stole my boyfriend," Karen said flatly and folded her arms across her chest.

"What?" said Chris and then she laughed. She ran the fingers of her right hand through her thick hair and said, "Do you mean Kenny Maguire? Sure you only went out with him for a couple of weeks. You're not still bitter about that, are you?"

"No, I'm not bitter," said Karen evenly, "but it just goes to show you the sort of person she is. Not to be trusted. And she'd rather freeload off you and Paul than pay her way."

"Now, Karen," said Chris, truly stung, "I don't think you're being fair. Bernie is my oldest and dearest friend."

"Is she?"

"Well, she was. And just because we've drifted apart over the last few years doesn't mean that we're not still friends. You know what it's like when you have a family. You don't have the time to keep up with everyone and with Bernie never marrying or having children, I guess we didn't have much in common for a while."

"You know what the trouble is with you?" said Karen, not unkindly, without pausing for an answer. "It's that you're always so determined to find the good in people."

"And what's wrong with that?"

"Nothing really," said Karen after a thoughtful pause. "Except that sometimes you're too trusting. People take advantage of you." Then she brightened suddenly and said, "Though I suppose it's miles better than being like me. I'm too cynical. And I'm not sure that's a good thing."

"Well, I don't know if being as naïve as I am is a good thing either."

"I didn't say you were naïve. Sure you're an intelligent woman and a fully qualified solicitor."

"Being bright doesn't make you street-wise. And I'm as naïve as a forty-year-old wife and mother can be. I know I am, especially when it comes to judging people," she said wryly. "That's why I chose to specialise in property conveyancing! If truth be told, I prefer dealing with bricks and mortar than people."

"Oh, but you're great with clients! They love you."

"Maybe. But I'm at my most comfortable dealing with hard facts and figures rather than complex and sometimes unfathomable human emotions. I guess, basically, I don't understand people very well." Chris sighed, looking at the base of her wine-glass.

"I think you're being a little hard on yourself," said Karen kindly.

Chris smiled. Then suddenly she thought of her husband Paul and the smile fell from her face. Was her unhappiness a cause of their relationship problems or was it, rather, a symptom of a marriage gone stale? Was it her lack of – of understanding, of empathy, that had caused the gulf between them? It was as though they were on the opposite sides of a huge chasm, too wide to enable them to communicate meaningfully with each other. So many of their conversations these days revolved around trivia. She couldn't remember the last time they talked about how much they loved each other or showed each other true kindness. They seemed to be locked into a pattern of terse comments and low-level bickering. But what was to be done about it? How could she repair that gulf? She didn't know how.

"Chris?" said Karen, bringing Chris out of her reverie. "Are you all right?"

"Yes, I'm fine," she said, forcing a bright smile, too reserved – or was it proud? – to confide these dark thoughts even to her sister.

There was a brief silence and then Karen asked, "And how does Paul feel about Bernie coming to stay?"

"Oh, you know Paul," said Chris lightly. "He's so easy-going he doesn't mind at all. He loves people popping in and coming to stay and the house always being full of kids. Drives me mad."

"It's good though, him being like that. It means the kids want to bring their friends home. And they're better here where at least you know what they're up to."

"Yes, you're absolutely right, Karen. And I do like it too – most of the time anyway."

"Can't see Tony being so accommodating when our two are grown," said Karen thoughtfully, referring to her son Jack, who had just turned seven, and four-year-old Chloe.

"Mmm. I imagine it would be a bit like a busman's holiday," observed Chris of her brother-in-law, who was headmaster of St Patrick's Secondary School. "Having spent all day with teenage kids he'll hardly want them sitting round his house all evening too!"

Noticing that her sister's glass was nearly empty, Chris lifted the bottle of wine out of the cooler and held the neck over Karen's glass.

Karen put her hand over the rim, glanced at the kitchen wall clock, and said rather half-heartedly, "No more for me, thanks. I'd better not."

"Are you sure?"

"Well . . . Oh, go on then. I can always get a taxi."

"I'm sure Paul will run you home when he gets in."

"Where is he?"

"He's on a night out – it's Sol Glover's retirement do."

"Oh, he's retiring at last, is he?"

"Not before time, I hear," said Chris. "He was starting to make mistakes. Prescribed some poor old dear the wrong tablets for high blood pressure. If the pharmacist hadn't noticed, well, God knows what might have happened.

9

Anyway, you know Paul never drinks at these things. He hates cheap wine. So I'm sure he'll run you home."

"That'd be great. I'll need to watch though," said Karen, taking a sip from her glass. "I'll have to get up early. Tony's got a school football match tomorrow morning at Tillysburn Park in Belfast."

Chris topped up her own glass and said, "I didn't know Tony had to go to football matches on Saturdays. Isn't that the games teacher's role?"

"It is, but this year the under-sixteens have done really well. They're in the final of the Senior Cup and Tony's got to show face. So an early start tomorrow. And of course there's my little darlings too."

"How are they?" said Chris, picturing with fondness her gorgeous little niece and nephew. It was hard sometimes to believe that her two surly and uncommunicative teenagers were once so innocent and adorable. She loved them to bits of course but the cuteness of childhood had long worn off. She couldn't help but long for those days when they placed her on a pedestal and their world revolved around her. How precious those times had been.

"Oh, they're great. It's just that they don't know the meaning of the words 'lie in'. Oh, I forgot to tell you," Karen was suddenly animated, "Jack lost his first tooth last night at teatime."

"The wee soul! That tooth's been wobbly for ages, hasn't it?" laughed Chris. "He told me about it weeks ago."

Karen nodded. "Well, he was just sitting there and he put his hand out and there it was in his palm. Tiny as a seed pearl."

"Did it bleed?"

"Not much."

"Oh, bless. Here," said Chris and she delved into her handbag which happened to be slung over the back of the adjacent chair and pulled out a five-pound note. She pressed it into Karen's hand and said, "Give that to him and tell him it's from Auntie Chris's Tooth Fairy."

"That's far too much, Chris!"

"No, it's not," tutted Chris, remembering the many kindnesses Karen had shown Hannah and Finn when they were little and she and Paul didn't have the money they had now. They'd married whilst still at Queen's University where Paul had studied Medicine and she Law and Hannah came along not long afterwards. Karen had met Tony much later in life and hadn't started her family until she was well into her thirties.

"He's already had two pounds off Tony and me – sorry, the Tooth Fairy," said Karen with a grin and then she added, "That's the going rate for the first tooth, apparently, and one pound for each one thereafter."

"That's inflation for you. In our day it was ten pence, wasn't it?"

"That's right. Well, thank you very much, Chris. At this rate he's going to have more money than me!"

"If he does as well as you, Karen, he'll be doing all right."

Karen raised her eyebrows noncommittally.

"How are things going at the nursery?" asked Chris. Karen was owner and manager of Wee Stars, one of Ballyfergus's two private children's nurseries.

"Good. I've finally put those staffing problems behind me and things are ticking over nicely. Yep," she said, nodding, "It's good."

"So what's your next project?"

Karen shrugged. "I don't have one."

"Don't give me that," said Chris good-humouredly. "You always have a project on the go, Karen. You're never content with the status quo."

Karen's face went a little pink and she readjusted the belt around her waist.

"What?" said Chris, looking at her sister's waistline. "What is it?"

"Promise you won't tell anyone? And I mean anyone," said Karen rather sternly.

"Of course. Cross my heart and hope to die," said Chris, as the tingling thrill that only a shared intimacy can induce ran through her veins. She took a quick slug of wine and waited, wide-eyed, not knowing what to expect. Was Karen pregnant? Or had she decided to sell up, buy another nursery, change career? Nothing would surprise her about her dynamic sister.

"Well," said Karen, "I've been thinking about this a lot recently and my next project is going to be me."

Chris screwed her face into a frown. "What d'you mean, 'me'?"

"Precisely that. Me. Karen Susan Magill. Businesswoman, wife, mother."

Chris waited for her sister to go on, not understanding.

"I want to change the way I am, Chris."

"I don't follow," said Chris shaking her head.

"The way I look."

"But why? You look great."

"No, I don't. I'm a mess. Look at my tummy," she lowered her voice, glancing down at her lap. "It's disgusting. My boobs are too big – I'm sure that's the cause of my backache – and I hate these hooded eyes," she touched the noticeable fold of skin over her left eye. "The thought of

12

another summer having to show all my bits and pieces . . . it just doesn't bear thinking about."

"You're not a rake, Karen," said Chris interrupting, "but you're hardly fat either. What size are you? A sixteen?"

"About that," confirmed Karen miserably.

"Well, that's not fat. You're tall for a start and you dress so well –"

"Don't say 'for my figure'," interrupted Karen.

"But you do. You always look great. I wish I was half as glamorous as you."

"You don't have to try as hard as me, Chris. I'm the one who inherited the 'fat genes'. Anyway, being a little overweight doesn't really bother me that much. It's more the shape of me. No matter how much weight I lose, my breasts never seem to get any smaller and this – this apron of flab – there's no other word for it," she said, holding a ring of flesh around her tummy. "It only gets worse the slimmer I get."

Chris regarded Karen carefully and said, "So what are you going to do about it? Go on another diet?"

"You know I've tried every diet from Atkins to the Zone and none of them work."

"I know you've tried them, Karen," said Chris gently, "but you never stick to one for long enough. You have to be prepared to change your eating habits forever. Not just for a few weeks."

"Oh, don't lecture me on something you know nothing about," said Karen crossly and Chris stiffened. "I've already explained that losing weight isn't really the issue."

"Maybe I don't know anything about the diets," said Chris carefully, knitting the fingers of her hands together and leaning her elbows on the table, "but I do think that you're . . . let me put it this way – you always appear to be looking for a quick fix."

"I'm not looking for a quick fix," said Karen sternly, "and I totally disagree with you about my dieting. I have followed diets religiously, some of them for months, and they've made no real difference to my tummy or my breasts. Whereas you can eat what you like and never put on weight."

"Hmm," said Chris, ignoring the last comment, not because it was true but because she didn't want to be drawn into an argument. Changing subject she asked, "Have you ever thought it might be your thyroid? An underactive thyroid can cause weight gain."

Karen sighed heavily and folded her arms across her ample chest. "I wish it was that simple. But I've been to the doctor and she's checked me out for that – and a host of other possible conditions – and says there's not a thing wrong with me."

"So," said Chris slowly, "if you're not going to diet, what are you going to do?"

Karen looked over her shoulder at the kitchen door through which Hannah had exited as though expecting someone to burst through it at any moment. Then she turned her attention to the glass on the table, took a long drink of wine and set the glass down again. She stared at Chris, her left eyelid twitching involuntarily.

"What?" said Chris, her heartbeat quickening slightly. "What is it?"

"I'm thinking of having some cosmetic surgery."

"Oh my God!" cried Chris as a raft of images hurtled through her brain. Images of the extreme TV makeovers she'd seen – the only experience she had of the business. True, she'd heard rumours about women in Ballyfergus

14

who were reported to have had 'work done' but none of her friends or close acquaintances had. Or if they had, they weren't telling her. She realised suddenly that this was something about which she was almost completely ignorant. Karen was looking at her but Chris didn't know what to say. She'd always viewed those poor women on television as desperate, weak characters who believed the answer to all their problems lay in improving their appearance. She suddenly realised that she didn't approve.

"Well," said Karen, "is that all you have to say?"

"I ... I ... you've taken me by surprise, that's all. I had no idea you felt that strongly ... well, that's not completely true, is it? I know you dislike some aspects of your physical appearance. But not enough to go this far."

"You make it sound as though I'm threatening to boil bunnies. People have these operations every day."

"What operations?"

"Definitely a tummy tuck," said Karen and Chris found her gaze drawn involuntarily to Karen's stomach, "and a boob reduction. And maybe I'll get something done about these eyelids," she added, pointing to the slightly overhanging hood of skin above each eye.

"Sure, I have those too," said Chris, touching her right eyelid. It was a feature they had both inherited from their mother. "They're not that bad, Karen." Though they were more pronounced in Karen's case than in her own.

"In themselves, maybe they're not but if I'm getting these other things done, I might as well go the whole hog and get everything done at the same time. If that's possible."

"I see," said Chris and she bit her bottom lip.

"You don't approve, do you?" said Karen rather miserably and Chris felt rotten.

15

"I just don't think it's worth exposing yourself to the risks, Karen," she said, thankful for the angle that had just popped into her head. "These aren't minor procedures. They're serious operations. You'll have to have a general anaesthetic, won't you?"

Karen shrugged. "Yes."

"That in itself carries big risks," went on Chris. "Never mind the dangers of the surgery itself. And it might not turn out the way you expect it. You might be disappointed. It's not as though you have some sort of horrible deformity or anything. I can understand why people want to, need to, have surgery under those circumstances. But you're very attractive, Karen. And your personality is far more important in creating that attractiveness than your appearance ever will be."

There was a long pause and then Karen said with a smile, "Is that the lecture over then?"

"Sorry," said Chris and she smiled weakly, recognising her tendency to get on her high horse.

Karen leant forward and spoke quietly into Chris's face. "Believe me, I've done loads of digging, Chris. I know the dangers. Haemorrhaging, haematoma, seroma, infection and the rarer complications like thrombosis, pulmonary embolism, necrosis." She was ticking them off like a list on her fingers for Chris's benefit, to prove that she'd done her research.

If Karen was trying to bamboozle Chris with medical terminology she was succeeding. She'd never heard some of those terms.

"Plus lots of unpleasant, but mostly temporary, side effects," went on Karen, "and of course the danger of being disappointed with the results. But I think my expectations are realistic. I know this isn't going to make me into Claudia Schiffer."

"Okay, okay!" Chris raised her hands in the air in a gesture of surrender. "You've done your homework. Point taken."

"Thank you," said Karen and she gave a little satisfied sniff. Then she added, "So, if you don't think I should go down the surgical route –"

"No, I don't," affirmed Chris quickly.

"Then what's the alternative?"

Chris shook her head. "You just go on as you are. Looking great."

Karen gave a snort of derision. "The thing is, Chris, you can't convince me that I look great. I'm not happy with the way I look and that's what matters. It's how I feel about myself when I look in the mirror that counts, not what you – or other people – tell me. I'm the mother of two young children and I feel like I'm sixty. I don't want people mistaking me for their granny at the school gates."

"Don't be daft. Of course they won't."

"They will, the rate I'm going," said Karen flatly.

The antique kitchen wall clock struck the hour and Chris, stressed by the nature of the conversation, refilled their glasses to the top. Karen did not protest.

"Does Tony know about this?" asked Chris, as she set the wine bottle down carefully on the table.

"Well, he knows I've been looking into it. I've sent off for brochures and printed a lot of stuff off the internet so he's seen that lying about. I even made an appointment to go and see a consultant."

"You have?" said Chris in alarm. "What did he say?"

"Oh, I haven't seen him yet. I'm going up to the

17

Malone Cosmetic Surgery Clinic – everyone just calls it The Malone – next week to meet a Dr Mezz. He comes highly recommended."

"Why Dr Mezz? What do you know about him?"

"I did my research. He has an entire alphabet of letters after his name, sits on several cosmetic surgery committees and has been doing tummy tucks for over twenty years. Anyway, it's just a preliminary chat. No obligation or anything. Just to see if he thinks if I would be a good candidate for surgery."

"Is Tony going with you?"

"Mmm," said Karen, becoming suddenly coy. "I haven't told him about the appointment yet. But I will."

"And what does he have to say about it all? He must have an opinion?"

"Well, he hasn't really said very much. Just that I don't need surgery which, of course, is complete rubbish. I don't think he realises yet how serious I am. But I think once he understands what this means to me, he'll be supportive. He usually is."

"What about the cost? Isn't it going to be very expensive?"

"About seven thousand pounds," said Karen.

"That's steep," said Chris, making a whistling sound through her teeth.

"That's just for the tummy tuck. The breast reduction could be anything up to six thousand and the eyelids, three thousand. Worst case, that is."

"Jesus, Karen," exclaimed Chris, before she could stop herself, "that's – what? Seven, six and three. Sixteen thousand pounds!"

"I know. It is rather a lot of money, isn't it?" said Karen, and she shifted uncomfortably in her seat and rearranged the chunky jewellery on her left arm. "I know it's selfish of me to think of spending all that money on myself when there's so many other things we could do with it."

"Won't Tony mind?" said Chris, ignoring Karen's last comment because she could not bring herself to disagree. It did seem like an incredible indulgence, especially when Tony earned a relatively modest income as a headmaster. Sixteen thousand pounds would go a very long way towards a brand new car (Tony's seven-year-old Saab was starting to look a bit worse for wear), several years' worth of family holidays or pay off a healthy chunk of the mortgage. And, looking to the future, if invested now it would most certainly be enough to pay both Jack and Chloe's way through university, should they wish to go.

"My business has done really well this year," said Karen. "I'm going to pay myself a big bonus. So it won't be coming out of the household budget or our savings."

"It sounds as though you've thought about everything," said Chris glumly, staring at the pale yellow liquid in her glass. She took a long drink, which she suddenly felt in desperate need of, and asked, "Have you definitely decided to go ahead, then?"

"You know, I think I have," said Karen, with sudden confidence. "I think I'm going to do it."

Lost for words, Chris did not reply. She let the moment pass and then said, rather hesitantly, "Karen?"

"Yes?"

"Has Tony said anything to you about your appearance?"

Karen shook her head. "No. Why?"

"I just wondered what's made you want to do this all of a sudden."

"It's nothing to do with Tony . . ." began Karen and her voice trailed off. "It's to do with me."

Chris couldn't help but feel that her sister was keeping something from her, but she didn't have the opportunity to grill her further for the sound of Paul's car pulling up outside could be heard.

Karen grabbed Chris's hand and said, very urgently, "You're not to tell Paul, now. It's bad enough getting a lecture from you, never mind him starting on me as well!"

Chris nodded her agreement, the back door opened and Paul came in. He was dressed in a smart navy trench coat over a suit jacket and co-ordinating grey slacks. He was a tall, well-built man of forty-five, now tending a little towards the heavy side. His smile came easily, he still had a full head of brown hair, and twinkling blue eyes. In spite of his slightly heavy jaw and weak chin he was, overall, handsome.

"Good evening, ladies," he said a little wearily and carefully set down his briefcase on the Chinese grey slate floor.

"Hi, love," said Chris automatically, the term of endearment too well-worn to mean very much. "A good night?"

"Oh, the usual," he replied as he shed his coat and jacket and threw them over the back of a chair. "Nearly everyone intoxicated, indecent behaviour. And that was only the doctors."

Karen giggled and Paul said, "Is there anything to eat?"

"Didn't you have a meal or something at the do?" asked Chris.

"If I had, I wouldn't be asking for food, would I?" said Paul, just a little tersely and Chris forced back the snippy retort that sprang to her lips. "It was disgusting," added Paul. "Greasy chicken wings and sausage rolls. I couldn't eat it."

"There's some coq au vin left in that dish, if you want it, and there might be some potatoes left too – try that pot there," said Chris, pointing at the stove but not getting up.

Paul lifted the heavy iron lid of the blue Le Crueset dish and peered inside. Drops of condensation dripped off the lid onto his polished black brogues and he jumped back as though he'd been scalded.

"Damn!" He bent over and brushed at the droplets of water with his left hand, still holding the lid of the casserole dish in his right. Paul was very particular about his appearance. Then he peered inside the casserole again. "*Sero venientibus ossa,*" he said dryly.

Karen looked quizzically at Chris and she translated, with a roll of her eyes, for her sister's benefit, "The bones to the late-comer."

"Latecomers," corrected Paul.

"I wish you'd let me know," said Chris. "I would've kept you a proper meal."

"No, this'll do. I'll survive," said Paul in a tone of stoic endurance.

Chris felt herself getting angry. If it was fine why make sarcastic comments?

"Well, Karen, how goes it in the heady world of childcare?" said Paul and she laughed.

"I'd hardly call it heady," she said. "More like headachy. Do you remember that wee girl over in England somewhere that fell into a pond and drowned while in the care of a nursery?"

"Yeah," said Chris, with a shiver. "I remember."

"Well, I'm getting another gate built at the entrance to the nursery so that it's doubly secure. I can't afford to take any chances. All it takes is one person not paying attention . . ." Karen shook her head and exhaled loudly. "I have nightmares over it, I can tell you."

"Still, it pays the bills," said Paul pragmatically as he served himself a plate of food and popped it in the microwave.

"Yes, it does," agreed Karen, "and for the most part it's a great wee business. As long as you've got good staff, you're fine."

"Now what have we got here?" said Paul and he lifted the wine bottle out of the cooler and, a little shortsighted, peered at the label. "Ah, let me see. You have treated yourselves to a bottle of my finest – what is it? Oh, yes. Amayna Barrel Fermented Sauvignon Blanc. Two thousand and four if I'm not mistaken."

"Sorry, Paul," said Karen, flashing an unrepentant little smile at Chris. "You weren't keeping it for something special, were you?"

"For you, my dear sister-in-law," said Paul with a theatrical flourish of his hands and a bow like a waiter, "nothing is too good."

He topped up Karen's glass which she then raised to him in salute and said, "Thanks you, Paul."

"I think you mean 'thank you'," he said with a smile.

Karen frowned. "That's what I said." She raised her eyebrows, then shook her head the way you do when your ears are full of water after swimming.

Chris blushed, thinking it rude of Paul to correct Karen whose speech was ever so slightly slurred by the wine she had consumed.

"Good? Yes?" said Paul and he rolled the now empty bottle in his hand.

"Mmm, very nice," said Karen.

"It comes from the Leyda Valley in Chile," he said, weighing the bottle in his right hand. "These guys are obsessive. Not only are the grapes handpicked and sorted in the vineyard, they are then re-sorted grape by grape in the winery. Needless to say, only the best ones make it and –"

"Really, how interesting," said Karen with an almost imperceptible lift of her left eyebrow. She glanced at Chris and smiled.

"Now tell me what you taste," said Paul to Karen, all intense and serious.

She rolled a mouthful of wine around in her mouth for a few moments, then the corners of her eyes creased and her lips turned up in a smile. For one awful moment Chris thought she was going to spray Paul, the table and herself with wine. Thankfully, she managed to swallow it and gave a relieved sort of grin.

"It tastes of . . . of . . ." she said, and stifled a giggle.

Chris put her lips to the wineglass to stop herself from joining in her sister's mirth. Paul did not like to be laughed at.

"Of?" prompted Paul.

"Of . . . well, of wine!"

Chris burst out laughing.

Paul gave her one of his withering looks, then turned his attention back to Karen, ignoring the bleep from the microwave. "Don't you taste the hazelnuts and melon and fig? And isn't that buttery, spicy style to die for?"

"Oh, Paul dear," said Karen, wet tears of mirth seeping out of the corners of her eyes, "I'm sorry. To me . . . well, it's just a glass of white wine. A very nice glass of wine, mind you. But just a glass of wine all the same."

"Philistines!" said Paul in mock disgust, as he retrieved the meal from the microwave with oven-gloved hands, set it down gingerly on the table and sat down.

"It's wine we're talking about, Paul," said Chris, slightly irritated by his superior manner towards herself and Karen. "Not a work of art."

"Ah, but that is where you are wrong, Chris," said Paul, as he picked up his fork. "A well-made wine is a work of art."

Suddenly Chris realised that she was married to a wine bore. She quickly turned her gaze away so that Paul would not see the change in her facial expression. She imagined it was one of horror. Her heart beat too fast inside her breast and she gulped down the uncomfortable lump that had formed in her throat. She stared at the tiny flecks of white flour caught in the ridges and hollows of the table, like microscopic snow. Had he suddenly become a bore? Or had he always been one? Was it possible that she had only just now, just this moment, noticed? She felt a falling-away sensation inside her stomach and touched the familiar, dimpled surface of the table to calm herself.

"What?" said Chris when she realised that both Paul and Karen were staring at her.

"Paul says he'll drop me off home right after he's finished eating."

"Oh, thanks, Paul, that's great," said Chris and she noticed how, for all his other refinements, Paul was shovelling his dinner into his mouth like a slob. She looked away.

Karen stood up. "I'll get myself ready to go then." She took her handbag and left the kitchen on her way, Chris presumed, to use the toilet.

"So, how was your day?" said Paul and Chris put a bright smile on her face and told him all about her rather stressful day in the office.

* * *

Later, as she watched the taillights of Paul's Range Rover disappear into the night, Chris folded her arms against the cold, stepped back inside the house and shut the heavy oak front door. She let her palm rest for a moment on the ornate brass fingerplate that adorned the door. And not for the first time she asked herself what was wrong with her?

She lived in a beautiful home, had two wonderful children (albeit they could be very annoying at times) and a good husband. And he really was good, she told herself firmly. He had always provided well for her and the kids – in the days when she didn't work. He had no vices to speak of, loved his children, and was kind and thoughtful. It was just . . . she tried to push the thoughts from her mind . . . it was just that she didn't really like him very much anymore. The things that she used to like about him, even the things that had initially attracted her to him – like his confidence and air of superiority – now irritated her.

She allowed herself to consider, just for a moment, what life would be like without him and suddenly the prospect filled her with panic. Where would she be without her marriage? It was the security blanket in which she'd wrapped herself these last twenty-odd years. What would she be without Paul? She couldn't extricate her identity from his. Married young, they'd practically grown up together. She couldn't envisage a life without him. She couldn't separate her identity from his. Friends jokingly called them 'PAC' – short for 'Paul and Chris' – and that summed up how she felt. They were so much a part of each other that they had become one identity.

And all marriages went through bad patches, she reminded herself. They'd been married for nearly two decades after all. It was perfectly natural that their feelings for each other would wax and wane over the years. No doubt there were times when Paul felt the same about her. She was feeling stressed at the moment, that was all, and that contributed to the way she was feeling. Her disenchantment with him would pass and life would get back to normal again.

Disturbed by these uncomfortable concepts, Chris responded in the only way she knew how – by keeping busy. She went upstairs to her study, ignored the noise coming from Finn's room, and set to work on drawing up a petition against the proposed new supermarket in Ballyfergus.

Two

Chris stood on the edge of the crowd gathered around the luggage carousel at Belfast International Airport and craned her neck looking for Bernie Sweeney. In spite of the blurred photo Bernie had e-mailed of herself, in which she looked like a hippy, Chris found it hard to imagine her looking any different than she did when she was a teenager. Back then, Bernie was into Spandau Ballet and all things 'New Romantic'. She even copied their style of dress at one time with flounced-sleeved shirts, waistcoats and Adam Ant-style feathers in her hair. She looked for a while, Chris recalled with a fond smile, like a cross between a highwayman and a red Indian.

Chris remembered with sudden clarity that Bernie had once borrowed five pounds from her to buy a coarse blue serge military-style jacket from a second-hand shop in Ballyfergus. She had never paid her back. It was clear that Bernie, swept up in her infatuation with Tony Hadley (dimpled-chinned lead singer of Spandau), had simply forgotten. But Chris had been too embarrassed to ask for it back. And the more time that elapsed, the harder it became to raise the subject and so she never had. That five pounds had been hard-won, from many hours spent baby-sitting.

She realised, feeling foolish, that she still felt resentment over it.

Seeing no sign of her friend, Chris retreated to the seating area nearby, and sat down in a green fabric-covered chair. She put her handbag on the seat beside her and crossed her legs. Inside she felt no different from the awkward teenager she had been back then. She panicked, suddenly worrying about what she would say to Bernie. They'd spoken a few times on the phone to make the arrangements for this trip but that wasn't the same as meeting face-to-face. Would they have anything in common?

Chris glanced down at her Burberry Mac belted over smart grey trousers and black patent high heels. She knew she appeared well off and sophisticated, but inside she felt she had not changed. What if Bernie had changed? What if they had nothing to say to each other? It could be a long month.

Suddenly Chris's brain was flooded with memories from her youth, jostling with each other like children playing rough and tumble. She remembered the laughter and the fun times they had and the tears when Bernie's beloved dog, Archie, died. The long hours spent holed up in each other's bedrooms listening to the Top 40 on wet Sunday afternoons, talking about boys and swooning over the Kemp brothers. Analysing in intricate detail each metamorphosis Spandau Ballet went through from their kilt-wearing phase to the later sharp suits, skinny ties and lashings of hair gel.

Chris smiled and then she remembered something else – the barely disguised competition between them – and the smile fell from her face. The underlying rivalry that had defined their relationship from that first day at Ballyfergus Grammar School, aged eleven, when they'd sat down beside each other in assembly. They had both attended the same Catholic primary school but had never been friends, and suddenly they were thrown together at the largely Protestant Grammar School. Their relationship was defined by the mutual need that had bonded them from that first meeting – the need to cling to their own in a sea of unfamiliarity.

She realised suddenly that Bernie had been as much her rival as she had been her friend. Chris had been cleverer but Bernie prettier and more of a hit with the boys and each one envied what the other had not.

Chris searched anxiously among the crowd, panicking, wondering if she could leave now and abandon the whole plan. Why had she agreed to it in the first place? Why hadn't she told Bernie she didn't have room, she was busy, any number of perfectly plausible reasons why she couldn't accommodate her?

But she knew why. She was too honest to make up lies and then there was Bernie's mum. Or rather the absence of her. Bernie had hardly known her mother because she had died when Bernie was four. Chris's mother was never done telling her how lucky she was to have her and talking about 'poor wee Bernie Sweeney'. And Chris had never overcome her own guilt at having what Bernie did not. And their relationship had, as a result, never quite been on an equal footing, for Chris always made allowances for the yawning maternal gap in Bernie's all-male household. She was prepared to overlook the occasional catty comment and the boyfriend-stealing – not that Bernie had ever done that to her. She put it down to the fact that Bernie suffered from a lack of sound feminine influences in her life.

But what if Karen was right? What if Bernie was just using her home as a convenient and free hotel? What if she had some horrible ulterior motive for coming back to Ballyfergus? Chris told herself not to be ridiculous. She was letting her imagination run wild. What harm could Bernie do her and what motive would she have for doing it?

They were both adults now and they were equals. She was a mature woman and so was Bernie. The infantile rivalry that had characterised their earlier relationship was a thing of the past. And it was only one aspect of their friendship.

There were many much more positive aspects to dwell on, like their shared memories of their schooldays. And the intense, all-consuming relationship peculiar to teenage girls which they had shared and which Chris had subsequently observed between Hannah and her best friend, Cat. No, she had nothing to worry about, she told herself. All would be well. Chris took a deep breath and brushed some imaginary dirt off her Mac.

A petite woman wearing dark clothing walked towards her pulling a luggage trolley behind her and Chris, absorbed in thought, automatically lifted her handbag from the adjacent seat, assuming that she too wished to sit down.

"Chris," said a voice and Chris looked up.

"It's me. Bernie," said the woman she had just ignored.

"Bernie!" cried Chris and she focused on her properly for the first time.

She ran her eye over Bernie in a split second, the way only women can do, taking in almost every detail of her appearance. She wore a buttoned-up chocolate velvet jacket and her tie-twisted patterned silk skirt reached to the floor.

Her blonde hair was tied back, little tendrils like straw-coloured vines escaping at the nape of her neck. She wore large gold hoop earrings and several chunky ethnic necklaces and some thick metal bangles on her left arm. Her complexion was pale, her face slightly strained, no doubt from the arduous journey. And her face was different from how Chris remembered it —it was thinner now and not quite as pretty. There were lines at the corners of her eyes and some creases round her mouth but, all in all, she looked remarkably well for a woman of forty not wearing any make-up. The corners of her mouth turned up in a wry little smile, her lips remaining sealed.

"You didn't recognise me, did you?" she said in a slight Australian accent and her large eyes, the colour of dark chocolate, danced with mischief.

"No, I'm sorry, I didn't," said Chris and she smiled and stood up, towering over Bernie in her high heels and feeling like an ungainly giant. Had she grown or had Bernie shrunk? Then she noticed with relief the flat pumps on Bernie's feet which partly explained the five-inch difference between them.

"It's good to see you," she said, stepping forward and giving Bernie a hug. She smelt exotically of patchouli and sandalwood, like the inside of Celestial Touch, the shop on Main Street that sold books on astrology and aromatherapy oils. Chris only knew this because Hannah took her there once – it was not the sort of place she would ever shop. Bernie looked like she was wearing their entire stock of ethnic jewellery.

"And you too," said Bernie, returning the embrace. Then she pulled back a little, her hands gripping Chris's forearms. "It's been too long, hasn't it?" she said and her bottom lip quivered ever so slightly over impossibly white and perfect teeth.

All Chris's reservations about this meeting melted away. She felt her eyes moisten with tears. "I should've made more of an effort to stay in touch."

"Me too. But it doesn't matter. I'm here now," said Bernie, smiling broadly, her face lighting up like a sunrise.

Chris took a step back. "You look so different, Bernie. I was half-expecting you to be wearing a frilly shirt with a feather in your hair and war paint on your face!"

"Oh God, I cringe when I think of it. I thought I was so trendy, didn't I? But thank God my Adam Ant days are far behind me!" She gave an earthy chuckle that seemed incongruous with her petite size. "Jesus, do you remember the time I went to the school disco dressed like that? Everyone must've thought I was a nutter."

"No, they didn't. They thought you were hip. The rest of us were so boring in comparison. Look at me; I'm as conservative now as I was back then."

Bernie cocked her head to one side and folded her arms across her chest while she examined Chris. Then she pursed her lips and said, "You look well, Chris. You look very . . . smart and sophisticated. Like a lawyer."

"Well, there you go. That explains it. I look exactly like what I am. Here, let me help you with that bag." Chris held out her hand and Bernie handed her a large soft cotton ethnic-looking shoulder bag.

Chris swung it over her shoulder. "The car's just out here."

"This is all changed," said Bernie, looking around the small, low-ceilinged arrivals hall as she followed Chris. "I can hardly remember what it was like before. But I'm sure it didn't look like this." She peered at the car-hire cubicles arranged in a line on their right-hand side.

"It has been the best part of twenty years, Bernie. Northern Ireland's moved on a lot."

"It needed to."

"Yes," said Chris thoughtfully, "it did."

They walked a few steps in silence, their pace dictated by the large wheeled suitcase Bernie pulled behind her. Chris remembered that, as a teenager, Bernie had been desperate to leave Ballyfergus and Northern Ireland far behind her. As soon as she could, she got out – by taking up a place at art college in London. Chris tried to remember the exact cause of Bernie's disenchantment with her homeland but could only recall a mixed muddle of emotional conversations revolving around the parochial, small-mindedness of the Province. She wondered what Bernie would make of it now and smiled to herself. Much had changed about Northern Ireland but Ballyfergus was still the sort of place where everybody knew your name and your business.

"So," said Chris, "when did you change your style to . . ." She paused, not wishing to give offence.

"Hippy?"

"No, that's not really the word I was looking for," said Chris honestly. She thought Bernie's clothes were eccentric rather than hippy. "I was thinking more your clothes conveyed a strong sense of personal style and individuality."

"Thank you."

"I guess, like me, you look like what you are. An artist."

"Not quite. I don't think being an illustrator qualifies as an artist."

"Oh, but it does. It's so creative. Don't do yourself

down, Bernie. I've looked at your website. Your stuff is great. It's more than great – it's fantastic. It's completely unique."

"I draw food labels for God's sake, Chris. What's so exciting about that?"

"But you've had a couple of exhibitions too, haven't you?"

"True. But the food label and other commercial stuff are still my bread and butter. Excuse the pun."

They had exited the building through sliding glass doors and they stood on the pavement outside in the spring sunshine. Chris fished a pair of Armani sunglasses from her bag and put them on.

"We just need to cross here," she said and pointed at the car park across the road.

"Chris . . ." said Bernie and hesitated.

Chris looked at her and Bernie went on in that peculiar Australian-Northern-Irish accent, "Thanks for having me to stay. You're a real mate."

Three

Bernie wished the car journey to Ballyfergus, in the plush cream leather-upholstered saloon car, would last forever. She loved looking out at the beautiful scenery but, more than that, she needed time to conquer the emotions welling up inside her. There was no doubt about it. Setting foot again on Irish soil had unleashed a whole raft of feelings that astounded her with their strength.

She listened to Chris talk about her husband and children, her entire monologue interspersed with terse little derogatory comments about them which she presented as harmless jokes. Bernie wondered if Chris had any idea how lucky she was. She knew teenagers could be challenging – hadn't she been one herself and quite a handful if she remembered correctly? Sure, Chris and her husband had been together a long time and no doubt, like all relationships, they'd had their ups and downs. But the upside was that they had stood by each other through thick and thin, they were still together and, most fortunate of all, they had been blessed with children.

And to top it all Chris looked great – far better than she had done as a teenager or a young woman. Bernie sneaked a long glance at Chris in the driving seat beside her, her face animated as she talked. She had finally found a hairstyle – a short bob – to suit her thick, unruly hair. Her pale skin-that-would-never-tan had, as a result, retained its elasticity – her complexion would have made any woman half her age proud. She was thinner now than she had been back then and very well groomed and she wore clothes that suited her tall lean figure. Some women grew into themselves over the years, their increasing confidence adding to their allure, and Chris was definitely one of those women.

As Bernie well knew, attractiveness has as much to do with the inner person as the outer shell. Many of the people she knew and considered attractive were not classically good-looking. Much of their appeal came from their personalities. And so it was with Chris – she was in her prime. Bernie wondered vaguely if her own had already passed . . .

"You must be tired," said Chris after some ten minutes, when Bernie had seen enough of the countryside to learn that it had not changed.

"I am." Bernie closed her eyes and rested her head against the seatbelt and pretended to be asleep.

Bernie knew now that she would never have children. She would never know what it was to be loved unconditionally by an infant and to return that love. It was the greatest regret of her life. And there was nothing that she could do about it. It wasn't just the illness that had robbed her of the chance – adoption would have been a possibility. But only if Gavin had stayed with her. She would not raise a child alone because it wouldn't be fair to deny a child a father and because she wasn't entirely sure she could cope on her own.

All those years she'd wasted on Gavin! When she

thought about it, she literally tasted bitterness on her tongue, so she tried not to dwell on it. But if only she could have them back! All those years convincing herself, and him, that she really wasn't the conservative, stay-at-home type, agreeing that they both needed to be free spirits, agreeing that marriage was just an institution created by society to control people. Believing that they, in spite of his views, had a future together and that he loved her. Accepting his reasons for not giving her the child she wanted.

"I don't want to be tied down, Bernie, and if you're honest with yourself, neither do you," he had said one night over the second bottle of Two Hands 'Canny Butcher' Grenache (Gavin liked his wine). "Ankle biters," he had said, pausing to light up another cigarette. He inhaled, made a tiny smacking sound with his lips and said, attempting and failing to be humorous, "They do nothing but throw up and poop and then, when they're older, answer you back and leave you bankrupt. Seriously Bernie, who'd want them?"

I do! I do! she screamed inside her head. But she had looked at her lap and deferred to his judgement the way she always did, not trusting her own. If she had been honest with herself, she would have told him there and then that she wanted to be married and have a child and that if he didn't want the same then it was time to call it quits.

But she had not because she loved him. She told herself that he simply wasn't the marrying type and, as long as she could have him, the rest did not matter. And inside she nurtured the fervent hope that he would change his mind before it was too late.

But time passed and then she became ill and, to give

him his due, he stood by her throughout the terrible treatment and her long recovery. Too consumed by the shipwreck of her life and health, she did not fully register the subtle changes in his behaviour towards her. And what changes she did notice (the withdrawal of physical contact, the feeling sometimes that his mind was elsewhere) she put down to the emotional, and understandable, strain of supporting her. But there was more, much more to it than that.

A fortnight after she came home from hospital he left her for a supermarket checkout girl half his age. Her name was Shirley Fair. It was Saturday morning and, full of a renewed zest for life (having brushed shoulders so recently with the real prospect of an untimely death), she was sitting on the bed, leafing through brochures for adventure holidays in Queensland.

"Gav!" she had shouted down the hall. "Why don't we go diving at the Great Barrier reef? I'd like to do that."

She waited, then called again.

"Gav! Will you come here?"

He appeared in the doorway dressed in slacks and a lilac button-down shirt. His worn tan suede jacket was slung carelessly over his left shoulder, hooked on his index finger. He looked like he was ready to go somewhere. She noticed the peculiar expression on his face and remembered, suddenly, that it was the same one he had wore at his mother's funeral. And then she noticed a small black suitcase by his feet, one of a pair she had bought only two days ago for the holiday they were planning to celebrate her recovery.

She dragged her eyes back to his face, unable to speak. It became very hard to breathe. She calmed her nerves, took a long deep breath and waited.

"I'm sorry Bernie," he said, pausing to clear his throat with a familiar raspy cough. "I've met someone."

She watched as the brochure in her hands fell to the floor and she realised suddenly that she was naked. Hastily she fumbled for a robe and pulled it on. She tied the belt and clutched the towelling lapels under her neck, tight, as if to hold herself together.

"You've met someone?" she repeated, part of her brain understanding full well, another part refusing to process the words she had just heard.

"Yes. And I think it would be best if I moved out." A pause. "Now."

"Are you . . . you mean you are going to . . . to live with . . .?" she said, her voice trailing off.

He nodded and glanced over his shoulder as though there was someone waiting for him in the next room.

"But who, Gav? Who?"

"It doesn't matter who, Bernie. You don't know her."

"Who is she?" demanded Bernie, almost screaming.

"All right. Her name's Shirley Fair. I think I'd better go now," he said and nodded firmly as if confirming something to himself.

"But . . . Gavin . . . you can't! You can't just go! I – I can't live without you. You know I can't."

"I knew you'd do this," he said calmly, though his face was red.

With what? Embarrassment? Shame? Anger?

"Do what?" she said, the pain of his rejection hurting like the delayed searing pain that follows a knife-cut.

"Try to use the sympathy vote to stop me going."

"Is that what's kept you here, Gavin? Sympathy?"

He looked at the floor. Silence.

"I thought you loved me," she said, and tears trickled down her face, settling like cold dewdrops on her chin. She brushed them away.

"I did. Until recently."

"But what happened? You can't just – just stop loving someone. You can't just stop loving me."

"Well, I have, Bernie. I'm sorry. I can't give you a time and a place when it happened. It just did. One day I woke up and I knew that it was over. I can't explain it but that's the way it is. I've stayed because I couldn't leave you when you were so ill. I couldn't do that to you."

"Is it because of my illness?" she said, remembering how terrible she had looked and how dependent she had been at times. Not to mention the vicious scar across her abdomen. Had that changed the way he felt about her?

"It has nothing to do with your illness. Nothing at all," he said and she did not quite believe him.

"Please, Gavin. Please don't leave me now," she said and started to sob. "I need you now more than I have ever done."

"No, Bernie. It won't work," he said. His face suddenly drained of colour and the muscle in his right cheek twitched – the way it did when he was angry or stressed. "My mind's made up." And then, in a softer tone, "Please don't cry, Bernie." He brushed his cheek roughly with the back of his hand and said, "I'm going now."

He walked the short distance to the door of the apartment they had shared for the last eight years. She would not let him go, she would stop him. She did not care what it took to keep him. She knew no humiliation. He was her life, her everything.

He turned the key in the lock and put his left hand on

the chrome door handle. Suddenly she leapt from the bed like an uncoiled spring and, racing out of the bedroom and across the small lounge, she wedged herself between Gavin and the door. She leaned against the smooth wood surface and heard the door click quietly closed behind her back.

"Please, Gavin," she sobbed into his shirt front, her eyes too blurred with tears to see his face clearly. She put her arms around his neck and burrowed her brow in his rugby-player's chest. "Don't do this, don't leave me," she whispered.

"I'm sorry, Bernie. I really am," he said, extricating himself from her embrace, lifting her arms away like they were sticky tentacles. "We always said we would never stay together if we didn't love each other. We always said that we would be honest. Now please let me pass."

"But I love you!" she cried, standing firm.

"I know you do and I wish that you didn't. Because I can't change the way I feel. I'm sorry. I really am. Don't make this any worse than it has to be."

"I'll kill myself!"

He regarded her for a few seconds, his head tilted backwards and his lips slightly parted. "No, you won't," he said. "You're a fighter, Bernie. Look how you beat the cancer."

She put her head on his chest then and sobbed quietly, knowing that he was right. Knowing that she had no argument in her arsenal that would win this battle. He sighed with a sound like the air escaping from a lilo, and then she felt him gently ease her out of his path. Her knees gave way and, very slowly, she crumpled to the floor. Then he slipped softly out of the apartment without, she was sure, a backward glance.

She found out later that Shirley Fair was pregnant by him. Six months later she gave birth to a healthy little baby girl and Bernie was consumed with jealousy of the child that should have been hers. Through mutual friends she learned that Gavin had surprised everyone by turning into the archetypal doting dad and Bernie tried very hard not to despise him, Shirley and the child. She did not want to be consumed with hatred, she did not want to become bitter and sad. So she stopped seeing the friends that were also friends of Gavin, moved to another part of the city and, by and large, had been successful in building a new life for herself.

That was four years ago. She still thought about him every day but time, like everyone said, was a great healer and there were worse things than having your heart broken, weren't there? Like not being alive. She knew more than most how fortunate she was to wake up every morning and for this alone – the gift of life – she thanked God every day. She had learned to expect, and ask, for nothing more.

"Nearly here now," said Chris and Bernie awoke from her reverie with a start.

She blinked in the bright sunshine and looked around, suddenly frightened. They were speeding down the gentle incline of the dual carriageway that led into Ballyfergus. Her heart fluttered like the wings of a nervous butterfly. She caught a glimpse of bright new houses on the left and then, where the turn off to the Marine Hotel used to be, they came abruptly to a new roundabout.

Disoriented, Bernie sought frantically for familiar landmarks, while Chris drove confidently straight across the roundabout, slowing the car's pace by only a fraction to check for oncoming cars. A few hundred yards further on, she took the slip road into Ballyfergus.

Bernie, damp under the arms, felt a little queasy. She thought briefly of opening the window and then thought better of it – she didn't want to attract Chris's attention. She didn't want her to notice her discomposure. Eighteen years had passed since Bernie had last set foot in her hometown. She had planned this trip so carefully and suddenly she was here and she wasn't prepared.

For this was no ordinary nostalgic holiday to the 'old country'. This journey was a quest. And what Bernie sought were answers to the many questions that had troubled her since the moment she had conscious memory. Would she find what she was looking for?

The car moved more slowly now and they cruised along Pound Street while Bernie reminded herself that she wasn't a child any more and to stop acting like one. She took a few deep breaths and paid attention to her surroundings. They passed three tall blocks of council flats that Bernie recognised instantly. Their sheer size and location – in the basin of the valley which was home to Ballyfergus – ensured that they were the most predominant architectural symbol in Ballyfergus. They had been given a makeover (in the form of blue paint and graphic artwork) but it wasn't enough to disguise the ugly 1960's architecture.

"They're due to come down," observed Chris wryly, with a nod in the direction of the flats. "Not before time, I'd say. They're an eyesore."

"The place won't look the same without them though," said Bernie, because for her they had been defining landmarks of her childhood.

Chris chatted on and sped past the 'Tech', where Bernie had gone for car maintenance classes (anything to avoid PE at the Grammar). She caught a glimpse of the low grey building and saw herself, a girl of fourteen in a navy blazer and grey socks, standing there looking back at her.

They passed the 'new' library on their left and then the old Carnegie Library which Bernie remembered visiting as a small child – before the powers that be determined that the town needed a bigger, state-of-the-art purpose-built facility.

"That's a museum now," said Chris as they passed the imposing red-brick building. "You should go and see it. They did a lovely job of refurbishing it."

On the car sped, along Victoria Road, past the high-fenced courthouse and the quaint Smiley Cottage Hospital where Bernie's Aunt Jean had worked as matron until her husband's job took her away to far-flung Coleraine. Bernie remembered waiting for her at the entrance to the hospital as a child – always hopeful of one of Aunt Jean's lemon bon-bons and rarely disappointed. She smiled, recalling the way Aunt Jeanie dispensed the sweets with a gruff, "Now, get away home with you now."

"The Smiley closed years ago," Chris informed her. "Ballyfergus Council have their offices in there now."

"Really? Where's the hospital now then?"

"Oh, you have to go to Antrim."

"Antrim!" said Bernie, feeling suddenly incensed. "But that's miles away!"

"Only half an hour in the car, or so they say. It's all about savings and rationalisation now. The Smiley just wasn't economical."

They came to the junction at the end of Victoria Road and turned left onto Glenarm Road. Up ahead Bernie could see the tall old brick wall which hid the Bowling and Tennis Club from view.

"Do you remember the summer we decided to learn tennis?" said Bernie, the happy associations with this place coming to the fore in her mind.

"I do," said Chris. "And we made our own tennis skirts."

"God, yeah. It took us weeks."

"Yours was okay. Mine was awful. I couldn't get the box pleats right at all. Do you remember? It looked like a pleated lampshade gone wrong. You were always good with your hands though. You could turn your hand to practically anything and make a success of it."

"The thing was," said Bernie ignoring the compliment which she felt she did not deserve, "I thought I was bloody Billy Jean King."

"And me Martina Navratilova!" exclaimed Chris.

Bernie laughed. "But we weren't actually any good at it, mate!"

"Do you remember," said Chris, laughing so hard now that she couldn't continue talking, and Bernie feared for their safety in the car. Chris paused to compose herself, wiped a tear of mirth from her cheek, and glanced at Bernie. "Do you remember the time Owen Cosgrave was watching us play and I was trying to impress him and I kept throwing the ball up in the air to serve and couldn't hit it. Not once!"

"It kept landing on your head!"

"Oh God! How embarrassing was that?"

Bernie smiled, remembering that one of the things she had always liked about Chris was her ability to laugh at herself.

"I wonder what happened to him," she said.

"Owen? He became a quantity surveyor. He's in the States now. Married some Filipino girl. Look, here we are now."

Chris indicated and turned left into a street a few hundred yards past the Tennis Club. She pulled into an open gateway and crunched along a short, hedge-lined drive which led to an impressive Victorian mansion. It had a covered, tiled-roof porch that protruded from the main flat-fronted building, which was built of grey weathered stone.

"This used to belong to Mr Wilson, the dentist," said Bernie, when she got out of the car. "I didn't know you lived here."

"Didn't you?" said Chris, opening the boot of the car and lifting out Bernie's case, which she set down on the gravel drive. A big black, four-wheeled drive Range Rover was parked by the front door.

"I knew the address obviously from our correspondence but it didn't click with me that it was the same house," said Bernie, squinting up at the handsome façade. "I used to come here every six months for checkups."

"We changed the name when we bought it from him. It used to be called –"

"The Elms."

"That's right but now the trees are gone," said Chris, as both women surveyed the beech hedge that lined the driveway. "They had to be cut down – Dutch elm disease apparently – so it seemed a bit silly to keep the name when the trees were gone."

"You called it Castlerock."

"That's right. We had some good times up there, didn't we?" said Chris, referring to the seaside town on the north coast where her parents had kept a static caravan and where Bernie had often joined them on short holidays.

"Brilliant!" said Bernie, picking up her suitcase. "All that freedom, long summer nights and no worries or responsibility."

"We didn't know we were living," agreed Chris. "You know," she added, as she led the way towards the house, "Paul and I have been looking at holiday properties up there. You wouldn't believe the price of them. Twenty years ago you could buy a three-bedroomed terrace house in Portstewart for under five thousand pounds. And now they're looking for hundreds of thousands for two-bedroomed apartments in the area! And the prices just keep going up. Paul reckons they're a good investment though. Anyway, welcome to our home!"

They crossed the threshold of the house and Bernie found herself in a wide, impressive and traditionally decorated hallway with a sweeping oak staircase, black and white tiled floor and dark red walls. On the elegant hall table was an enormous display of white lilies, opened to perfection, as though timed for her visit. The entrance was unrecognisable from its former life as a dingy dental surgery. She couldn't help but compare it to her own small apartment back in Melbourne and think that she hadn't done very well in life. Materially or, she thought glumly, otherwise. She didn't begrudge Chris her obvious success but it was hard to face the fact that your life was a failure.

"It looks a lot better than it did in Mr Wilson's day," said Bernie, forcing herself to sound cheerful. "I remember the paint peeling off the window-frames and the place was freezing in the winter."

Chris nodded. "Yes, we've done a lot to it over the years. Replaced all the windows, put in central heating, new kitchen, new bathrooms, extended. Everything really."

"It's beautiful," said Bernie quietly.

"Paul!" shouted Chris. She waited a few moments, listening with her head cocked slightly to one side. "Don't know where he is. Why don't you come on upstairs and I'll show you your room and you can meet Paul later. Can you manage that bag?"

"No problem," said Bernie, used to coping on her own in spite of her petite size. She mounted the red-carpeted stairs behind Chris and lugged the suitcase up two flights to the top attic floor.

"We put the guest suite up here," said Chris, opening the cream panelled door onto a large, neutrally decorated room with combed ceilings and two single beds. "There's a bathroom just here," she added, pushing open a door on the landing to reveal a sparkling white, state-of-the-art bathroom with roll-top bath and separate shower. "It's not en-suite but no-one else comes up here, so it's just for your use."

"It's fantastic," said Bernie, thinking that it was far more luxurious than anything she could have afforded for her planned month-long stay. The cost of the flight had put a serious dent in her holiday budget. "I really can't thank you enough."

"You don't have to," said Chris with a wide grin. "I'm just glad you're here. Well, why don't I leave you to get unpacked? Would you like to join us for dinner? It'll be ready in half an hour or so. Or would you like to sleep – you must be very tired?"

"I feel okay at the moment," said Bernie. "Maybe it's best if I eat something and try and stay awake a little longer before turning in."

"Great. I know the kids and Paul are dying to meet you," said Chris with a big smile. "And I promise we'll not keep you talking all night!"

Four

Paul wandered into the kitchen from the conservatory where he had been reading the most recent copy of *The Lancet*. He liked to keep up with the latest in the medical world, though part of him thought it was a waste of time. As a GP in a small town like Ballyfergus you weren't exactly at the cutting edge of medical science. Half of the specialist medical advances he read about he'd never see, use or experience.

Chris was bustling about the kitchen in what he recognised as, and called, her 'hyper' mode – a state of heightened anxiety that was induced by guests, even just the one. She smiled distractedly at him, and then continued with her task of hurriedly cutting bread and throwing it in the bread basket. Murphy sat at her feet waiting for food to fall to the floor. A piece of bread missed the basket, slid off the counter and landed on the slate. Before either Paul or little Murphy could react, Chris swooped down on it and deposited it in the bin. Less haste, more speed, thought Paul, but had the wisdom to say nothing. He took a piece of bread, still warm from the breadmaker, out of the basket – Chris ignored him – and continued his line of thought.

It wasn't that he was grumbling about being a GP, far

from it. He was relatively contented with his job and the niche he'd chosen within the medical world. There were undeniable advantages to being a GP in a town this size. People knew who you were and, in the modern world where so much was disrespected, you were still regarded as a pillar of society. Anonymity bore no attraction for Paul – he rather liked the feeling of being a big fish in the goldfish bowl of Ballyfergus.

Paul's father had been a GP in the town in the days when it really meant you were somebody and Paul had enjoyed all the privileges his father's status afforded him – private boarding school, annual skiing holidays in Switzerland and sailing in the Med in the summer, membership of Ballyfergus Golf Club, frequent cultural trips to seventies London. He had grown up in the certainty that he had only one destiny – to follow in his admired father's footsteps. And Paul was good at his job and well-liked by his patients and colleagues. He knew his life was somewhat privileged but that did not stop him enjoying his success and the material benefits that came with it.

And yet, and yet, there was a part of him that remained unfulfilled. He had, at one time, desired nothing more than to become a doctor. Now he wasn't so sure he'd made the right choice. For a start he lacked the passion and dedication that his father had shown for the job. In fact the only thing he felt passionate about these days was wine.

But there were bills to be paid, university fees to be met and all the outgoings necessary to maintain the comfortable lifestyle his family enjoyed. He had been a doctor, or training to be one, for over twenty years – what else could he possibly do at this stage of his life? He glanced at Chris, her brow now furrowed with concentration as she adjusted the place settings on the table. She would have no time to entertain such notions in him – or in herself. She believed in doing your duty, working hard and being practical. She would tell him to wise up.

"There. That should do it," said Chris, visibly relaxing as she surveyed the table.

"So where is she then?" said Paul, plucking a large green olive stuffed with a whole creamy white almond from the dish sitting on the kitchen island. "This mysterious guest of yours?"

"Shhh . . . she'll hear you," said Chris in an exaggerated whisper and she put her index finger to her puckered lips. "And she's not mysterious – you know fine well who she is."

"Haven't met her before though," said Paul, popping the olive in his mouth and chomping for a few seconds. "Those are delicious!" He wiped his greasy fingers on a piece of kitchen roll. "And your sister has me rather intrigued. She makes this Bernie sound like the black witch."

A fleeting smile crossed Chris's face and she said, "Please, Paul! She really will hear you. Oh, I nearly forgot," she said, changing both tone and tack, "did you put the potatoes in when I told you?"

"Yes."

"And did you remember to turn them?"

"I'm not a complete imbecile," said Paul, irritated that she didn't trust him to do even the simplest of tasks in the kitchen.

"I know you're not, darling," she said soothingly.

Paul wondered, not for the first time, why Chris didn't accord him the respect he expected – and deserved. Only at home did he feel undermined in this way. Maybe he shouldn't have married a woman as well-educated, successful and as smart as Chris. Maybe he should have married someone less gifted. Someone, he thought ruefully, who would appreciate him more.

Chris, armed now with oven gloves, was ready to do battle with the culinary disaster she imagined she would face when she opened the oven door.

"Look at you!" said Paul. "Will you just relax and calm down. Everything's under control. You're buzzing about the place like a hyperactive wasp."

"I am not!"

"Yes, you are."

She opened the oven door, pulled out the tray of roast potatoes, shook them about a bit and shoved them back in. She closed the oven door and stood up. "They look okay," she said, frowned, and fiddled with the temperature control knob on the range. "I'll just turn the oven down a bit."

"I told you. Everything's under control. Dinner will be ready to serve in precisely thirty-three minutes."

"Oh," she said and removed the oven gloves, pairing them carefully before setting them down on the speckled granite surface. "Then I'd better go and freshen up."

"And I'll pour the gin and tonics," said Paul, with what he hoped was a withering lift of his right eyebrow.

Chris disappeared and, moments later, a small woman with long blonde hair entered the kitchen. She headed straight for Paul with an oversized smile, but before she could open her mouth she was accosted by a very excited Murphy.

"Oh, what's your name? You're gorgeous!" she exclaimed, at once sinking to the puppy's level, her long brown skirt pooling on the floor, and cupping his little grizzled head in her hands.

"That's Murphy," said Paul with a smile, as the hyperactive dog leapt and snapped the air with joy at finding a new friend. His tail wagged so hard it seemed to dictate the movement of his body which wiggled excitedly in an 'S' shape. "Just be careful though. He tends to urinate when he's a bit —"

But it was too late. Just at that moment Bernie stood up and Murphy showered her curiously bare feet with a light spray of warm, pale urine. She had a thin silver bracelet round her left ankle and, on the middle toe of the right foot, a silver toe-ring. Her toe-nails were painted aqua blue.

"Oh dear, I am sorry," said Paul, taking Murphy by the collar and depositing him in the puppy pen in the utility room. "He can't help himself. Chris calls it an excitement wee, though I can think of other names. We're hoping he'll grow out of it."

"No worries," said Bernie calmly. "I'll just go and clean up."

She left the room and Paul disinfected the floor where the dog had peed, cursing Chris under his breath for getting a puppy. Their previous dog, Rascal, had come fully grown and well-trained from a dog home and had slotted into family life with barely a blip. Paul was no great lover of animals and Murphy, cute as he was, had turned out to be quite a lot of work. Chris had to come home from work at lunchtimes to let him outside — and mine-sweeping the garden for little brown worms of puppy-poop was now an unwelcome routine task, which he flatly refused to undertake. Rascal could be relied upon to defecate like clockwork, once a day on his early morning walk.

"Just as well I had no shoes on," said Bernie with a laugh as she came back into the room.

"I am sorry," he said again. "Do you often go barefoot?"

"All the time. It's better for your feet and your posture." She held out her hand and said, "I'm Bernie. You must be Paul. I've heard a lot about you."

"Likewise," he said, taking her slim, strong hand in his and squeezing it firmly. Paul was a great believer in firm handshakes. "It's great to have you here. Chris has been looking forward to your visit. We all have. Gin and tonic?"

"Mmm, yes, please," she said and put out both hands to receive the Waterford crystal tumbler, like a child accepting a cup of hot chocolate. "Mmm," she said again, turned her back to the kitchen island, leant against it, took a sip of the drink (still cradled in both hands) and surveyed the room. She was wearing a turquoise tight-fitting top over good breasts and chunky wooden jewellery. She was exceptionally slender – he could've encircled her tiny waist with one arm. Her perfume was powerful – old-fashioned, he thought – with strong undercurrents of neroli and bergamot. It reminded him of the classic perfume, Mitsouko, his grandmother used to wear.

"This is nice," she said and looked at him. Her brown eyes, like oiled chestnuts, fixed him with a steady gaze across the lip of the glass. "And something smells good."

"Yes, Chris is a great cook," he said firmly, feeling the need all of a sudden to be loyal to his wife. He walked over to the range, away from Bernie, and then turned to face her again – this time with the island unit between them. Why did he feel as though those eyes were penetrating him, reading his thoughts?

"Please," he said, nodding at the collection of white china dishes clustered together on the beech surface. "Try some Italian queen olives stuffed with almonds. Or the honey-and-thyme preserved garlic. And the *prosciutto crudo* is particularly good. You must try that."

Bernie looked down at the food, revealing a slick of iridescent teal-coloured shadow on her eyelids.

"Where did you get them from?" she asked.

"The deli on Main Street, at least that's where I think Chris got them."

"I didn't know Ballyfergus offered such cosmopolitan sophistication."

He shrugged and, taking slight exception to her patronising tone, said, "You've obviously been away a long time, Bernie. Ballyfergus has finally caught up with the rest of civilisation. I think we can offer a culinary experience the equal of anywhere in the world."

"I didn't mean to cause offence," she said, and he immediately felt responsible for, and regretted, the pained expression that crossed her diamond-shaped face. "I didn't mean to imply that Ballyfergus was some sort of backwater. It was just when I lived here, the most exotic thing I ate was a mandarin orange at Christmas."

"Here, try something – airline food is the pits of the earth – you must be starving," he said by way of apology and he went and stood beside her. "You must try one of these." He offered her the olives.

She lifted one carefully between small fingertips and looked at it as though considering what to do with it.

"Eat it whole," he said. "There's no other way. If you try and bite it, the almond shoots out like a bullet."

"Okay," she laughed.

She opened her mouth and he watched as she inserted the olive behind teeth the colour of the almond and closed her moist lips. A globule of olive oil ran down her chin, leaving behind a greasy trail but she appeared not to notice. The olive, too big for her mouth, bulged suggestively in her left cheek.

"You've dribbled some oil on your chin," he said.

"Have I?" came the mumbled reply. She made no move to wipe it away with her hand or seek a cloth but held out her hands, palms upwards, helplessly.

"Let me get it," he said, then lifted the teacloth that was lying on the counter and gently dabbed her chin with the corner of it.

"Thank you," said Bernie and she smiled at him, her wide bark-coloured eyes framed by long curved lashes.

He realised then that, not since the children had been little, had he felt such a sense of being needed. He was so used to living with his fiercely independent and capable wife that he had forgotten what it was like to take care of a woman.

"I see you too have met each other," said Chris cheerfully, coming into the room and Paul immediately dropped the cloth onto the floor.

He picked it up again just as quickly, telling himself not to be so jumpy.

"Yes," he said. "Bernie was just asking where you got the antipasti."

"Heggarty's on Main Street. Do you remember David Heggarty from school, Bernie?"

"Can't picture him, but the name rings a bell."

"He runs it with his Italian wife, Carmela. She's lovely. And it's doing really well. The other day when I was in there, he was talking about looking for bigger premises."

"Well, that garlic is superb," said Bernie, crunching on a whole pickled clove.

"Good," said Chris with a pleased look on her face. "Have the children been through to say hello yet?"

"No. I think they're both upstairs," said Paul. "I'll go and call them."

Minutes later Hannah and Finn shuffled into the room in that practised nonchalant way of teenagers that managed to grate ever so slightly on Paul's nerves. They weren't bad kids, not at all, they just weren't as clean cut as he would like them to be. Finn insisted on slouching around in baggy jeans, hooded sweatshirt and a strange knitted hat – he called it a beanie – which bizarrely he wore inside the house as well as out. And most of the time Hannah looked like an extra from the *Rocky Horror Show* with her grungy gothic clothes, and heavy make-up.

Nagging them to "smarten up their act" had only resulted in Hannah getting a nose piercing and Finn refusing, for a while at least, to eat with the rest of the family. Under advice from Chris, Paul's new tactic was to completely ignore any errant behaviour or weird dress code in the hope that his lack of censorship would cause them to lose interest in their particular fixation. So far it hadn't worked.

"Hi there, nice to meet you," said Hannah to Bernie, with a genuinely pleasant smile that surprised her father.

It had been several months since he had seen her teeth exposed in a smile. He stared at the slightly red flesh around her nose piercing. Unlike ear-piercings, the wound in the nose never truly healed. It must have been extremely uncomfortable, painful even, but Hannah insisted it wasn't. He didn't believe her.

"I'm Finn. Good to have you here, Bernie," said Finn, equally pleasantly, and Paul thanked the Lord that, in spite of their appearance, their basic good manners were still intact.

"Mum says you're from Aussieland," said Finn. "Cool."

"I think so," said Bernie. "Have you ever been?"

"No but I would *soooo* love to," said Hannah, her childlike enthusiasm at odds with the grim external image she portrayed through her dress and demeanour.

"Surfing's ace down under, isn't it?" said Finn. "One day I'm going to ride the waves on Bondi Beach. Now that would be cool." He bent his knees and swayed his body as though riding on an invisible surfing board. His handsome face broke into a broad, happy smile. Hannah rolled her eyes and Bernie laughed.

"Tell you what. If you come to visit me, I'll take you surfing," she said. "Not to Bondi, mind. That's Sydney. But in Melbourne we have some of the best surfing in the whole country."

"Isn't that where the Twelve Apostles are?" asked Hannah. "Those pillars of stone that rise out of the sea?"

"That's right. I'll take you to see them too."

The children led Bernie into the conservatory, and their conversation soon became inaudible, save for the outbursts, now and again, of laughter. He could tell by their easiness in Bernie's company that they'd both taken an instant liking to her.

"Well, what do you think?" said Chris in a loud whisper.

"Of Bernie?" said Paul, practising the same nonchalance he had observed in his children only minutes earlier, for some reason he couldn't even explain to himself.

Chris rolled her eyes and said, "No, the Pope."

"She seems very nice," he said, choosing to ignore

Chris's sarcasm. "Hannah and Finn seem to like her."

"Yes, I think they do. That sister of mine had me all worked up to high doh about Bernie's visit. And do you know what?" she said with a relieved look on her face. "I think this visit is going to turn out just fine. In fact, I think it's going to be a big success."

She lifted the roast from the oven, pierced it with a metal skewer and examined the juices that leaked out.

Paul took a sip of his gin and tonic and his thoughts turned to Finn. What, he wondered, what he had done to deserve such a mindless son? Educated at Ballyfergus Grammar School, a respected local grammar, Finn's education had been completely wasted on him. To his father's horror, Finn had left school at sixteen – against both parents' wishes, needless to say – and was now an apprentice joiner. Thinking about it made Paul physically shudder with distaste.

He loved his son with all his heart but he could not bring himself to give Finn the approval and acceptance that he knew he ought. Chris said that the most important thing was that Finn was happy. There were a lot worse things he could be doing, she reminded him, but Paul struggled to imagine what could possibly be worse than having a tradesman as a son. He tried very hard, he really did, but there was no getting away from it – Finn was a great disappointment. It was humiliating, especially when the children of local brickies and dockworkers were winning prizes at school and going on to obtain university degrees.

Paul pursed his lips and suppressed the burning resentment he felt when he considered his children's education. Chris had not wanted either of them to attend boarding school – she said it was inhumane to send small children away from their parents. And by the time the children were ready for secondary education they both refused point blank to attend school outside of the local area. They had, in short, been spoilt.

Chris said they would get a perfectly good education at Ballyfergus Grammar School – wasn't she a former pupil and head girl herself? – and he had allowed himself to be persuaded.

But he now realised that they had been too indulgent with the children in allowing them to have so much say in the critical matter of their education – and it was one of the greatest regrets of his life. He should have insisted that they were sent away to private school – a stint at somewhere like Gordonstoun in Scotland would have sorted Finn out. But by the time it was obvious that Finn's academic career wasn't going anywhere, no private school would have him.

On the other hand, there was hope for Hannah. In spite of the awful way she looked, there was actually a brain in there. She'd attained excellent GCSE results and was on her way to attaining straight 'As' at A-level in Biology, Physics, Chemistry and Maths. Best of all, though – and Paul couldn't help but beam with pride at the thought – she had applied, and been accepted (conditional upon exam results, of course), to read medicine at Edinburgh. Not his first choice of medical school, but still, very gratifying.

"What are you smiling at?" came Chris's voice.

"Oh, nothing," he said and the smile fell from his face.

"What?"

"I was just thinking about Hannah and how well she's doing at school, compared to her brother."

"Yes. She is," said Chris, suddenly tight-lipped, anticipating correctly where the conversation was going.

"And," he said, unable to contain himself though he knew that his comments would only lead to friction between himself and Chris, "I was thinking the exact opposite of Finn."

Silence.

"I must say, for a boy of his natural ability, he has done exceptional poorly, hasn't he?" Paul went on, unable to keep the bitterness out of his voice.

"Perhaps. But he had every opportunity available to him at The Grammar, the same as his sister," said Chris in a crisp, I've-had-this-conversation-before sort of voice. "The difference is she's taken advantage of them. The same way I did."

"I still maintain that private schooling would've been the making of Finn, you know. Firm discipline. A strong guiding hand. That's what the boy needed. And now it's too late."

"Are you still flogging that old horse, Paul? Will you not give it a rest? Finn had no interest in academic achievement. Private school wouldn't have made any difference."

"I don't agree," said Paul and waited for a response but Chris, lifting plates out of the cupboard, remained silent. He could sense the tension in her hunched shoulders. "Well, it's too late now anyway, isn't it?" He was surprised with the depth of his anger. "The damage is done. I just wish I'd taken action sooner. But you were so set on them going to The Grammar –"

"And you agreed with me at the time. It served me well enough, Paul," she interrupted, refusing to concede. "And maybe Finn hasn't reached his potential yet. Now I think we should stop talking about it. We have a guest, remember."

There was a long pause and then Paul, remembering his duties as host, said, "Shall I get some wine?"

"Oh, haven't you chosen it already? It won't be the correct temperature."

"The red'll be fine and the white can be chilled in the wine chiller. It'll only take a couple of minutes," said Paul, not wanting to admit that he'd forgotten to select the wines earlier.

"If you would, that'd be great. Thank you," said Chris, all civility again.

Paul went to a small north-facing stone-built room off the utility that had once served as a larder for the old house and was now his wine store. It wasn't ideal – the house had no underground cellar – but the walls were thick, he'd blacked out the window, installed wine racks, a de-humidifier and heating (for the rare occasions in the winter when it was needed). By painting the roof white, a simple tip he'd picked up from *Decanter* magazine, he'd managed to lower the internal temperature of the room by two degrees.

Paul reached into the inky darkness and switched on the light, then closed the door behind him. A bare light bulb hung a few inches above his head and bottles of wine, lying on their sides in steel floor-to-ceiling racks, filled the entire length of the narrow room. It felt cool in comparison to the cosiness of the kitchen and smelled of musky dust.

Paul checked the maximum/minimum thermometer hanging from a wire near the centre of the room. It said eleven degrees centigrade – perfect. He took a deep breath, closed his eyes and tried to let go of the anger he felt towards Chris.

Of course, he never actually managed to do that – to let go of the anger – he just caged it away somewhere where he didn't have to deal with it. And the next time it emerged, it was as raw and as intense as ever. And because he spent his time suppressing the anger and never resolving it, it never went away. It just compounded, with the result that he felt increasingly more resentful.

Although he knew the failing was mainly on his part he couldn't help but apportion some blame to Chris. She thought she was always right. He could count on the fingers of both hands the number of times in their marriage that she'd admitted to being wrong. Sometimes, even when it was blatantly obvious that she was wrong – like over the issue of Finn's schooling – she would argue 'til she was blue in the face. Once he had laughed at this trait in her – now it infuriated him.

He took a deep breath of the still, cool air and reminded himself that Chris was, on the whole, a good match for him. It was unrealistic to expect perfection in a partner and Chris had many admirable qualities. She was a thoughtful and generous person who was always willing to lend a hand to someone in need. Underneath her rather serious exterior there was a warm and loving mother and, though not often glimpsed, a fun-loving spirit. She was conservative in her tastes, as he was, and she ran an efficient and orderly home. On balance, they were as happy as the next married couple, weren't they?

One thing Paul had learnt early on – in fact it had been instilled in him by his mother – was that you should never look to just one source for your happiness. Otherwise, when that one thing or person failed you, you were setting yourself up for a crushing disappointment. Therefore Paul looked not only to his wife, but to his children, his friends, his work, hobbies and his passion for wine for fulfilment.

And it was a strategy that, by and large, had served him well.

He socialised at the Golf Club after a round of a Saturday morning, enjoyed the company of the more erudite of his colleagues at work and immersed himself in his passion for wine. He and Chris were part of a busy social and dinner party circuit that ensured almost every Saturday night was taken up with some engagement or other. So, all things considered, if someone had asked him, he could honestly say that he was a happily married man.

The humidifier hummed away quietly in the background and Paul opened his eyes and cleared his mind of these unsettling musings. He stood in front of the wine racks and rubbed his chin thoughtfully. When he concentrated on wine, it helped to erase all the irritations in his life.

A nice Pinot Noir would go well with the simple menu of celeriac soup and roast lamb followed by apple crumble. Paul removed a bottle of Californian Iron Horse 2002 from the rack, looked at the label and wiped the dust from the bottle with a cloth hanging from a peg that he kept especially for that purpose.

With the red wine chosen, he turned his mind to white – an Australian wine would be a nice touch for their guest. He had a very special Chardonnay from Petaluma, one of Australia's most famous wineries in the Adelaide Hills founded by Brian Croser in the nineteen-seventies. Best paired with fish, of course, but roast lamb would be a very acceptable partner. He looked at the label, trying to remember exactly what he had paid for it – at least fifteen pounds a bottle – and wondered if Bernie would appreciate it. Or would it be wasted on her palate? Better to err on the cautious side until he learned how much she knew about wine – and anyway he and Chris would most certainly enjoy it. He wiped the dust from the glass and, gripping both bottles of wine by their necks in his left hand, opened the door, switched off the light and let the sprung door slam shut behind him.

In the kitchen he popped the bottle of white into the wine cooler, switched it on and opened the red. He poured it carefully into a crystal decanter leaving, as always, the last inch or so of wine in the bottle and took it through to the dining room. The table was elegantly laid with white Irish linen, cutlery and Waterford 'Alana' crystal (a wedding present from his parents).

Tiny arrangements of fresh spring flowers – freesias, primula and gypsophilia – studded the length of the table, linked to each other by ivy vines, like beads on a necklace. The heavenly, peppery smell of the white freesias filled the room and burning tea lights, interspersed between the miniature floral arrangements, twinkled like lights on a Christmas tree in the failing evening light.

"I think the food's just about ready," said Chris, standing in the doorway. "Did you get the wine?"

"Yes, that's the red. I'll just bring the white through now."

"Good. I'll ask everyone to sit down then," said Chris and she turned to go.

"Chris."

"Yes?"

"The table looks marvellous."

Chris made momentary eye contact with him and she gave him a brief, pleased-with-herself smile. "Thank you."

When Bernie came into the room Paul was standing with his hands on the back of the walnut carver chair at the head of the table. She gave out a little gasp, waved the crystal tumbler in the air and said, "Why, this is gorgeous!" She had a way of swaying her body, gracefully, from the waist as though she was a delicate flower stalk blowing in the wind. There was something almost insubstantial about her.

Paul followed her eyes to the pale yellow walls, the crushed buttermilk-coloured silk curtains, and the Burr walnut furniture, trying to imagine how the room, so familiar to him, might appear to the eye for the first time. Chris and he had spent a long time perfecting this house and it was gratifying to see the effect it had on Bernie.

"Why, what beautiful flowers, Chris!" said Bernie. "Did you do them yourself?"

"Oh, it was easy," said Chris modestly, though Paul could tell she was pleased that Bernie had taken the time to notice them. "I copied the idea – of a row of little vases and tea lights up the middle of a table – from a magazine."

"Well, I think they're just lovely," said Bernie and she picked up one of the little arrangements on the table and held it to her nose. "Freesias!" she cried with childlike zeal. "Is there anything nicer?"

This last remark was directed at Paul and he smiled widely, caught up in her breathless enthusiasm. "No," he said just to please her and keep the smile on her face. "I think not."

The children and Chris were now hovering around the table.

"Would you like to sit here?" he said and Bernie paused to consider the question as though what he'd asked was of great importance. He waited for her to speak for what seemed like an age.

"No," she said at last. "That's your chair."

He shrugged. They didn't often eat in this room – only

when they had guests really – and he always offered the carver to the guest of honour.

"It's your home," went on Bernie, "and I think the man of the house should always sit at the head of his table."

Chris pulled a face that said 'What did I just hear?' behind Bernie's back and Paul smiled. If those words had come out of any man's mouth they would've been daubed old-fashioned, anti-feminist and chauvinistic. Coming from a single, independent, and apparently successful woman like Bernie, well, it just went to show that appearances could be deceiving. If anyone had asked him he would have assumed that she was a strong-minded feminist.

"Well, then," he said, trying not to show his amusement for fear she would take offence. He pulled out the dining chair on the right-hand side of the carver. "How about this one? You can sit beside me and tell me all about Melbourne."

Bernie took the seat offered to her and placed the tumbler, which had held her gin and tonic, on the table.

"Let me take that," said Paul, lifting the glass and setting it on the sideboard before taking his seat at the head of the table.

Finn sat beside Bernie, Hannah sat on her father's left-hand side and Chris took the seat nearest to the door – a convention that had simply evolved during their long years of marriage, without ever being talked about, so as to minimise disruption when serving a meal.

"What's for dinner, Mum?" said the ever-hungry Finn. He grasped his knife and fork in a child-like manner and added, "I'm starving, Mum."

Paul rose from his seat to serve the wine while Chris laughed and said, "You'll see in a minute." Then she addressed Bernie with, "I can't feed this lad. Honestly, as soon as a meal's over he's in the fridge looking for more food. One time he came in from rugby training, ate dinner and then consumed an entire loaf of bread and a pint of milk!"

Finn smiled proudly as though he'd just been applauded for a great achievement.

"I can't help it, Mum," he said, shrugging his still-skinny shoulders in a helpless manner, and smiling coyly. "I'm a growing boy."

"More like a glutton," mumbled Paul grumpily, as he leaned over Chris's shoulder, and Bernie cast him a reprimanding glance. Inexplicably he blushed and sat down.

"Paul, a toast?" prompted Chris, her eyebrows moving in a most exaggerated fashion like they had a life of their own.

Paul raised his glass. "I propose a toast to Bernie. Welcome to Ireland and to our home. May your stay here be everything you wish for!"

Everyone clinked glasses and murmured their assent.

Bernie smiled and said, "Thank you. I can't tell you all how grateful I am to you for having me to stay. It's so much nicer to be here, Chris, with your family than some horrible impersonal hotel."

"We wouldn't want it any other way," said Chris and Paul was surprised to notice tears in her eyes – Chris was not normally given to sentimentality. She took a sip of white wine, said, "I'll serve dinner," then left the room.

Bernie turned to Paul and said, "Surely you were the same when you were Finn's age, Paul? Eating everything in sight?"

He shrugged, genuinely not remembering.

"From what I understand," went on Bernie, "it's all to

do with hormones. There really is nothing you can do about it. Same goes for sleeping in. I read somewhere that it's scientifically proven that teenagers' brains are wired so that they find it difficult to go to bed at night and need to sleep late in the morning. Why that should be, I don't know."

Hannah clapped her hands in glee and said, "Are you listening, Dad? Maybe you'll get off my case for a bit. You're always nagging me to get up at the weekends. It's bad enough having to get up for school during the week."

"Do you know what I've often thought," said Bernie, carrying on as though Hannah had not spoken.

"What?" said Paul, thinking that they had enough trouble with Hannah and Finn without Bernie stirring things.

"Why don't they change the time of the school day to coincide with the natural peaks and troughs in the average adolescent mind?"

"Cool!" said Finn. "Like you mean not start school 'til two every day?"

"Why not? Then you'd be tapping into the time when teenagers are naturally at their most receptive."

Chris came in with a large tray, set it on the sideboard and placed three serving dishes on the table – one contained slices of lamb, the other two roast potatoes and vegetables. "What's this you're talking about then?" she said, sitting down.

"Bernie's just suggested that school should be scheduled to fit round the bio-rhythms of adolescents," said Paul.

"Really?" said Chris and Finn said, "Bio-whats?" while pinching a bit of lamb crackling with his fingers. Chris cast him a warning look that would have turned milk sour.

"Oh, it's a well-known fact that teenagers naturally follow a different sleep pattern to adults or children," said Paul, grateful for the opportunity to show off his knowledge. "Not only do they need more sleep – as much as nine hours a night – but their bodies dictate when they need it. Whereas the rest of us operate on a twenty-four-hour cycle, or circadian rhythm, the internal clock of the typical teenager runs much slower, on a cycle of twenty-six to thirty hours. At eleven at night their internal clock is showing eight pm. And when the alarm goes off at seven in the morning, their body tells them it's only four."

"That's fascinating," said Bernie, her eyes locked onto his.

Encouraged by her rapt attention he went on, "It's all to do with the release of the hormone melatonin, which promotes sleepiness, Bernie. In teenagers it's secreted much later than adults."

"Bernie, please help yourself to some food," said Chris, and then she turned to Paul and said, "So you agree with Bernie that secondary schools should start later?"

"In theory, yes. But the problem comes with the teachers. Understandably they don't want their working patterns altered because they, unlike the students they teach, are at their most alert in the morning and they want to go home to their families at a sensible time."

"But has anyone lobbied for change?" said Bernie.

"As far as I know, these findings have been put to the teacher's unions but they argue that their students are most receptive in the mornings."

"But that can't be true. What do you think, Hannah?" said Bernie.

"I'm bright enough in the mornings, I guess. But it's true that by lunchtime I'm shattered."

"You're bright all the time, Hannah," said Paul and turning to Bernie he added, "Did Hannah tell you she got ten straight 'A's in her O-levels?"

"Dad!" protested Hannah.

"That's wonderful," said Bernie.

"What?" Paul said to Hannah and held his hands out, palms upwards. "It's nothing to be ashamed of, Hannah."

Her pale cheeks went a shade pinker and she muttered something incomprehensible.

Chris said, "Hannah's the top student in her year. And she's on course for straight 'As' at A-level too, aren't you, darling?"

This time it was Chris's turn to bear the brunt of Hannah's reproach. "Mum, I wish you wouldn't," she all but snarled and glared at her mother.

Paul couldn't understand why Hannah didn't take pride in her achievements. While he had no desire for her to be boastful about her extraordinary intelligence, he sometimes felt she played herself down a little. He thought she lacked confidence.

"Okay, okay," said her mother with a wry little smile, backing off. "We just want you to know that we're proud of you, Hannah, that's all."

There was a short, awkward silence and Bernie said, "Getting back to what you were saying, Hannah, you'll be tired by lunchtime because you haven't had enough sleep overall, not because you're naturally more receptive in the morning."

"I guess so," said Hannah.

"Well, it's a problem that we've had to live with for centuries," said Chris, in her bringing-a-conversation-to-an-end voice. "The world can't revolve round teenagers, can it? There's also an element of just having to get on with it."

"But that's so unfair, Mum," said Hannah with feeling, as the notion of injustice rose within her. "If people know about this then why isn't something being done to change things?"

"For the reasons your father's explained. Why should the rest of the world have to change to accommodate the needs of a minority group like teenagers? What about babies and toddlers, who go to bed early and wake up at the crack of dawn, like Finn and you did when you were little? Or old people who hardly sleep at all? Should the world revolve around their sleeping patterns?"

"That's different."

"No, it's not. The majority of people in this country are adults so I'm afraid they get to set the rules."

"Mother –" began Hannah but she was interrupted by Bernie, just in time to avert a heated exchange.

"This wine is exceptionally good. Australian, if I'm not mistaken?" she said, squinting to read the label on the bottle.

"That's right. A chardonnay from Petaluma in the Adelaide Hills," said Paul.

"But I thought Petaluma was in California," said Chris.

"It is," replied Bernie. "Brian Croser, the founder of the winery, named it after the Californian town where he had spent some time in the early nineteen-seventies. He studied at the University of California in Davis, you see – that's about seventy miles from Petaluma."

Paul closed his eyes for a second and silently gave thanks that he had chosen the wines for the meal wisely. Here was a woman who clearly knew her stuff.

"Of course Brian Croser isn't involved in Petaluma any-more," Bernie went on, addressing Paul who nodded as though he already knew what she was telling him, which he didn't. "It was taken over in 2001 by Lion Nathan. Brian stayed on as a figurehead for the group, finally bowing out in 2005. He's now involved in a joint venture called Tapanappa with the Bollinger family and Jean Michel Cazes."

"Oh yes," said Paul, grateful for the chance to display some knowledge, "the charismatic French owner of Chateau Lynch Bages."

"You've met him?" said Bernie.

"Only briefly at a tasting in London I went to a few years ago. Have you ever met Brian Croser?"

Bernie laughed. "No, I've never met him but I feel as if I have." Then, while everyone waited for further explanation, she reddened slightly at the base of her neck. At last she said, "I knew someone once – I mean one of my friends – a close friend, that is – was a bit of a wine buff. I suppose it's rubbed off on me."

"Is your friend in the wine business?" asked Paul and immediately regretted it because, for some reason, the redness that had started at the base of Bernie's neck now consumed her face entirely.

"No, strictly amateur," she said hastily. She looked down at the table then and fingered the stem of the glass with fingernails painted the colour of the sea.

"Seconds anyone?" said Chris and everyone but Finn, who up until now had been too busy eating to contribute to the conversation, refused. His mother served him a plate of food almost as large as the first portion.

Just before he tucked in, he said, "The red's nice too, Dad. What is it?"

"Iron Horse from California. But I wouldn't get too

fond of it, Finn. You won't be able to enjoy wine like that on a joiner's wage."

Chris, who until that moment had been staring at the remains of the food in the serving dishes before her, flashed Paul a searing look.

He shrugged his shoulders and said, "What?"

Finn looked at the food on his plate as though it had suddenly gone off and let out a sigh. He laid his cutlery down carefully and, without lifting his eyes from the table, said, "Why do you always have to say things like that?"

"Because it's true?" said Paul, realising even as he said it how awful he sounded. It was a brutally hurtful thing to say and yet he could not stop himself.

Finn became suddenly animated and stood up, almost knocking the chair over in his haste. His face was flushed now, the muscles in his neck and arms pulsing with emotion. He fixed a long, hard stare on his father. "I don't want any of your scabby old wine, anyway. It tastes like piss."

"Finn!" cried Chris, her voice squeaking with anger. "Don't speak to your father like that!"

"It's okay," said Paul, raising a hand to quieten Chris and pretending to be far less embarrassed than he was by Finn's behaviour.

He glanced at Bernie and she smiled thinly at him and Chris, before politely averting her gaze so as, he imagined, to spare them further embarrassment.

"Thanks for dinner, Mum," said Finn and he threw the starched white linen napkin on the table, "but I'm not hungry any more. I'm going upstairs." And he stormed out of the room.

A few moments of uncomfortable silence followed

which was broken by the sound of the clock on the mantelpiece chiming eight o'clock.

"Is that the time?" said Bernie. "I'm tired all of a sudden."

"Bernie," said Chris quickly. "I'm terribly sorry about Finn. He and his father –"

"Chris," interrupted Bernie, "you don't have to apologise to me for anything."

"But you must think –"

"I don't think anything. And who am I to rubbish anyway? What I know about raising teenagers you could write on the back of a durry packet. That was a corker of a meal. Now, if you'll excuse me, I think I'll turn in."

"But you haven't had any dessert," said Hannah.

"Save me some for tomorrow, will you?" said Bernie with a broad smile.

Paul stood up as she rose from the table. She leaned over and, to his surprise, planted a demure kiss on his cheek. She smelt of mango and watermelon.

"Thanks for a lovely evening," she said. Then she embraced Chris and Hannah and floated out of the room.

As soon as she had disappeared, Hannah and Chris turned a combined fierce gaze on Paul.

"What?" he said again, feigning innocence, but he knew fine well by those critical, censorious stares what was coming next.

"What did you have to go and say that to Finn for?" said Chris. "We were having a perfectly lovely evening and you have to go and spoil it."

"I was only pointing out the truth. What's wrong with that?"

"What's wrong, Dad, is that you were being nasty," said Hannah, narrowing her eyes until she looked just as mean as could be. "It wasn't nice. And I'm not sitting round here any longer waiting for you to pick on *me*."

And with that she stood up, threw her napkin on the table with a flourish and flounced out of the room.

"Well, I hope you're happy now," said Chris, in a voice that conveyed the exact opposite sentiments. Then she stood up, formed her lips into a hermetically sealed line and set about clashing plates and cutlery together as she cleared the table.

"I didn't mean it to come out like that," he said feebly. "I just want him to understand the implications of what he's choosing to do with his life."

"But don't you see, you stupid man," cried Chris, waving a dirty knife menacingly in the air, "every time you make snide remarks like that you're simply hardening his resolve to go against you. I don't like it any more than you do but you're going to have to learn to keep your mouth shut. You're just making things worse."

"No, Chris," said Paul, feeling wounded. "That's not fair."

"It is fair. Like it or lump it you're going to have to come to terms with Finn's choice in life. If you keep on at him like that, we're going to lose him."

"We're not going to 'lose' him," snorted Paul dismissively, not entirely understanding what she meant.

Chris lifted the stack of dirty plates crowned with cutlery and walked to the door. "If you don't lay off him, he'll be out of here before you know it and he won't want to have anything to do with you ever again. Is that what you want?"

Five

Bernie fell into bed exhausted and surprised herself by not waking until the following lunchtime. She pulled on a dressing gown and stumbled downstairs into the hall, embarrassed to have slept so long.

"Morning!" she called out, fixing the cord on the dressing gown, but no-one answered. "Morning!" she called, more loudly this time but got only the puppy's high-pitched yapping in response. The sun shone through a fan-shaped window above the door and a wave of pleasure came over her at the prospect of spending time alone in this beautiful building.

She went into the deserted kitchen. The door to the utility room was open – Murphy threw himself against the sides of his wire prison, panting, beside himself with joy at her presence.

"Hi there, little one," she called out but, mindful of last night's urinary performance, she did not let him out of the pen at once. First, she read the note on the kitchen table. *'Morning, Bernie'* it read, *'Hope you slept well. Help yourself to anything you want – nice organic bread in breadbin. Could you let Murphy into the garden at lunchtime? It'll save me having to pop home? Cheers. And could you give him the bowl of dog food that's sitting on the counter in the utility room? C. XO.'*

"Better put you out then, little one," said Bernie and smiled at herself for addressing a dog.

He sat down with his head cocked to one side as though waiting to hear what else she had to say. Every muscle in his body quivered with anticipation while she unfastened the gate on the puppy pen. Then he burst forth into the room, leaping and bounding like a puppet on a string and snapping the air with his pin-sharp little teeth. His gums and tongue were the colour of the inside of a pomegranate. The excitement was too much for him – a thin trickle of urine criss-crossed the floor beneath his paws.

Bernie wasted no time in leading this over-excited bundle of fur to the patio doors that led into the garden. As soon as she opened them, he squeezed through the crack and, crouching like a bitch, immediately relieved himself on the grass right outside the door. He had not yet learned to cock his leg.

"Good onya! Clever dog, Murphy."

He came running back to her then, his tail wagging back and forth like a demented metronome. He nuzzled her legs with his wet nose and licked her bare feet until she giggled. She tickled him under the chin and he stared at her for a few seconds with adoring eyes the colour of coffee. Then he then charged off in the direction of the trees at the bottom of the garden, and Bernie went back inside feeling her spirits lifted by the encounter with the puppy.

First she cleaned up the accident in the utility room. Then, ravenous, she poked about the kitchen cupboards and drawers until she found what she needed to make herself a good breakfast of cereal, boiled eggs, wholemeal toast and coffee. After she had eaten she sat in the conservatory in a wicker chair, drinking coffee and watching the battle of wits between a clutch of brightly coloured finches and Murphy. The birds sat on the wall, well out of harm's way, while Murphy yapped and pawed the ground, his tail wagging like the propeller on a plane. Soon he lost interest and proceeded to shred a nearby pampas grass.

"Daft dog," she said to herself with a smile.

She'd never fancied a dog herself – too tying and she'd always preferred less boisterous feline company – but she could, in Murphy's loveable and affectionate nature, see the attraction. She thought about the family dynamics she had witnessed the night before and it saddened her to realise that she had observed no evidence of affection between Chris and Paul. True, they had been married a long time, but she had been with Gavin for eight years and strangers would always have known, just by watching them, that they were lovers.

But Chris was Chris, hardly changed at all from school – serious and reserved. It comforted Bernie to think (while not really believing it) that Chris wasn't the sort to engage in public displays of affection. Hannah and Finn she had found enchanting – youth was so refreshing – though their very existence confronted her with the bleak absence of children in her life.

It was so unfair, she thought, allowing herself this one brief moment of bitterness. She swallowed the last tepid mouthful of coffee and sighed. It was just so unfair. She would have made a wonderful mother. How she envied the women she saw everywhere, trailing tearful kids around in their wake, grim-faced and determined, clearly less than elated in their role as parent. Didn't they realise how lucky they were? But she mustn't dwell on her disappointment.

She must focus her wayward thoughts, ever ready to slip into doleful self-pity, on something more pleasant.

Like Paul. Well, there was no doubt about it, she found him . . . intriguing. Charming and interesting, he was clearly a well-read and intelligent man and, when he talked about wine, she caught a glimpse of his passionate nature too. And yet, in spite of his erudite sophistication, he was totally incapable of communicating with his son. She had understood immediately, from the few words Paul had uttered, what a letdown it was for him that Finn was a tradesman. It saddened her to see a father-son relationship so soured by anger and disappointment.

If she was entirely truthful with herself, and she blushed at the thought even though there was no-one there to see her, she had been more than intrigued by Paul. She was attracted to him and she was quite sure that he felt the same way about her. The way he seemed nervous and jumpy in her presence, the way he hung on every word she said, too easily impressed by her scant knowledge of Australian wines – and desperate to impress her with his.

This was not the first time that Bernie had found herself in this position – married men often took a shine to her and she understood, without being in any way bigheaded, why. She was slightly-better-than-average-looking, single, and available and the grass was always greener, wasn't it? Most of them wanted nothing more than to flirt with her, proving to themselves that they still could still pull. Some, however, wanted more.

Married men in this category figured that there was no-one to get hurt in a relationship with her just so long as the wife never found out. It surprised Bernie to find out that her feelings were, very often, not considered at all. So experience had taught her to be very cautious around married men and she would employ that cautiousness with Paul as she had done with those before him.

She would enjoy his company but, not knowing what his intentions were, and just to be on the safe side, she would be sure not to mislead him into believing that their friendship was anything more. The last thing in the world she would ever do, she reminded herself, was threaten Chris's marriage. Not for the sake of a meaningless fling.

The clock in the dining room chimed two and, reluctantly, Bernie heaved herself out of the chair. She opened the patio doors and called to Murphy who loped happily across the grass to greet her. She coaxed him inside, secured him in his pen and fed him, then climbed the three flights of creaking stairs to the top floor and ran herself a hot bath. She examined the selection of luxury oils and foams on a glass shelf and chose a bottle of purple bath oil by Pecksniff's.

She poured some slowly into the bath where, on contact with the hot, clear water, it burst into rings of rainbow colour – like drops of petrol in a puddle – and released the summery smell of lavender. Bernie placed her toes in the water to check the temperature, then stepped in and lowered her body gingerly through the oily film into the soothing water. Then she closed her eyes, concentrated on relaxing, and tried not to think too much about why she was here.

Later, when she was dressed, made up and fully unpacked – in other words when she had procrastinated for as long as was humanly possible – she sat down on the bed in her room and glanced at the radio alarm-clock, thoughtfully placed there for her convenience. Chris thought of everything. God, if she could see the sort of artistic squalor her friend lived in she would be absolutely appalled, thought Bernie, and she smiled. One of the nice things about being away from home was that you could pretend to be what you weren't – and that included, but was not limited to, being neat, tidy and organised. All the things she knew she ought to be but wasn't.

The digital display on the clock changed, catching Bernie's eye. It was nearly half past three. She imagined Hannah would be home from school soon and she should really make a start on preparing dinner.

So, if she was going to call her brother, she'd better get on with it. She couldn't put it off any longer or questions would be asked, and offence taken, such was the delicate nature of her relationship with her siblings. A little swell of panic rose up inside her like indigestion. She put a hand between her breasts to calm herself. She tried to reach for the phone but her arm felt heavy as lead.

She let it drop by her side and recalled the last time she'd seen Michael. It had been in the hallway of the semi-detached house on Ladas Drive where they'd grown up and where her father had lived until he died. Michael had kicked at the carpet with his scuffed work-boots while she stood before him, his hands shoved into the pockets of his too-tight jeans. Never a great one with words, he'd muttered something about Australia being a great place and maybe he'd come and visit one day. Then he'd offered her a limp handshake and placed a dutiful kiss on her cheek, like she was a maiden aunt with an overpowdered face.

"Good luck, then," he'd said and stood at the doorway and watched her load her case into the boot of the ageing yellow Renault 5. She'd got into the passenger seat beside her father and looked back at Michael one last time. But he was already gone from the threshold, the Astra glazed door like a giant glassy eye, firmly shut where he had stood.

The memory of that closed door had left an indelible mark on Bernie's memory and had come to sum up everything about the relationship, or rather lack of it, between Bernie and her brothers. Was it possible that they were just absolutely incapable of showing affection – as she hoped? Or did they really not care about her – as she had always believed?

She took a deep breath to suppress the flutter of nerves that made her hand shake when she opened her address book, and carefully dialled the number.

"Hello, Michael," she said into the mouthpiece, sitting on the edge of the bed as though ready to jump up at a moment's notice. "It's me. Yes, yes. I arrived safely. Last night." Pause. "The journey was fine. How are you all?" She listened to him for a few minutes and then said, "Yes, that would be lovely. No need, I'll hire a car. Yes, I have the address. Okay, I'll see you Sunday then. Me too."

The conversation ended abruptly with no exchange of endearments beyond what was necessary to pass for politeness. Bernie put the phone down, sat with her hands between her knees, and exhaled slowly. To say she had never been close to her brother Michael, and her other brother Jim for that matter, was an understatement.

Jim was her elder by ten years, Michael by twelve. She had spent her childhood wondering why they did not like her and trying, unsuccessfully, to curry their favour. But it had never worked – they never seemed to care for her. In spite of her pathetic efforts to endear herself to them – like dressing up pretty for them to admire her and, when she was old enough, making rock cakes for their packed lunches to take to work – they had taken little or no interest in her.

Their world was one of steel-capped work-boots, angry yellow-headed pimples, deep husky voices and aftershave-sodden Saturday nights at The Candlelight disco. They fought with her father and made fun of her Adam Ant posters and her devotion to Spandau Ballet. And, as soon as they were old enough, they had moved out, leaving the house permeated with sadness like damp and her alone with her father in the quiet misery that passed for a life.

Who could blame her for wanting out? Who could blame her for going as far away as she could – to the other side of the world? What was the alternative? Stay at home and care for her father only to find out, at the end, that he never cared for her? It had been bad enough finding out how much he despised her when he died last year. How much worse would she have felt had she devoted her best years to him?

So, all things considered, she told herself, the phone call had been a good start. It was the first step in the process of discovery that had brought her all the way from Melbourne to Ballyfergus – and the sole reason for this trip. She'd arranged to go and see Michael and his family on Sunday. With any luck she'd get to spend some time alone with Michael and maybe start to unravel the mystery that she had come here to solve.

She heard sounds from downstairs and stood up. Yes, she had a few bridges to build on this trip and the phone call to Michael was just the start.

* * *

Hannah and Finn had already left the table in the kitchen where they were dining and Bernie watched Chris bring cheese and fruit to the table.

"That was absolutely divine," said Paul, kissing the tips of his fingers in the dramatic, Mediterranean fashion, "*Ab ovo usque ad mala*". The clever Latin words rolled off his tongue confidently, like a prayer. He seemed to address this comment to no-one in particular and then offered, to Bernie's relief, a translation. "It means 'from beginning to end'. Delicious from start to finish!"

Bernie looked at the remains of the simple chicken and rice dish she had prepared in the serving bowl and blushed. The meal did not compare favourably with the banquet Chris had served the night before and it certainly did not deserve such praise.

"Thank you," she said.

"Did you go out today?" asked Chris when she had finished serving the cheeseboard and sat down at the table again.

"It sounds awful but no. I never set foot across the threshold," replied Bernie. "I hope that doesn't make me sound completely lazy but I didn't wake up 'til lunchtime. By the time I'd had something to eat — that bread was delicious by the way — did you make it, Chris?"

"Well, the breadmaker did."

"It was gorgeous. Well, by the time I'd eaten and had a bath, the day was just about done. It's just so lovely in your house. I had no desire to leave it."

"Ah, a day of supine indulgence by the sounds of it," said Paul wistfully, popping a shiny aubergine-coloured grape into his mouth. "How I envy you. While the rest of us labour at the coalface of illness and injustice."

"Well, I am on holiday, you know," said Bernie, in a playful tone. She rearranged the linen napkin on her lap and looked up at Paul through mascara-coated lashes.

"Quite. Nothing wrong with a day of indulgence now and again," said Chris icily, directing her comment to Paul, apparently misunderstanding the light-hearted nature of their conversation.

Bernie doubted if Chris had ever had a day of indulgence in her life. She was just too – too serious.

"And aren't I the greatest advocate of it?" said Paul, raising his eyebrows just a little in mock surprise at Chris and casting Bernie a conspiratorial glance. "Why, I prescribe it to my patients," he said and smiled wickedly.

"You prescribe 'it'?" said Bernie, starting to giggle. "What precisely is 'it'?"

Bernie realised with a jolt that she far preferred Paul's company to Chris's and this made her feel guilty. She stopped giggling immediately and bit her lip.

"Unashamed self-indulgent pleasure. Sometimes people need a license to be good to themselves. People are so busy working and doing, they don't take enough time to do the things in life that give them pleasure. Take Chris for example."

"Now don't you start," said Chris, folding her napkin and laying it on the table.

"No, listen," said Paul. "I'm serious."

"I know you are."

Paul chose to ignore the warning tone in Chris's voice and said to Bernie, "Chris works too hard, you know. If it's not office work it's one of her charities or fighting Tesda."

"Tesda?" said Bernie.

"The big supermarket chain," said Chris. "They want to build a massive supermarket in Ballyfergus."

"And that's a bad thing?" said Bernie, hesitantly.

"Why, yes," said Chris quickly before Paul had time to speak, suggesting to Bernie that they did not share the same views on this subject. "It'll kill all the independent shops in the town centre. They won't be able to compete with the buying power of a big supermarket."

"Not everyone would agree with that analysis," said Paul quietly.

"You see, Paul and I don't see eye to eye on this topic."

"It's just not as black and white —" began Paul but Chris interrupted him, not unkindly.

"Let's not go into all that again, Paul," she said wearily. Then she stood up and added, "But on that very subject, I have some work to do for PINBAT. Sorry, that stands for People In Ballyfergus Against Tesda, Bernie. We've got an important meeting coming up with the planning authorities soon and I need to go over some papers. Leave the dishes — I'll tidy them later."

"Sure, no worries," said Bernie and Chris left the room. There was silence for a few moments during which Bernie rearranged the napkin on her lap.

"Why were you blushing earlier?" said Paul.

"Was I?" said Bernie, forcing herself to look him in the face and feeling the familiar hotness in her cheeks again.

"There. You're doing it again," he said directly and if it had been anyone else she would've considered them rude. But not Paul. His directness seemed to stem from a child-like inquisitiveness.

"You're embarrassing me," she said, sliding her gaze off his face onto the slate floor. "Stop it," she added, smiling at her girlish silliness, and she flicked him a brief glance.

"I didn't . . ." he said and paused.

She stole a look at him. He was staring at her with furrowed brows as if considering something quite perplexing.

"I made you blush," he said at last, a statement rather than a question. His brow was smooth again, all signs of concentration gone.

"Let's talk about something else."

"Okay," he said. "What?"

"Ask me why I'm here. On this trip."

"Bernie, why are you here in Ballyfergus?"

"Do you really want to know?"

"Yes. And you want to tell me, Bernie, don't you?"

"I do. I want to tell someone."

"Not me especially then. Just anyone."

"No, I didn't mean it like that," she said quickly.

He laughed, threw his head back a little and settled his steady gaze on her face again. "It doesn't matter. Go on."

"But it does matter. I want to tell you."

"Why me?"

"Because . . . because I think you'll understand."

He nodded his head slowly, considering this and then said, "So, what is it you have to tell?"

"Well . . . I . . ." she began and faltered.

He waited while she fumbled for the words like lost keys.

"I came here on a quest, Paul. To solve something," she said and felt the hotness in her cheeks worsen. "That makes it all sound very mysterious, doesn't it? Like a murder mystery or something."

He was quiet. Serious. Waiting for her to go on.

"My father died last year," she began.

"I'm sorry. I didn't know."

She shrugged and found herself forced to pause because her breath was suddenly shallow.

"Are you all right?" he said, the frown returning and settling on his brow like a scar. She hated to see it. She had a sudden desire to put her hand out and caress it away.

"Yes. I'm fine," she said and forced a bright smile.

"So, your father?" he prompted, resting his head on the upturned palm of his right hand while lazily taking a sip of wine. "Tell me about him."

"I didn't come home for his funeral, you know."

She waited for his expression to alter – for a hint of shock or disgust to cross his face. But his features remained impassive, non-judgemental, supported comfortably on the palm of his hand.

"I couldn't," she went on. "I'd communicated very little with him over the years and when the news came, well, it was as though a stranger had died. I was sick at the time. I guess I wasn't thinking straight. I'm not sure I could've travelled . . . I sound like I'm making excuses, don't I?"

"Are you? You don't have to. Not to me."

She smiled gratefully. He was a good listener. "I just didn't want to be there. I couldn't. I can't explain why. My brothers weren't very pleased . . . but, I didn't come home. And then, a few months later, I got the most awful shock. Not that I had been expecting anything. Nothing could've been further from my mind."

"Expecting anything?" he asked gently.

"My father never left me anything in his will," she said, her voice suddenly high-pitched like a child's. She cleared her throat and went on, "Not that there was an awful lot to leave but that wasn't the point. He didn't just omit me from the will. I was mentioned – but clearly and specifically written out of it. His inheritance was split equally between my brothers."

"You read this for yourself?" said Paul, sitting upright suddenly.

"No, but Jim – my brother – told me. He called especially to tell me. He was very embarrassed about it. He said so on the phone. That he didn't know why Dad had done it and he was sorry to be the one to have to tell me. I think he thought I was bothered about the money."

"But you weren't?"

"I couldn't have given a rat's ass."

Paul smiled.

"Sorry," said Bernie. "But I really didn't, and don't, care about the money."

"Did your brothers offer you restitution?"

Bernie stifled a laugh which came out as a sort of unpleasant snort. "You don't know my brothers, Paul. Anyway, I don't care about the money. I mean it."

"I know. But you want to know why you were written out of the will?"

"Yes."

"And do you have any idea why your father did it?"

"None. None at all. Only . . . only I've always had this feeling . . . Oh, I can't explain it. It'll just sound daft."

"Try me."

"Well," she said and hesitated, squashing damp crumbs of Roquefort into her plate with the flat of a knife, "I always felt that Dad didn't love me."

"What made you think that?" he said carefully.

"I don't know. No, I do know. He never showed me much affection as a child. I don't remember him kissing me or cuddling me."

"That doesn't mean he didn't love you. Men of that generation often had difficulty showing affection to their children."

Hot tears sprang to her eyes and she bunched both fists in her lap in an effort to hold them back. "I'm finding this difficult," she said, blinking hard to hold back the tears.

Suddenly he reached out and took a balled-up fist in his hand. He pulled it towards him across the cluttered table and slowly unfurled her stiff fingers.

"I know," he said and gently stroked her palm with the tips of his fingers. She thought for one moment that he was going to kiss her palm but he simply sat there staring at it, like a fortune-teller.

"The thing is," she went on, trying to ignore the heady sensation created by his touch, "I felt it as well. In here." She pressed the other closed fist to her left breast. "I felt as though I was an obligation. Something that had to be dealt with out of a sense of duty rather than love."

"Did he treat your brothers any differently?"

"It's hard to tell. There was such an age gap between us – over ten years – so I don't know what he was like with them when they were small. But I think he was – he was – kinder somehow to them than me." She found it hard to concentrate – little ripples of pleasure stole up her arm and fuddled her brain.

"Yes, I'm almost sure he was. And then, when he wrote me out of the will, I just had this very strong, overpowering feeling that I had to get to the bottom of this. That I had to find out why he did it. For there must be a reason, mustn't there? You don't just write your only daughter out of your will for no reason. I felt as though he was telling me something from beyond the grave. I just have to work out what."

"So it is a mystery of sorts," said Paul, his hand suddenly still.

"I guess so."

"Well," said Paul and he folded the healing fingers of his large hand over her small, delicate digits and said, staring into her face so intently this time that she flinched, "I'm going to help you solve it."

Suddenly she came to her senses. Chris was in a room upstairs only a matter of feet from them. What was she thinking of? What was Paul thinking of?

She withdrew her hand sharply, still burning from his touch, and stood up so abruptly that she nearly toppled the chair over.

"That's great, Paul," she said and then, injecting as light-hearted a tone as she could muster, she added, "Come on, help me clear away these dishes. It's not fair to leave them all for Chris."

She could hear his intake of breath as he opened his mouth to speak but she did not want to hear what she knew he had to say. She grabbed something off the table – a half-full water jug – and stumbled towards the kitchen. With her back to Paul she poured the contents of the jug into the sink and still she could sense his presence bearing down on her.

And then, to her relief, Finn ambled into the room looking for something to eat even though he'd eaten less than an hour ago and the leftovers from dinner were barely cold.

* * *

Chris sat in the study on the second floor with a sleeping Murphy at her feet, staring at the photographs on the wall. There was one of Finn as a blonde-haired cherub sitting bolt upright in his pram at six months old. And one of a skinny Hannah on Portstewart Strand, when she was just five-and-a-half years old, with Murphy's predecessor, Rascal. Limbs like a stick insect in her bright pink swimming costume, and a smile like a sunbeam radiating pure innocence. Two perfect children, living safe and blessed lives. How precious those days had been, though too busy with the business of parenting, she had not known it then. How had her glorious babies turned into the disgruntled creatures she hardly recognised these days?

She lived in the hope that things would come full circle, as people assured her they would. That her children would one day come back to her, in the sense that she would have a close relationship with them once more, that they would confide in her and ask for her help in the way they used to as small children. This state of affairs, impossible to imagine now, would come to pass, she was told, when her children themselves became parents. Parenthood would make them see their parents in a different light.

Suddenly she and Paul would no longer be the over-protective killjoys they were currently perceived to be. Parenthood would be the glue that would bind the generations together once more – along with, she thought cynically, free childcare, baby-sitting on demand and restorative Sunday lunches at the grandparents'.

Chris sighed. Hannah and Finn were still very young – it would be a long time before either of them were parents. Meantime Chris had her work and many interests (as well as spearheading PINBAT she was chairwoman of the local fundraising Ladies Circle) to keep her busy. And of course Paul.

She wet the ring finger of her left hand with her tongue and worked her engagement ring and wedding band free. She laid them on the desk and stared at the little bands of gold. She picked up the engagement ring, a solitaire diamond, its brilliance dulled by layers of grime – she could not remember when she had last cleaned it. She set it down gently and examined her finger. The rings, slightly too tight now, had left indentations at the base of her finger. She wondered if she stopped wearing the rings would the marks fade or would they be a permanent reminder of Paul?

Oh, how things between them had changed! There was a picture of him, handsome with sunburn and crinkle-eyed with laughter on a long-ago summer holiday to Puerto Pollensa. When did they stop laughing together? When had she ceased to be impressed by his Latin quotations and come to consider them pompous instead? When did his passion for wine become a bore to her?

And when had she stopped being fun? Was it when she stopped loving Paul in the way she once did? Immediately, she pushed this thought – the idea that she didn't love him – away. For the idea of being married to someone she did not love was something that she could not bear. She believed marriage was for keeps – it was about weathering the storms and keeping it together. Sometimes passionate love mellowed into a sort of companionship and, if that was your lot, then you got on with it and made the best of it. It was better than being alone, like Bernie, wasn't it? It was better than breaking up an otherwise happy home.

Chris felt like she had been feigning interest in Paul, his

life and his hobbies for a long time. Nothing that he said or did intrigued her any more. Not the way it used to, when the highlight of her day was talking to him over a late supper and a cheap bottle of plonk (in the days before they could afford good wine) with the kids safely tucked up in bed.

But, in spite of his flaws, he was a good man and she knew it. Maybe that was what made it hard. Knowing that he was decent made her faultfinding seems mean and cruel. It was, she knew, simply a case of making the effort. Now that Hannah and Finn were growing up and almost away, they should make more time for each other and try to reignite the passion that had once bound them so intimately. Just how this was to be achieved though, was beyond Chris.

She remembered a time when she used to hang on every word he said, just as she realised with sudden clarity, Bernie had done tonight, mesmerised by his ever-so-slightly-cocky confidence and sharp intelligence. But Chris had long since discovered that Paul was not as confident as he appeared. He was a man who needed constant reassurance – no – admiration, to thrive. And it had been some years since he had got that kind of hero-worship from her. It just wasn't in her nature to massage anybody's ego, Paul's included.

From under the desk came a grinding noise and she looked down at Murphy. He was lying on his side, his legs jerking in his sleep, his jaws chomping away on some imaginary delicacy. He thrust his muzzle forward, the way he did when foraging in the undergrowth, and made a snuffling sound. His visible ear, rust-coloured and edged in black, was folded like the flap on an envelope. If only her life could be as simple and as happy as a dog's. Had humans as a race, she wondered, lost the ability to be truly happy? Everyone she knew, and she included herself and Paul in this analysis, was so busy these days and their lives so very complicated.

There was a brief knock on the door but, before she had time to answer it, Paul opened it. He did not come in but stood on the threshold.

"How's it going?" he said.

"Fine," she said, guiltily sliding a piece of paper over the rings to hide them from his view. "Nearly done. I just need to check that all the objections are properly documented for this planning meeting."

Paul said nothing in response and Chris swivelled round in the office chair to face him. He had a bemused, faraway look in his eyes induced no doubt by too much of that fine wine at dinner.

"Chris," he said theatrically, "what do you say to us going away together for a romantic weekend?"

"Just the two of us?" she said and was filled with utter panic. What would they do for a whole weekend in each other's company? He was offering her the opportunity for intimacy that she had, only a few moments ago, decided her marriage needed. And yet her immediate reaction was to avoid the situation at all costs.

"Yes, just the two of us. That's the whole point," he said a little irritably. "How about somewhere romantic like Paris? No, we've done that, haven't we? And Rome. What about Venice then?"

"Oh, I don't know. Would this be the best time of year to visit Venice? Mightn't it be busy?"

"No, now would be a perfect time to go. How about next weekend?"

"Next weekend?" she repeated with a frown.

"Yes, let's just book it and go!" he said, surprising her with his spontaneity.

"Hmm. Can't do next weekend," she said, clutching desperately at straws. "Don't you remember we have that dinner at the Websters'? It's already been rescheduled twice. And the following weekend you have a medal competition at the golf club. And we can't really go away when we have a house guest, can we?"

"I'm sure Bernie will find things to do," said Paul and Chris was surprised that Bernie's name on Paul's lips suddenly made her feel . . . uncomfortable.

"Still, it wouldn't really be the done thing to leave her on her own, now would it?" She felt her face flush slightly and looked at her knees.

There was a pause.

When she looked up he was staring at her and he said rather sharply, "No, I suppose not."

He was disappointed in her, she could tell. And yet she couldn't bring herself to change her mind. What on earth would they talk about for a whole weekend in Venice anyway? What had made him come up with this madcap scheme? It was so out of character.

"Another time, perhaps?" she suggested half-heartedly. "When we're not so busy?"

"Yeah, another time," he said, dispiritedly.

Chris breathed a silent sigh of relief and congratulated herself on her successful sidestepping of the issue. She hoped he wouldn't bring it up again. But she couldn't help but wonder how on earth they were going to fill holidays together from now on. Finn had come with them on their last holiday to France in January but only because they were skiing. Next time, they would most likely be alone. Maybe they could get someone to come with them – another couple perhaps?

"Chris," came Paul's voice.

"Yes?"

"Are you okay? You look worried."

"I was just thinking," she said and paused. "I was just thinking about work."

"Don't you ever switch off, Chris?" he said, sounding exasperated and she smiled blankly at him, refusing to be drawn into an argument.

So, changing subject, she said, "Where's Bernie?"

"Just this minute gone up to bed."

Chris glanced at her watch. "What were you two chatting about for so long?"

"Not a lot," said Paul, transferring his weight from one foot to the other.

"God, Paul. You've been down there for nearly two hours. You must have been talking about *something*."

"She was telling me about her quest, as she calls it."

"Quest?"

"Yes," said Paul thoughtfully, his eyebrows knitting together as he frowned. "You know, the business of her father's will – and the fact that he never left her a penny. He left everything equally between her brothers. She thinks there might be some sort of sinister reason why he wrote her out of the will. And she's here to find out what it is."

"She didn't mention that to me."

"Didn't she? I just assumed she would have. You being best friends and all. Oh dear, maybe she meant for me to keep it a secret. I wonder why she told me? She must've felt she could confide in me . . ."

"Don't worry, I'll not say anything. And I'm sure she

will tell me. We just haven't had that much time to talk yet," said Chris, feeling a little bit put out that Bernie had confided in Paul rather than herself. "I'd heard Tommy Sweeney died last year," she went on. "Mind you, it's not unusual for sons or daughters to be disinherited. People often settle old scores through their wills."

"But what beef could Bernie's father have with her? She's completely mystified."

"Mmm," said Chris and this time it was her turn to frown. "I have no idea and I really can't imagine. But you know what?" she added, suddenly animated. "She could contest it, I'm sure she could." She swivelled round in her chair to face a raft of books on a shelf above the desk. She stood up and ran her index finger quickly along the spines of the books, some of which dated back to her student days, with her head inclined to the right so that she could read the titles. "It's not my speciality of course but . . ."

"I don't think she wants to contest the will, Chris."

"She doesn't?" said Chris with a French-manicured index finger poised on the spine of a book.

"She's not interested in the money. In any case, I don't think there was that much involved. It's more about finding out the reason why her father did this to her. It must be very hurtful."

"Well, yes, I imagine it must be," said Chris, turning back to look at Paul. She peeled off her reading glasses and rubbed the spot between her eyebrows. "To be disinherited without any explanation. It must've come as a shock. Funny that she never came home for his funeral though, isn't it?"

"That's another story," said Paul, and the tone of his voice suggested that he was not to be drawn further on this subject. "Look, will you be long?"

"Another forty minutes or so should do it."

He was staring at the papers on the desk as if he hated them, but all he said after a short pause was, "Well, I'll say goodnight then. Bernie and I cleared up the dishes."

"Thank you. You really didn't need to, especially Bernie. I must tell her that in the morning."

"She was glad to do it," he said and then added, "Goodnight, Chris."

"Night."

"Love you," he said, as he always did.

"Love you," said Chris automatically and she waited until she heard the door shut behind him.

Then she leaned back in the chair and examined the phrase she had just used. It was so well-worn she wondered if it had any meaning left. She said it every day to the children – to their utter mortification – and in their case she felt it meant something. But when she said it to Paul she felt like fraud. Because she couldn't be sure that the feelings she had for him were strong enough to be called love in the traditional sense.

She sat slumped in her chair, arms crossed defensively across her chest, and ruminated over these thoughts. Then she said out loud and rather crossly, "This doesn't help, Chris!"

Mulling over morose thoughts had never been her style. She was a doer and keeping busy had always proved a better ally to her in times of crisis than any form of introspection. So she replaced the rings on her finger, gave her head a little shake to activate her brain cells, sat upright in her chair again and applied her over-active mind to the tricky matter of the planning application.

When she came to bed some time later Paul was in a

deep sleep, the reading light still on and the journal he had been reading lying on the carpet. She undressed and then went around to his side of the bed and picked the journal up off the floor. She set it on his beside cabinet and paused a moment to stare at the lines and contours of his face, looking for the man she had married. His features were so familiar to her and yet lying there with his face a blank, undistorted by emotion, she wondered if she knew him at all. Then she put her hand to the switch on the wall and extinguished the light.

Six

The alarm went off at six fifteen and, beside her in the bed, Tony moaned. Immediately alert, Karen quickly switched the buzzer off, slid out of bed and locked herself in the ensuite bathroom.

Tony was a heavy sleeper and could be relied upon to slip back into a deep and restful slumber. Only one of the children hollering in his ear, jumping on top of him or trying to open his eyes with stubby little fingers was guaranteed to wake him. And, with any luck, the kids wouldn't waken for another twenty minutes or so. Just long enough.

She sat down sleepily on the toilet and tried to ignore the apron of flesh that rested on her lap. Then she stood up, peeled off her nightshirt (pyjamas were out of the question with her shape, being both unsightly and uncomfortable) and stepped into the shower. She showered very quickly, lathering her hair with a Toni and Guy shampoo and conditioner for highlighted dyed hair. Then she stood under the strong jet of hot water and thought that life was so unfair. Even her best attribute – her highlighted blonde hair – was fake. There was nothing about her natural body that she liked.

The thing was that people had absolutely no idea that she felt this way. She dressed well and fashionably, though more carefully than people could ever imagine, every purchase weighed and measured in terms of its slimming effect versus style. She knew that her obsession with her body was unhealthy but she was powerless to stop herself.

Karen stepped out of the shower and dried herself briskly with a soft white towel. She went to extraordinary lengths to avoid any situation where she would have to reveal more flesh than she wanted. For example, only she knew the real reason for her early-morning alarm calls. She told Tony that she was an early bird and that she liked to get things done in the morning. Truth was, she was just as much of a night owl as he, but the bright spring morning light was especially unkind to those with a fuller figure.

She squinted up at the two velux windows in the sloped ceiling which let in far more natural light than was desirable. When they'd brought the house she'd thought them an asset – she dreamt of long, bubbly nighttime baths, gazing up at the stars. They'd lived here for five years and she could count on two hands the number of times she'd lain in the bath and watched the stars. She was always afraid that Tony might come in and watch her or, worse, want to join her. The only place Karen felt comfortable with her body was in bed at night in the pitch dark.

It wasn't just her shape that bothered her. The weight was accompanied by horrible disfiguring cellulite. She replaced the damp towel on the heated towel rail and examined the top of her right thigh in the long mirror that hung on the bathroom wall. Orange peel, my arse, she thought. What a misnomer if ever there was one. Her legs looked more like the pitted surface of the moon, scarred by the fat deposits lurking beneath her skin. She'd tried using fake tan to minimise the dimples – a tip she'd read in a magazine – but it made little difference.

Averting her gaze because it was too depressing to look any longer, she applied moisturiser to her face, deodorant to her underarms and talc on her damp bits. Then she quickly applied her make-up and put on the clothes that she'd laid out on the flat marbled surface at the end of the bath the night before. The objective was to get dressed (i.e. covered up), and looking presentable, before Tony woke.

She heard the dull sound of the children's footsteps on the hall carpet and smiled – she was ready just in time. She applied a slick of fuchsia lipstick and stared at her reflection in the mirror.

If she looked at her face in a certain flattering light, and from a moderate distance, well, it was tolerable. Even better when she smiled, so she did and, satisfied that she had made the best of her meagre assets, she unlocked the bathroom door and went into the bedroom.

The children were bouncing on the bed with the excitement that only a four- and a seven-year old can generate first thing in the morning. Tony was doing his best to ignore them, his head buried determinedly under the cream duvet which he held in place with a clenched fist.

"Come on, you two," said Karen, in her best firm voice. "You know you're not allowed to jump on the bed. Now go back to your bedroom, both of you, until it's time to get up."

"But – it – *is* – time – to – get – up!" said Jack, breathless with exertion, and pausing momentarily between each word as he jumped.

"No, it's not. You're not supposed to get up, or leave your room, until it's ten past seven."

"*You're* up."

"I have to get up earlier than you to get myself ready before you get up," said Karen.

"But why can't we just get up at the same time?" he demanded.

"Because."

There was a muffled moan from under the covers and Karen smiled to herself. What she was doing running a nursery God only knew, when she couldn't even handle her own kids. She was far too soft with them, she knew that, but the truth was she had no desire to toughen up. She worked full-time and she wasn't going to be an ogre in the little spare time she had to spend with them.

"Not fair!" chimed in Chloe and Karen knew she had committed the mortal sin of engaging in dialogue with children.

In the fantasy world of childcare manuals, many of which lined her shelves at the nursery, she was supposed to give orders and the children were supposed to obey. Pity the real world didn't work like that.

"God, don't you start and all, Chloe," she said, swiping at Chloe's legs playfully with the crumpled nightshirt she held in her hands.

"I don't know why you let them come in here every morning and do that," came Tony's muffled voice.

"Oh, don't be such a grouch!" said Karen, waiting until both the children had scampered back to the bedroom they shared. Then she sat down on Tony's side of the bed and peeled the covers from his face.

He screwed up his face and blinked. Just looking at him made her happy. His lashes were thick and dark and the black stubble on his rough-looking chin stood out against his fair skin. She ran her hand through his thick hair, damp and sweet with the smell of fresh nighttime sweat.

"Wakey, wakey, sleepy head! Time to get up."

"Is it?"

"Mmm," said Karen planting a kiss on his sweaty forehead. "'Fraid so."

"Your hair's wet," he said, recoiling slightly.

Karen laughed and leaned over so that long strands of cold wet hair fell on his face.

"Ugh! That's horrible! Stop it!"

The sound of squabbling voices floated in from the hallway. Karen turned her face to the door and shouted, "Have you got your clothes on yet, Jack? And you too, Chloe?"

"Thought you said it wasn't time to get up," came Jack's voice from the doorway, quiet and challenging.

"Well, you might as well get dressed now that you're up," she said, realising that she had lost the battle of wills, and logic, yet again. "Now off you go."

Jack slouched off, mumbling resentfully as he went.

"You're not very good at that, are you?" said Tony.

"What d'you mean, cheeky?" said Karen, knowing full well that his comments applied to her parenting skills.

"Being consistent. You say one thing, then contradict yourself."

"Oh, shut up," said Karen playfully and she suddenly pulled back the covers to reveal his naked, well-toned torso. "That'll teach you to be cheeky to me!"

"Don't do that, Karen! Leave me alone," he said grumpily and pulled the covers up over his head again. "You know I'm not a morning person," he mumbled from underneath the covers once more.

"You can tell me that again. Will you look at the time!

I'd better get this hair dried."

By the time she'd styled her hair, finished dressing Chloe, pointed out to Jack that his trousers and sweatshirt were on the wrong way round and went downstairs, it was half seven. She stuffed a load of washing in the machine, emptied the dishwasher, frowned at the empty bottle of white wine sitting in the kitchen sink – did they really finish that last night? She'd only meant to have one glass – and popped it in the recycling. Then she called the kids through from the playroom for their breakfast just as Tony appeared in the doorway fiddling with the top button of his shirt.

Casper, their fluffy white cat, poked her head through the cat flap in the back door, then leapt through and picked her way haughtily across the tiled floor, her tail stiff and erect like a feline aerial.

"Morning, Casper," said Karen brightly.

"Why can't we have a puppy?" said Jack.

"There's lot of reasons," said Karen as, with one eye on the clock, she watched Jack tip Special K into his bowl. "For one thing there wouldn't be anyone here during the day to look after a puppy and that wouldn't be fair on it, would it?"

Chloe took a mouthful of Special K and chewed thoughtfully. Then she said, her bottom lip protruding suddenly as a sense of injustice hit her, "Auntie Chris has a puppy."

"Yes, I know she has," said Karen with a sigh, suddenly hankering for the days when kids were seen and not heard.

"Auntie Chris works and so does Uncle Paul," chipped in Jack. "Auntie Chris is a liar and Uncle Paul's a doctor."

"I think you mean 'lawyer', Jack," said Karen, and she shared a smile across the table with Tony.

He laughed and ruffled Jack's hair with his big bony hand.

"Well, yes," Karen continued, silently cursing her sister and looking to Tony for assistance as he filled his bowl with the same cereal as the children, "but they're not as busy as we are. When parents have children your age, and they both have jobs, well, it's too much work to have a puppy."

"Now Karen, you know that's not the only reason," said Tony, setting his spoon down on the table slowly and carefully. Then he rested his elbows on the table and clasped his hands together under his chin.

"Isn't it?" said Karen, relieved that the spotlight was momentarily off her.

Tony waited for the children to give him their full and undivided attention.

"What is the reason then?" asked Jack as he and his sister watched his face expectantly.

Karen grabbed the cereal packet and tipped it over her bowl. A few crumbs fell out and she sighed. How was she ever to lose weight when every time she bought slimming foods the rest of the family ate them? She got up, found a box of All-Bran in the cupboard, filled her bowl and sat down again.

After a long pause Tony spoke. "There are too many dogs in The Paddock already for us to have one," he said with a deadly serious expression on his face. "Let's count them," he suggested and the children followed his lead by folding down a finger for every dog he mentioned. "There's Milo in number two, Tess and Lassie in number four, and Max in number six. If we got a dog too, well, it would be too many for the street. You see, you can only have four dogs for every six houses."

Chloe stared at him open-mouthed as though he'd just revealed some great truth. Jack screwed up his eyes and stuck his tongue out the right-hand side of his mouth – an indication that he was thinking hard about something.

Karen smiled and munched on the straw-like cereal, full of admiration for Tony's ability to engage with the children in a way that she couldn't. By capturing their imaginations he was able to take them along with him, making them feel part of the decision-making process. He had a real talent for working with children of all ages – a talent that she didn't share. People thought that, because she ran a nursery, she had some sort of gift with children. But she didn't. She was primarily a businesswoman. The demanding task of dealing with the children in her care fell to the wonderful staff she employed.

"There's only six houses in The Paddock," announced Jack at last.

"That's exactly right, Jack," said Tony.

"So does that mean we can never have a dog?"

"Not while the other dogs live here."

"What if one of them died?" said Jack and Karen raised her eyebrows at Tony, a warning to be very careful about what he said next.

"That would be very sad, wouldn't it?" said Tony, playing for time.

"But then we could get a puppy," said Jack, brightening.

"Not necessarily," interrupted Karen, reluctant to allow the conversation to drift into these dangerous waters. "As I said there are a lot of other things to think about. Now will you look at the time! Jack, time to do your teeth. Chloe, go to the toilet."

"I don't need to go."

"You have to try," insisted Karen, mindful of last Monday morning when she'd had to stop the car on the way to the nursery so Chloe could go to the toilet behind a bush in the front garden of a big house on The Roddens. Thankfully, no-one had spotted them.

"But I don't need to."

"Do as your mother says," said Tony.

Chloe dragged herself away from the table and soon the sounds of squabbling could be heard from the downstairs loo where Jack was already brushing his teeth.

Karen decided to ignore them.

"Quiet, you two!" shouted Tony as he folded up the stiff collar of his white shirt and fumbled with the necktie. The children's bickering quieted down without ceasing altogether.

"Here, let me," said Karen and she adjusted the collar and tied his pink silk tie without fuss. Tony ran a strict school and demanded high personal standards of his pupils. So his image was important in setting an example and maintaining discipline. For that reason he always wore a suit to work and a shirt and tie.

"Are you remembering about tonight?" said Karen, the palm of her right hand lingering on his chest. Not for the first time she marvelled that he loved her enough to marry her.

"What's happening tonight?" he said and Karen smiled because he never remembered about social engagements.

"Chris and Paul are coming over for dinner and they're bringing Bernie Sweeney with them."

"Oh, yes," he said, remembering or pretending to remember, she wasn't sure which. "Who's Bernie Sweeney again?"

"You know. That friend of Chris's who's over from Australia. They went to school together."

"Right," he said and nodded. "Didn't realise it was tonight. Have you sorted dinner? Do you need me to do anything?" A little note of anxiety sounded in his voice.

"Not a thing. The Tesco man's coming at four. I made a lemon tart when you were out at football last night and I'm just going to do salmon and vegetables. Something nice and easy."

"Sounds great."

"It will be."

Tony adjusted his tie in the small octagonal mirror that hung by the American-style fridge and said to his reflection, "Thought you said you didn't like her."

"Bernie Sweeney?"

"Yeah."

Karen paused for a moment to analyse her feelings towards the woman she had not seen in two decades. Looking back all those years, they had been little more than children really, though they'd thought themselves so grown-up and sophisticated.

"I didn't used to," she replied, stacking the dirty breakfast bowls. "But I'm probably being unfair. That was a long time ago. I'm sure she's changed. We all have."

"What was it about her that you didn't like?"

"Well, she stole my boyfriend for one thing," said Karen, trying and failing to keep the childish pettiness out of her voice. She collected the used spoons and dropped them with a clatter into the topmost bowl on the stack.

"Oh, Karen!" laughed Tony, and he paused with his hand on his belly. He turned to face her with a big good-humoured grin on his face. "I can't believe anybody would choose any woman in the world over you."

"Well, Derek Irwin did," said Karen as she threw the empty Special K cereal box in the bin, refusing to laugh at herself. The ignominy of being dumped at the school disco in full view of the entire sixth year had left its mark. She put a plastic clip on the inner bag of the All-Bran cereal and picked the box up off the table.

"What a fool Derek Irwin was," said Tony, trying to suppress the mirth that crept into his face, curling the corners of his lips upwards.

"You're making fun of me," she said reproachfully and now he was laughing outright again. In spite of herself, a bubble of mirth wriggled its way up her throat and erupted from her mouth as a chortle – well, more of a guffaw really.

"Come here, you!" Grabbing her, he pulled her to him and kissed her on the lips. "That's why I love you."

"Why? Because I was dumped by Derek Irwin in sixth year?"

"No, because of that laugh. It's so sexy."

She considered, not for the first time, that he might be lying but, no, his expression was earnest, true. He must be mad then – her laugh was most unattractive. If pressed, the only thing she could liken it to was a cow in labour.

Suddenly, he swung her round until she became unsteady on her feet, tipped her backwards and planted another kiss on her lips. She still held the cereal box in her right hand.

"You're going to drop me," she cried, flustered and acutely aware of her weight.

He heaved her upright, not without difficulty, and she blushed.

"Right! I'll love you and leave you, you sexy woman!"

Then, more loudly for the children's benefit, "Time for me to go. Come and say goodbye, kids!"

"You've lipstick on your lips!" called Karen after him.

He wiped his mouth with the back of his hand as the children came running in.

"Why were you doing that to Mum?" said Chloe.

"Doing what?" said Tony as he bent over to kiss Jack on the head and give him a swift bear hug. Jack stood on his tiptoes to plant a surprisingly delicate kiss on his father's cheek.

"That's my boy," whispered Tony.

"Why were you swinging Mummy round like that?" said Chloe. "I saw you!"

Tony scooped Chloe into his strong arms, her small frame apparently weightless to him. He kissed her gently on the forehead under her fringe of fuzzy brown hair.

"Why'd you do that to Mummy?" she persisted, with the tenacity small children usually demonstrate when told they cannot do or have something. She played with the knot in his tie. The image of father and daughter standing there in the hall, with their features silhouetted against the light that poured through the glass door, was picture perfect. Karen felt a little lump in her throat.

"Because I love Mummy," said Tony and Chloe smiled a secret little smile to herself, satisfied that everything was right with her world.

Just as it was with Karen's world if only she could do something, once and for all, about her appearance.

★ ★ ★

Preoccupied with planning the dinner party that night

Karen worked absentmindedly in her office behind the nursery which was housed in the lower part of an old Victorian villa on Victoria Road. She signed off the staff wages, checked the staffing schedule for the following week, and advised a relieved working mother that a place had finally become available for her child. She interviewed a candidate (second interview) for the job of nursery nurse and gave the job to her, a nice girl called Sarah from Glenoe.

There was always more to be done than she had time for, but she was good at time management. She always did what was crucial first – the nice-to-haves, like ordering desperately needed new office furniture, would have to wait until she had the time.

At twelve o'clock she went downstairs to collect Chloe – one of the advantages of owning your own nursery was flexible and free childcare – said goodbye to the staff and drove to the primary school to collect Jack. She parked in the car park and she and Chloe got out and walked the short distance to the very large exposed playground where, on arrival, Chloe ran off to play with a little girl she knew from nursery. Karen waited along with the other parents, invariably mothers, for the end-of-school bell to sound.

The primary school was adjacent to the high school where Tony taught and she found herself staring involuntarily at the building, imagining him inside, going about his work - holding a staff meeting perhaps, or patrolling the corridors (Tony believed a Head should be visible to pupils, not holed up in his office all day) or perhaps wading through the bureaucratic paperwork he complained about so often.

There were several very attractive teachers and office staff at the school – any one of them could catch Tony's eye. Karen folded her arms protectively across her chest. Compared to the school receptionist Helen (stunning) or even the buxom maths teacher, Sandra Knight, Karen thought she looked like a heifer. She shivered all over – a brief involuntary spasm caused not by a sudden blast of cool air in that draughty playground (it was a warm, still spring day) but by the pang of worry that gripped her heart. She shook her head crossly. Her fears were utterly irrational, she told herself. Wasn't Tony always telling her how much he adored and loved her? Had he ever given her cause for concern? Never.

"Hi, Karen! Over here! Hieeee!" called Angela Fletcher from across the playground as she ran across the tarmac in her Tod's driving shoes, one of those girlish, printed skirts from Boden and a co-ordinating jersey jacket – the very embodiment of a stay-at-home middle-class mum. Angela worked tirelessly for the Parent Teacher Association, was chair of the local scouts, fund-raised for every charitable cause going, served as a community councillor and appeared to organise everyone's social life.

Karen didn't envy Angela's life but she didn't despise her lifestyle either. Karen might have chosen to work more or less full-time but she appreciated the valuable role such mothers played in keeping the local community vibrant and thriving. Karen hadn't time to draw breath, never mind get involved in clubs and committees.

Karen presented Angela with a bright smile – not entirely forced for, though she and Angela were very different, Karen was genuinely fond of her.

"Gosh, I'm glad I caught you just now," said Angela, placing a hand on Karen's arm and pausing to catch her breath. "I want to talk to you," she went on in a low voice, increasing her grip on Karen's arm and scanning the playground with small beady black eyes. Everything in Angela's life was a drama.

Karen noticed for the first time that her black hair, tied in a ponytail, was greying slightly at the temples. She touched her own hair involuntarily and thought that she must check for grey hairs that very afternoon. At the moment she was still at the stage of pulling them out with tweezers but it wouldn't be long before she was forced to graduate from highlights to a full-blown dye job. That was the trouble with ageing – it crept up on you stealthily in all sorts of cruel little ways. She tuned in to what Angela was saying.

"It's Pat Flynn's fortieth this year and she doesn't want a fuss but we're organising –" here she paused dramatically and scanned the huddles of chatting mums again – she lowered her voice even more and continued " – a surprise line-dancing night for her at the Scout hall!"

"Wow!" said Karen. "That sounds like fun."

"And you're invited!"

"Brilliant. It'll be a laugh," said Karen. "And I think Pat'll love it. When are you thinking –"

"Oh it's all booked. Saturday twenty-seventh," said Angela interrupting, a fault caused by her infectious enthusiasm for everything and, therefore, forgivable.

"Saturday twenty-seventh," repeated Karen, trying to commit the date to memory.

"Yes," said Angela. "And you've got to wear jeans and a Stetson, checked shirt – that sort of thing. We must all look the part, mustn't we?" And she burst into a fit of giggles.

"Of course," said Karen, wondering where on earth she would get a cowboy hat in Ballyfergus. There was always the internet of course – the working woman's saviour.

"Now, will you remember Saturday twenty-seventh? Or do you want me to send you an e-mail?"

"Yes, you'd better," said Karen.

Angela rooted around in her bag. "Now where is it?" she mumbled to herself, then pulled out a red flock-covered notebook and waited, pen poised.

Karen gave her the e-mail address as she watched a crowd of boys spill through a door into the playground. Jack was amongst them, small and serious, scanning the crowd anxiously.

"Over here, Jack!" she called out and waved.

As soon as he saw her his face broke into a wide, wonderful smile and he started to run towards her.

"That's great, Karen," said Angela. "One more thing though."

"Yes," said Karen, not taking her eyes off Jack.

"I'm asking everyone to bring some food. Could you maybe bring along a salad?"

"Yes, of course. I'd be delighted to."

Jack reached her just then and ran into her with some force, wrapping his arms around her waist.

"Hello, darling," she said and kissed him on the top of the head. Thank God he was still too young to be embarrassed by public displays of affection.

"Must dash," said Angela. "I need to have a quick word with Joanna Steven."

"Thanks, Angela!" Karen called as Angela darted across the tarmac. "Thanks for organising and for inviting me!"

Angela waved her hand in the air by way of acknowledgement and was gone.

"Thank Crunchie it's Friday!" said Karen, parroting the

catchphrase from the eighties TV ad for Crunchie bars.

"What does that mean, Mum?" said Jack.

Karen let out a long sigh. Some things were just too hard, or too much effort, to explain to a just-turned-seven-year-old.

"Never mind. I'll tell you another time," she said brightly as Chloe ran up to them grinning like something demented. "Look, here's Chloe!"

The rest of the afternoon was spent in a busy frenzy – a quick lunch at home, ferrying Chloe to ballet lessons and Jack to karate. And, in between, hastily tidying the house and trying to pull together the preparations for the dinner party that night. In her haste at lunchtime, she had eaten only a small plate of salad and an apple (convincing herself that she would eat nothing else until dinner) but, by three-twenty-five, waiting for Jack outside the community centre, she was starving.

She battled with the munchies for a few minutes, her eye constantly drawn to the corner shop. Unable to stand it any longer she got out of the car, went into the shop, checked no-one she knew was in there and bought two large packets of tomato-flavour crisps – her favourite. She stuffed them into her capacious handbag, went back out to the car, got into the driver's seat and consumed both packets in under two minutes. Then she hid the empty crisp packets in the glove compartment and sat back, sated. Almost immediately she regretted what she had just done. Self-disgust followed soon after.

She knew what Chris would say if she could see her: "If you'd eaten a more substantial, well-balanced lunch then you wouldn't have felt the need to snack." And of course she would have been right. It was a vicious circle. The less

Karen tried to eat, the more she ended up eating. She was pathetic; she had no willpower. It was moments of weakness like this, more frequent than she liked to admit, that undermined her. She knew it. It was almost as though, for a few seconds, something possessed her. A force, compelling her to eat something fattening *right now*, that she was completely unable to resist.

She let out a long sigh, and wiped the delicious sweet salty taste of the crisps from the corners of her mouth and tried not to be so hard on herself. The odd bag of crisps wasn't responsible for her droopy eyelids and the apron of flab on her abdomen. No amount of dieting was going to change those aspects of her appearance. And it was a one-off, she told herself, it really was. She would try harder next time. She really would – she would not give into temptation. She applied fresh lipstick, got out of the car and arranged her usual pleasant expression on her face. Then she joined the little throng of women outside the community centre door wondering, as she did, how many of them also battled daily with their demons.

* * *

When Tony walked out of the main school door at four thirty he did so with a sigh of relief. It had been a tough day. He'd had a meeting with the parents of the fourteen-year-old Ramsey twins and, as usual, it had been a waste of time. Declan was in trouble this time – serious trouble – for bringing a knife onto the school premises. And not just any old knife but a six-inch long switchblade. Where on earth, Tony wondered, did one even buy such a thing?

Jimmy Ramsey's only question, his muscled, tattooed arms folded across his too-tight black T-shirt, was, "Did he threaten anyone, like?"

When Tony answered in the negative he replied, "I dinne see what the problem is then," and seemed to tune out of the conversation.

The mother, Moira, who was hollow-eyed, had long, lank hair and looked half-famished – he was sure he'd never seen a woman so thin – was just as bad. Fidgeting with an imaginary cigarette between the bony yellow-stained thumb and forefinger on her right hand she said, "I canne do anythin' with them boys, Mr Magill. I've tried everythin', I really have, so I have."

When he told them that Declan was banned from school for a fortnight, Jimmy stood up abruptly, muttered something about lads having the right to defend themselves, propelled his malnourished wife by her skinny arm from the office and slammed the door behind them both.

As if that wasn't enough, Joan Baxter, the English teacher and one of his most experienced staff, came to see him at the end of the day to tell him that she was intending to resign. Her husband, several years her senior, had taken early retirement six months ago and they had now decided to move back to Enniskillen to be near her recently widowed mother. She would not leave the school in the lurch, she explained, she would see out the end of term but, come the new scholastic year, she would be gone.

God knows who he'd get as a replacement. Probably some kid just out of training, still wet behind the ears and unable to control one Declan Ramsey never mind a class half-full of them.

There were some bright kids at St Pat's but the troublemakers were so disruptive, and took up so much of the teaching staff's time, that Tony felt they didn't get the education they deserved. But, as the only state-funded Catholic secondary school in the Ballyfergus area, they were obliged to take what they got and educate them, or not, to the best of their ability.

Still, he reminded himself, if he'd wanted an easy ride he would've chosen a different career, or moved to Scotland or England to work in a private school where pupils were handpicked according to ability and, being brutally honest, background. You wouldn't find any Declan Ramseys in a fee-paying school.

But Tony had made a commitment to public education a long time ago and he would not be diverted from his goal of running the best school he knew how. He knew it was perverse logic but he thought that the good he did here would somehow balance out the mistake he had made in his past. He saw it as a sort of penance for the thing he had once done and could not forget. But when unhappy memories from the past clouded his otherwise contented life, he reminded himself that he had been young and foolish. Accidents happened, it was true, but the taking of a life . . . well, he just tried not to think about it too much. And because he could not forgive himself for what he had done, he would atone for it. Surely if he did enough right in this world it would cancel out the one wrong?

Tony only remembered about the dinner party on the drive home and his heart sank a little. He wasn't an anti-social man by any means, but tonight he could do without it. What he wanted more than anything was to chill out in front of the TV with a beer in his hand and maybe watch a movie with Karen snuggled up beside him on the sofa. At least it wasn't people they hardly knew coming over. Apart from Antipodean Bernie, tonight was a family affair and Tony was fond of his sister-in-law and her husband. And he knew Karen was looking forward to hosting dinner – for her sake, he would make the effort.

She amazed him sometimes. After a hard week at work she had bags of energy for entertaining. He enjoyed company and having people round but Karen was definitely the driving force behind their social life. She was just great – she loved people, fun, laughter. She was always organising some bash or other, going out with her pals and generally living life to the full. Girlfriends were always asking her places and he was sure they received so many invites as a couple because of Karen – she really was the life and soul of any party. He wondered sometimes what she saw in him. He hoped she never found him dull.

Just as he pulled into the driveway of their four-bedroom detached modern house, the Tesco van drove off. Inside it was chaos. The kids were playing a noisy game that seemed to involve chasing each other with murderous intent, toys were strewn all over the floor and bags of groceries swamped the island unit and spilled onto the floor. The kids paused in their game momentarily to welcome him, then ran out of the kitchen shrieking. The smell of fish fingers filled the room and, in the midst of it all, by the cooker, stood Karen wielding a potato masher over a pot billowing steam.

"How are you, love?" she shouted over the din, her cheeks a little red and strands of hair falling over her face. "Welcome to the madhouse!"

"Don't you just love family life?" he said sardonically

and Karen flashed him a smile of resigned agreement. He found a bottle of beer in the fridge, opened it and took a swig.

He pulled a few black grapes off a bunch protruding from one of the shopping bags, popped them in his mouth and, looking round at the scene of disaster, said, "When is everyone expected?"

"Seven thirty for eight," said Karen, a little distractedly as she bent to retrieve the potato masher which had somehow clattered to the floor. She quickly rinsed it under a hot tap, and continued mashing the spuds in the pan. "Don't worry. I'm more ready than I look. The starter's in the fridge, salad's made and the salmon's all ready to cook."

She divided six fish fingers between two small plates, and added a dollop of fluffy mashed potato and a scoopful of bright green peas to each. "If you could just call them in for their tea," she said, untying the apron round her waist, "and maybe put away the groceries?" she added with an if-you-don't-mind-please smile. "Then maybe I could grab an hour just now and go get myself ready?"

"Take as long as you want, darling," said Tony, rolling his sleeves up. He glanced round the untidy room and stifled a sigh.

"Are you sure?" said Karen, quick as always to pick up on every nuance of a conversation.

"Absolutely fine," he said. God, what he wouldn't give for five minutes with his feet up! "You go on and I'll sort this lot out."

One hour of hard work later and the kids were fed and sitting in pyjamas watching TV, the dishwasher was stacked, groceries put away and the kitchen tidied. Just as he was finishing up, Karen came into the kitchen wearing a well-fitting black skirt, high-heeled, shiny black shoes and, unusually for her, a glamorous red-sequinned tunic top.

"You look fantastic," said Tony. He threw the damp tea-towel in his hand to one side and walked over to Karen. Taking her in his arms, he said, "You know I love you in red."

"Well," she said, with a smile that looked a bit forced, "you know I'd rather wear black."

"Why do you want to wear black all the time?" he asked, releasing her from his embrace, which he sensed was slightly unwelcome.

"You know why," she said, smoothing the front of the skirt and avoiding eye contact with him. "It's more slimming."

"You don't need to worry about that. Black's boring. And you, Karen, are anything but boring."

She stared at him hard, without smiling, and bit her bottom lip.

Sensing something amiss, he said, "What?"

"I've made an appointment to see a cosmetic surgeon at a clinic next week up in Belfast."

"You have not?" he said in disbelief.

"I have."

"I didn't know you'd got that far down the road with this – I mean I knew you were looking into it but . . . well, that is a surprise."

"I've given it a lot of thought, Tony. In fact, doing something about my tummy and my breasts is something I've thought about – no, obsessed about – for years. And since I've had the children, well, it's just reached a point where I can't stand it any longer. You know that. Plus, finally, I have the money to do it."

"What sort of money are we talking about?" he said, as a way of buying time, of diverting the conversation away from his feelings on the matter. He only had a vague notion of what the procedures might involve, but he knew enough to feel suddenly squeamish. The thought of a surgeon's knife piercing Karen's beautiful body, made him wince. And the fear that she might be damaged in some way, or worse, that he might lose her, filled him with terror. He suddenly realised how brave she was to be seriously considering this.

"I have to be honest with you, Tony. It's very expensive. But the figures for the nursery this year are excellent. For the first time, I'm going to be able to pay myself a really good bonus."

"That's great news," he said calmly, but inside his emotions were in turmoil.

He dearly wanted to support her because he really did understand how much it meant to her. But, at the same time, he baulked at the whole idea of her going under the knife, of inflicting this on herself unnecessarily. He wasn't against cosmetic surgery in principle – he just truly believed that Karen did not need it. Not enough to justify surgery anyway.

And yet, although her figure didn't honestly bother him, he could understand how she felt. Every day, she was bombarded with images in the media of flat-chested, slim-hipped girls, barely out of puberty. Presented as the desirable figure of womanhood, very few real women could conform to this demanding ideal – and Karen fell so far short, he could see how demoralising it must be for her. She often complained how difficult it was to find flattering clothes for her figure, though he always thought she looked great.

But, frustratingly, she paid very little heed to his constant praise and positive comments on her appearance. They rolled off her like water off a duck's back, bringing a brief, insincere smile to her lips, but not penetrating in any way. She always seemed faintly amused by them, as though she thought it some sort of joke that he should find her body attractive. As though she didn't believe him.

"If I have everything done, including my eyes – you see, I was thinking of getting these lids fixed too . . ."

He heard her explaining though he was too wrapped up in his own thoughts to pay much attention.

"There'll not be much change out of sixteen thousand pounds."

That brought him to his senses.

"What?" he said, incredulously.

"Sixteen thousand pounds. I know, it's a lot of money, isn't it?" she said, wringing her hands together.

You can say that again, thought Tony. But he said instead, "Okay," and nodded his head slowly in a sage fashion, to indicate he was letting this sink in, that he was giving it the consideration it deserved. That he wasn't dismissing it out of hand. Inside he wanted to scream, 'Are you mad, woman?' But how could he? She was staring at him with eyes as wide as a frightened doe's, her pretty face distorted by worry.

"It's your money, Karen. You don't have to ask my permission to spend it."

"I would like to have it though. I would like to have your agreement to spend it on *this*."

"I wish," he said, and sighed deeply, closing his eyes briefly, "I just wish you would rethink this whole plastic surgery thing."

"Cosmetic surgery," she corrected.

"Cosmetic surgery. Call it what you like. It's not the

money, Karen. I don't care about that. It's just that I love you the way you are. And I don't think that it's worth undergoing surgery, no matter how dismissive you are about the risks." He went over to her and took her right hand in his.

He was shocked to find her hand cold and shaking and he noticed, now that he was close to her, that her eyes had welled up with tears that threatened to spoil her freshly applied make-up. Briefly, he felt a flash of anger with her for her foolishness but it was quickly eclipsed by his compassion. He clasped her hand in his and held it to his breast.

"Please don't say that, Tony. You're wrong, you know. I'm not dismissive about the risks at all. I realise these are serious operations and that many things can, and do, go wrong. I know there's a possibility, albeit a very slim one, that I could even die and leave the children without a mother." She paused to utter a little sob, then composed herself before going on. "Don't you see? The fact that I'm even contemplating going ahead, in spite of what I know, in spite of what could go wrong and what that would mean for you and the children, is evidence of just how desperate I am and just how much this means to me. I thought you would support me."

"I do. It's just . . ."

"Don't, Tony. Please don't," she said, sounding close to tears. "Don't you understand? Nothing you can say will make any difference to the way I feel about this."

"I know that, Karen, my love," he said gently, bringing her hand to his lips and pressing the gentlest of kisses on the back of it. His heart was heavy with sadness. "And that, of all things, is what hurts me so."

"Oh Tony, please, don't be like that!" she cried.

The tears came suddenly and he pulled her to him and held her in a ferociously tight embrace.

They clung to each other for a few moments and then Tony spoke into her sweet-smelling hair, his voice choked with emotion. "If it's what you want, Karen, then you know I'll support you. I don't necessarily agree, but I'll go along with it. But only if you're absolutely sure it's what you want."

"It is," she said firmly. She pulled back from him, and looked up into his face. Her cheeks were streaked with mascara but her gaze was fierce and steady. "I've never wanted anything more in my life. Except for you. And the kids."

He kissed her on the forehead and said, in a soothing tone of voice he usually reserved for the children when they were distressed, "Okay. Okay, sweetheart. You'll have your surgery. But let's not talk about it any more, eh, Karen? Not tonight. It's upsetting you."

"No. I'm not upset anymore," she said with a smile through her tears. "Not now that I know you're okay about it."

"Well, I'm glad to hear it because it breaks my heart to see you distressed. Listen, will you look at the time? We need to get the kids to bed and get ready for our guests."

"You're right," she said, with a sniffle. "Has my mascara run?"

He nodded. "You look like an inky spider's gone amok all over your face."

She laughed and said, "I'll need to pop upstairs then. I'll be down shortly to take over with the kids. Give me ten minutes, will you?"

She walked out of the room and he called after her, "You do know I love you, don't you?"

She stopped in the hallway, turned and said, "Yes."

"I mean really, really love you?"

"Yes. I know that. And I love you too."

"Go on then and sort yourself out and then I'll take a shower."

As he watched her teeter up the hallway in sexy high heels, he thought that she had no idea how much he loved her. Nor did she know his dearest wish: that she could learn to love herself just the way she was – perfect in his eyes.

Seven

There was definitely something of the hippy about Bernie – Tony noticed that one of the first things she'd done on arriving with Chris and Paul, was to kick her shoes off. So now she sat long-skirted and bare-footed in their lounge, dwarfed by the deep sofa on which she perched. Her feet did not quite reach the floor and she took long sips of gin and tonic by dipping her head down to the glass rather than the usual manner of bringing the glass to one's mouth. The gesture reminded him of an awkward child.

"This is a lovely room," she said, taking in appreciatively the rather unconventional style of décor.

It was all Karen's doing of course as Tony had little interest in such things. A black crystal chandelier hung from the ceiling, one wall was covered in a turquoise and gold ornately patterned wallpaper and the wooden parquet floor was almost entirely covered by a huge rug with bright circles of colour on it. On sentry duty by the window stood a near life-sized antique statue of a Scotsman in full highland dress, the aged paint chipped and worn. The curtains were sheaths of sea-green silk swept back with ornate gold-tasselled tiebacks and the comfortable sofas, one of which Bernie now sat upon, were upholstered in a natural coloured hessian-like fabric.. An assortment of objects were carefully arranged on the coffee table – a small vase of dried flowers, a sliver tray bearing three candles in the form of small fruit tarts, an embossed silver canister they'd bought back from a holiday in Greece; a small pile of books. The overall effect was both chic and relaxing.

Beside Bernie on the couch Karen looked uncomfortable, her legs crossed primly at the ankle, her arms pressed in at her sides. Tony could guess why – by now he was pretty good at understanding how her mind worked. She would not like sitting beside the small-framed Bernie with her almost doll-like proportions. She would think she looked huge in comparison. And she would think everyone was looking at her and thinking that she was fat. His heart ached for her.

And she was wrong of course. With her luscious breasts and attractive curves, her body was womanly and inviting compared to the insubstantial, bird-like physique of Bernie, with her sharp edges and jutting angles. But Tony had long ago given up talking sense into Karen when it came to her size. What she failed to appreciate – though he had told her until he was blue in the face – was that he liked her figure the way it was. For him a few flabby bits did not spoil the overall package and, anyway, he was obsessed with her mind as much as her body. And who was he to judge anyway, he thought, sucking his tummy in just a little. He was hardly Brad Pitt himself.

In spite of her unprepossessing physical appearance, Bernie turned out to be an interesting little sprite of a thing. She was lively and engaging and she entertained them with tales of her life down under and her slightly alternative views; for example, she said that she believed that the ownership of material things brought unhappiness. She added an interesting dimension to the conversation which otherwise would have gone down the rather predictable route of most middle-class dinner parties – property prices, second homes and holiday destinations. In fact, so long had Tony known Chris and Paul that their conversations were often repeats, albeit slightly reworked, of ones that had gone before. He welcomed the diversion.

"So, Bernie," he asked, when there was a pause in the conversation, "were you friends with Karen as well as Chris at school?"

"Oh, no," said Karen quickly. "Remember I'm two years older than Chris and Bernie. No offence meant, girls," she said, staring at Bernie while she said it, "but a two-year gap at that age is huge. I had my own friends."

Tony winced at Karen's uncharacteristically blunt comment, which he took to be a sign of her discomfort. She definitely wasn't the life and soul tonight and when she'd said she hadn't liked Bernie, she really meant it.

"You ran around with Margaret Wharry and what was that other girl's name, one of the Gallaghers?" said Bernie.

"Liz Gallagher," supplied Karen.

For a few minutes the women reminisced about their schooldays and then Karen stood up, wiggling her hips until the hem of her skirt settled once more just below her knees. "God, I didn't realise the time! You must be ravenous. Come on through – we'd better eat before we all faint from starvation!"

Everyone followed her through to the conservatory which served as the dining room. Outside dusk was falling, and the room was lit by dozens of scented candles and fairy lights strung round the rafters like bunting. Karen had laid the table the night before with fresh white linen and fresh flowers – tiny pink rosebuds in crystal glasses. The atmosphere was magical. If there was one thing that Karen and her sister knew how to do, thought Tony, as he looked round the room approvingly, it was entertain. Though he thought his wife did it better. Chris was an accomplished hostess and cook but Tony never quite relaxed at her home. It felt a little too formal for his liking. Here Karen set the scene in the same way but her warm, informal approach put everyone immediately at ease.

At the table the conversation flowed more readily, oiled by a few very nice bottles of wine supplied by Paul. He seemed to be enjoying himself and, seated beside Bernie, they engaged in a quiet, intense conversation. This registered briefly with Tony as being a little odd but when he looked at Chris, listening to Karen who sat on the other side of her, she seemed oblivious, and rather preoccupied.

"How are things going with PINBAT, Chris?" said Tony, when Karen left the table to attend to the main course.

"Okay, I think," said Chris, "We presented our objections and the petition to the planning authorities on Thursday. Now all we have to do is wait."

"How many signed the petition in the end?"

"We've over four thousand signatures."

"Pretty impressive."

"Yeah, well," said Chris with a shrug, "we'll see. I hope we've done enough but it'll be months before we know the outcome and I daresay there'll be more open meetings too."

"And work, how's that going?" said Tony, suddenly realising that he was annoyed with Paul and Bernie, still talking exclusively to each other. They weren't pulling their weight as guests. It was rude to ignore the rest of the party round the table. Positively infantile in fact.

"Busy," said Chris. "Bob McMillan retires on Friday and it's all change from next week. The new boss, Sam McIlwaine, starts on Monday. A big gun sent down from Belfast to sort us all out, no doubt."

"Have you met him before?"

"No, but I've heard he's very well regarded."

"He must think it a good business," said Tony, realising suddenly that both Paul and Bernie were a little drunk. There were two empty wine bottles on the table, the lion's share of which he reckoned Paul, Bernie and Karen had polished off between them. Chris, so serious and focused in all aspects of her life, rarely drank more than a couple of glasses and tonight was no exception. She was still nursing an almost full glass he'd poured for her in the lounge. Tony had stuck to beer.

"He must do," agreed Chris.

Tony nodded momentarily and then, turning his attention to Paul and Bernie, he said suddenly, "So, Paul, aren't you and Bernie going to share with the rest of us what it is you two are so engrossed in? What's the big secret?"

"There's no secret," said Paul evenly, and he looked at Bernie. "We were just talking about the Third World."

"Really?" said Paul and waited.

Just then Karen came in bearing two plates, one in each hand. She set one in front of Chris and the other on the table in front of Bernie. A shell-pink fillet of salmon swathed in a rich creamy dill sauce sat in the middle of each plate.

"That looks divine!" said Bernie.

"Can I give you a hand?" said Chris, already on her feet.

"No, no, you sit and enjoy yourself," said Karen, reinforcing her words with a waving-away motion of her hand. "Tony, could you just give me a wee hand with the veg?"

He followed her out into the kitchen and brought through dishes of baby boiled potatoes and asparagus while Karen served the rest of the salmon. Then they sat down to eat.

Tony said, "This looks fab."

Karen flashed him a smile, a genuine one this time.

Halfway through the main course, after the source of the fish (wild, not farmed) and the relative health benefits had been discussed, and everyone had complemented the cook sufficiently, Tony judged it timely to return to a previous topic.

"Paul," he said, "you were saying earlier that you and Bernie were discussing the Third World?"

"Yes, that's right," said Paul and he dabbed the corners of his mouth with a napkin before setting it carefully by his plate. Paul was a man of precise habits. He glanced at Bernie and went on, "Bernie was just sharing a radical theory with me about how to end world hunger."

"That sounds very interesting," said Karen, who seemed more her usual self now that she'd consumed several glasses of Chardonnay. "Do tell us more."

Everyone, including Paul, looked at Bernie and she seemed suddenly embarrassed to be the centre of attention. She chewed self-consciously for a few seconds and then washed the food down with a mouthful of white wine.

"Well," she said, and cleared her throat before going on,

"it's really very simple. I was just making the observation that the answer to world hunger lies in getting the western world to stop overeating."

"I'm sorry, I don't follow," said Chris, always anxious to hone any discussion down to facts and figures she could analyse, measure and understand. She wasn't a fan of woolly concepts and sweeping statements.

Paul threw her an impatient look and said, "If you'll just let her finish."

"Yes, please go on," said Tony to Bernie, intrigued to hear the logic behind the theory.

"Well," said Bernie, "development agencies estimate that the cost of providing enough food, clean water and basic healthcare in the Third World is thirty to forty billion dollars a year. The total annual health bill in America for conditions caused by obesity is nearly forty million dollars and Americans spend nearly as much every year on dieting – diet foods, plans and the like. And that's just the US. If you add the rest of the Western world to those figures there's more than enough money to solve the problem."

"But," said Chris, "solving the problem is much more complicated than just throwing money at it, right? The main problem in many of these countries is corruption."

"That's right," said Tony. "Didn't a lot of the Live Aid money get siphoned off by the Ethiopian government?"

Bernie nodded, as though acknowledging these comments, but when she spoke she continued on in her train of thought, as if she had not heard them.

"You see, one way of viewing this relationship between the overweight and the hungry of the world is that it's causal. People are starving because others overeat. But the radical view, you see, is to say the opposite. People are eating too much *because* others on the planet are starving. And," she said, becoming suddenly animated, "there's actually scientific support for this idea. In the nineteen-thirties, a Russian called Sergei Speransky conducted some experiments on mice. He divided a community of mice in half, placed them in different locations and proceeded to starve one group. The amazing thing that he found was that the other group began to eat much more as if some subtle sympathetic communication was at work."

Karen frowned, expressing the scepticism that, in spite of his Herculean efforts to remain open-minded, was now settling over Tony. He glanced at Paul who leaned back in his chair with his fingers entwined across his stomach, nodding thoughtfully. But Bernie wasn't finished yet.

"His findings indicate that there are deep connections at work. You see, we're all connected spiritually to every human being on earth. I believe that the fact of our essential unity communicates itself unconsciously through our biology. Those with overeating issues," she said and he could've sworn she threw a glance at Karen, "should view themselves, not as those responsible for world hunger, but as those most sensitive and unconsciously sympathetic to it. Their weight issue is a symptom of their sensitivity to humanity, not of their lack of humanity."

An agonising silence ensued during which Tony glanced round the table. Chris and Karen shared the same expression he imagined he did – one of incredulity and embarrassment. Only Paul looked impressed as though he divined some sort of truth from this mystical nonsense. This surprised Tony. Paul was a man of science and, in the past, had displayed little time for any concepts outside the conventional.

"That is . . ." said Tony, desperate to break the tension, and he paused. "That's a very interesting thought, Bernie."

"Yes, fascinating, isn't it?" said Paul with enthusiasm and Tony could almost feel Chris's astonishment crackle in the air like static.

"I think I follow you so far," said Tony cautiously. "But how does this theory translate into solving world hunger?"

"The next step would be to allow the unconscious sympathetic response to move out of the body and become conscious by addressing it directly. Instead of spending money on diet and exercise programmes which do not address the underlying issue, that money could be used to respond consciously to the food needs of others. Instead of charity, money given becomes a real investment in human welfare, which directly impacts their own."

"So the first practical step," said Karen hesitantly, "would be what? To educate people to think like this? To accept the concept that we are all linked spiritually through our biology to one another and that this is affecting our eating habits?"

"Exactly!" said Paul and he shared a small, almost triumphant, smile with Bernie.

"I don't mean to sound negative," said Chris, "but this approach still doesn't address the fundamental issue of how we distribute that wealth. Even if the west did suddenly, by some miracle, stop overeating and donated all this money to the developing countries, you would still have the problem of corruption to deal with. And that has nothing to do with the west and everything to do with the dishonest governments in place in the Third World."

"I don't have the answer to that," said Bernie equitably. "What I do know is that our current approach to solving the problem isn't working so perhaps it's time for a radical rethink. Many of the west's efforts are motivated by fear or guilt and often result in a further division between the giver and receiver of aid. The radical view I've outlined offers the opportunity to generate a partnership that recognises and acts on our underlying unity."

"I see," said Chris and she smiled politely in a manner that indicated, to Tony at least, that she did not see at all.

Taking advantage of the momentary lapse in conversation Karen stood up and said brightly, "Anyone for pudding?" and Tony could've hugged her there and then for bringing this uncomfortable, and rather bizarre, conversation to a close.

He got out of his seat quickly, thankful for the diversion, and made himself busy gathering plates and cutlery, scraping food off plates and stacking the dishes before carrying them through to the kitchen.

"Let your belts out, boys and girls," said Karen as she left the room. "It's home-made full-fat lemon tart."

There were approving murmurs from round the table.

In the kitchen, Tony put the plates in the dishwasher and whispered to Karen, "What a strange conversation. Where does she get her ideas from?"

"Search me," said Karen as she headed out of the kitchen with the dessert. "But I did warn you."

Back in the conservatory, Karen served generous slices of tart with lashings of whipped cream and fresh raspberries. The delicious dessert lived up to its name – the lemony filling was the perfect combination of tangy and sweet and the pastry was delicate and light.

"This is fabulous, Karen," said Chris. "Did you make the pastry?"

"Not quite," said Karen and she screwed up her face in that endearing way of hers and giggled. "The food processor did it, really. You just put everything in and zap! Job done."

"Well, I think it's fabulous, Karen. As always," said Paul and he raised his glass. "Here's to the hostess with the mostest!"

Everyone laughed and clinked glasses.

There was a short pause, then Karen said to Chris, "Do you remember yesterday you called me and said you'd been talking to Raymond on the phone?"

Raymond was Karen and Chris's bachelor brother. Older than Karen by a decade he worked as a structural engineer all over the Far East – the last they'd heard he was living in Thailand. Tony had only met him three times during the ten years he'd been married to Karen: on their marriage, then again when Karen's father had died five years ago and, most recently, two years ago when Phyllis, his mother-in-law, was poorly. He seemed a likeable person, if a little self-centred, and his sisters, who seemed to overlook his shortcomings, were very fond of him.

"Chloe fell and cut her lip in the middle of our phone call," Karen went on, "and I got distracted and then you had to go. You never did get to finish telling me what he said."

"Oh!" exclaimed Chris and she put her hand to he mouth. "How stupid of me! How could I forget!"

"Forget what?" said Paul. "Is it something serious?"

"No, not really. Nothing bad, I mean. But yes, it is important."

"What is?" said Karen.

"Raymond's getting married."

"He is *not*!" exclaimed Karen and she slapped her right

thigh in the manner of Doris Day's Calamity Jane. "Well, if anything calls for a celebration that does!" She jumped up. "Let's get the champagne out! Tony, have we got a bottle on chill?"

"I think so," he said, good-humouredly, thinking that it was going to be a long night. "I'll go and look." Rising suddenly from his seat he realised he was slightly drunk. He held onto the table for a few seconds to steady himself, then went through to the kitchen and opened the stainless-steel fridge.

When Tony came back into the room armed with the champagne, and holding the stems of five slim glasses precariously in his left hand, Karen was bombarding Chris with questions. "Why didn't he say anything about her before? How long has he been engaged? Does Mum know yet?"

"One thing at a time, Karen, please," said Chris good-naturedly, holding up her hand as a physical barrier to the onslaught of questions from her sister.

"Here," said Paul to Tony, relieving him of the bottle, "let me help you with that." He peered at the label and said, managing to sound just a little disappointed, "Ah, yes. Moet et Chandon. Always —" and he paused, "reliable."

Tony knew that Paul liked to source his champagne from small, obscure champagne houses he had never heard of. The fact that Paul probably considered Moet and Chandon champagne rather common, amused rather than insulted Tony. If Paul ever got a bit too pretentious with Tony he was quick to bring him back down to earth with a good-natured riposte. And so, as brothers-in-laws often thrown into each other's company by circumstance rather then by choice, they rubbed along well enough.

"Like us Paul, eh? Reliable?"

"To the end!" retorted Paul.

Paul started to remove the foil from the mouth of the bottle. Tony set the glasses down carefully on the table.

"I don't think he's told Mum," Chris was saying. "Actually I forgot to ask him if he was going to phone her himself or if he wanted me to tell her."

Tony thought that, knowing Raymond, he'd expect his sisters to tell his mother for him. But he knew better than to say anything for Chris and Karen would not hear a word said against him. Raymond's rather casual sense of duty towards his ageing mother irritated Tony just a little. Karen and Chris were dutiful daughters, always taking their mother out, having her round for meals etc. but she treasured more than anything the slightest crumb of contact from Raymond – such as one of his very infrequent postcards from some farflung country or a rare phone call.

Tony's mother had died when he was in his twenties – before he'd reached the age where he truly understood and appreciated all the sacrifices she'd made for him. It was a source of great regret to him. If he had the chance again, he would be a better son.

"Shall I?" said Paul, when he'd competently eased the cork out of the bottle without sending it smashing through the glass roof.

"Sure," said Tony good-naturedly and sat down and watched Paul pour the drinks and hand a glass to the others.

Then Paul sat down, raised his glass in the air and said, "Karen."

At this cue, she lifted the flute and said, "I propose a toast to our big brother, Raymond, and his fiancée. What's her name, Chris?"

"Shona."

At the mention of a name he had not heard in a long time, Tony's heart tightened just a little. He took a deep breath and relaxed.

"To Raymond and Shona!" said Karen theatrically. "Wishing them all the luck and happiness in the world!"

"To Raymond and Shona!" repeated everyone and there was a moment of almost reverent silence while they all took a drink of champagne.

"It's good to have something to celebrate, isn't it?" said Tony, smacking his lips. "It's about time this family had a good old knees-up!"

"We haven't even started yet," said Karen, with a wicked laugh. "Wait until the wedding! Have they set a date yet, Chris? Oh, I can't wait. We'll have to make it worth the trip, Tony. Go for at least three weeks. The kids'll love it. We'll have to see if they can make it during the school holidays. Maybe Christmas!"

"Hold on a minute!" said Chris laughing. "Don't be making your travel plans just yet, Karen."

"Why not?" Karen, her words starting to sound a little slurred.

"You haven't heard the best of it," said Chris and she paused momentarily for effect. "Raymond's contract ends in a couple of months and he says that they're going to come back here to live."

"What, permanently?" said Tony in disbelief. Raymond had always struck him as the rolling-stone type. "I never thought your Raymond was the marrying settling-down type."

"Neither did I," said Chris seriously, "but we had quite a serious chat on the phone about that. The ex-pat life is wearing a bit thin and Raymond doesn't want to end his days living in some outpost in the back of beyond. I guess he's got that wanderlust out of his system. And of course now he's met someone and fallen in love."

"Now, let me get this right," interjected Karen with her radar-like focus. "You mean they're coming back here to live *after* the wedding?"

"I don't think so," said Chris, sounding pained to burst her sister's happy bubble.

"What? No beach wedding in Phuket?" said Karen.

"'Fraid not by the sounds of it," said Chris.

"Uhhh, I was really looking forward to a holiday in the Far East," said Karen, her voice and demeanour sagging with disappointment.

"Never mind, pet," said Tony, hating to see her hopes dashed. He reached across and patted the back of her hand which was resting on the table. "We can go another time."

Karen face brightened and she mouthed, "I love you."

Pleased, but also slightly embarrassed, Tony winked at her and pulled his hand away.

"So are they going to get married here then?" said Bernie.

"That's the plan but Raymond was very vague about a date. Said they'd sort all that out when they got here."

"So tell us, Chris," said Paul, "what do you know about this Shona?"

"Well, her full name's Shona Johnston," said Chris. "She's forty-three and she's a nurse working with one of those medical charities – which one is it now?" She frowned and paused momentarily.

Tony looked at the table and tried to quell the rising anxiety in his breast. The name was right, the age was right.

She was a nurse. Surely it couldn't be? What were the chances? No, it was impossible. It had to be.

"Medicines Sans Frontier?" said Paul.

"Yes," said Chris. "I'm sure that's it. MSF. She's working on some Aids/HIV project with street kids in Bangkok."

Tony wondered if anyone had noticed that the smile on his face had turned to a grimace. He worked hard to keep it there, terrified what expression might replace it should he let the manic grin fall from his face. Unwelcome memories came flooding back of the Shona Johnston he'd known two decades ago. Time had not erased the intensity of those images – he fought hard to push them from his mind and was more than grateful when Bernie spoke.

"Isn't that wonderful?" she said. "I've always wanted to do something worthwhile like that."

"I think MSF need qualified medical people," said Chris doubtfully.

"I mean in general – doing something worthwhile with your life. Instead of getting caught up in the rat race like everyone else. Don't you think we could all be doing something more worthwhile? More altruistic?"

"Well, your priorities change when you get married," said Chris quickly – anxious, Tony imagined, to avoid a lecture from Bernie on philanthropic living. Her views on the solution to world hunger had been mind-boggling enough. "Maybe they've had enough of living abroad. Or perhaps they want to start a family."

"At forty-three?" said Karen, and Bernie looked at the table and was quiet.

There must be more than one Shona Johnson in the world, thought Tony. It was most likely just a coincidence that Raymond's fiancée shared her name, he told himself

145

firmly. The panic in him subsided a little.

"That's not late nowadays," said Paul. "The age of women having their first baby is rising all the time. But how do you know she doesn't already have kids?"

Chris shrugged. "Well, I don't. But I think Raymond would've mentioned it. I wouldn't imagine, living the life she does, working out there in that environment, that she has children. Would you?"

Paul shook his head, agreeing. "Unlikely. Though I wonder if she's been married before?"

"Don't know," said Chris. "It's weird to think that Raymond's engaged to someone we've never met, isn't it? I'll have to get him to e-mail a picture of her."

"Oh, I do hope she's nice, Chris," said Karen, "Won't it be lovely to have a sister-in-law after all this time? I hope she likes us."

The speculation regarding Shona continued for some minutes, giving Tony time to compose himself. Once he could trust himself to speak without betraying emotion, he waited for a lull in the conversation and asked casually, "Did Raymond say where Shona was from?"

"She's Scottish apparently," said Chris. "He didn't say where exactly. But she did her nursing degree over here at the University of Ulster. Isn't that interesting?"

Tony's heart began to pound so fast he put his hand on his breast. He felt the cold prickle of sweat on his brow. It *was* her. Please, please God make it not, he prayed. There was always the chance it was someone else – but he'd known many of the nurses in Shona's year, and the year above and below, and none of them had ever mentioned another Shona Johnston.

"At Coleraine?" asked Paul.

"I think that's where they did the nursing degrees back then. And they did their training at Altnagelvin, didn't they, Tony? Don't know if it's the same now."

"That must've been round about the same time as you, Tony," observed Karen and Tony stared at her, unable to speak.

"Does the name ring a bell, Tony?" said Paul.

"She would've been a couple of years behind him though," said Chris to Paul, momentarily diverting attention away from Tony, "so he probably wouldn't have known her."

"Excuse me," said Tony and he rose from the table too quickly – his head spun with the alcohol and the madness of what he'd just learnt. Karen's brother was marrying Shona Johnson. It couldn't, shouldn't be – but it was. His stomach churned with anguish and he thought he was going to be sick. He groaned softly.

"Are you all right, love?" said Karen's anxious voice.

"Yeah, I'm fine. I think I drank a bit too much, that's all," Tony managed to blurt out before leaving the room.

He locked himself in the downstairs toilet and turned on the cold tap with shaking hands. He splashed icy water on his face over and over until his features were numb, then turned the faucet off and stood there for a long time, water dripping off his face into the sink, thinking, thinking, thinking. What should he do? What had he done already?

He had lied by omission. By not owning up immediately that he knew Shona, he had led everyone, including Karen, to believe he did not. With hindsight, that had been a stupid thing to do. But he'd panicked. In his haste to keep the lid on his past he'd overreacted. He should just have said something casual like that the name rang a bell and left it at that. But the moment was past and now it was too late.

He had never lied to Karen – not about anything that really mattered. Like any man he had told the odd white lie to spare her feelings – or those of others. But this lie was different and he knew it. This time he had something to hide.

How could he face Shona after all these years and exchange small-talk and pretend that he did not know her? Pretend that they had not once been lovers and that they did not share the most shameful secret. He wondered if she had remained a Catholic – if her faith mattered to her the way it did to him. Maybe she had lost her faith and he could not blame her if she had. What happened had undoubtedly been much, much worse for her than it had for him.

And yet they were both culpable. It had been a joint decision, both of them motivated, he now saw, by selfishness and fear. Oh yes, fear. Fear of the unknown. Fear of the recriminations of their families and those they held dear. Fear of being bonded to each other for the rest of their lives. They had managed to extricate themselves from the mess they had made and, to his shame, Tony had felt nothing but liberation.

But that freedom had come at a cost and that price for Tony was a guilt that grew rather than diminished with time. In that instant he had grown up and he knew that it had changed him forever. The experience had made him wiser, more forgiving than he had been before. His faith was a flexible and elastic one – while he believed in the tenets of the Church, his application of them in daily life was more forgiving, less judgmental than it might otherwise have been. He knew what it was to err and just how difficult it was to live a blameless existence.

He wondered if Shona ever thought of him. He wondered if she hated him. His primary emotions when he thought of her, and that frequency had dwindled greatly with the passage of time (until tonight), was guilt and remorse. He wished with all his heart that he could turn the clock back and undo what they had done. And then his slate would be cleansed of mortal sin.

Worse of all, he was a hypocrite. While he prided himself on not judging others, he created the impression that he was superior. In his role as headmaster of a Catholic school a large part of his job, and life, revolved around setting the example for others, including staff, to follow. He wondered what they, and the pupils, never mind their parents, would think of him if they knew.

"Are you all right in there, Tony?" It was Karen's voice, concerned, from the other side of the door.

"Yep, I'm okay, love. Just coming," he replied, as chirpily as he could muster.

"I'm just making some coffee!" she said.

"Right!" he shouted. "I'll be out in a minute!"

He waited until he heard her footsteps retreating along the wooden floor, then breathed a sigh of relief.

It was Karen he cared about most of all. What on earth was he going to tell her? What would she think of him? She believed him to be a better man than he was. He could not risk losing her admiration. He could not bear the disappointment that he knew would ensue when she found out he had kept such an important part of his life a secret from her. He could not risk jeopardising the happiness that had once proved so elusive and was now his on a daily basis.

He was a coward, he knew it, but he also wanted to spare Karen any pain. It wasn't that he doubted her ability to forgive him a past mistake – given Karen's generous, loving nature that would probably come quickly and readily.

But Shona's appearance in Ballyfergus, and being forced to socialise with her as part of the family on a regular basis, was another matter. If Karen knew about the former relationship between Shona and Tony, it would be extremely difficult, if not impossible, for her to endure.

He loved Karen dearly but her one glaring flaw – apart from her skewed self-image – was a tendency to jealousy. She seemed to think that every attractive woman with whom he crossed paths, was a threat. A former lover lodged in the heart of the family as her brother's wife would be unbearable for her. And there was too much pain and guilt and shared history between him and Shona to pretend that their relationship had been just a light-hearted student fling. It really would be better if Karen never found out.

He wondered if Shona knew his identity. At Uni his nickname had been Doctor, after Doctor Doolittle, on account of the fact that he had, at one time, kept two goldfish, a mouse, a snake and a dog called Harvey as pets in his student accommodation. She knew his real name, Anthony, of course, but no-one called him that nowadays and when she knew him he was studying Geography. His career in teaching was yet to come.

He also doubted if Raymond even mentioned him to her except, in passing, as Karen's husband. She might recognise him from photos – if Raymond bothered to show her any – but he had changed considerably. He'd worn a moustache and glasses when Shona knew him (his shortsightedness had been cured three years ago by the miracle of laser surgery) and he'd been a lot thinner then.

"Come on then, Tony! That's the coffee ready!" called Karen, beginning to sound impatient.

"Coming!"

He flushed the toilet and let the taps run for a few moments. He splashed his face with water again.

On balance he doubted that Shona would guess. So she was in for a hell of a shock. He did not know how he was going to do it, but somehow his and Shona's past must remain a secret. It was in nobody's interests to go raking over it all, least of all Shona's. And too many people would get hurt – aside from Karen there was Raymond to think about. He hoped Shona would share this point of view but, if she didn't, then it was his job to very quickly persuade her otherwise.

He turned the taps off, pulled the hand-towel from the rail and dried his dripping face. He stared at the reflection in the mirror and did not like what he saw. He looked beyond the handsome face, into the piercing blue eyes, and saw a man whose past was about to catch up with him.

Eight

Paul sat in the front passenger seat of the car beside Chris on the way home: Bernie sat in the back, directly behind Chris. They were both a little too drunk to drive. Chris didn't mind driving – she needed a clear head because she wanted to get up and go for a run in the morning. And if it meant that Paula and Bernie could have a few drinks and enjoy themselves, in a way that she realised she was almost incapable of, then that was fine too.

"That was a lovely evening," said Bernie and she hiccupped.

Chris could hear the slap of her hand against her mouth as she covered it and then she burst out laughing. She composed herself quickly, and said, "Excuse me," before hiccupping again which sent Paul into a fit of the giggles.

"I'm sorry," he said, holding his belly with his right hand, tears of mirth streaming out of the corners of his eyes. Chris had never seen him act so – so, well, silly was the only word for it.

The two of them were worse than Hannah and Finn. Chris felt like she was the only adult in the car. And a very staid and disapproving adult at that. They made her feel old.

A little series of stifled hiccups, followed by girlish giggles, came from the back seat.

"Oh, don't! Bernie, stop it! I can't stop laughing," cried Paul.

"You're not –" said Bernie, pausing to hiccup again, "you're not helping!"

This foolishness continued for much of the short journey home. Chris tuned out of their conversation, such as it was, and thought of Raymond. She was delighted that he was to be married. And to have him back in Ballyfergus. It was just the best news ever.

Mum would be so pleased. She contemplated the change in dynamics within the family. It had been some years since there had been an engagement, marriage or birth and the prospect of welcoming someone completely new was an exciting one. She hoped this Shona Johnston was a likeable person. It would be so nice to have sister-in-law that she and Karen really liked and could, one day, come to love. And, forty-three or not, there was the possibility of children to look forward to as well. The thought of a precious new baby filled Chris with nostalgia for her own, now grown.

By the time they pulled up at the house, Bernie's hiccups had, at last, abated and Paul was entertaining them with his version of 'Music of the Night' from *The Phantom of the Opera*.

"Hey, that's pretty good, Paul!" shouted Bernie above the sound of his singing as she opened the door to get out.

Chris flinched and glanced at the black windows of the adjacent neighbours' house. The night was silent and still and she worried that the noise would carry and disturb them at such a late hour.

"Come on, Paul," she said, got out of the car and shut the door, waiting for him to do the same so she could lock the car. "Yes, didn't you know?" she said to Bernie. "Paul's played the male lead in Ballyfergus Operatic Society for the last three years."

"You are joking?" said Bernie.

"No, he really is a man of many talents," said Chris wryly.

"I'm beginning to realise that," said Bernie thoughtfully.

Paul stumbled out of the car, Chris locked it and they all went inside, Chris picking her way carefully across the gravel drive in her high heels.

"Right," said Paul, rubbing his hands together briskly. "Who's for a nightcap?"

Chris hesitated, thinking of her plans for a run in the morning.

"Oh, go on, Chris," said Bernie and she nudged her playfully in the ribs, making her feel like a killjoy.

"Okay, just the one then," she said, relenting. "I'll have a Baileys, please, Paul. What'll you have, Bernie?"

Paul organised the drinks and Chris went through to the kitchen. She let Murphy into the garden while she made coffee. After relieving himself, the puppy came bounding back into the kitchen, jumping and snapping his sharp little teeth in sheer delight at her presence. She stopped what she was doing, bent down and stroked him, sending him into more raptures of joy. She couldn't help but smile and wished that she could be as happy.

Once he'd calmed down a bit, she left him in the kitchen where he was unlikely to get up to much mischief – he wouldn't have the run of the house until he was properly housetrained. She carried a silver tray laden with a white china coffee pot, cups and saucers through to the elegant drawing room where Paul and Bernie seemed to have sobered up a bit.

"This really is a lovely room," said Bernie as Chris set the tray on the coffee table.

Chris smiled and glanced around the classically decorated apricot and green space. The windows were dressed in elaborate silk curtains trimmed in glass beads, the floor was covered in oriental rugs, a big antique marble clock ticked quietly above the mantelpiece and crystal chandeliers hung from the high ceilings.

The room had evolved over several years; many of the pictures, smaller pieces of furniture and ornaments had come from Paul's side of the family. And much time, and money, had been spent on the acquisition of everything else. Not that everything in the room cost a fortune – some of the lamps and knick-knacks had come from TK Maxx! But the placement of every item in the room was the result of careful consideration and deliberate thought. It always pleased Chris when the room was admired. She was proud of it.

"Thank you," she said.

She poured the coffee, sat back in the comfortable pale apricot sofa cradling a cup and saucer and said, "So what are your plans for the weekend, Bernie?"

"We were just talking about that earlier," said Bernie, nodding in Paul's direction.

"What's that?" said Paul, his voice sounding a little slurred.

"Remember, I'm going to visit my brother in Ballymena on Sunday," said Bernie.

"Is that Jim?" said Chris.

"No, Michael, the eldest. He's married with three boys."

Chris tried to recall Bernie's taciturn elder brother. Although Chris had spent many hours in the same house as him, watching TV or playing records in Bernie's room, she realised she had hardly ever spoken to him, or him to her. Her clearest recollection of Michael was of him sitting in his dusty work clothes in front of the evening news on TV eating his dinner off a lap-tray. Her memory, though fuzzy with time, was that he had not been a particularly good brother to Bernie. He basically ignored her most of the time though, even as a child, Chris could see how Bernie craved his attention. Strange to imagine him now married with a family of his own. She wondered if his nature had improved with age.

"When are you going?" said Paul.

"Sometime in the afternoon."

"Will you stay the night?" said Chris.

"I'm afraid my brother doesn't have the space," Bernie said, and broke eye contact with Chris. "If it's okay with you, and Paul, I'd like to come back here Sunday night."

"Of course it's okay," said Chris quickly and genuinely, anxious to dispel the slight discomfort she detected in Bernie. "You don't need to check with us. As I said before the third floor is yours for the duration. You have your own key – just you come and go as you please."

"Thank you, Chris. That really is sweet of you. And Paul."

"Tell you what," said Paul, after a pause. "I'll run you over to Ballymena."

"You will?" said Chris, surprised, spilling a little coffee into her saucer. "But we're supposed to be going to Mum's."

"Oh, I don't need to be there, do I? It's just for afternoon tea and she really only wants to talk to you – and Karen. I just get in the way. You'll have a better time without me."

156

Whilst this may well have been true Chris was, nonetheless, peeved. Regular Sunday visits to her mum's were part of the family routine. It was hard enough persuading Hannah and Finn to come along once in a while. It didn't help if their father opted out at the slightest opportunity. And Mum was looking forward to seeing Bernie – though, in fairness, that could easily be arranged later in the week. If there was one thing Mum had plenty of these days, it was time. But it would be the height of rudeness to withdraw the offer of a lift from Bernie, now that it had been made. Paul knew this. Chris smiled sweetly.

"No, I suppose you're right," she said, setting the saucer down on the coffee table. She placed a paper napkin in the shape of a fan under the cup to absorb any spillage.

"Anyway, how would Bernie get over to Ballymena?" said Paul. "It's only a skeleton bus service on Sundays."

Hire a car like anyone else, thought Chris, but she managed to maintain the smile on her face and nod in agreement. Immediately she reprimanded herself for having such an uncharitable thought.

"It's really very kind of you, Paul," said Bernie, "but it's not necessary, really. If I can't get there by public transport I'm sure my brother would come over and pick me up."

"And have him drive back to Ballymena, bring you over here again and have to drive back home to Ballymena again on his own? I wouldn't hear of it."

On reflection, Chris knew that in offering Bernie a lift Paul was only doing the courteous, gentlemanly thing. He put her to shame.

"I need to get a few things over in Ballymena anyway," he said.

"You mean in the shops? On a Sunday?" said Chris,

trying to remember when Paul last went shopping.

"Yes, it's Finn's birthday next month. I'll see if I can pick up a few presents for him."

"Well, that'd be great," said Chris, wondering what had brought about this change in Paul. The procuring of birthday presents had before now always fallen into her domain. While she welcomed the change, it was slightly unsettling. Her reaction reinforced how set in their ways she and Paul had become.

"Well," said Chris, when she'd finished her coffee. She glanced at her watch and winced at the late hour, calculating how little sleep she would have before having to get up and attend to Murphy. Paul would need to sleep off the effects of the alcohol. There was no danger of Hannah or Finn being up before noon and Bernie was no early riser either. "I don't know about you two but I'm just about done in. If you don't mind, I'll say goodnight." She stood up and hesitated a moment. "I'll see you in the morning then." Paul and Bernie said perfunctory goodnights, without either of them making signs of following her.

"Will you be sure to put Murphy in his pen?" said Chris. "And lock up?"

"Yes, yes," said Paul, sounding as though he was impatient for her to be gone.

At the door she stopped and glanced back.

"Is private medicine a big thing over here now, Paul?" said Bernie and Paul launched into a diatribe about private medicine and how it was damaging the National Health Service. He held surprisingly egalitarian views on public access to medical care.

She felt as though she was invisible. And yet she hovered there a few moments longer to watch Bernie lean forward, hanging on every word Paul uttered. She couldn't put her finger on it but, if she believed in intuition, she'd have sworn that something wasn't quite right. Something inside was setting off warning bells and she wasn't sure why.

* * *

"This really is very good of you, Paul," said Bernie as Paul's huge Range Rover pulled out of Ballyfergus onto the dual carriageway.

"No problem," he said, glanced in the mirror and accelerated quickly.

She'd always thought that Land Rovers and their bigger brothers, Range Rovers, were meant for use on farms and the like. But this car couldn't have been further from a utilitarian farm vehicle. It reminded her of what she imagined the cockpit of a private jet would be like, sitting up high, ensconced in leather and luxury. Briefly, she felt queenly, superior even but then she reminded herself that this was a gas guzzler and the type of car pilloried by environmentalists all over the world. Still, she couldn't deny that she understood the attraction. She had to remind herself firmly that she hated cars like this and the people who drove them.

She looked across at Paul in the driver's seat and suddenly realised that this generalisation was not true. Her heart raced just looking at him. His head was turned slightly towards the side mirror, his eyes obscured by sunglasses. With his attention momentarily on the traffic, she took the opportunity to appraise him. She liked the way his brow wrinkled like folds in a cloth when he was focused, like now. She liked his slightly weak chin and the set of his full lips. His expression, even in repose, was always pleasant. He was upbeat, an optimist – she admired that too. She imagined, from the little she knew of him, that he hadn't experienced the sort of disappointments in life that had, over time, led to her general pessimism.

Perhaps this accounted for his unshakable confidence, which made him seem to her like a rock. She wanted to cling to him – to attach herself to someone solid and stable who was free of doubts and fear. She wanted some of that magic to rub off on her. She felt that when she was with him she was different. He made her different. He made her feel safe and certain about the world, which, up until now had proved a trying place for Bernie. Because her life had not fulfilled its early promise.

Here she was at forty, single and, since the break-up with Gavin, struggling to make ends meet. She would never have children and at the rate she was going she would end up old and alone. She kept reminding herself to be thankful she was alive but, since she'd come to Ireland, that in itself wasn't enough anymore. In the company of Chris and Karen, both so successful in their chosen fields and blessed with wonderful homes, nice husbands and healthy children, she felt a failure. Life had dealt her a crap hand. And that was so unfair.

She bowed her head and balled her hands into tight angry fists, then released them quickly. It didn't have to be that way always though, did it? The past wasn't a precursor to the future. Wasn't she entitled to a bit of happiness like everyone else? She was sick of struggling on alone. If the chance came her way, shouldn't she take it? She glanced nervously at Paul. What if they had a future together, like she was beginning to suspect? What if he wanted to take care of her? Her heart raced with the possibilities. Would she – could she? – do what was necessary to make it happen. She blushed with shame and tried to push these treacherous thoughts from her mind.

She concentrated on the purpose of today's trip to see her brother – to find out what she could to help unravel the mystery of her father's will. She had pretended to Chris and Paul, out of a sense of embarrassment, that she was looking forward to seeing Michael and his family. The truth was, she was dreading it. She and Michael rarely spoke on the phone; they just didn't have anything to say to each other. They still played out the roles of the distant big brother and the annoying little sister. At least that's how it felt to Bernie – that's how Michael made her feel. Stupid and boring.

Because of the distant relationship with her brother, she had been a poor aunt to his three boys. Occasionally she sent presents at Christmas but, she was ashamed to say, she did not remember their birthdays and knew very little about their lives. Maybe it was best she'd never had children of her own – on reflection, she might not have made a good mother after all.

She had never met Michael's wife, Lesley, of nine years either. They'd spoken on the phone of course and she seemed a pleasant, if rough, sort of woman. She had no real desire to meet her face-to-face.

Only her desire to find out as much as she could from Michael drove her to go through with this. She expected the visit to be awkward and uncomfortable but it would be worth it if Michael was able to shed some light on why her father had disinherited her.

"You're very deep in thought," said Paul suddenly, disturbing Bernie's reverie. He glanced at her lap and she realised, embarrassed, that she was wringing her hands together in anxiety. She pulled them apart and hid them in the folds of her peasant skirt.

"Oh, I was just day-dreaming," she said.

She blinked and looked out the window, seeing the landscape properly for the first time. They had passed through Kilwaughter and were now on the bleak stretch of road that went through part of the Ballyboley Forest. The road was flanked on one side by pine tree plantations and on the other by open moorland. They were lucky today – it was fine and bright. Bernie remembered that this section of the road, because of its high altitude, was often shrouded in icy hill fog or mizzle for much of the year.

"What were you day-dreaming about?" he said.

"Just thinking about Michael and his family," she replied.

He leaned forward and adjusted the heating control – a faint waft of aftershave, something sweet and spicy, came her way. She shut her eyes and inhaled it deeply. She wanted to touch him.

There was a long silence in the car then, broken at last by Paul.

"I like this. Just you and I," he said.

The question, disguised as a comment, caught Bernie by surprise. She glanced quickly at him but his face was impassive, his gaze directed at the road ahead. She turned her gaze on a copse of trees to her far left. Her heart pounded against her breastbone. She did not trust herself to speak.

This was what she had been waiting for, she suddenly realised. She didn't have to respond of course – she could choose to ignore his comment or change the subject. But she knew what Paul was doing and why. He was testing her. What she said now would determine the course of their relationship. They would remain friends or become much, much more to one another, based on her reply.

She had known him for less than a week. Was it possible to fall in love with someone so quickly? She told herself it was. She'd fallen for him almost as soon as they'd met, her passion fanned by the fact that Paul seemed to reciprocate those feelings. She could tell by the attention he paid her, by the way his face lit up when she came into a room, by the way he confided in her his innermost thoughts.

She wasn't just imagining it. She'd been round the block a few too many times to mistake his intentions. But did he really love her? Or just fancy her? There was a big difference.

He had a lot more to lose than she – a wife, a family, a home. Would he really jeopardise all that for her? She thought guiltily of Chris and was ashamed of what she was contemplating. But, she reminded herself ruthlessly, she wasn't responsible for the failure of their marriage; it had obviously been on the rocks long before now. She'd been in the company of Chris and Paul enough times now to know, even if they didn't, that their relationship was dead. She had not seen one sign of genuine affection between them. Rather, they seemed to bristle along in a low-level state of semi-irritation with each other. They did not, it appeared to Bernie, love each other.

She knew that Chris would hate her for what she was about to do. So would Karen. She would hate herself too. But the alternative as she saw it – a life lived out alone and without companionship – filled her with horror. She was sick of struggling, of being poor, and she was honest enough with herself to admit that part of Paul's attraction was his wealth. And there was nothing wrong with that. In her position, she had to be pragmatic. Wouldn't it be wonderful for once to have someone look after her, pay the bills, provide money for all the little luxuries she needed? She would be hard pressed to do better than a well-paid doctor, even one with financial commitments to two nearly-grown children.

And though Chris would not see it this way, Bernie told herself that she would actually be doing her a favour by rescuing her from a marriage that had gone cold and stale. She tried not to think too much about Hannah and Finn. They were nearly adults, she reasoned – old enough, surely, to cope with their parents' break up, if it came to that? And it must be as obvious to them as it was to her that their parents' marriage was not a happy one.

While these thoughts flitted in and out of her brain in random paths like butterflies, one overriding thought prevailed. Above all others, one voice persisted. Whispering and insistent, it seduced her with fantasies of bliss. This, said the voice, this is your chance at happiness, Bernie. Take it. Take it now before it's too late.

"I like it too," she said cautiously and there was a long pause while she fought to control the emotion in her voice. "What I mean, Paul, is that I like you. I like you a great deal."

Without looking at her he reached out and found her hand and squeezed it, a gesture so full of promise it made Bernie's eyes fill with tears. The line had been crossed and there was no going back.

* * *

"Hello, Bernie," said Michael when he answered the door of his modest semi-detached home, greeting Bernie as though they'd last seen each other two days ago rather than two decades. He was wearing a pair of jeans and a polo shirt with some sort of football logo on it. "You'd better come in."

Bernie turned and waved to Paul, waiting in the idling car on the broad street, and watched with longing as he drove off. Then she stepped into the narrow hall and Michael gave her a perfunctory kiss on the cheek. When he pulled away his face was pink with embarrassment and he looked down awkwardly at his feet.

Time had not been kind to Michael. He was instantly recognisable but it was as though the younger, almost-handsome man that he had once been was trapped inside a fat suit. Not that he was grossly obese, just overweight in that middle-aged-spread way that afflicts so many. His skin, never good in his youth, still bore the marks of the fierce acne that had plagued him in his teens. His hair had started to recede and he had attempted to disguise the emerging bald patch by sweeping a long, greasy lock of hair over it.

His appearance saddened Bernie and filled her with a sense of nostalgia for their youth. Michael had never been very handsome but he had once been slim and strong – and full of life and promise. Now he looked washed out, tired, worn down by life. Panic gripped her. If Michael had aged like this then so must she. Was this how she appeared to others? Were her attempts to retain a youthful figure and disguise the ever increasing lines and wrinkles a waste of time? Was she fooling herself? Instead of looking trendy, did she look ridiculous in her hippy clothes and beads? Did she, God forbid, look old?

"Who was that?" said Michael, watching over her shoulder as Paul's car indicated right and disappeared down an adjacent street.

"Chris's husband, Paul. He gave me a lift over."

"Uhh," grunted Michael, followed by, "Must be loaded driving that monster."

"He's a doctor," she said by way of explanation and felt herself faintly blush. There was an awkward pause. She looked down the street in the opposite direction in which Paul had driven.

"I suppose we'd better go through," he said and led the way into a comfortable sitting room.

It was on a modest scale but pleasantly decorated in a modern style and furnished with two very large cream leather sofas. They were angled so that both faced the enormous flat-screen TV in the corner of the room. The house was spotlessly clean and tidy, not at all what Bernie had expected from the little she knew of Lesley, a divorced former hairdresser who was from one of the rougher areas of Ballyfergus and had come to the marriage with an eighteen-month-old son in tow. Bernie walked into the centre of the room and stood on the shaggy brown rug in front of a bright brass fire surround. The coal-effect gas fire in the grate was lifeless.

"Well," she said to fill the awkward silence, "it's good to see you, Michael. How have you been?"

"You know," he shrugged, jamming his hands into the front pockets of his jeans. "Getting by. Work. Home. Kids. They take up your life, kids do. I'm knackered most of the time. Not that you'd know anything about that," he said and sniffed.

Bernie felt her stomach muscles tighten. His rudeness was compounded by the fact that he had unwittingly touched upon a subject most painful to Bernie. He knew she had had cancer – he did not know that she was sterile as a result of the treatment she had received. She was starting to remember why she disliked him so much.

"You know," she said severely, "I was under the impression that children were something to be enjoyed, not endured."

"Yeah, well. Have a couple of rug rats yourself and come back and tell me about it in ten years' time," he replied dismissively. He rolled back on his heels, folded his arms across his chest and made eye contact with her for the first time so that, she imagined, he could assess the effect of his words on her. Why, she wondered, did he dislike her so much? What had she ever done to him?

"Still, it must be a nice life, just having yourself to worry about."

His tone was lightly mocking now – or was she imagining it? She shot him a hostile look, disappointed that the conversation looked set to follow the same old predictable routine of their shared adolescence. It infuriated her that Michael still treated her like a child and accorded her so little respect.

"Well, if you find raising a young family so exhausting, Michael, maybe you should have thought twice before having them."

"What d'you know about it?" he said quickly.

"And," she added sharply, choosing to ignore his last comment, "you know nothing about what it's like to be me, Michael. So can we talk about something else, please?"

"Suit yourself," he said with an almost-smile, pleased with himself for having riled her. Just like the good old days when she was a child except he was old enough now to know better.

Bernie sat down on the opposite end of the sofa to her brother and, in a better frame of mind now, Michael talked about various relatives and what they were all up to now. Bernie was surprised to hear that feisty Aunt Jean had finally had to be institutionalised in a nursing home in Portstewart, where one of her daughters lived. "I'd hate to be working in that place, looking after her," chuckled Michael. "She's still got all her marbles, that one, and let me tell you, she gives them hell."

There was an awkward pause.

"Just a minute, I'll get the boys in," he said then. But instead of rising from his seat to go and find them, he hollered, "Boys!" so loudly, that Bernie flinched. "Come and meet your Aunt Bernie!"

Almost instantly, three boys ranging in age from six to about eleven appeared in the doorway of the room wearing football shorts, tops and trainers. They were well-built with coarse brown hair, freckled cheeks and cheeky demeanors. The youngest, with his hand in his mouth, appeared to be chewing on it. At first glance there was no doubt that they were, all three, brothers.

"Hi, boys! It's good to meet you," she said, looking for any evidence of a different father in the features of the eldest, Rory. But there was none – the boys looked remarkably similar and all three strongly resembled their mother. She wondered briefly what kind of a father her brother was to this boy. Did he treat him as his own? Or did he favour his own blood?

The children stared at Bernie like she was an alien until Michael said, "This is your Aunt Bernie, all the way from Australia. Say hello now."

The children mumbled reluctant hellos, the youngest

boy, Dennis, dancing excitedly from one foot to the other.

"We were just going out, Dad," said Rory.

"Wait a minute – I have something for you," said Bernie, pulling from her capacious bag three hand-crafted wooden boomerangs and navy T-shirts in three different sizes with a stylised map of Australia on the front of each. She handed them out to the boys.

"What do you say?" said Michael, with a warning tone in his voice.

"Thanks, Auntie Bernie!" they chorused.

Toby, the middle child, held the T-shirt up for examination and stared at it for a few seconds. "That's where kangaroos and koalas come from, right?"

"That's right," said Bernie.

"We did that in school," he explained.

"What's this for?" said Dennis, holding up the curved, wooden missile.

"It's a boomerang. It was made by a native of Australia, an aborigine. It's a sort of weapon, designed to return to you when you throw it. Look, there's instructions on the leaflet in the package. You might need a little practice though. I still can't throw one to save my life!"

"Wow! I've never seen one of these before," said Rory, turning the boomerang over in his hands. He ran a finger over the smooth curves, and examined the line carvings and yellow drawings that decorated it. "That's pretty cool."

"Yeah, cool," said Dennis, his interest stimulated by his elder brother's approval. Suddenly, he threw the boomerang across the room. It bounced on the sofa and fell to the floor.

"Hey! Not indoors!" said Michael, raising his voice. Then his tone softened and he added, "Away with youse now and give us some peace," surprising Bernie with the affection in his voice. At his command, Dennis retrieved his boomerang from where it had landed and the three boys scampered quickly from the room.

Just then a woman, whom Bernie recognised as Lesley from the registry-office wedding photos, appeared in another doorway that led, she presumed, to the kitchen or dining room. She was dusting her hands together and the smell of home baking accompanied her into the room. She was much bigger than in her wedding pictures and solidly built but she had a pretty face and kind smile. She was younger than Michael, Bernie remembered, by nearly fifteen years.

"Hello, love," she said genially, came over quickly and Bernie stood up to receive a warm bear hug. Lesley's straw-like dyed-blonde hair tickled her face.

"She brought those T-shirts for the boys," said Michael, "and boomerangs."

"Oh, you shouldn't have!" said Lesley, examining the T-shirts admiringly. "I hope they said 'thank you', did they, Mike?"

"They did but then they ran straight out."

Lesley rolled her eyes. "Don't you mind them now, Bernie. Boys'll be boys and all they want to be doing is playing outside – isn't that right, Mike?"

Just as she said this there was a dull thud from outside and a blue and white football was kicked high into the air in full view of the window, closely followed by two boomerangs. Michael jumped up, surprisingly agile, opened the window and shouted out, "Not near the house! How many times have I told you? Rory, you keep an eye on your wee brother now. See he doesn't come to any harm."

Michael stared out the window for a few seconds then,

satisfied that his orders were being obeyed, sat down heavily on the end of one of the cream sofas.

"They're lovely boys," said Bernie, sitting down again and swallowing back the little pang of envy that threatened to descend into self-pity. "You're very lucky," she added brightly.

Lesley smiled happily and said, "Yes, they're good boys by and large. Now, will you take a cup of tea, Bernie? I've just made some fresh scones." She ran her eye quickly over Bernie's small frame and said rather doubtfully, "You do like scones, don't you, love?"

Bernie smiled broadly, warming to Lesley by the minute, and said reassuringly, "I love them. And yours smell absolutely delicious. It's years since I've tasted a home-made scone. The Aussies don't go in for them much."

"Then they don't know what they're missing, do they?" said Lesley, sounding pleased, and she left the room.

Bernie remembered that their father had been bitterly disappointed in Michael's choice of bride. He thought that Michael could've done better. Personally Bernie thought Michael had been lucky, at the age of forty-two, to persuade anyone to marry him – let alone a warm person like Lesley. And yet she could understand why Lesley might have married her taciturn brother – for security, a father for her son, simple companionship. As a single, overweight mum on a low income in Ballyfergus, her options would've been pretty limited. In that context, Michael mightn't have seemed like such a bad bet.

"So, Bernie," said Michael, that irritating smirk of his hovering just below the surface, "you're not with that Aussie bloke any more? What was his name?"

"Gavin," she said, realising that she had not uttered his

name in over a year. Before she'd met Paul, the mere mention of him would've unsettled her for the rest of the day. Now she realised, with sudden shock, that she was free of him. Paul had effected an instant cure that four years of distance and determined independence had been unable to deliver.

"Yes, Gavin," repeated Michael.

"No, that didn't . . . work out. We went our separate ways a while back."

"I see," said Michael and there was a long pause.

Bernie looked out the window at a group of kids playing in the street. Her nephews were nowhere to be seen. Michael lived near the end of a wide sweeping cul-de-sac surrounded on all sides by identical new-build homes with red roofs and white harled walls, a popular finish on houses in Northern Ireland. Though small they were aspirational and the estate had a pleasant, family feel to it.

The leather creaked as Michael adjusted his weight on the sofa.

"You should've come back for his funeral, Bernie," he said in a quiet voice.

Bernie froze, her gaze fixed on the scene outside the window. "Maybe I should've," she whispered, conceding that she might have been wrong. But she didn't want to start an argument. She was here for answers.

"You left everything to me and Jim," said Michael, bitterly. "Clearing out the house, deciding what to do with all his stuff – all the old letters and photos. It wasn't easy."

"I'm sorry about that," said Bernie.

"Why didn't you come back?"

She sighed, wearied by the burden of explaining

something she could not fully understand herself. "There didn't seem to be any point. Dad and I . . . well, you know we never saw eye to eye. And we hadn't spoken to each other for years – not since I moved in with Gavin. You know he didn't approve of us living together. You know how old-fashioned he was about things like that." She gave a nervous little laugh. She glanced at Michael but he remained stony-faced. The smile fell from her face and her voice softened. "After he was dead, well, it felt like it was too late to . . ." she paused and then added, "too late to come home. I just couldn't face it. I'd been very ill, you know."

"I know you had a rough time, Bernie, and I'm sorry for that, but," his voice hardened, "you don't not go to your own father's funeral. I mean, do you think Jim and I enjoyed it? You don't go shirking your responsibilities just 'cos you don't feel like it."

Bernie listened, trying hard not to react. She should've known better than to expect Michael to understand.

"Everyone wondered where you were," he went on.

"I don't care what other people think."

"I can see that."

They glared at each other and just then, to Bernie's relief, Lesley came into the room bearing a large tray. She set it on the glass coffee table and proceeded to unload cups and saucers, a teapot and a plate of oversized fruit scones which were split, buttered and spread with dark red raspberry jam.

She went back into the kitchen and came back immediately with a traditional three-tiered china cake stand which, disconcertingly, Bernie recognised. It used to sit, collecting dust, in the display cabinet in the lounge of her father's house. Now it was being used as it should – or would have been, she imagined, had her mother lived. It was laden with old-fashioned home-made treats of the sort Bernie had not seen since her childhood – slices of Victoria sandwich, iced gingerbread, flapjacks, and millionaire shortbread.

"Did you make all these?" said Bernie in wonder.

"I did," replied Lesley, making no attempt to conceal her pride.

"My goodness, Lesley, this looks just lovely! You've gone to a lot of trouble."

"It's no trouble really," she replied, making light of the effort. "I bake all the time, don't I, Mike? And there's never anything wasted in this house, not with Mick and the boys, is there, Mike?"

"No, love," said Mike tamely.

Bernie felt herself envying the homely domesticity that evidently reigned in this house. It was so far removed from the urbane, and often lonely, lifestyle she enjoyed in Australia. It reminded her of long ago visits to Auntie Jean who, mindful that they had no mother at home, would always try to stuff her and her brothers with home baking.

Bernie battled her way through a huge scone while Lesley chatted amiably about this and that. Then, having forced a slice of Victoria Sandwich and another cup of tea on her guest, Lesley heaved herself out of the armchair, dabbing in a ladylike manner at her mouth with a yellow paper serviette.

"I suppose I'd better go and see what those boys have done with wee Dennis," she said. "He's only just six. The big ones sometimes go up to the playing fields to play football and I worry he'll wander off on his own. I'll see you before you go now, Bernie." She patted Bernie on the knee and left with a smile.

As soon as Lesley shut the door behind her, Michael said, "Look, Jim and I have talked about it. We weren't very happy about you being left out of the will. It didn't feel right. We'll share the money out equally between the three of us. The way it should've been divided up. We think it's the right thing to do."

"What are you talking about, Michael?"

"The money that Dad left in his will."

"I'm not interested in his money," said Bernie dismissively but Michael went on as though she had not spoken.

"I know it's not much, Bernie. If he'd bought the council house like we told him to all those years ago he could've been sitting on a healthy little nest egg. But you know what he was like. Too stubborn to take advice, least of all from his sons." He shook his head in despair at his father's financial incompetence. "We've not spent a penny of it, you know. It's still sitting in the bank."

"I don't want his money," said Bernie, firmly.

"But isn't that why you're here?"

"No. What makes you think I came here for money, Michael?"

He shrugged, appearing to be at a genuine loss, and said, "What else was I to think? I haven't seen you in years and then all of a sudden you turn up on the doorstep." He paused and set his teacup, too dainty for his meaty hands, on the coffee table. Then he leaned against the back of the sofa and folded his arms across his chest.

"Is it just a social visit then?" he said, with an edge of sarcasm in his voice.

"Not exactly."

He raised his eyebrows.

"I hardly know where to begin," said Bernie, feeling foolish. "It is about Dad and the will but not in the way you think. I'm not interested in the money – in getting any of it – I mean. But I do very much want to find out why Dad left me out of his will."

He raised his eyebrows and shook his beefy jowls. "I don't know the answer to that, Bernie. Maybe Dad was confused when he wrote the will. I don't know."

"But you told me on the phone that the will had been written six years before he died. He was perfectly lucid then."

Michael shrugged.

"So we both know that he wasn't confused when he wrote it," said Bernie. "Which leads me to the conclusion that what he did was quite deliberate."

Another shrug.

Bernie sighed deeply, glanced for a moment at the china figurines of little children that adorned the mantelpiece, and then looked sideways at her brother again. He was staring straight ahead.

"Michael," she said and paused. "Michael, did Dad ever talk to you about me?"

"What d'you mean?"

"Did he ever say anything that might indicate why he did this thing?"

"Of course he mentioned your name from time to time. But I can't think of anything . . ." His voice trailed off. He rubbed his chin with his right hand and shook his head. "Well, he was very put out by you taking up with that Gavin, of course."

Bernie shook her head. "I don't think that's it. I don't think that's why he disinherited me."

"Why do you say that? What other reason could he have had?"

"For one thing Gavin and I had broken up a couple of years before Dad died. And anyway, it goes much deeper than that. It goes back to when we were growing up."

"What're you on about, Bernie?" Michael said with a little snort.

"I . . . oh, I can't really explain it except to say that I've always had this feeling that . . . that Dad didn't like me."

"Don't be daft!" Michael blurted out, and he laughed, dismissing her like a schoolgirl.

"I knew you'd react like this," she said stiffly.

"What do you expect me to do when you come off with stuff like that?" he said, mirth still playing round the corners of his mouth. "You're imagining things, Bernie."

"I tell you I'm not," she replied firmly, determined to make him take her seriously.

He regarded her thoughtfully for a few moments, the smile gone from his face and then said quite solemnly, "Bernie, I have absolutely no idea what you're trying to get at here."

"I'm trying to tell you that something wasn't – wasn't quite right. It was the way I'd find him watching me sometimes with a hard look on his face and when I smiled he'd look away. Sometimes he'd ignore me completely. Like I'd walk into a room and ask him something and he'd just say without even looking up in this deadpan voice, flat as a pancake: 'Go away.'"

"He never did that."

"He did. He just never did it to you and Jim or when

anyone else was around. In front of other people, well, he acted like a normal dad."

"Bernie, the man was widowed, left with two teenage boys and a wee girl to raise on his own. What'd you expect him to be like? He must've found it hard. He must've been depressed a lot of the time."

"I understand that and I appreciate everything he did in raising us on his own. I'm not questioning his commitment, and the sacrifices he made."

"What are you questioning then?"

Bernie paused, thrown by the question. She was ready to list a long litany of complaints about the way her father controlled her with a vice-like grip. The way she wasn't allowed to have boyfriends or stay out later than ten at night, even as a nearly grown woman. The way he refused to let her wear make-up or the latest fashions, go to school discos, read teenage magazines and complained about her listening to pop music.

She remembered how he insisted on knowing exactly where she was at all times and with whom. And how he would explode with rage if she was so much as five minutes past the curfew and ground her for a month in punishment. It was as though he wanted to infantilise her, to stop her growing up into a woman. The way he treated her was, of course, the reason why she had rebelled and got as far away from him – and Ballyfergus – as she could.

She believed that none of the things her father did had been done out of protective love. She never remembered him once saying that he loved her and he never made her feel loved. She tried so hard to win his approval, but she never succeeded. She didn't remember him ever kissing her, not once. Everything he did for her had felt to Bernie like it was a chore.

Of course, when her mother had been alive it had not mattered. She had precious little memory of her dad from that time – a shadowy figure on the periphery of her life, either at work or out doing whatever he did in the evenings and on weekends – the pub, football, playing pool. She realised suddenly that it wasn't until her mother was gone that she had became aware of how much her father resented her. But what had she done to incur such antipathy?

"I don't believe he loved me. And I want to know why," she said with a gasp, at last uttering the words that had been lodged in her heart for two decades. "I want to know why," she repeated.

"Rubbish," said Michael, with a look of incredulity on his face. "You don't know what you're talking about."

"You were never there, Michael!" she cried. "You were working or out all the time. You never paid any attention to me or what was going on at home. You don't know what it was like for me."

Michael shook his head in disbelief. "You haven't changed a bit, have you? You're still selfish and attention-seeking just the way you were when you were a kid. It was always 'me, me, me' with you. Always thinking of yourself and demanding this and that. You had Dad's head turned, so you did. And the rest of us."

"That's not fair!" cried Bernie, wounded.

"The problem with you, Bernie, is that you're too self-centred. You don't come to Dad's funeral and then you turn up here and all you want to talk about is yourself. You should get married and have a couple of kids and then you'll have someone to worry about instead of yourself."

"And you're just the same pig-headed ignoramus you've

always been, Michael Sweeney," said Bernie and she rose to her feet. "You were a shit to me when I was small and you've not changed one little bit. And if you think I'm staying here to listen to any more of your abuse you've got another think coming."

From outside in the hall Bernie heard the sound of the front door opening and Lesley coming in with one or more of the boys. She seemed to be scolding someone.

"Go on then, go," said Michael and he nodded at the door. "Run away like you always do."

Ignoring him, Bernie snatched the door open to find Lesley sitting on the bottom stair with Dennis, her youngest child, balanced, sniffling, on her knee.

"Will you look at the state of that," said Lesley to Bernie and pointed at the child's dirty, bloodied knees. "Now you're going to have to have a bath, young man, to get that dirt out." She sighed heavily in mock exasperation but her tone was good-natured. "Kids. Can't let the little beggars out of your sight for five minutes!"

"I have to go now, Lesley," said Bernie.

"So soon?" said Lesley and her head snapped up suddenly, concern creasing her rounded features.

"I'm sorry," said Bernie and she opened the front door and stepped outside.

"But we haven't even had a proper chat yet," called Lesley, as she struggled to her feet, depositing Dennis, still crying, on the stair.

"I'm sorry – I have to go!" Bernie called over her shoulder as she strode purposefully away from the house.

She reached the end of the path, put her hand on the wooden gate and fumbled with the latch.

"Bernie!" came Michael's voice. "Wait!"

She paused and glanced behind to see him walking down the path towards her.

"Don't go just yet. I have something for you," he said gruffly, and she hesitated.

"I don't want it," she said, sounding churlish. But, her curiosity aroused, she couldn't help but notice that he held something in his right hand, his fingers curled round it in a fist. She lifted the latch, the gate swung open and she stepped onto the street, pulling the waist-high gate shut behind her.

"Please," said Michael and she stopped and turned to glare at him.

"What?" she said coldly.

"Jim and me – well, we thought you should have these."

He unfurled his work-worn hand to reveal a small burgundy flock-covered jewelry box. She frowned at him questioningly.

"Open it," he said and thrust it into her hand.

She prised the sprung lid open to find a brooch, gold chain and two rings entangled together. She nudged them gently with her index finger, turning one of the gold bands over to reveal one side of it encrusted with little shards of diamonds.

"Mum's?" she said and he nodded.

"Dad never said what he wanted to happen to them. Me and Jim'll never use them now we're both married and neither of us have girls to pass them onto. I don't suppose they're worth much anyway."

Bernie glared at him and closed the hinged lid with a snap. Trust Michael to put a monetary value on what was beyond price. She let her arm drop to her side and the little box burned in her hand.

"Look, don't be silly, Bernie," he said, looking first up and then down the road, avoiding her gaze. "You can't just go off like this. At least let me give you a lift back to Ballyfergus?" His eyes settled on her at last.

"No, Paul's going to take me back. It's all arranged. All I have to do is call him. He'll be here in a few minutes." Without waiting for a reply, she turned and walked away.

She heard Lesley's footsteps on the path and the urgent, low sound of her voice as she no doubt grilled Michael as to what was going on. But Bernie did not look back. She marched to the end of the street and only slowed her pace when she had rounded the corner and was out of sight of the house.

She fumbled in her bag for her mobile, her hands shaking. She dialled Paul's number and nearly cried with relief when he answered. He would never speak to her the way Michael had just done. She needed him desperately. She needed him now.

"Paul!" she cried into the phone. "Can you come and get me?"

"Already? But you haven't even been there an hour."

"I know. But I want to go now," she said, pacing urgently up and down outside a house that looked identical to her brother's.

"Okay," he said slowly. "Are you all right, Bernie?"

"I'm fine," she said quickly.

"You don't sound it. Tell me what's wrong?"

"Just come and get me please."

"Okay. I'm on my way now," he said, his voice full of concern.

"Paul."

"What?"

"Don't pick me up at the house. I'll meet you at the end of the street, just round the corner from Michael's house. You'll drive past me on your way in. I'm right beside the post box. You can't miss it. Hurry please."

Bernie put the phone back in her bag and stood self-consciously by the red pillar box, aware that she struck an incongruous figure on this busy Saturday afternoon estate. On the other side of the street two men, close neighbours, were in their driveways washing their cars. They paused now and then to chat and threw curious glances in her direction. She looked away. Further along, a woman, kneeling on the grass, tended to an already immaculate garden while what seemed like dozens of noisy children played in the street.

The front door of the house she stood outside opened and a woman poked her head out. She held a tiny baby in her arms and a blond, wide-eyed toddler clung to her leg.

"Can I help you?" she shouted across the small garden laid in grass, not sounding like someone who wanted to help at all.

Bernie gave her a weak smile. "I'm waiting for a lift. Should be here any minute."

The woman, smiling coldly, shut the door and Bernie fought back tears. Michael's cruel words echoed in her head and etched themselves into her memory. Was she as self-centered and obnoxious as he said? Is that the reason why her father had not loved her? Because she had been an unpleasant, horrible, demanding little girl? Was she still like that?

Her stomach knotted with anxiety. She did not want to believe Michael but she had to face facts – what other explanation was there? Her dad did not love her simply because she was unlovable. Was that why Gavin had left too? Because he found in his new love something that was lacking in her? Was she too selfish? And had the last few years living alone made her even worse?

There was no mystery to her father's will, after all. He simply hadn't liked – or loved – her. In the twilight of his life she had not been a good daughter to him. She had escaped Ballyfergus just as soon as she could and visited only once from Australia when Jim got married. Her neglect had always been a source of shame – now she was glad. Glad that she hadn't played the dutiful daughter only to be spurned by him from beyond the grave.

She looked at the box in her hands and mourned the mother she had hardly known. She could not remember what she looked like. She could not remember her smell or the sound of her voice. She just remembered that once, when she was very little, someone had loved her unconditionally. A warm presence, spiritual and physical, had been there for her every waking moment. Her life was defined by her mother's early death – there was the time before it and the time after it. And she could not help but feel that her life would've been so much different – so much better – had her mother lived. How she missed her!

When Paul's car pulled up at the kerb she got in quickly and put her head down to hide the tears that sprang suddenly from her eyes.

"Bernie," cried Paul, "what's wrong?"

"Drive, Paul," she managed to say between sobs. "Just drive, will you?"

The car shot forward like a bullet. Paul expertly navigated the way out of the housing estate with its warren-like network of narrow winding streets and dead ends and residents going about their lives. Bernie stared at the scenes of everyday domesticity as they sped past and felt her heart would break. She wondered when she would ever see Michael again.

"Jesus, Bernie," Paul said aghast, "what happened?"

"It was Michael. He was horrible to me. He told me that I was selfish and self-centred."

"But, Bernie," he said in a half-laugh, "you're none of those things. Don't pay any attention to him."

"He said that was why Dad didn't like me. That's why he left me out of his will. He said that I was . . ." she sobbed and could not go on.

"It's okay, it's okay," said Paul urgently and he squeezed her hand in his.

Soon they had left Ballymena behind them and were on the country roads. At the first available opportunity Paul pulled into a lay-by and killed the engine.

He turned to face her and she could not look at him. She put her hands to her face to hide her distress and the jewellery box fell into her lap.

"What's that?" said Paul.

"It Mum's jewellery – her wedding and engagement rings," she said, her voice choked with emotion. "Michael gave them to me."

"Is that what made you cry?"

"Partly," said Bernie and she found a handkerchief in her pocket and dabbed her eyes. "Dad didn't love me, you know, Paul," she said and her voice started to break again. She composed herself and went on, "That's why he left me out of the will. I thought there was some big mystery to unfold but there's not. He just didn't love me."

"Oh, Bernie. I'm sure that's not true," began Paul but she shook her head vigorously, disagreeing.

"It's the only explanation. His own flesh and blood. How could he do that? How could he?"

Paul was quiet, and it was his turn to shake his head.

"I wish my mum hadn't died," she blurted out, buried her face in her hands and wept afresh.

"Oh, darling," said Paul and he pulled her to him then and held her tightly in an awkward embrace, the handbrake digging into her right hip. She closed her eyes, and let her body meld with his. She put her arms around him, buried her face in her neck and inhaled the scent of him.

She so desperately wanted to be loved. To be held and adored and told that none of the horrible things Michael said were true. She knew it was wrong to take comfort from another woman's husband, especially when that woman was her friend and she was a guest in her home.

But so much about her life had been wrong. She'd been dealt too many bad hands. Here was her last chance of happiness. She would be a fool not to take it. If only he wasn't Chris's husband. If only her happiness didn't rely on the destruction of a marriage. But what was she to do? Walk away now? Turn her back on a man who loved her? A man who could take care of her for once in her life?

He moaned softly, turned his head and his lips found hers. His kiss was bitter and sweet and beautiful. She closed her eyes and tried not to think about Chris or Hannah or Finn.

Nine

When they got back to the house, Chris's car was gone from the drive and inside the house was silent and deserted as a mid-week graveyard. Paul hated himself for what he was about to do but he was driven by a force he could not control. A force he didn't want to control.

Bernie followed him inside to the hall and Paul shouted, "Chris! Finn! Hannah!" They stood in the silence that followed and stared at each other and waited for a reply. There was none.

Slowly and deliberately Paul set his keys down on the walnut console table in the hall and bolted the front door, then closed the inner glazed door. He knew that Chris would not be back until after six – it was only four o'clock. His heart raced and his breath came in shallow, quiet gasps. He knew that to take Bernie in this house was wrong and he knew that he took a great risk in doing so. But his desire for her consumed him. He could not stop himself. He didn't want to.

He was tired of living a life of weary predictability. Of enduring life with a woman who, at best, was warm, never passionate, a woman who never made him feel that she needed him sexually or any other way. A woman who made him feel that if he was not there she could manage quite well without him, thank you very much. He was sick to death of feeling like he was half dead, his senses dulled with lack of use. He wanted to live before it was too late.

He could hear Bernie's rapid breathing in the relative gloom of the inner hall. She stood motionless, hands by her sides, staring at him, her beautiful face tear-stained and full of sorrow. No woman had ever before induced such feelings of protectiveness in him – certainly not Chris. His feelings for Bernie were fiercely possessive. She belonged to him – she would be his.

"Bernie," he croaked, his voice little more than a whisper, "you know I love you."

She nodded. He stepped towards her and touched her shoulder, his entire body alive like never before. He stoked her face, gently, with the back of his shaking hand and a solitary tear slid down her cheek. He leaned forward and licked it greedily, the brine sharp on his tongue.

"Don't cry," he said, imagining her naked, her slim toned body astride him. His body yearned for her. He cupped the back of her head with his hand and his thumb brushed against a long, beaded earring. He whispered into her right ear, "I want to make love to you."

"No, no, we mustn't," murmured Bernie but she moaned softly, her body arching into his touch. Then, suddenly, she pulled away. His hand fell awkwardly to his side.

"If we do this," she said solemnly, "it changes everything. I will have to go. I can't stay here, under this roof." She glanced uncomfortably around the handsome hall, and her dark eyes, steady and serious, settled on him once more. "You know that, don't you?"

He nodded because she was right. The act of making love would change everything. He had never been unfaithful to Chris. He thought of the life he had shared with her for the last twenty years and much of it had been good. They had both been highly driven people, motivated by the acquisition of the good things in life. If anything he'd been more avaricious than she.

But somewhere along the line, and it had started long before Bernie came along, he had changed. Perhaps it was because he and Chris now had, more or less, all the material things they had striven for over the years. No longer distracted by endless home improving, he had the opportunity for retrospection and, with that, came the harsh realisation that their life together was lacking in intimacy, warmth, true love.

With maturity, the demands of the children had dwindled too. Now all they really needed or wanted from him and Chris, or so it seemed, was money. Had the busyness of family life over the years blinded him to the fact that he and Chris had, somewhere along the line, lost each other? Perhaps. But whatever the cause of their estrangement he knew he had no desire to re-kindle what they once shared. For he had within his grasp a better love – shining bright with newness, untarnished by decades of dull matrimonial history.

He tried to imagine another twenty, thirty, forty years with Chris. A predictable life, not without its pleasures and compensations. But, still, a life devoid of passion. Panic seized him. He was too young to accept such a fate. Many people did, many people made the best of things, for better for worse, for the sake of children and grandchildren yet to come. But he wasn't one of them.

It was true he cared about appearances, and his standing in society, but he didn't care enough to sacrifice his soul to them. He had only lived half his life, for Christ's sake! He wanted to love and to be loved. What he was about to do was utter madness, but the alternative – saying no, denying himself – would destroy that part of him that still kept faith. The part of him that believed that there was more to life than this. The part that still believed in love.

"*Omnia vincit amor*," he whispered to himself.

"What?" said Bernie.

"Love overcomes all things, Bernie."

"Does it, Paul? Does it really? Can it, for example, make this – us – right?"

"I believe so, Bernie," he said and stroked her hair gingerly. "Do you?"

She stared at him and he did not breathe. The wait seemed interminable.

"Yes," she said at last and his heart leapt.

"Oh, Bernie," he said and took her small hand and folded her fingers over his. Her smooth nails, each one a perfect shiny oval, were pale pink like the inside of a shell. He kissed each one tenderly. "You will not regret this. I promise you, my darling."

Then, unable to bear the suspense any longer, he took her by the hand and led her to her bedroom on the topmost floor of the house. There he pushed her down gently into a sitting position on the bed and knelt before her. He laid his face in her lap and placed his palms on the outside of her thighs. Even through the crinkly fabric of her skirt, her skin felt hot. He raised his head and pulled her gently to him, her thighs parting to let him get close enough to kiss her gently on the lips. Her chest rose and fell rapidly against his, and when he put his hand to her neck he could feel her pulse racing.

"Wait," she said, pulling away from him. "Let me close the blinds."

There was no real need to do so for privacy for the windows were velux ones and the only living things that could see inside the room were the birds. But he did not argue; he released her. She wriggled out of his embrace and pulled the blinds on both windows down, plunging the room into almost total darkness. Then she raised one blind a fraction of a centimetre, just enough to allow a sliver of light into the room. Enough to see her form and shape as dark shadows against the light, but nothing more.

"Just wait," she said as he stood up. "Your eyes will adjust in a minute."

He heard the rustling of fabric and sensed, more than saw, her remove her clothes. He heard a soft rushing sound as they fell to the floor and felt the air move as she came towards him. She placed a hand on his shoulder, her breath warm on his face. In answer he put his arm around her waist, thrilled by the touch of bare flesh. He moved his hand down, onto the smooth curve of her bottom, and then up, only to meet with a barrier. She had removed only her skirt and pants – her upper body was still clothed.

"I have scars," she said. "I don't want you to see them."

"That's okay," he said and removed his clothes. Then, both naked from the waist down, they lay on the narrow bed in the guest room and, pushing all thoughts of his wife and family from his mind, he made love to her like a man possessed.

Afterwards, he cradled her in his arms and kissed her forehead. Her tousled hair smelt of coconut oil.

"Are you all right?" he said.

"Mmm," she murmured contentedly and wriggled against him.

"I could do that all over again, you little minx!" he teased and she giggled.

"I believe you could, you tiger!" she said, growling the last word. They both burst out laughing.

Then she leaned up on her elbow, pulled the sheet over her hips and sucked in her bottom lip. She traced a line down his face from forehead to chin with her finger and a little frown puckered her smooth brow.

"Paul?"

"What?"

"What do we do now?"

He glanced at the clock. It was ten minutes past five.

"*Tempus fugit!*" he cried, throwing the covers aside. "We'd better get dressed before Chris comes home." He leapt out of bed.

"I didn't mean right now. I meant what happens next. To us. After this?"

"Oh," he said, feeling foolish. He sat down on the bed and pulled the edge of the sheet across his lap to hide his nakedness. "I don't quite know, Bernie. I mean I haven't worked that out yet. This has all . . . well, I have to say it's taken me by surprise."

Her face fell a little and she turned her head away from him to look at the wall.

"And it's wonderful," he reassured her, gently cupping her chin in his hand and guiding her face back towards him. "And you're wonderful and I love you. And I promise you, we *will* be together," he said, surprising himself with the words as he said them.

It wasn't that he didn't mean them – his heart certainly meant them – it was just that they came from his mouth before his brain had the time to process them. He hadn't actually given any thought to the future – to what would happen after he had slept with Bernie. Now that burning physical desire had been quenched, he suddenly realised that he didn't want it to end there. He didn't want to have sordid little affair behind his wife's back, nor did he want to stop seeing Bernie.

So, emboldened by this confession, he bared the contents of his heart.

"I've had enough of – of living like this, Bernie. I respect Chris. She's a good person and I don't want to berate her in any way, but I don't love her. I love you. I want to feel alive again and you are the only woman who can make me feel like that. I want us to be together, to have a future together."

"So do I."

"Then we will find a way to make this happen."

She put her hand on his arm and smiled fleetingly. "I can't stay here – in Chris's house – after what we've done. You do see that?"

"I understand how you feel. I feel awful too. But let's not do anything rash." She gave a little gasp and he placed his hand on her arm. "No, listen. I have a lot to think about, Bernie. The children for one thing." He pulled his hands over his face and moaned, remembering. "Hannah's in the middle of her exams, for Christ's sake!"

Tears filled her eyes and she flopped down on her back on the bed and stared at the ceiling.

"You're not going to leave her, are you?" said Bernie, flatly. "You should tell me the truth."

"Oh, Bernie! How can you think that?" he said and pinned her to the bed with the sheet, his hands either side of her shoulders, pressing down. He covered her face in urgent kisses and got an erection. He longed to make love to her all over again.

"See what you do to me?" he said.

She glanced down and a shy grin spread across her face.

"I'm mad, crazy in love with you, woman. Can't you see that?"

"And I'm mad, crazy in love with you too, Paul Quinn," she said and smiled her lovely smile.

"You just have to trust me on this one, Bernie," he said, suddenly serious. "I – we need to decide exactly how we're going to do this. I have the children to think of as well as Chris. And there's just so much to sort out – the house, finances . . ."

"We can walk out the door right now," said Bernie, her eyes ablaze as she pulled herself into a sitting position.

"It's not that simple."

"It is, Paul. It is if you want it to be."

He shook his head. "This is all happening very fast, Bernie. We need to think things through." Her face hardened. "I just need you to promise me one thing."

"What?" she said, her arms folded resentfully across her chest.

"I need you to promise me that you won't go back to Australia," he said, prising one of her arms away from her chest. She resisted at first and then let him take her hand. "Not for good anyway. Now that I've found you, I can't just let you go."

"Why don't you come with me to Australia?"

"Maybe one day. But for the time being I want to be near the kids."

She nodded. "So you want to stay in Ballyfergus?"

"Yes. What about you, Bernie? Would you be happy living here?"

"I'd be happy anywhere as long as I was with you."

"And you wouldn't mind living in Ballyfergus? In the short term anyway?"

"No. It's a different place than the one I left. I think I rather like it here." She paused then and sighed.

"What is it?"

"I just worry that, though you say you love me, you won't leave Chris."

"Why do you say that?"

"For all the reasons you said. The house, the kids, finances, duty."

"I understand why that might worry you but it's simply not going to happen, Bernie," he said patiently. "But you must see that I can't just run out the door. I have responsibilities and I must attend to those before I am free."

"But what do you mean by that, Paul? How long is it going to take before we can be together?"

"Not long, Bernie. I have to wait until Hannah's exams are over for one thing and you must have matters to attend to in Australia?"

She nodded.

"But I agree with you," he said, thinking on his feet. "It would be best if you moved out as soon as possible. We need to get you somewhere more permanent to live and then I'll join you later. I'll wait until Hannah's exams are over then I'll break the news to Chris and the children."

He suddenly realised what a huge logistical, financial and emotional undertaking lay ahead of him. This was the most exciting thing that had happened to him since the birth of the children, but it was also the most daunting.

He felt a stab of terrible guilt when he thought of Hannah and Finn. His relationship with them wasn't as close as he would've liked (and he knew he only had himself to blame for this, as Chris was fond of telling him) but he loved them. And he knew that no child wants to see their parents split up. Children, he had discovered, whilst anxious to be seen to break the bounds of conventionality at every available opportunity, were incredibly conservative when it came to how they wanted their parents to behave. And staying married was high up on the list.

"Are you okay, Paul?" said Bernie softly.

"Yeah, fine," he smiled, though inside his stomach was tied in knots. "I was just thinking things through. But you do understand that this isn't going to happen overnight, Bernie?"

"But when?" she said, clutching his forearm. "When?"

"As soon as it can be arranged. As soon as it's – practical," he said firmly. "A month or so, maybe longer. I have a lot to sort out."

"Are you having second thoughts about me?"

"No, not about you, darling," he said and planted a reassuring kiss on her forehead. "It's just that . . ." He sighed. "It's just that I have a lot more than you to lose, Bernie. This is very hard for me. I've worked all my life for this house and the lifestyle I enjoy."

"I appreciate that."

"Leaving this place and the kids . . ." he said and his voice trailed off. "Well, let's just say I won't be doing it lightly."

"You're not leaving the kids. You're leaving Chris."

"Well, let's just hope the kids see it like that."

He stood up then and found his clothes quickly. She watched him while he pulled on his trousers and belted them.

"Aren't you going to wash?" she said.

"I don't have time."

"But won't Chris, you know . . ."

"Bernie, it's been a long time since Chris and I were intimate," he said in reply.

"You'd better hurry up, then," said Bernie. "I'll get myself straightened and follow you down in a minute."

He paused at the door. "Love you," he said.

"And I love you too."

* * *

Paul was in the kitchen with his head in the fridge, trying to concentrate on the subject of supper. But all he could think about was Bernie and what they had just done. His feelings oscillated between intense joy and a sickening fear of discovery. Just when he thought he had his emotions under control, the doorbell rang. Not once but several times, cross and insistent. It could only be Chris. He stood frozen with his hand on the fridge door handle, listening, unable to move.

His heart pounded in his breast. Gently he closed the fridge, then wiped his hands down the front of his shirt and patted his trouser pockets, checking foolishly for telltale signs of his infidelity. Who was he trying to kid? Chris would know. She would know just by looking at him. Guilt, he knew, was written all over his face. He would not be able to look her in the eye.

Dear God, he prayed, help me. He moved towards the hall. He dreaded what must come next. If Chris confronted him he wasn't sure he could lie. And yet he needed to buy some time. He needed a little space to think clearly, to work out his next move. He knew what he wanted – he wanted Bernie – but he had a lot of hurdles to overcome before they could be together. Walking out would create such a .. . mess. There was no other word for it. The last two hours had changed the course of his life, but it would take more than one afternoon to undo the knots and ties that bound him and Chris together.

"I'll get it," came Bernie's steady voice from the hall and he stopped in his tracks. He heard her light skip across the tiled floor, the sound of the bolt being drawn back and the creak of the old hinges as the door opened. He stepped into a vantage point in the alcove in the lounge where he could see but not be seen.

"What's the bolt drawn for?" said Chris, brushing past Bernie like she was some kind of minion and Paul felt his face redden in anger at her dismissive treatment. She glanced behind the door as though looking for something. Finn followed her, mumbled a greeting to Bernie and bounded straight up the stairs two at a time.

"Oh, that was me. I closed it when we came in," said Bernie with a lighthearted laugh that sounded forced and unnatural to Paul. But Chris did not seem to notice.

"We only bolt the door at night and sometimes not even then," said Chris patiently, like she was explaining something to a child.

"Well, I'll know next time, won't I?" said Bernie brightly, a competent actress. She winked at him over Chris shoulder and he felt the weight of his dread begin to lighten. Chris suddenly seemed . . . ridiculous. He hadn't realised until right now, right this moment how much he disliked her. And if Bernie could act out a pantomime, then so could he.

"Where's Hannah?" said Bernie.

"Gone to one of her friend's – Cat. I think you met her. They were here one night last week."

"Oh, yeah. I remember. Was she the one with the spiky blond hair and the black lipstick?"

"That's the one," said Chris wryly.

"I thought she was nice."

Chris threw her keys into the marble bowl that was placed on the console table for just that purpose. She picked up Paul's keys from the top of the table where he'd left them earlier, made a slight tutting sound, and threw them in the bowl on top of hers.

"That'll damage the table," she muttered under her breath. Then, changing to a lighter, more pleasant tone, she asked of Bernie, "Back long?"

"Not long," said Paul, coming into the hall, and planting a kiss on her cheek. It smelt faintly of perfume. "How was your mother?"

"Oh, you know. Fine. Just the same as always. She sends her love."

"That's nice. Was Karen there?"

Behind Chris, Bernie mouthed, "I love you" and Paul struggled to keep the smile from his face.

"Yes, Karen was there," said Chris, "and there's no need to be sarcastic."

"Me? I'm not being sarcastic. I like your mum."

"I saw that smile on your face."

He coughed and said, "I was just about to start supper. I was thinking of doing something with those chicken breasts. A stir-fry maybe?" He hated himself for making the last sentence into a question. Why did he always have to defer to her judgment on domestic matters?

"No, no, no," snapped Chris, talking to him like he was

an idiot, whilst already making tracks for the kitchen. "The chicken's for tomorrow night's dinner. Don't you remember – I was going to make a chicken casserole?"

Before, such treatment would have caused an argument between them. Now it served only to harden his resolve to extricate himself from the situation and start a new life with Bernie. The practicalities would have to be worked out of course, but the main thing holding him back was the children and the effect his leaving would have on them. Especially Hannah, when so much depended on the outcome of her A level exams.

The thought of leaving Castlerock, and all the material things he had worked for, filled him with regret also. But equally, the place had become something of a prison. A prison he now longed to escape with Bernie at his side.

Thrilled and appalled in equal measure by his ability to deceive so easily, Paul followed Chris into the kitchen. And for the first time he realised how so much of the time she acted like his mother, rather than his wife. It was partly his fault, he acknowledged that. She did it because he let her get away with it.

"We'll have pasta," she said, pushing up the sleeves of her fine silk knit over thin arms and filling the kettle with water for the pasta. "I've a jar of sauce in the cupboard somewhere. And I can rustle up a salad in no time. It'll only take a minute."

"Sounds good," said Paul and he went about setting the table, amazed at how quickly he was able to detach himself emotionally from the bizarre situation in which he now found himself. Perhaps, with Bernie's help, he would be able to do this after all. People did it every day.

The newsagent Paddy Watson, father of four, had left his

wife Rose to set up home with the milkman's wife, Lorraine Gallagher. One of the GPs at work had run off with the practice nurse. It was far from uncommon. Yes, it caused a stir – and provided several weeks of office gossip fodder – but soon boredom set in, people forgot and got on with their lives.

He thought briefly of his own philandering father – not that he drew any comparison between his father's reprehensible behaviour and the situation he now found himself in – and wondered why he had never left his mother. Things were different back then in the sixties, of course, but perhaps he'd never found his true love. Perhaps his wife – in spite of his disgraceful behaviour towards her – had been his true love after all.

As he pondered how to break the news to Chris, Paul realised that there was no such thing as protocol in such matters. Some people carried on for months, even years, behind their spouse's back, but he could not bear the subterfuge and deceit – it wasn't in his nature. And for all her faults, which seemed to magnify hourly under his very recent scrutiny, he owed it to Chris to treat her with honesty. A clean break really was best and the sooner the better for everyone.

Except, perhaps, for Hannah. Her exams weren't over for weeks yet and he really would never forgive himself if his actions jeopardised her future. If only he could get Bernie to slow down a bit, to see the big picture and the longer view. But Bernie had made it very clear that she was no longer comfortable staying in the house. He could persuade her to bide her time, but not for long. He would have to find somewhere for her to live until he was able to join her. And soon.

And yet, and yet . . . the very thought of taking action to set the necessary train of events in motion filled him with terror. The very idea of voicing his disquiet and revealing his treachery appalled him. How could he tell Chris, his loyal wife of twenty years, that their marriage was over? How could he tell her that he no longer loved her? What was he to say to the children? And yet he must.

Was he brave enough to start over? Brave enough to leave all this behind him? The house would have to be sold. He couldn't afford to live like this, and support the kids, on a GP's salary alone. From what Bernie had told him, she earned only a modest income as an artist. As he contemplated all these difficult issues, his heart pounded in his breast and he felt cold beads of sweat on his brow.

"Can I help?" said Bernie's voice and he looked up to find her standing across from him on the other side of the table.

Her face was illuminated by the candles he had just lit. She glowed like a goddess — strength and certainty emanated from her and he was calmed by her presence. He could see the gentle rise and fall of her chest and the hint of cleavage at the top of her blouse. The taste of her was still on his lips — and he knew in that moment that she would give him the resolve that he needed.

At dinner Bernie told lies about her visit to her brother's, making no mention of the argument, early departure and the tears.

Chris responded with a description of her visit to see her mother, interrupted by the children's humorous, but not unkind, quips and jokes, mainly at the expense of their grandmother's failing memory and many malapropisms.

And, while the others swapped banter and chuckled, Paul sipped quietly on a fine Chianti from Veneto and chewed thoughtfully on the good, simple Italian food Chris had prepared. But the wine did little to quell his troubled soul and the food in his mouth was tasteless.

Someone brushed his leg with their foot and he glanced at Bernie. She frowned a little, then smiled encouragingly. He nodded almost imperceptibly. And then he looked round grimly at the faces at the table and realised that, though they did not know it yet, their days together as a family were very much numbered.

* * *

When she came down for breakfast dressed in her work clothes a week later, Chris was relieved to find no sign of Bernie in the kitchen. She let Murphy out to pee, made a fuss of him for a few minutes, then put a pot of coffee on. She was still mulling over her appalling behaviour to Bernie the previous Sunday. She shouldn't have taken it out on her, but the visit to her mother's had been trying.

The children were grumpy because she'd forced them to go (she only asked them to visit their grandmother once in a blue moon, for goodness sake!) and on the short drive home she'd felt a migraine coming on. By the time she got there, tired and hungry, being locked out of her own house was the last straw. She had been a little sharp with Bernie about the bolt on the door and with Paul about the chicken for supper. But she'd been too embarrassed to apologise then and now, a week later, it was definitely too late.

Since then a slight distance had evolved between her and Bernie. It was hard to put a finger on what, exactly, had changed because on the face of it nothing had. It was just that Bernie was a little more reserved with Chris than before and she kept her business more to herself. She had, for example, suddenly taken herself off for the best part of the previous week on a trip to see distant relatives in Donegal. Chris couldn't have accompanied her because of work, but it would have been nice to have been asked.

She missed Bernie's beguiling openness but she knew she had only herself to blame. She had been unforgivably rude. She pondered why she found apologising so hard and came to the conclusion that she was stubborn and proud – attributes of which she was thoroughly ashamed. She hoped her better qualities were enough to counteract these less savoury ones.

Chris poured herself a bowl of muesli and sat down at the kitchen table with a heavy sigh to peruse the morning paper. She tried to push these unpleasant thoughts from her mind but, a few minutes later, unable to concentrate, she folded the paper and set it down on the table.

Having a long-term house guest was proving harder than she'd anticipated. It wasn't that Bernie was difficult or demanding – far from it. She was helpful and polite and excellent company.

It was just that you couldn't relax in quite the same way when a stranger was in your home. The best bit of the last week for Chris, when Bernie hadn't been there, was chilling out in front of the TV in her fleecy dressing gown and slippers, stuffing her face with chocolate (a secret treat to which she succumbed now and again), and not having to make small talk over supper every night.

Speaking of small-talk, Paul had been unusually poor company – quiet and irritable – this last week. She guessed that, in spite of his bonhomie and general cheerfulness, even he was feeling the strain. Bernie had come back yesterday from Donegal and Paul had hardly said a word at dinner. Afterwards he'd gone to the study and stayed in there until he came to bed well after midnight, when he thought she was asleep.

Bernie was due to go back to Australia in a week and Chris was determined that her visit should end on a happy and successful note. Putting the past behind her, she resolved to make the rest of Bernie's stay as enjoyable as possible. She smiled to herself when she thought of the things she had planned.

Just then Paul came into the kitchen in his dressing gown, looking dishevelled.

"Aren't you due at the surgery this morning?" she said, surprised.

"I am. I'm just going in a little late, that's all," he yawned, opened the loaf of bread sitting on the counter, put two slices in the toaster and switched it on. "I'm sure they can manage without me for part of the monthly meeting. Nothing but bureaucracy gone mad anyway." He sounded quite heated about it. "It's a complete waste of time, if you ask me. Everyone sits around moaning about what's wrong with the place and then we all go back to work."

"Are you not feeling well?" said Chris, thinking this bad-tempered outburst was uncharacteristic of Paul.

"I didn't . . . I didn't sleep too well last night, that's all."

"You do look a little peaky. Perhaps you're working too hard," she said, wondering if that was the explanation for his recent grouchiness.

He opened his mouth to speak then closed it. The toast popped up and he transferred it to a plate. He began, methodically, to butter one slice.

"Guess what?" she said. "I've got a surprise planned for

Bernie tonight," and she couldn't help grinning.

"You have?" he said flatly and stood stock still, staring at her with the knife suspended in mid-air.

"Don't look so horrified! I've only invited Mary Ramsey and Lorraine Kane round. I don't think you know them – you know I had quite a job tracking them down – but we all went to school together."

"Have you told Bernie yet?"

"No, silly. It's supposed to be a surprise! I'll tell her we're expecting company but not say who. We'll crack open a bottle or two of wine. It'll be a good laugh."

"I'm not sure that's such a –" began Paul but Chris, disappointed in his lack of enthusiasm for her scheme, interrupted.

"She'll love it. You know how she loves company. And she was almost inseparable from Mary and Lorraine when we were at school. I wonder if she'll recognise them – I haven't seen them in ages either."

"What about food?" said Paul lamely and Chris could've sworn he was determined to spoil their fun.

"We'll get a carry-out," she said, puzzled. Paul was usually so keen to see the house filled with people – 'being used properly' he called it.

"I'll make myself scarce then," said Paul and he shuffled into the conservatory.

"Paul?" said Chris, rising from her seat to follow him.

"What?" he said as he settled down heavily on the wicker sofa and put his bare feet on the coffee table. The sun was just starting to creep into the garden and Murphy was lolloping awkwardly round the garden in pursuit of a football.

"You don't seem yourself," she said, regarding him critically.

"I'm fine," he said, staring out the window.

"Are you sure?" said Chris doubtfully. "It's just that you seem so down on me having these women round tonight. It's not like you."

"I'm not down on you," he said crossly. "I – I have other things on my mind, that's all."

"Look on the bright side, honey," said Chris, making the assumption that he was referring to work. "Once we're both retired we'll never have to work again! Only twenty years to go, darling!"

He gave her a half-hearted crooked smile and said, "Chris, you'd better get to work or you're going to be late."

Chris glanced at her watch and said, "Shit!" under her breath. She really couldn't be late this morning, of all mornings. "You're right. I've got to run. The new boss wants us all there for a meeting first thing. And I've got papers to go through first."

She dashed out into the hall. Hannah was coming down the stairs wearing her night things.

"Morning, Mum," she said, sleepily, rubbing her mascara-stained eyes.

"Am I the only person getting dressed this morning?" said Chris tetchily.

"I was up 'til one studying last night, Mum," said Hannah, sounding a little wounded.

"Of course. I forgot. Sorry, love," said Chris, her irritation evaporating.

Hannah's A-level exams had started the previous week and would run for nearly a month. Her entire future depended on the results and Chris did not envy her daughter the task ahead one little bit. "Good luck with the studying, Hannah. Oh, you wouldn't do me a favour, would you?"

"Uh-huh?" came the sleepy reply.

"Could you take Murphy out for half an hour at lunchtime? I don't know what Bernie's doing or I would've asked her. And I'm meeting Aunt Karen for lunch so I can't pop home." The lunch date was an indulgence for Chris – usually she never left the office at lunchtime.

"Sure. No problem."

"You're a lifesaver," said Chris with a smile. "I've got to run now or I'll be late for work. I'll see you at teatime." She gave her daughter's cheek a hasty peck. She grabbed her coat and car keys, hesitated for a moment, then threw a light raincoat over her arm. She picked up her bulging briefcase and said, "Isn't that brother of yours up yet?"

"'Course I am," said Finn's decidedly cheery voice as he bounded down the stairs and into the hall, where he planted a kiss on Chris's cheek. "See you, Mum!" He disappeared into the kitchen.

Chris smiled to herself, opened the door and went out to the car. In spite of his father's objections (and her own disappointment) she was coming round to the idea that Finn had done the right thing in leaving school. He really hadn't been academically gifted and he loved his job. He was learning a valuable trade and, who knows, one day he might own his own business. With all the new building that was going on over the province and the price that tradesmen charged these days, he could be millionaire in no time, she thought ruefully.

She picked her way across the gravel, careful not to scrape the heels of her smart shoes. She opened the car door and, just before she got in, glanced up at the closed curtains on the topmost floor where Bernie slept. She could've sworn she saw the curtains twitch, then told herself she was imagining it. She got into the car and drove off reminding herself to phone Bernie mid-morning.

* * *

Sam McIlwaine was an imposing man in every way. He was nearly six feet six inches tall with broad well-built shoulders, a slim waist and, from what Chris could discern through his starched white shirt as he moved about, a toned abdomen. His navy suit jacket was thrown carelessly over the back of the seat in the cramped office space that served both as conference room (on the rare occasions, like today, when it was required) and meeting room for clients.

Present in the room along with Sam and Chris were the rest of the staff: Rose, the legal assistant; Mandy, the secretary; Lynette, newly qualified solicitor and granddaughter to Bob McMillan (the kindly, old-fashioned gentleman who had sold out to Stevenson and McIlwaine); and Declan, a slim eighteen-year-old of dubious sexual orientation who helped with the admin.

Sam was on his feet, moving actively about the room (as best he could with the limited space available), with a marker in his right hand. The room felt too small for him. He gesticulated a lot with his long, lithe arms and scrawled action points on a flip-chart squeezed in the corner. His style was so very different – so very much more dynamic – than Bob McMillan's sedentary and pedestrian ways. His energy was mesmerising. Chris worried that he might find them all, to a certain extent, apathetic.

Things had been done in the same way for so long under Bob McMillan's tutelage that she feared this might be the case – they were all rather set in their ways. The place probably did need shaking up a bit. And a new challenge was just what she needed to revitalise her professional life which, like her personal life, seemed to have fallen into a bit of a rut. She resolved to do her best to be receptive to the changes that would inevitably come with new ownership.

Sam's graying salt and pepper hair, rather then ageing him, made him look handsome and distinguished. It was cruel, Chris thought, that the same ageing on a woman would make her look like a grandmother. Sam had also been blessed with a good-looking face – strong chin, full lips and soft grey-blue eyes. He wasn't perfect – his eyes were a little too deep-set and close together – but he was definitely handsome in a rugged sort of way. When her musings were, unexpectedly, interrupted and she became the focus of attention, Chris blushed.

"So what percentage of conveyancing clients are converted into other products, Chris?" asked Sam.

"Converted?" said Chris.

"You know. To what percentage of them do we onsell other products and services – wills, powers of attorney, family law advice, financial advice, tax planning. You must have targets for that sort of thing, surely?"

Chris glanced at Rose, her assistant, who raised her eyebrows slightly, crossed and uncrossed her knees. Chris said, "I – I'm not sure. I have to confess I've never thought of what we do in those terms. I've always seen our role as providing a professional service. Not selling."

"Well, call it what you will, selling is what it's all about nowadays, Chris. You specialise in conveyancing, right?"

She nodded.

"Well, when people move house they're often at a vulnerable stage in their lives. Think about it," he said, peeling back the used piece of paper on the flip-chart to reveal a virginal sheet. He compiled a list of bullet points, in his scrawling hand, while he spoke.

"Birth, marriage, divorce, death. Stages when clients most need our services, even if they don't realise it themselves. We're perfectly poised to take advantage of this – whilst always keeping our clients' best interests at the forefront of everything we do, of course."

Sam flashed Chris a dazzling smile, which she suspected might be the results of chemical whitening, and she looked quickly at her feet.

She wasn't entirely comfortable with the idea of herself as a saleswoman. She hadn't studied law for all those years just to sell things, whatever they were.

"Are you with me on this, Chris?" said Sam, and she realised she was still staring at the floor.

"I think I understand you, yes," she said, in what she hoped was a pointed manner, and she met his gaze with a steely one of her own. She understood all right, she just wasn't sure she liked the direction in which Sam McIlwaine was taking the firm.

"And now that you're part of the bigger Stevenson and McIlwaine group, with wide expertise in all fields," he said, addressing the whole room now, "we can offer your client base a really topnotch service."

And fleece them for all they're worth, thought Chris – a little unfairly. It was just that all this talk of cross-selling and targets made her uncomfortable. She told herself to remain open-minded. She was being unworldly – this was the way a commercially minded firm had to operate nowadays. And they probably did need to be roused from the sleepy hollow of legal practice into which they'd fallen.

She smiled at the thought of Bob McMillan – he would be mortified if he was in the room now, listening to this conversation.

Sam thought she was smiling at him and gave her one of his eye-blinding grins in return. He thinks he's won me over, she thought.

After the meeting, as everyone was filing out of the small meeting room, Sam said, "Have you got a moment, Chris?"

"Sure," she said, sat down again and smoothed her skirt over her knees. Although his behaviour towards her was in every way proper, Sam made her feel uncharacteristically self-conscious. His overt masculinity made her acutely aware of her womanliness. Never having looked at anyone but Paul in twenty years, she wondered if this meant she fancied him. She immediately dismissed the notion as ludicrous and turned her mind to business. No doubt Sam wanted to pick her brains about the firm. She crossed her hands primly in her lap.

Sam waited until the last person had left the room, then shut the door and sat down in the seat beside Chris, turning his chair by forty-five degrees so that they were facing each other sideways, in a relaxed, informal sort of way. He crossed his long legs and tapped the back of his left hand with a gold fountain pen.

"I used to come here to play rugby," he said. "When I played for my school, Ballymena Academy. Ah, great days. We'd come over here to play Ballyfergus Grammar."

"I thought you were from Belfast."

"No, no. My roots are in County Antrim, Chris. That's one of the reasons I was keen to come down here to Ballyfergus." He shifted his gaze to the window and stared out distractedly at the clear blue sky for a few seconds. "I fancied a change from Belfast. Needed to get away really. To start again."

Her curiosity aroused, she wanted to ask him what he meant by this enigmatic comment but contented herself instead with, "You mean you're going to move down here? I assumed you'd commute."

"No, no. I'm in the process of buying the Old Manse on the Grammar Brae. I hope to move in within a month."

"Oh," said Chris. "I'd heard it was for sale with Brian Todd."

Chris knew the house well from her schooldays. It was a large property with five bedrooms. She wondered if Sam had a big family. She guessed him to be in his early fifties – his kids, like hers, would be almost grown by now.

"You approve? Is it a good buy?"

"It's a lovely old house. But whether it's a good buy or not depends very much on what you paid for it."

He laughed and said, "Quite right. It needs a fair bit of work though to bring it up to standard."

"Yes, I know," said Chris. "I used to go there regularly in the early eighties when the Reverend McFarlane lived in it – his daughter Heather went to school with me. The house is handsome but it was neglected even then. The church couldn't afford the upkeep. I'm afraid old properties like that just eat up cash. I should know. We're never done spending money on ours."

"And where do you live?"

She explained briefly and he said, "Sounds very nice. And your husband? You are married?"

"Yes."

"What does he do?"

"Paul is a doctor here in the local surgery."

He stared at her for a few seconds, very hard, then said, "Well, I'll look forward to meeting him."

There was a pause, during which Sam looked through the glass partition into the main office.

"Rose," he said, all of a sudden. "What do you think of her? Is she good?"

She followed his gaze to catch sight of Rose, hunched over with the phone under her chin, while she rummaged through a pile of papers on her desk. By her elbow was a mug that said 'Special Auntie' on it – a recent present from her sister's little girl – and an empty crisp packet. Rose, though in her early thirties and living with her partner, John, had no children of her own.

"She appears a little disorganised," said Chris, feeling very defensive of the friend whom she had worked with for the best part of eight years. "But she's good at her job. She's very clever, you know. She could've gone far, if she'd had the chance."

"And Lynette?"

"Lynette," said Chris, turning her attention to the pretty young blonde at the desk by the window and smiling. Her feelings towards Lynette bordered on the maternal. "Lynette has a sharp mind and an engaging manner with people but she's young – she's only just qualified. She needs a bit more experience, but I think she'll make a fine solicitor."

"Good, good," said Sam nodding.

"You're not thinking of making any staff changes, are you?" said Chris, suddenly concerned for the welfare of the others. She glanced out at the office and frowned.

"No, I don't think so. Not at this stage. If anything, we're looking to grow the business not shrink it." He paused and regarded her thoughtfully. "As the senior member of staff here, Chris, I'm relying on you to help me implement the changes we need. I need you to ensure that the staff are with me as the business evolves. It can't stay the way it is, you do know that, don't you?"

Chris nodded, and said, feeling a little hypocritical, "Yes, of course. I'll do my utmost."

"You and Bob have built up a good solid business here, Chris. But Ballyfergus is a growing town. There are great opportunities to be found and we're going to make the most of them. And," he suddenly introduced a more lighthearted tone, clapping his hands together, "one of the first things we're going to do is find bigger premises. You need an office as well as me. And this . . ." he glanced around as he wrung his hands in a peculiar hand-washing motion, "well, it's a bit cramped, isn't it?"

"I suppose it is," said Chris, trying to hide her surprise. But out of loyalty to Bob, she said, a little defensively, "But it's served us well enough over the years."

"But now it's time for a change, don't you think? Something bigger and better?"

She looked around critically and suddenly saw the faded wallpaper, stained carpet and worse-for-wear furniture in a different light. It did look shabby and, lacking adequate filing space, it was untidy. Paperwork spilled out of bookcases and over desks. All in all, it represented a homely but rather shambolic face to the public.

"I'm waiting to hear if our offer for that old bookshop on the corner of Agnew and Main Street has been accepted."

"You've put in an offer on it?" said Chris, somewhat rhetorically, rather taken aback by the speed at which Sam

McIlwaine was effecting change. She recovered her equanimity and added, "Old Steven McFaul owns that place. It's been on the market for ages. I should think he's desperate to sell."

"Let's hope so."

"It has potential though. High ceilings, nice tall windows," mused Chris. "It used to be a bank, you know."

"And then there's the change of name to think about. We're going to need new signs, stationary, business cards. The lot."

"Sounds like we're going to be very busy!"

"I hope so," said Sam and he gave her one of his wide, full grins. "I very much hope so."

Ten

By the time Chris got back to her desk, it was late morning. She hadn't expected the meeting to go on so long and she hadn't noticed either. But there was something infectious about Sam's enthusiasm. She was genuinely excited by the prospect of working with him. She'd even started to visualise her shiny new office and had to reign in her fantasies of chic pale wood and acres of lush beige carpet.

She glanced at the clock and silently prayed she hadn't missed Bernie. She picked up the phone and dialled home. She was in luck. Bernie answered.

"Hi. It's me, Chris. How are you?"

"Good. I was just about to go out," said Bernie. "I have . . . I have some business to attend to."

"Listen, I can't talk long. It was just to tell you that I've invited some friends round tonight at seven thirty."

Silence.

"Bernie, can you hear me? Are you still there?"

"Yes. I'm here."

There was a pause and Chris said, "Is that okay?"

"Well, I don't know," said Bernie, sounding very doubtful. "I mean, who is it?" she asked, without any of her usual enthusiasm.

"I'm sorry for the late notice," said Chris, suddenly realising that perhaps she should have consulted Bernie before organising the evening's entertainment. "I was rather hoping to surprise you. It's just some old school friends I've managed to round up. I thought we could get a carry-out and crack open a couple of bottles of wine."

"Great," said Bernie, not sounding very keen and Chris supposed she was still cross with her.

"I can cancel if you'd rather," said Chris quietly.

"No, it's – it's eh – that sounds great. I'll look forward to it."

"Good."

"Chris?"

"Yeah?"

"I have some . . . oh, never mind."

"Some what?"

"It'll keep. It'll keep until I see you later," she said firmly.

After exchanging a few more pleasantries Chris hung up, a little deflated and perplexed. Bernie had sounded rather distracted on the phone and, though she'd agreed to tonight's get-together, her response had been less than ecstatic. But, Chris reasoned with herself, she had rather sprung the whole idea on her friend. She'd taken her by surprise, that was all. It was only natural that she sounded a little taken aback. Bernie would soon warm to the idea – she would be thrilled to see her old friends after all these years. So, with her reservations hastily dispatched, Chris put the matter out of her mind.

She could have done with getting her head down and catching up on the pile of work on her desk but it was the first Monday of the month – the day when she and Karen took time out of their busy schedules to meet for lunch.

They never broke the engagement unless absolutely necessary.

So come noon, Chris stepped out of the offices of Stevenson and McIlwaine on Main Street, as they were now to be called, to discover that the fine morning had disappeared. A strong wind tugged at the hem of her grey skirt, the sky had clouded over and black clouds threatened rain. She struggled into her raincoat in the strong breeze, and dug deep in the bottom of her handbag for a compact umbrella and car keys. Then she briskly walked the short distance to her car which was parked on a side street, got in and headed out of town.

At the opposite end of the Main Street from her office she took a short-cut down Cross Street to avoid the traffic lights. She was just about to turn into Circular Road when she glanced up to see Paul's car, distinctive because of its personal number plate, parked on the narrow, quiet street. She frowned, wondering what he was doing there at this time of day. Paul didn't often take a proper lunch break, usually grabbing a sandwich on the hoof.

She paused at the junction, and looked down the road again, straining to see Paul. Then she saw him, stepping out of the offices of Hunter Campbell, the estate agents, with a woman at his side. He turned to speak to her and Chris strained to see more clearly. The woman was Bernie and she was holding what looked like a thin sheaf of white papers in her hands. They moved quickly across the pavement to the car. Paul opened the passenger door for her, with a proprietary hand on the small of her back, she got in, and he followed on the driver's side.

"That's odd," said Chris out loud. The driver in the car behind her tooted his horn and she was forced to drive on, trying to make sense of what she had just seen. The plausible explanations came to mind first – they had just bumped into each other, Paul had offered Bernie a lift, she had asked him for some sort of help. (Chris had noticed Bernie's tendency to be a little needy, especially when around men. The feminist in her found it a bit pathetic.)

Maybe it had something to do with the sale of Bernie's father's property? She dismissed this thought almost as soon as it came to mind – she was pretty sure Mr Sweeney's house had been rented. So it was highly unlikely that there was unfinished business in connection with that.

And swiftly on the heels of these thoughts, came more questions that did not present with readily supplied answers. Hunter Campbell sold and rented property. What were Paul and Bernie doing in their offices? What possible reason could either of them have for visiting there? Unless, Paul was making further enquiries about a second home on the North Antrim coast. But if so, why was Bernie with him? And why hadn't he mentioned it to Chris? No doubt he would, in time, thought Chris as she waited for the lollipop man outside the school where Tony worked to wave her on. Quite often she forgot to tell Paul about important things until days later simply because they both led such busy lives.

Still, the matter perplexed her and was still on her mind when she joined her sister at a table in The Mill, a popular family-owned pub and restaurant on the Old Glenarm Road, on the outskirts of town. When they were teenagers it had been the hottest venue in town and they had spent many sweaty nights in the crammed bar being deafened by bands. Now it was strictly over twenty-ones and catered for a more mature crowd. The exposed brickwork, painted white, gave the place a slightly industrial feel and the atmosphere, on this busy lunchtime, was relaxed and friendly.

The waitress, a girl about the same age as Hannah with plain features and a perfect complexion, showed Chris to the table, though there was no real need. She and Karen always booked the table near the door, which was flooded with natural light from the glass roof above. Karen was already there, looking stunning in a black skirt and black silk blouse. She wore chunky costume jewelry just right for her frame and her face and hair were, as always, immaculately groomed.

"I'm sorry I'm late," said Chris, peeling off her coat.

"That's okay," said Karen, getting up to give her a brief peck on the cheek. "Wine?"

"Mmm. Yes, please," said Chris, sitting down heavily and placing her bag under the table at her feet.

Karen ordered her sister a glass of Sauvignon Blanc, her usual tipple, while Chris tried to flatten her windswept hair as best she could with the flat of her hand.

"How was your morning?" said Karen.

"Fine. Okay. And yours?"

"Manic as usual," said Karen. "But let's not talk about that. Tell me what this Sam McIlwaine was like."

"Well, he's very," said Chris, searching for the right word. "He's very… dynamic. I can see he's quite determined to shake us all up."

"What do you mean?"

"Well, he's planning to move us to new offices for one thing."

"Where?"

"You know the old bookshop on the corner of Agnew and Main Street?"

"I see," said Karen, raising her eyebrows and pulling her face into an exaggerated expression of mock astonishment. "Very posh."

"Yes, I expect it will be – once it's all refurbished. And he spent the morning giving us a lecture on cross-selling."

"You sound as though you don't like him very much."

Chris paused, remembering how she felt in his presence – intrigued, stimulated, excited. "I don't dislike him," she said. "Not at all. In fact I think he's going to be quite fun to work with. He's just very different from what I'm used to. I worked for Bob McMillan for the best part of the last twelve years, remember. And Bob, lovely man that he is," she added, with a sardonic lift of her right eyebrow, "can hardly be described as dynamic."

Karen laughed, and said, "And what does he look like? Is he handsome?"

Chris paused and said honestly, "He is. He looks a bit like an American chat-show host."

Karen giggled and said, "What on earth do you mean by that?"

"You know. Well groomed, steel-grey hair, suntanned, super-white teeth – I thought they were just whitened but, come to think of it, they might even be veneers."

"He sounds a bit like Bob Monkhouse."

"Oh, that's too cruel," laughed Chris. "Sam's only in his fifties and he doesn't dye his hair. Yet."

The waitress came with a glass of wine on a silver tray and set it in front of Chris with a flourish. She took a welcome sip, savouring every drop. As she was driving, she could only allow herself the one glass.

"We should order," said Karen, stifling her mirth as she perused the menu.

"Okay. I'll just have the usual," said Chris to the waitress. "Caesar Salad to start with and the monkfish."

Karen looked up from the menu and said, "I don't know why I bother looking either. I always order the same thing too. I'll have the pâté to start with and steak and chips, please."

Chris, mindful of her recent conversations with Karen about her weight, was about to point out the calorific nature of her choice, but decided against it. Her advice would not be welcome and would only create an atmosphere between them.

Once the waitress had moved away, Karen raised her glass and said, "Here's to us!"

"Us," said Chris, "and health and happiness."

They clinked glasses and drank.

"Well, that all sounds very exciting," said Karen, setting her glass down. "A nice new office, hey? That can't be bad."

"Mmm," said Chris distractedly, licking the wine from her lips and thinking about Paul and Bernie.

"What, Chris?"

"Oh, nothing. At least I think it's nothing."

"What is?" said Karen.

"It's just that I saw the strangest thing and I can't make sense of it."

Karen waited for her to go on.

"I was leaving the office to come and meet you just now when I saw Paul's car parked on Circular Road. It's not a route I usually take. Well, anyway, a few seconds later I saw him and Bernie come out of Hunter Campbell together and get in the car."

Karen frowned. "What were they doing in there?"

"I have no idea. Bernie had some papers in her hands. Schedules for properties, perhaps?"

"But what for?" frowned Karen.

"Search me. The only thing I could think of was that Paul might be looking at more properties up north. You know the way he's keen on a second home?"

Karen nodded.

"Though why he would involve Bernie in that, I don't know."

"Unless she just tagged along," said Karen, doubtfully. She paused a moment, twirled her wine glass by the stem and said. "You're not going to want to hear this, Chris."

"Go on."

"It sounds a bit fishy to me."

"I knew you'd say that."

"Because I don't like Bernie?"

"Yes," said Chris, irritably. "I mean, what are you suggesting, Karen? That she's having an affair with my husband?" She gave a hollow laugh and tried to lighten her tone. "Don't be ridiculous. Paul wouldn't look at her. For one thing, she's not his type. She's far too hippy and left-wing."

"I don't know what I'm suggesting, Chris. I'm only saying that it seems . . . suspicious," she said and paused. Karen took a deep breath, gave Chris a sharp look and then went on, "And how has Paul been recently?"

Chris shrugged. "Same as always. A bit distracted lately but he's busy at work. We both are. And I've been spending far too much time on the Tesda stuff. Though hopefully the worst of that is over now the petition's handed in. It's in the hands of the planning authorities now." She tapped the side of her glass with a manicured fingernail and said softly, "It's just. Well . . . we don't seem to have much time for each other these days."

224

"You have to make time," said Karen, sounding every bit the elder sister.

"I know, I know," mumbled Chris, remembering Paul's abortive attempt at arranging a weekend away in Venice for the two of them and the complexity of feelings that particular failure had aroused – a gut-wrenching mixture of blessed relief and bitter disappointment. Her sadness had come, not from the fact that the weekend itself hadn't worked out, but from the glaring flaw it had revealed in her and Paul's marriage – neither she nor Paul really had the interest or drive to make it happen. Karen wouldn't understand because she and Tony were very much in love. For this reason it was both lovely and painful to be in their company: lovely to see two people so attuned and painful because their oneness only served to highlight the divide between her and Paul.

"Look," said Karen, rather unconvincingly as she had already said it was suspicious, "I'm sure there's a perfectly innocent explanation for what you saw today. Why don't you ask Paul about it as soon as you see him?"

"I intend to," said Chris, sounding more confident than she felt. Inside she was feeling inexplicably nervous. But she did not want to show her discomposure to Karen.

The waitress came with the starters. Chris toyed with the salad, turning the leaves over with her fork, her appetite suddenly gone.

"Guess what?" she said, by way of changing subject. "I've organised a surprise for Bernie tonight. Do you remember Mary Ramsey and Lorraine Kane from school?"

"Of course I do," said Karen, spreading an oatcake with pâté and balancing a dollop of glutinous chutney atop. "Mary Ramsey had the most terrible knock-knees. Do you remember?" She took a bite of the oatcake and smiled mischievously.

"Oh, you are wicked!" laughed Chris.

Karen swallowed quickly and added, "And Lorraine Kane had a brother. Now, what was his name?"

"Derek."

"That's the one. Oh, he was gorgeous, wasn't he?"

"I didn't know you had a soft spot for him," said Chris.

"Everyone did. Except you, Chris," said Karen, good-naturedly. "You were too busy studying all the time to notice boys."

"Maybe," said Chris, though it was not true. She had had her fair share of crushes but it wasn't in her nature to share them with others, especially not her rather brash sister. She was altogether a much too private person and, much as she loved Karen, she never quite trusted her to keep such delicate matters to herself. "Anyway, I've invited them both round tonight for a carry-out and a drink. I thought it'd be nice to reminisce a bit about school. I thought Bernie would enjoy it."

"I'm sure she will," said Karen. "I hope she appreciates the trouble you've gone to."

"It's no trouble really," said Chris. "You know she goes home in just over a week's time? I thought I'd try and give her some nice memories to take away. I feel like I . . . well, I don't think I've been the best hostess."

"Nonsense! I don't believe that for a minute," said Karen firmly, cutting dead any further exploration of the topic.

Chris gave her a weak smile, loving her for her loyalty.

"Come on, eat up," said Karen. "We haven't got all day."

Chris acquiesced with a smile. She had no desire to elaborate on her shortcomings as a hostess. The salad was good – she realised she was hungry after all – and, after a short pause while they both ate, she suddenly remembered about Karen's visit to the clinic.

"How did your appointment at the clinic in Belfast go last week? What's it called again?"

"The Malone. Well, I saw Dr Mezz on Thursday. He was very nice, very professional. He gave me a thorough examination and asked me lots of questions and then he said that I was an ideal candidate for a tummy tuck and breast reduction. Isn't that fantastic?" She went on without waiting for a reply. "He told me that my abdominal muscles have herniated because of the pregnancies and no amount of dieting or exercise is ever going to repair that damage. Oh, Chris, you can't imagine what it feels like to hear that! For someone to say, basically, that it's not my fault. That there's something medically wrong that need fixed. I nearly broke down and cried."

Karen paused to wipe a tear from the corner of her eye and Chris felt ashamed of herself for her earlier uncharitable thoughts. Karen composed herself and went on.

"He said that he thought, given my general health and the tone of my skin, that I would heal very well too. And being a non-smoker apparently goes in my favour. He said he thought I would get very good results from the surgery. The only disappointing thing is that he won't do all the procedures at once. He wants to wait six months before doing the breast reduction and eyelids."

"That sounds very sensible," said Chris, relieved that the doctor seemed to be taking a cautious approach.

"I've decided to go for the tummy tuck first because that's what bothers me the most."

"I see. And was he happy with your weight?" She knew Karen had been trying for some weeks to get her weight down but she hadn't noticed any discernible difference.

"Yeah. He said it was fine. He didn't seem concerned by that at all."

"Did he talk about the risks?"

"Yes, of course. But he said that complications were rare. Apparently it's the fourth most popular cosmetic procedure and it has one of the highest customer satisfaction ratings."

She paused and Chris smiled as best she could. It was also one of the most painful, most risky and most expensive. That much Chris had learnt from a quick trawl on the internet. Karen was an intelligent woman yet she'd chosen to filter out these negatives, focusing instead on the upside.

"Chris," she said solemnly, her face flushed with excitement, "I told him I want to go ahead. I'm booked in for the second of July. Less than two months away! Oh, Chris, I can't wait. I'm so excited."

Karen reached across and squeezed her sister's arm and Chris smiled evenly. She had made her reservations known, yet Karen was still determined to go ahead with the surgery. There was nothing to be done now but support her as best she could, in spite of her misgivings. So, trying not to sound as horrified as she felt, she said brightly, "So what happens next?"

"I go up a couple of weeks beforehand for a full medical, blood tests etcetera, and then, assuming the test results are okay, I just turn up on the day."

The expression on Chris's face must have betrayed her true feelings for Karen leant over and patted her comfortingly on the back of her left hand, which was resting, idle, on the table. "You mustn't worry, Chris. Dr Mezz told me he wouldn't do it unless he was one hundred percent sure it was safe for me."

Chris nodded begrudgingly.

Karen withdrew her hand and went on, "It's just a bit frustrating, not being able to get everything done at once. It's the amount of time I'll have to take off work that's the problem. That and caring for the kids, of course. I'd need a fortnight off for the eyes; another for the breast reduction; and four weeks for the abdominoplasty."

"The what?"

"The tummy tuck. That's two months in total. I can't afford to take all those holidays off in one year, or expect Tony to take care of the children. I so wanted to have everything done at once but the doc says no. It looks like I'll have to spread it out over a couple of years." She was talking more to herself than to Chris.

"Maybe that's no bad thing, Karen. It'll give you body time to heal between surgeries, and give you more time to make sure you're doing the right thing."

"Mmm, I guess so," said Karen doubtfully. "The tummy tuck takes the longest to recover from but with any luck I'll be back on my feet in four to five weeks. Six at the most."

"Assuming it all goes to plan," said Chris darkly.

"It will," said Karen firmly, the tone of her voice a warning to Chris to ditch the negativity. Clearly, she did not want to hear Chris's concerns.

"Can you afford to take that amount of time off work?" said Chris, taking the hint and changing tack.

"Oh, I'm not planning on being off work for the full recovery period."

Chris said nothing but raised her eyebrows in disbelief.

"Oh, don't look at me like that, Chris!" said Karen scornfully. "The doctor said I should be able to do most things a few weeks after the operations. Anyway, you know me. I'm no good being stuck at home – I'll be tearing my hair out with boredom after a week."

"From what I've read, you'll be lucky if you can get your hands above your head a week after this surgery, Karen."

"You really have no need to worry – Dr Mezz is one of the best guys in the business. Now where was I? Oh, yes, work. The nursery's quiet during the Twelfth fortnight – a lot of people go on holiday then – so I'll be off the first fortnight. After that, I should be able to keep an eye on things from home and, later, maybe manage a few days in the office if I'm feeling up to it. I couldn't really contemplate this if it weren't for Tony being off for the summer. Not that he'll have to mind the kids all the time. He can put them into the nursery as much as he wants, though I'm sure he'll want to spend time with them as well."

"You know I'll help," said Chris quickly and Karen smiled.

"I know you will," she said.

"And how long will you be in hospital?"

"Just a few days, all being well. Though I think I'll be pretty wiped for the first week or so."

The waitress cleared the plates and, almost immediately, another set the main courses down in front of them. They began to eat.

"So what does Tony think about the surgery?" said Chris.

"To tell you the truth, he's been a bit funny about it all."

"Understandable," said Chris.

Karen nodded, pointed her knife at the food on her plate and said, "Mmm – this is good. Yours?"

"Excellent."

"When I think about it," she went on, "he's been very quiet the last wee while. I think he is worrying about it. He says he can't understand why I want to do it. He says he likes me the way I am. Of course," she added quickly, "I don't believe him."

Saddened by this last comment, Chris opened her mouth to speak then shut it just as quickly. She suddenly realised that nothing she or Tony, or anyone else, said would make the slightest bit of difference to Karen's self-image. And if cosmetic surgery could make Karen love herself then perhaps it would be worthwhile after all.

Chris did not believe for one minute that it would dramatically change Karen's appearance in the way she feared her sister expected. Yes, she had a flap of stomach that protruded, but didn't all women, especially those who had borne two or more children? Though in Karen's case she did allow it was excessive. All Chris prayed for was that Karen got through it without any ill effects. But if it made Karen *feel* differently, and thereby made her more contented within herself, then perhaps it was worth every penny – and the risks. Chris was still concerned about the risks but, in light of the sudden realization about what it meant to Karen, she felt her moral objections melting away.

She let the subject drop then while they ate and then Karen announced that she had heard from Raymond on the phone late the night before.

"He says they're coming home in the middle of July. Raymond's got a job with a firm of structural engineers in

Belfast. He sounded very excited about it. He said jobs here are hard to come by in his field and that he was lucky to get it."

"Why, that's fantastic news," said Chris.

"It is, isn't it?" said Karen and then she frowned. "I hope my swelling's gone down by then."

"I'm sure it won't be too bad," said Chris thinking that she really shouldn't be issuing such assurances as she had no idea what she was talking about. What did she know about the after-effects of such surgery? Nonetheless she added, "By the end of July you're going to look just fantastic. Now we must give some thought to a welcome home party for him and Shona, don't you think?"

"It'll be an engagement party too, don't forget," said Karen, spearing the last of the chips on her plate with her fork.

"Of course. Won't it be just wonderful?" said Chris. "We haven't had a proper party for ages."

And the two sisters set about happily making plans for Raymond and Shona's bash. Over coffee, they discussed their respective children and Karen entertained Chris with tales of Pat Flynn's line dancing night until Chris thought her sides would split with laughter. Then, both realising the time, they hastily paid the bill and made their way out to the carpark.

"Let me know how tonight goes," said Karen.

"I will. Bye, love," said Chris and she gave her big sister a peck on the cheek, got in the car and drove back to town. And if it hadn't been for that niggling uncertainty about what she'd seen that morning, Chris would've felt happier than she had done in some time.

* * *

"Aw, Mum, what did you have to go and invite people round for tonight? Don't you know the footie's on?" pleaded Finn, sounding more like a six-year-old than a sixteen-year-old. He stood in the doorway of the drawing room with his hands shoved deep in the roomy pockets of his slouchy jeans, his too-big feet encased in dirty-looking trainers.

"Finn!" cried Chris, more concerned with the state of her cream carpets than with Finn's complaint. "What are you doing walking round the house in those shoes?"

She was feeling harassed, having only got home from work less than an hour ago. She'd changed, re-applied her make up and squirted on some Flowerbomb by Viktor and Rolf, a present from Paul at Christmas. It was a favourite of hers, a sweet floral scent that she hoped hid the fact that, annoyingly, she'd not had time to shower or wash her hair.

After that, she'd given the drawing room and kitchen a quick tidy, laid out glasses, crockery, cutlery and nibbles for tonight. Then she'd taken a couple of bottles of wine from Paul's cellar, chilled them in the wine cooler and popped them in the fridge.

During all of these preparations Bernie was nowhere to be seen, only appearing at the foot of the stairs five minutes ago. To give her credit, she had asked if Chris needed any help. But it was all done by then and now Bernie sat in the lounge listening silently to the exchange between mother and son, and the soft background music of Madeleine Peyroux.

"My mates are coming round specially to watch it,"

went on Finn, as though Chris hadn't spoken.

"No, they're not, Finn," said Chris, with a heavy sigh. She was trying to create a relaxing atmosphere, which Finn was single-handedly managing to wreck. "Not unless you watch it on the TV in your bedroom."

She returned to the tricky task of lighting candles. The box of long matches was finished and she was trying to ignite the candles with short cook's matches from the kitchen, without burning her fingers. They were fine for the tea lights but not so good for the tall pillar candles that had burned down into a deep hollow. These she had to hold horizontally and insert the lighted match into the centre until the wick caught light.

"But that TV's shite, Mum. It's out of the ark."

"Language please," said Chris and then, softening, she turned to him and added, "Look, I really am sorry Finn. But I didn't know and now it's too late to change the arrangements. I can't just cancel on them."

Bernie, who until now had sat on the sofa listening silently to their exchange, opened her mouth to speak, appeared to think better of it and closed it again.

"It'd be rude, Finn. I'm really sorry," said Chris, displaying more patience with Finn under Bernie's scrutiny than she normally would have done. "Now will you go and take those shoes off before you trail mud all round the house? Your father'll go nuts if he comes home and finds you wearing those trainers indoors."

"But why can't we watch it in the family room?" he persisted.

"Because," said Chris wondering, not for the first time, why children, and teenagers, could never just accept 'no' for an answer but spent their young lives pushing boundaries, "you'd make a racket. You couldn't help yourself. And the house isn't that big that the sound wouldn't travel. Anyway, Hannah needs peace and quiet to study."

"She's going to have to listen to you lot cackling away in here," he said grumpily and then added, with a shy smile, "Sorry. Not you, Bernie."

Chris, suddenly seeing the funny side, had to suppress her laughter. At least he'd remembered his manners and had the decency to exclude their guest from the insult. She shared a wry smile with Bernie.

"I suppose I'll just have to go round and watch it at Sparky's," he said crossly, in the absence of any satisfactory response from his mother.

"That sounds like a good idea," said Chris to his retreating back. And she shook her head, wondering how Finn could make going round to a mate's house sound like a hardship. Maybe she and Paul were too soft with them, giving them and their pals the run of the house – and often exclusive access to the big flat screen TV in the family room.

"There. Almost done," she said, as she finished lighting the last candle, threw the spent match in the log basket by the fireplace and stood back to admire her handiwork. The candles were not necessary of course on such a bright spring evening, but still, they added to the welcoming atmosphere. And the gorgeous Maxim's de Paris candle, that she'd brought back from a trip to the city with Paul last year, filled the room with a the sunny smell of watermelon mixed with musk and sandalwood.

She pulled her fine gauge cashmere sweater self-consciously over her slim hips hoping she looked decent enough to pass muster.

"You look nice," said Bernie who was perched, rather inelegantly, on the edge of one of the Chesterfield sofas. She was wearing trousers for a change, wide-legged in burgundy velvet, with a rather pretty cream blouse and her feet were bare of course. But her legs and arms were tightly crossed like she was fending off the cold, although the room was warm enough. She didn't look at all at home and Chris wished she would relax. She was making her feel uncomfortable.

"Thanks," said Chris. "So do you. I like the velvet trousers. Very tactile."

"You think so?" said Bernie, glancing down at the trousers with her head cocked critically to one side, as though viewing them for the first time.

"Yes, I think they look great. Now, what can I get you to drink?" she offered.

"Wine. White wine would be great," said Bernie.

"I've pinched a nice Sancerre from Paul's cellar," said Chris, pretending to look over her shoulder to check her husband wasn't lurking there. "He won't mind," she added with a giggle, wrinkling up her nose in humour.

But her laughter was shortlived for Bernie sat as still as stone and simply stared at her. Her face was the colour and texture of the pale yellow candles Chris had just lit.

"Are you feeling all right, Bernie? You don't look at al' well."

"Don't I? I feel – perfectly fine," and then, after a pause, "A little tired, perhaps."

"Haven't you been sleeping well?" said Chris.

"Not terribly well these last few nights," she admitted.

"I'm sorry to hear that. I hope the room's comfortable for you?" She was trying to imagine what little detail she might have overlooked that could account for Bernie's insomnia.

"Oh, the room's lovely, Chris. It's nothing to do with that. It's me."

A little perplexed, Chris excused herself, went into the kitchen, took the wine from the fridge and poured two glasses.

Back in the lounge she handed one to Bernie who said, "Cheers."

"Cheers," said Chris. They clinked glasses and put them to their lips.

"Mmm, very nice," said Bernie and then, "Shouldn't Paul be home by now?"

"Normally, yes," said Chris with an involuntary glance at the clock on the mantelpiece. "He called to say that he had to visit a patient, Derek Beattie, who's dying and being cared for at home by his family. Apparently he's in a lot of pain."

"That's tough on Paul," said Bernie, her voice full of real empathy.

Chris frowned, thinking it odd that Bernie should consider Paul's feelings before those of the dying man and his family. "Even tougher on Dr Beattie and his family," she said, before she could stop herself. However, realising she had been rather rude, she tried to make light of it with an embarrassed smile but it was a little too cutting to brush off that easily.

"Yes, yes, of course," mumbled Bernie quickly. "It must be awful for them."

Self-consciously Chris took a seat opposite Bernie on one of the sofas that flanked the fireplace, studiously avoiding eye contact with her.

"Paul didn't say anything about being on call," said Bernie.

"Strictly speaking he's not," said Chris, relieved to be moving the conversation on. However, it struck her as peculiar that Bernie should make it sound, through the inflection in her voice, as though Paul should have told her what he was doing. As though she somehow expected it from him.

"Dr Beattie used to work with Paul," she explained. "They became really quite good friends, in spite of the age difference, and have remained so even after his retirement. I don't think his wife, Doris, likes any doctor, other than Paul, tending to her husband. And he's glad to do it, on call or not."

After this little speech, Chris was slightly astonished to find her chest swell with pride. She admired Paul for his dedication to his work and on occasions such as this, she envied him for doing something so worthwhile. Legal conveyancing work, valuable and necessary as it was, just wasn't in the same league as saving lives and comforting the dying.

She understood very well why Paul was so devoted to his job; difficult though it was at times, it was also highly rewarding. For there could be no greater privilege, she thought solemnly, than to help a dying friend. She remembered Dr Beattie fondly and prayed he would be spared any suffering.

"You obviously know the family well too," observed Bernie.

"Not very well. I only met them a few times through work-related events, Christmas nights out, that sort of thing. But Derek and Doris are just lovely, lovely people. I feel so sorry for him, and for her." She paused, took a sip of wine, and said thoughtfully, "Death holds so much fear for us all, doesn't it? I mean we all know, intellectually, that we must die, that we all die in the end. There is no other way out of this world."

"That's certainly true," said Bernie.

"I read somewhere that around a hundred and sixty thousand people die every day. And for every two babies born, someone dies. And yet death is such a secretive, hidden activity and it's still such a taboo subject. And when it comes close, when it's our turn, we're filled with fear. I sometimes wonder whether if we as a society were more open to talking about it, death would be so feared."

"It's an interesting thought," said Bernie. "You know, for aborigines, there is no ending of life with physical death. Death is seen as part of a cycle of life. You emerge from the spiritual world through birth, and eventually you return there through death, only to emerge again."

"What? Like reincarnation?"

"Something like that. I imagine a belief like that would make you less afraid of death. You might even embrace it."

"Mmm," said Chris. "What do you think it is that people fear most – leaving behind their loved ones? Or what will happen to them when they die?"

"I know," said Bernie softly and she paused momentarily. "I mean, I understand from people who've faced the real prospect of death, that what they fear most is what happens when they die. Even those who believe in an afterlife."

"I'm not sure what I believe. I mean, imagine if there was nothing on the other side. If the end of this life really was the end of everything. It's impossible for me to comprehend the idea of nothingness." She paused, stared at

Bernie and said, "You know, I sometimes wish I had some sort of religious conviction. I do believe in life after death but what form that might take I have no idea. If I had faith, you see, I wouldn't have that uncertainty."

"Well, I think that, like the aborigines, we are spiritual beings and when we die we return to that state. I'm not convinced about reincarnation, though. I believe we only get one chance at this life on earth. That's why I believe we should seize the opportunities that fate presents to us. Don't you?"

"I guess so."

Bernie paused and said into her glass, so quietly that Chris barely managed to hear her, "Even if your actions bring unhappiness to others."

Chris wasn't sure if this was a question or a statement. She was quiet for a few moments and then said carefully, "I'm not sure about that. It isn't always possible, or right, to put your own desires, your own happiness, first."

"Why not?"

"Because putting yourself first all the time is selfish. If everyone did that, then we would live in an uncaring society where no-one did anything for anybody unless it was self-serving. Sometimes, you have to put the happiness of others before your own, even if it makes you unhappy. Children are a case in point. Parents endlessly do things they don't really want to do, but they do them for their children. They put their happiness before their own."

"Then they're mad!" said Bernie, with a laugh.

"You think so?" said Chris, reflecting on the many little compromises she made on a daily basis as an employee, wife and mother. Her life, and identity, were shaped and constrained to such a degree by these three roles, that the occasions were rare indeed when she truly felt she put herself first. Bernie, fulfilling none of these roles, probably wasn't forced to make the same compromises, the same sacrifices.

"Don't you think there's something noble about sacrificing your needs to others?" said Chris. "Helping others – putting their needs before your own at that particular point – gives people meaning in their lives and makes them feel that they're making a difference in the world? That's the reason why people volunteer their time to do charitable work, raise money for charity etcetera."

"Yes, I think it's important to do those things. But it's also important to look after yourself. Everyone needs a little me-time," she added, in a light-hearted tone and Bernie gave a nervous little laugh, breaking the tension.

Chris smiled and said, "Amen to that! We're getting very serious, aren't we? All this talk about death and self-sacrifice!"

"God. yes! We should talk about something else," laughed Bernie and she took a hearty swig of wine. "I wonder what time Paul'll get in?"

"Don't know," said Chris absentmindedly and she glanced at the clock on the mantelpiece again. Mary and Lorraine weren't due for another fifteen minutes or so. Time enough to ask Bernie what had been on her mind since lunchtime. The glass in her hand became unsteady all of a sudden and she took a large slug of wine to quiet her nerves.

She arranged her left elbow on the arm of the sofa and tried to appear calm. But, because the arms of the sofa were as high as the back, this position quickly proved uncomfortable. She removed her arm, shifted in her seat and looked at the fireplace.

She stared at the nest of coiled white fairy lights in the grate – which ensured that the magnificent Victorian fireplace remained, in spite of its unlit status, the focal point of the room – and wished she could put her sister's comments from lunchtime out of her mind.

Karen had been so suspicious when she'd told her that she'd seen Paul and Bernie together. Chris had put it down to Karen's dislike of Bernie, a juvenile hangover from the past which she had tried to dismiss. But Karen was such a good judge of character, it was hard to ignore her opinion. And she couldn't get that image out of her mind of Paul's hand on Bernie's back as she got into his car. There was something so – so at ease about the gesture that disturbed Chris.

"So are you going to tell me who these mystery guests are?" said Bernie, appearing to lighten up a little.

"Do you want to know?" said Chris, with what she hoped was a warm smile as she told herself to stop being paranoid. All she had to do was ask and the matter would be resolved instantly. Bernie would give her a perfectly logical explanation for what she had seen – and her fears, vague and unspecified as they were, would be banished immediately.

"I think so," said Bernie with a smile. "If you'll tell me. I'm not a great fan of surprises, you see. Sometimes they can be . . ." she paused, appearing to search for the right words, "most unpleasant."

"This one won't be. I've invited Mary Ramsey and Lorraine Kane round."

"Oh!" said Bernie with a delighted little squeal and a broad smile. "I haven't seen or heard from either of them since I left Ballyfergus!"

"I'm glad you're pleased," said Chris. She cleared her throat with a weak little cough and said, "Bernie?"

"Yes?"

"I never got the chance to ask you something earlier."

"What's that?" said Bernie, who by now had untangled her legs and sunk back into the soft cushions of the sofa.

"I was on my way to meet Karen, and I saw you and Paul outside the office of Hunter Campbell."

"You did?" said Bernie and she sat bolt upright, her face a slightly paler shade, if that were possible, than before.

"I don't want you to think I was being nosy or anything," said Chris, suddenly feeling the need to explain herself. "It was just that I happened to be driving past on my way to meet Karen at exactly the same time you came out of the estate agents. I chanced to glance up and there you were. I saw you get into Paul's car."

"Yes, Paul gave me a lift back here," said Bernie, through thin lips, her chin tilted upwards by a few degrees. Her expression reminded Chris of the defiant faces Finn used to pull as a child – indeed still did from time to time – when he didn't get his way. Or when he'd been caught doing something wrong . . .

"I don't mean to pry," said Chris, "but was Paul showing you some of the holiday properties we've been looking at up North? He's really keen to go ahead with it but I'm not sure."

"He never mentioned a holiday home."

"Oh," said Chris and there was a pregnant pause. "I thought you had property schedules in your hands. I thought the bits of paper were . . . I must've been mistaken."

"That's what I wanted to talk to you about earlier," said Bernie. Her face suddenly took on some colour and she put her glass down carefully on the antique side table beside the sofa. Chris had to suppress the urge to retrieve a coaster from the nearest drawer and place it under the glass. Water marks were so very hard to remove from polished wood.

"Do you remember this morning?" said Bernie, recapturing Chris's attention again, "I started to tell you on the phone but – well – then I thought it was probably better to talk face-to-face . . ."

"Tell me what?" said Chris and just at that precise moment the doorbell rang.

They stared at each other and Chris was torn between the need to hear what Bernie had to say and the desire not to.

After what seemed like an age, but could only have been a few seconds, Chris said "Can it keep?" Without waiting for an answer, she got to her feet. "That'll be Mary and Lorraine."

She set her glass down on the mantelpiece and caught a glimpse of her reflection in the mirror. The tired, harried woman she saw there made her pause for a moment and, mentally, she gave herself a ticking off. She reflected on poor Doris Beattie and thought how foolish she was to be worried. The only thing she had to be bothered about at the moment, she told herself harshly, was a rather hyperactive imagination.

She turned her back to the mirror, gave Bernie a big smile and suddenly realised that whatever Bernie's explanation might be for this morning, it didn't really matter. She would be on her way back to Australia in ten days' time. And then life for her and Paul and the children would be back to normal.

"Aren't you going to answer the door then?" said Bernie.

"Yes. Yes, of course. Right this very minute."

★ ★ ★

Chris and Bernie stood in the doorway and waved goodbye to Mary and Lorraine who, a bit worse for drink, were giggling like the schoolgirls they once were as they got in the taxi. Mary caught her heel in the hem of her skirt, which caused great hilarity when she nearly fell headfirst into the back seat of the car. Eventually she got herself untangled, all the doors were slammed shut and the car crunched down the drive.

"Is that them away?" came Paul's voice from inside, startling Chris. She hadn't heard him come in.

"I didn't know you were home," shouted Chris, as she closed the door.

"No," said Paul, "I decided to keep a low profile. I've been in the study."

"Yep, that's them away," confirmed Chris.

"Thank the Lord," said Paul.

Inside Bernie headed straight for the drawing room. Chris bolted the heavy front door, turned the key in the lock and threw the key on top of the others in the marble bowl. Finn would not need access through this door tonight – he had a key for the Yale lock on the back door. In the hall, Chris kicked off her taupe beaded evening mules and placed them on the bottom step of the stairs, ready to take up on her way to bed. The tiled floor felt cool on her bare soles, a welcome rest for her tired feet.

"Well," she said, with a bright smile, walking into the drawing room, "that turned out to be a very enjoyable evening, didn't it?"

Bernie and Paul were standing in front of the fireplace

talking urgently in low voices to each other. They stopped as soon as she entered the room and turned to face her. The smile froze on Chris's face as she took in the scene before her. She was not mistaken. They *had* ceased whispering as soon as she'd come in. That meant their conversation was not intended for her ears. She felt a sickening feeling in her stomach. What on earth could they be talking about that they did not wish her to hear?

"Yes, yes it was," said Bernie with a too-bright smile. Bernie had been edgy all night and now she looked positively unwell.

"Has Mary Ramsey always been so loud?" said Paul, only half-jokingly. "I could hear every word she said in the study upstairs."

"Sorry about that," said Chris, who had had three glasses of wine and was feeling every so slightly tipsy. She put her hand to her mouth to stifle a burp and said, "We were rather noisy, weren't we?"

"It was her voice I could hear above the rest of you. She was shrieking like a bloody banshee."

Bernie laughed at this, a tad nervously, and Chris said, "That's just Mary. She's always been a bit loud. She's very nice though. You should've come down and met her."

"I didn't have to," said Paul, wryly. "I feel that I know her intimately after tonight."

Bernie laughed again. Chris gave him a rather tired smile, too familiar with his sarcasm to find it humorous.

"I'm sure Hannah didn't get a thing done," went on Paul. "She needs peace and quiet to study. Her last exam is next week and if she doesn't get the grades . . ."

"I know, I know. She won't get to be a doctor," said Chris, emboldened by the drink. "Relax, Paul. One night of merriment isn't going to destroy her medical career. Anyway," she said, changing tack, "on the subject of medicine, how's Derek Beattie?"

"He's okay now, poor bugger. I upped his morphine. Doris and her daughter are quite determined to nurse him at home but I don't know how long the two of them can go on for. They look exhausted."

"Is he near the end then?"

Paul nodded solemnly and said, "Pretty near, I'd say. A matter of weeks."

"I am sorry to hear that," said Chris, wondering if there was anything she could do to assist them. A few home-cooked meals, delivered to the house, would probably be very welcome, but finding the time out of her busy schedule could prove challenging. Still, if there was a will, there was a way . . .

"Shall we sit?" said Paul and, with a theatrical sweep of his hand, he invited both women to take a seat.

Paul waited until Bernie sat on one of the sofas and then he sat down opposite her. He coughed to clear his throat and made a show of settling comfortably in the seat, his arms thrown wide across the back of the sofa.

He crossed his legs and a flash of sunflower yellow showed at his ankle. Paul had a fondness for brightly coloured socks: he said they were one of the few ways for a man to express his individuality through dress. Chris thought them ridiculous on a man of his age – as she had told Paul on more than one occasion, to no avail, a man's socks should always match his shoes.

Chris watched Paul let his gaze drift around the room, settling anywhere but on Bernie. There was something staged about his movements and demeanour. He was trying too hard, Chris thought, to look at ease.

"Have a seat, Chris," he said, but she found herself rooted to the spot, her hands clasped in front of her tummy, joined as if in prayer.

"I'm all right where I am," she said tersely and he gave her a sharp look.

He did not like her to gainsay him. She stood in silence and waited for one of them to speak, mystified as to why such a feeling of dread should have descended upon her.

"Chris?" said Bernie and she glanced at Paul. He nodded for her to go on. "Today when you saw Paul and me coming out of Hunter Campbell?"

"Yes," said Chris, nodding stupidly. Her heart felt as though it had stopped. She shut her eyes.

"I was looking at houses. Well, apartments."

"Houses?" said Chris and she opened her eyes. They darted quickly from Bernie to Paul and back again, her brain trying to divine some understanding from their blank expressions.

"Yes. To rent."

Chris put her hand to her heart and felt it pounding against the wall of her chest. She sat down suddenly on the same sofa as Paul and looked at him. He avoided eye contact with her and stared at Bernie, his expression utterly unreadable. Chris followed his gaze and waited for Bernie to say more, her brain befuddled with unasked questions, so unexpected was this news.

"As you know I am due to go back to Melbourne shortly," said Bernie, not addressing Chris exactly, rather focusing on a point some distance away over her left shoulder. "But as the time comes closer, I find I'm dreading it more and more. I've tried to imagine going back to my old life there and to be honest I just can't picture it. Things out there haven't worked out as . . . well, as I'd hoped. My life there has been quite lonely these last few years. Don't get me wrong," she said quickly, "I'm not complaining – that's partly been my choice. But as I get older I find I want to be nearer my family. And my friends," she added meaningfully and nodded at Chris who felt the unnamed fears that had haunted her all day start to dissipate.

"I've decided," said Bernie, "that I'd like to settle back here in Ballyfergus."

"Gosh!" said Chris, with a loud exhalation of breath. "That is a shock. I mean I'm delighted for you but it seems so – so sudden."

"I suppose it is rather," said Bernie with a nervous laugh.

Chris paused, not wishing Bernie to think she was in any way criticising her. "But," she said carefully, "you were always so keen to get as far away from Ballyfergus as possible. You don't think you'd find it too parochial here?"

"I don't think so. People can change," said Bernie and looked at Paul.

"Are you sure you've thought this through, Bernie?" said Chris. "I mean, what about your work? And your apartment in Melbourne?"

"As far as my work's concerned I'm geographically mobile. With e-mail and the internet I can work from anywhere. I rarely see my clients as it is. Most of my work is completed, and delivered, electronically. Anyway, I'm confident I can find work here if I have to."

"And your flat?"

"It's rented. I only have to give a month's notice."

Bernie paused and added, "I know it might seem like I'm rushing things but I've been thinking about this seriously for the last fortnight." She brightened suddenly as though lit from within and she said, looking first at Chris and then Paul, "No. I've been thinking about this for much longer than that, on a subconscious level anyway – I just didn't realise it at the time! Since the idea of this holiday took root, my life has been moving in this direction. I just didn't know it. I see it clearly now. Fate has guided me here! It was in my stars, you know."

"Really," said Chris, trying to hide her scepticism and anxious, given the lateness of the hour, to divert Bernie from expounding her views on astrology. She glanced crossly at Paul, rather put out that Bernie had not felt able to confide in her, but had obviously confided in him. "You knew?" she said and he turned to her and opened his mouth to speak.

But before he could say anything, Bernie said, "Paul only found out today by accident. He came into the letting agents while I was there."

"Yes," said Paul. "Keith Chalmers phoned me about a new development in Castlerock. He thought I might be interested."

"I see," said Chris again, feeling very slow on the uptake. Paul had not mentioned this call before. Perhaps Keith had only called this morning and he hadn't yet had the opportunity to tell her.

"There's a place on Bay Road available straight away," said Bernie, and Chris turned her head slowly to look at her.

As well as feeling baffled by the astonishing and rapid turn events were taking, she felt utter relief. Now that her suspicions had been proven unfounded she could articulate, to herself at least, what they had been. She had seriously, truly believed (egged on by Karen's suspicious nature) that Paul and Bernie were about to tell her they'd been having an affair. The idea, she saw now, was completely crazy. How could she have been so foolish? She found it hard to look at either of them without blushing with embarrassment.

"When were you thinking of moving in?" said Paul.

"I was going to move in tomorrow."

"But why so soon?" said Chris, confused. "I don't understand the rush."

"I don't want to lose the apartment. It's a lovely ground floor conversion in one of those big semi-detached houses and I absolutely love it. If I don't take it now I might not get another one as good."

"She's right," said Paul quickly. "There aren't that many good rental properties in Ballyfergus."

Chris opened her mouth to ask Paul since when had he become an expert on the property market but she managed to bite her tongue. This didn't make any sense, she thought logically, her brain finally kicking into gear. Why was Bernie rushing to rent somewhere when she and Paul were more than happy to host her? She had a flight back to Australia in ten days' time, already booked and paid for. It would be madness not to use that flight.

"But you're going to have to go back to Australia to sort things out there, aren't you?" said Chris and Bernie nodded. "And I imagine that's going to take some time? Wouldn't it make more sense to stay here with us until your scheduled flight, go back to Australia as planned and rent a place once you come back? If you start paying rent now you're only going to have to leave the flat empty while you go back to

Australia. And you know Paul and I are more than happy to have you here, aren't we, Paul?"

She looked to him for encouragement and he gave her a little nod of support. He rubbed his pursed lips with the tips of his fingers, a habit of his that usually indicated he was deep in thought. No wonder, thought Chris – he must be as taken aback by this turn of events as she was.

"No," said Bernie with such forcefulness it jolted Chris. Bernie lowered her voice and her eyes. She fingered the cuffs of her blouse and said, "I mean that's a very kind offer but I really can't trespass on your hospitality any longer." Then she added with a bright smile, "Anyway, I'm keen to start my new life!"

Chris's heart sank. Had she really been such a miserable hostess that Bernie wouldn't stay another day longer under her roof? She had acted meanly and she was truly ashamed of herself. And yet, now that it was done, Chris could not find within herself the burning desire to make Bernie change her mind.

"But what about furnishing the place?" said Chris, turning her mind to the practicalities to avoid dwelling further on these unpleasant reflections.

"It's already fully furnished. It's absolutely lovely. Two bedrooms, brand new kitchen, all brand new furniture and a lovely courtyard garden that gets the sun in the morning."

"But the expense –" said Chris and she stopped, not wishing to embarrass Bernie by alluding to the fact that she was obviously not awash with money. She hated herself for being aware of these things, but she couldn't help but notice that Bernie possessed nothing of value.

She wore cheap costume jewellery, a fake watch, her clothes were not well made and, on the one occasion that she'd ventured into Bernie's room to give it a quick clean – when Sabrina, the cleaner, was ill – she'd observed that none of her make-up, beauty products or perfume was of good quality. Sensitive to Bernie's circumstances, it had become an unspoken rule that, when they went out anywhere, they sought out inexpensive places to eat. And why two bedrooms? What did Bernie intend to do with the second one?

"I can afford it," said Bernie and Chris did a quick mental trawl of her knowledge of rental properties in the area. A two-bedroom apartment in popular Bay Road in the condition Bernie described would not rent for much less than five hundred pounds a month.

"I hope you don't mind me asking, Bernie. But has this decision something to do with your brother Michael? It was shortly after your visit to him that you went off to Donegal. And I … well, I sensed something had changed."

"Yes," said Bernie and she looked at Paul again. "Yes, it was probably round about then that I started seriously thinking about moving back here for good."

"So did something happen at your brother's?" said Chris. Seeing him and his family after all these years had probably made Bernie realise how much she missed them.

"No," said Bernie, shaking her head slowly. "Not exactly," and then, appearing to remember something, she added quickly, "Oh yes. There was the money."

"What money?" said Paul sharply.

"From Dad's will, Paul. Don't you remember I told you? Michael and Jim decided to split the money three ways. I really wasn't bothered but they insisted. And Dad had quite a little nest egg saved up. So money isn't an issue."

"That's good to know," said Chris.

"So you see, you really don't need to worry about me, Chris. I'll be just fine." And she gave Chris a reassuring smile.

"We should give you some sort of send-off," said Chris. "Shouldn't we, Paul?" Although she couldn't help but feel relieved that Bernie was moving out, nonetheless it didn't seem right to let her go without some sort of celebration.

"Really, Chris, there's no need," said Bernie firmly. "You and Paul have done enough for me already."

"But we should do something. How about a nice meal? I can ask Karen and Tony round –"

"No, really," interrupted Bernie. "I insist. I shall be perfectly happy in my new home."

"But –" began Chris, who was ashamed to admit that she did not want Bernie's rapid exit from Castlerock to reflect badly on her. She feared that it would look like she had been thrown out.

"I think," said Paul, who up until now, had said very little during the conversation, "that we should do what Bernie wants, Chris."

And with that he stood up, said goodnight to Bernie, and left the room, bringing the discussion abruptly to an end.

* * *

In bed that night, Chris squirmed restlessly while Paul sat propped up by two pillows, reading. He wore pyjamas now, winter and summer, though there had been a time when he'd worn nothing in bed, whatever the weather. She remembered how she used to love snuggling up to his warm body – and the inevitable making out that would follow.

It had been a long time since she had initiated anything in the bedroom. She often thought that she should make more of an effort but she never did. She read with incredulity about women in their forties discovering a renewed interest in sex. She had neither the time, energy or interest. She wondered if Paul was disappointed in her.

She glanced across at him. He had on blue checked seersucker pyjamas from Browns in Dublin that Chris had bought for him last year on a Christmas shopping trip with Karen. He seemed remote, untouchable. In some ways she knew him so well – or thought she did – in other ways he was a stranger to her. The lack of physical intimacy was, she knew, a symptom of the emotional distance between them. And yet, this state of matters did not pain her as much as she knew it should.

He peered through wire-framed reading glasses at the latest copy of *The Lancet*, apparently engrossed. Chris lay on her back, in pink satin pyjamas and crossed her hands on her chest. She let out a long sigh. Paul turned the page of the magazine and ignored her.

"Why were you and Bernie being secretive tonight?" she said.

"I have no idea what you mean," said Paul crisply, enunciating every word carefully. He continued to read.

"When I came into the drawing room, just after Lorraine and Mary left, the two of you were whispering together. And when I came into the room, you stopped."

"We weren't whispering. We were talking. She was telling me that she had decided to take that property in Bay Road."

"But why did she keep it from me? I mean she could've told me earlier in the day. She had ample opportunity. She could've popped into the office even or called me on my mobile for a chat."

"I think she was worried that you might take offence."

"Why would I take offence?" said Chris, sharply. "She's a free agent, isn't she?"

"See? She was right. You are annoyed."

"I'm only annoyed because my husband is in the habit of keeping secrets from me."

Paul sighed, took his glasses off, folded the arms of the spectacles with the tap-tap sound of metal against metal and set them on the bedside table.

"You always have to make everything about me, don't you? You twist things to make out like I've done something wrong. When actually what you're angry about is the fact that Bernie didn't confide in you." He closed the magazine and placed it alongside his glasses. "I bumped into her in Hunter Campbell's. I gave her a lift home and she told me what she was thinking of doing. And, in case it's slipped your mind, my dear, by the time I got home from work, you were entertaining guests. At what point exactly should I have interrupted you to reveal Bernie's oh-so-secretive plans?"

"You could've phoned me at the office."

"To share tittle-tattle? Oh grow up, Chris. It isn't my place to share other people's business with you."

"It is when that person is staying in my house."

"It was up to Bernie to tell you when she was good and ready – and she did. Now I'm going to sleep. Goodnight." He lay on his side with his back facing her, reached out his left arm and switched out the bedside lamp, plunging the room into semi-darkness.

"And goodnight to you too," said Chris and she

pointedly turned her back to his and stared at the wall. The digital display on the clock-alarm threw a pale blue light across the room shrouding everything in a ghostly hue.

She lay there, simmering with resentment, and thought of all the clever retorts she should have thrown at Paul. But she wasn't as quick-witted as he or as verbally dexterous and, as usual, her wits had come to her aid too late. She always lost arguments with him and, as a consequence, her main line of defence – developed over their many years of marriage - was to sulk. Childish and ineffective, she knew, but old habits were hard to break.

And yet, in spite of her anger, she was somewhat relieved. It would be great to get the house back to themselves and yet . . . and yet, the idea of Bernie living in Ballyfergus. Well, it had thrown her – that was the only word for it. Chris's mind had been set on the idea that Bernie's visit would soon come to an end. She would return to Australia and life would return to normal. And now that wasn't to happen.

Bernie's decision to stay here, like Raymond's decision to come home after all these years, would introduce a new dynamic into their lives. Bernie had become firm friends with Paul and the children and Ballyfergus was a small place - it would be almost impossible to avoid her, not that Chris wanted to, she reminded herself hastily.

It was just that the sudden turnaround in Bernie's fortunes made her feel uneasy – and for the life of her, she couldn't understand why. Perhaps it was because Bernie's visit had put a dent in Chris's fanciful notion of lasting friendship. People do change over time and she and Bernie had grown in different ways. Whatever their former friendship had been based upon (and looking back now, it had probably been nothing more than finding themselves thrown together in unfamiliar new school surroundings) it was no longer there. Or perhaps it was because the woman who had once been her dearest friend – and closer to her at one time than her own sister – seemed determined to get away from her as fast as she possibly could. And for that, Chris thought, she could only blame herself.

She lay in silence, feeling more alone than she had ever done in her life, as misery consumed her. And it was with uncharacteristic insight that she realised that her unhappiness had nothing to do with Bernie. But she couldn't think about that now. For she knew that if she started delving into her life for answers she would not be able to stomach some of the truths she would find there.

She put her hand to her temple and crossly brushed away the warm, unwanted tears as they slid onto the four-hundred-thread-count Egyptian cotton pillowcase and seeped into the white Hungarian goose-down pillow. She must put these depressing notions out of her mind and sleep. For one thing, she was going to ruin her much-treasured bed linen and for another, she knew that everything would seem better in the morning. She closed her eyes.

Eleven

It was the middle of June and Karen was in the car on her way to Belfast for her pre-op appointment at the Malone clinic. Her feelings were complicated: a mixture of apprehension, nervousness, and most of all, excitement. Part of her still couldn't believe this was actually happening!

"They say this hot weather's going to continue for the rest of the summer," said Chris, who was sitting next to Karen in the passenger seat, looking chic in cream linen.

"That's great," said Karen, turning the air conditioning up. "Pity I'll be spending most of it indoors though."

That was the only downside of having the surgery in July, thought Karen, as her smile faded a little – she wouldn't be able to spend much of the summer, or at least the first four weeks of it, with Jack and Chloe. But, she told herself, they would have their Dad to take care of them and later, at the end of August, they would all go away for a week's holiday to a wonderful hotel in Donegal.

"It'll be worth it though," said Chris positively. "And there'll be other years."

"I know," said Karen, brightly.

Chris was right. There would be other summers. Summers when she would be able to frolic on the sand with the children in a swimsuit, maybe even a bikini! Holidays abroad, when her primary concern would be how to get an even tan, not how to devise clever ways to hide her gargantuan stomach. Carefree days when she would be able to wear fashionable summer clothes and ditch her current wardrobe of tent-like linen creations - and over-sized chunky jewellery.

Her obsession with her figure bordered on narcissism, she fully accepted that. But she was also powerless to change that fact without changing the cause of the problem itself. She looked forward to the day when she would be able to forget, truly forget, about her body and free herself from this self-absorption. She looked forward to the time, now within her sights, when, for the first time since childhood, she would be liberated from the chains of acute self-consciousness. She couldn't wait.

When they joined the M2 motorway into Belfast the traffic was bad and they more or less ground to a halt.

"Must be an accident or something," said Chris, straining to see ahead. Unable to see any sign of what might be causing the problem, she slumped back in the seat and said, "Thank God we don't have to do this drive every day."

Karen rested her elbow on the steering wheel and said, "Yeah, there's not many people like us with commutes of under ten minutes. Five in your case. We really are very lucky, aren't we?"

There was short silence then and Chris said, "It's not by chance that our lives have worked out the way they have, Karen. I've worked hard for where I am now. And so have you."

This was true but there was also an element of luck involved, thought Karen. But she did not want to pursue the subject with Chris right now as she knew her sister did not believe in woolly concepts like fate and karma and luck. The difference between the two sisters, Karen often thought, boiled down to the basic fact that Chris believed she deserved her blessings, while Karen, underneath it all, did not.

And for this reason she often envied her sister and the certainty and assurance that came easily to her. She did not suffer from the self-doubts that plagued Karen. Whilst appreciative, Chris thought she deserved everything she had – her wonderful home, husband and kids. Karen woke up every day amazed that Tony was in the bed beside her, that her business was a success and that she had been blessed with two of God's most wonderful creatures in her children.

After a short wait, the traffic jam cleared and soon they were driving through the city, Chris navigating from written instructions. Karen made a mental note to get a car with sat-nav when this one was due for renewal. Mind you, with the amount of money she was spending on the surgery, a new car might have to be postponed for a while. She decided not to think about it.

The Malone Cosmetic Surgery Clinic was housed in a handsome, well-maintained Victorian building that had, in its heyday, been the impressive residence of a successful city merchant. Now it was disfigured by a huge modern block of an extension that filled whatever garden it must once have had, and connected it to the next door villa, a house of equally striking proportions.

This then was the clinic where her surgery was to take place. A Frankenstein of a building, the sharp, bright, modern, sandwiched between two relics of the past.

Curbing her imagination's tendency to run away with itself, Karen thought it wise to put such comparisons out of her mind.

She found a visitors' space in the small and busy car park, pulled in and cut the engine. She took the keys from the ignition and held them in her right fist. Her stomach churned with anxiety, her easiness from earlier now eclipsed by the unexpected onset of fear. Not fear of what was going to happen today, but fear of the next stage, of where today's appointment would, inevitably, lead her.

For Karen was well aware of the dangers ahead of her. She made light of the surgery, especially to Chris, who was apt to jump on the slightest hint of doubt or hesitation as a firm reason not to go ahead with it. Because she knew that Chris's heart wasn't really in it, indeed she knew that she harboured deep reservations about the whole idea of cosmetic surgery, she appreciated her sister's show of support all the more. The fact that Chris had come along today, and was keeping her concerns to herself, said a lot about her as a sister. They were always there for each other.

But what, thought Karen, was she doing? Putting herself at risk like this? Placing the children at risk, albeit a very small one, of being left with a damaged, or worse, dead mother. Things could go wrong, things did go wrong. Not every operation was a success.

She'd read on one of the many websites she'd trawled about the ongoing complications that could ensue, like infection and misaligned belly-buttons. Ugly 'dog-ears', aptly named folds of skin on the hip line, where the untouched skin met with the newly tightened section. Numbness, bad scarring, life-threatening blot clots and the hideous-sounding skin necrosis – where parts of skin literally turned red then black and died due to poor blood supply. Yes, Karen was aware of them all, along with the ultimate possibility of a failed operation where, after all this angst and expense, she could end up looking worse than when she started.

"We made good time, didn't we?" said Chris cheerfully, retrieving her handbag from the foot well and opening the car door. She swung her legs round, in a ladylike fashion, ready to get out of the car. "Come on!"

She glanced round at Karen. Something in her sister's face betrayed her emotions and Chris immediately pulled her legs back into the car and shut the door with a resolute thud.

"Right, if you're having second thoughts, Karen, it's perfectly natural," she said in her calm, neutral-toned lawyer's voice, using her graceful hands to emphasise her point. "I'm sure the clinic staff are well used to people changing their minds. Paul's heard through the grapevine that they're very reputable, very professional. So it won't be a problem at all. If you like I can go in and talk to them right now."

For a moment Karen considered the possibility of saying 'yes', putting the key in the ignition, turning on the engine and driving home. Of returning to her life unchanged, of carrying on as before. But, afraid though she was, that was inconceivable to her now.

She reminded herself how badly she wanted this, of the years spent fantasising about a flat stomach and taut abdominal muscles. And she had done her research; she had tracked down the best surgeon she could find and thereby minimized the risks as much as possible. She had got this far. She must find the resolve to see it through.

Karen gulped down a mouthful of air and said, "I'm not having second thoughts."

"What's wrong then?" said Chris, her expression changing from one of concern to bewilderment.

"I'm just a bit – a bit afraid, that's all."

Chris sighed and closed her hand around Karen's tight fist and the keys fell from her grasp into her black-skirted lap.

"Of course you are. It's only natural. But look, nothing's going to happen today. You said that yourself. It's just a few tests and then we go and enjoy ourselves at the shops!"

"Okay," said Karen, taking a deep breath and putting a brave smile on her face. "It's just an attack of last-minute nerves."

"Justifiable under the circumstances," said Chris kindly. "Are you ready to go in now?"

Karen nodded. "Yes, I'm ready."

"Right, come on then," said Chris with a forced jocularity designed to lift Karen's spirits. "We haven't got all day! I want to hit those shops as soon as possible. And I've a treat in mind for lunch. I'm taking you to Apartment on Donegall Square West."

Apartment was a trendy cocktail-bar-cum-restaurant popular with Belfast's 'in' crowd.

"So," said Chris. "The sooner we get this over and done with the better!" And Karen smiled, thinking that she really couldn't have asked for a better sister.

Inside the plush reception area, the well-preserved receptionist recognised Karen and greeted her by name. She asked her to fill out some paperwork and told her that a nurse would do all the necessary tests before the consultation with Dr Mezz. Karen smiled to herself, wondering why a visit to a NHS doctor was an 'appointment', but as soon as you went privately a doctor's appointment became a 'consultation'. There was something faintly pretentious about it.

They took a seat in the elegant waiting room, which was flooded with natural light from a glass cupola in the high ceiling. Both the room and the glass dome were oval-shaped which made for an unusual, if somewhat disconcerting space, without corners. In the middle of the inner wall, was an unused marble fireplace with dried flowers in the grate and, opposite it, three large picture windows that looked out onto the shrubbery in front and the street beyond.

At the end of the room was a set of white-painted double doors, now locked and bolted, which must once have led into the garden. Five large sofas, in soft tan leather, lined the edges of the room and, in front of each one, was a mahogany coffee table, each one boasting a fanned display of recent issues of glossy magazines.

"What a lovely room," said Chris. "It must've been the drawing room, don't you think?"

"I suppose so," said Karen, distracted, working hard to control her nerves.

A white-clothed middle-aged woman came up, introduced herself as Nurse Jenkins and Karen followed her along a carpeted corridor and into a room that looked like a doctor's surgery. She asked Karen to take a seat and sat down opposite her.

"Now," said the nurse, putting on a pair of glasses and consulting a sheaf of paperwork she picked up from the desk. "Mrs Karen Elizabeth Magill. Date of birth: 24th February 1965."

"That's me," said Karen, with a bright smile.

"And you're coming in for an abdominoplasty or tummy tuck with Dr Mezz on 1st July?"

"That's right."

"And how are you feeling about it?" said Nurse Jenkins.

"To tell you the truth, I'm a little apprehensive. No, that's not true," she said and let out a little gasp. "I'm absolutely terrified."

"That's only natural," said the nurse kindly. She put down the paperwork and removed her glasses. "If it helps to put your mind at ease, Karen, I can tell you that Dr Mezz is one of the best surgeons I've ever seen. The vast majority of patients are delighted with his work and the ones that aren't often don't have realistic expectations in the first place."

Karen smiled bravely, worrying that she was one of those people with unrealistic expectations.

"Now," said Nurse Jenkins, all business again, "Let's get on with these tests, shall we?"

★ ★ ★

"Well," said Chris, once they were back in the car and heading towards the city centre along the Malone Road. "How did it go?"

She took a quick peek at her Cartier watch, straining to see the digits on the dial, and wondering what on earth had taken so much time. Karen had been in there for nearly two hours.

"Fine. Absolutely fine. It was a very thorough physical – blood tests, urine sample, pregnancy test, pulse, weight, height. Did I forget anything? Oh yes, blood pressure and then I had a chat with Dr Mezz. He gave me these," she said, waving in the air with her right hand the wad of folded A4 sheets of paper she had placed in the driver's door pocket. She stuffed them back in the same place and said, dryly, "Pre-op and post-op instructions. I'll be living like a nun for the next month."

Chris laughed and said, "What do you mean?"

"Well, they've already banned me from the contraceptive pill – it increases the risk of blood-clotting apparently – so no sex without fear of pregnancy. Now I'm not allowed any drugs whatsoever, including alcohol, for a whole month."

"Hmm," said Chris, thinking of her sister's, and indeed her own, fondness for a glass of wine. "That is a tough one. However, every cloud has a silver lining."

"How come?" said Karen, pulling a face.

"Well, if you can't drink, you can drive. Which means I can have as much wine as I like at lunchtime."

"Don't you even think about it, Chris. That is so unfair!"

"Only joking," said Chris, glad to see Karen back to her old, humorous self. "I'll just have the one then." She paused for effect. "Maybe a nice Pinot Grigio or perhaps a crisp Sauvignon Blanc . . ."

"I'm warning you!"

Chris chuckled quietly to herself for a few moments and then, serious again, said, "All the same it's good to know that they're being so thorough, isn't it?"

"Absolutely. I don't think I could be in better hands."

Chris offered up a silent prayer that this was the case.

They parked in the multi-storey at Castlecourt Shopping Centre in the heart of the city. They wandered aimlessly around the make-up department in Debenhams, where Karen bought a new lipstick, and Laura Ashley, where Chris bought some pale green silk cushions trimmed with glass beads for her bedroom. In Olsen Chris bought off-white linen trousers and a sleeveless knitted grey silk top with matching wrap cardigan. It felt so decadent, so indulgent to spend a day like this. Chris tried to stop worrying and enjoy it.

They moved onto the shops on Donegall Place, and stopped for coffee at Paul Rankin's café on pedestrianised Fountain Street. They sat on chairs on the pavement in the hot sun, and Chris sipped a cappuccino.

"It almost feels like being on the continent, doesn't it?" said Chris.

Karen sighed contently. "It sure does. I wish we were going abroad. Not that we can this year because of my op. But maybe next. Are you and Paul going away this summer?"

"We haven't planned anything yet. We might do something at the last minute but to be honest we're holding off because of Hannah. Money for holidays might be a bit tight for the next while as Hannah won't get a grant and we don't want her leaving university in debt." Chris was only partly telling the truth. Hannah and Finn would not want to come on the sort of holiday Chris would like and the prospect of two weeks alone with Paul filled her with unease. "We're even toying with the idea of buying her a place – there's some sense in investing in a property rather than shelling out on rent all that time. Though I'm not sure about buying into the Scottish market. We'll have to see."

"Mmm," said Karen slowly and she set her cup down carefully on its saucer. "You know, Hannah popped in the other night."

"She did?" said Chris, surprised that Hannah hadn't mentioned this to her.

"She was round at Cat's," said Karen, referring to Hannah's friend who lived very close to Karen. "She called round on her way home."

"I see. That's nice."

"She . . . well, she seemed a bit worried to me," said Karen awkwardly.

"Really? I wonder what she got to be worried about? She's finished all her exams. And she's got a lovely long summer ahead of her with a well-paid part-time job in the day centre and loads of time to relax. Maybe it's post-exam shock. You know – worrying, now that it's all over, that she's not going to get the results she needs."

"Maybe . . ."

"You know I thought she handled the stress of the actual exams really well. I'm really proud of her." .

"I know you are – and rightly so. She's a very capable girl," said Karen and paused. "But has she ever said anything to you about not wanting to do medicine?"

"Not wanting to do medicine?" repeated Chris, incredulously. "Of course she wants to do medicine. She's had her heart set on it since she was six."

"Really?" said Karen in a flat voice.

"What did she say to you?" said Chris.

"Not much. Just that she was worried that she wouldn't get the results she needed. That she'd let you and Paul down. When I asked her if she still wanted to do medicine, she said she wasn't sure."

"That's just nerves talking."

"Still, it made me think."

"Think what?"

"That maybe she is having seconds thoughts."

"Well, it's bit late now, if she is," said Chris, crossly,

dismissing the notion that Karen would know what was in Hannah's heart better than her own mother did. "She's been accepted at Edinburgh. She went over for an interview in April and everything."

"People can change their minds," said Karen quietly and took a sip of coffee.

"Perhaps," said Chris, mainly to appease Karen but the idea of Hannah not doing medicine was almost inconceivable. She had never before expressed any doubt to her or Paul. Neither had she mentioned an interest in any other subject or course. Surely Karen was imagining things?

"So you'll talk to her?"

Chris nodded. "Of course," and then, changing subject, she asked, "So, what about you and Tony? I don't suppose you'll still be able to go to Donegal as planned now you're having the surgery?"

"Actually we are hoping to go. I contacted the The Shandon and we managed to change the booking for the last week of the summer holidays – luckily they had a cancellation. It's such a great place for the kids. And it's so beautiful there. I just hope I'll be okay, though. It'll only be six weeks after the operation. So I should be all right according to the literature."

"I'm sure you will be," said Chris reassuringly, "And it's not as though you're miles away in some far-flung country. You can always hop in the car and drive home should something go wrong. Which I'm absolutely sure it won't."

Karen smiled happily and finished the rest of her coffee. "Shall we go and have a look in Marks and Spencer?"

"Only if you want to," said Chris doubtfully. "I just realised that you probably don't want to be buying new clothes two weeks before your op because they won't fit you afterwards."

"But I want to look at all the lovely clothes I'm going to be able to buy once this tummy's gone!" she laughed, grasping a handful of saggy flesh at her stomach. "Come on. We're wasting valuable window-shopping time!"

It was after one by the time they got out of Marks and Spencers and made their way to Apartment at the side of the City Hall. The whole front of the restaurant was glass through which they could see that it was busy – on the second floor all the sofas by the huge windows which overlooked the City Hall gardens were taken.

The doorman told them there was a twenty-minute wait for a table and directed them to the cocktail bar on the second floor. They climbed the wooden stairs, found a place at the bar, dropped their shopping bags at their feet and perched (as elegantly as they could) on cream leather barstools. Tapping her heels on the metal footrest in time to the background music which, thanks to Finn, she recognised as Van Morrison sound-a-like Foy Vance from County Down, Chris surveyed the scene.

The bar was sleek and modern with an abundance of wood – on the floor, the fascia of the bar they sat at, it even flanked the walls. The colour-scheme was subdued and neutral: soft creams among the natural shades of wood, brown leather chairs, buttermilk straight-sided lampshades. The staff all wore black – the only bright colour came from the eerie blue glow of backlights behind the bar.

Under the flattering light from table and floor lamps the, mainly young professional, clientele were trendy and attractive. Almost half the women in the room were blonde (in a country where less than five per cent were born that way) and browned like toasted nuts, they looked like they had just come back from a foreign holiday.

At first glance the pale-faced young men in the room did not appear quite so attractive as the women, not having the benefit of these enhancements. But plainness cannot be disguised by dyed hair, golden skin and make-up so that, when Chris scrutinised the women more closely, few of them lived up to their initial favourable impression.

"What are you staring at?" asked Karen who had a big smile on her face and was clearly enjoying herself.

"Just the people in here," hissed Chris. "Isn't people-watching fascinating?"

"Yeah. Do you see that guy behind me," said Karen, indicating with a roll of her eyes, for Chris to look over her left shoulder. "The one at the end of the bar wearing black jeans and pale pink shirt."

"What about him?"

"Isn't he gorgeous?"

"Oh, Karen," laughed Chris. "Shush or he'll hear you. You're old enough to be his mother for heaven's sake!"

"Oh, thanks very much, Chris!" said Karen, struggling to hide a smile and adding, with just a hint of alarm in her voice, "We're not the oldest ones in here, are we?"

"No. Look at that couple over there. The lady with the red jacket and the man with her – the one with grey hair. They're older than us. And over there, by the loos. See those two rather glamorous women. I'd say they were in their fifties."

"Thank goodness," said Karen sounding relieved. She added lightheartedly, "Anyway age is just a number, isn't it?"

"So they say," said Chris, wondering for the first time if Karen's desire to change her body stemmed from her fear of ageing. Chris feared getting old too – didn't every woman? – but she knew her defences against it would be limited to much less radical solutions than her sister's.

"Shall we get a drink?" said Karen.

"Yes. Now let's see . . ." said Chris, scanning the extensive cocktail menu she held in her hand.

Soon two exotic cocktails – both non-alcoholic on account of Karen's prohibition from Dr Mezz and Chris's decision to show solidarity with her sister – were placed in front of them with a flourish by a cute barman. The drinks were presented in sugar-rimmed stemmed cocktail glasses. Balanced on the side of Karen's glass were small triangles of red watermelon, grapefruit and lime, and, on Chris's glass, a strawberry, slice of orange and sprig of fresh mint.

"Bottoms up!" said Karen. "Here's to the new me!"

"The new you!" said Chris and put the glass to her lips. "Oh, that's gorgeous!"

"Mmm . . . mine too. Even if there is no alcohol in it!"

Later, when they were seated at a quiet table for two, and their food order had been taken, Karen cleared her throat. "So, tell me. Have you heard much from Bernie since she left?"

"Not a thing since she went back to Melbourne. I guess she's busy."

"I see," said Karen and paused momentarily. "And before that?"

"Well, she sent round the most beautiful bouquet of flowers from that lovely flower shop in Broadway along with a lovely thank-you note."

"Yes, I saw them. They must've cost a fortune. A salve for her guilty conscience, I'd say."

"What guilty conscience? She didn't do anything wrong."

273

"Yes, she did," said Karen sharply. "Leaving your house with hardly a moment's notice. Treating the place like a hotel."

Chris shifted uncomfortably on the chestnut leather banquet-style seat and felt the colour rise in her cheeks. "I wish you would stop this, Karen," she said quietly.

"Stop what?" Karen turned her palms upturned in a gesture of innocence.

"You know what," said Chris, leaning into the table and eye-balling her sister. "Needling me about her all the time – making little comments. I know you don't like her very much but she's my friend. Maybe not my best friend – but still a friend. And if she's coming back to live in Ballyfergus, then it has got to stop."

Karen stared at her for a few moments and blushed. "Okay," she said, suddenly contrite. "You're right. I'm sorry. I won't do it again."

There was a momentary pause during which Chris took a sip of wine and Karen popped a marinated olive in her mouth.

"So," said Karen, chewing the olive on one side of her mouth, "have you actually seen her since she moved out?"

"No," said Chris. "We spoke on the phone a couple of times after she left. But she was busy getting the flat sorted and getting ready to go back to Australia."

"So you haven't actually seen the flat yet?"

"No."

Karen nodded her head thoughtfully. "So what does Paul have to say about it all?"

Chris shrugged. "Not much. Although I think even he would admit that things are better now she's gone. It is a wee bit of a strain having someone living under your roof for several weeks. I think it affected Paul more than me."

"How come?"

"Well, I think he's a lot more relaxed since she's gone. And things between us seem better."

"Are you and Paul having problems?" said Karen in astonishment.

"No, not problems really. Just . . . well, you know," said Chris, evasively. Even though she loved her sister dearly, she found it hard to talk about the difficulties in her marriage. She equated talking about them as tantamount to admitting her marriage was a failure. "Every marriage goes through its ups and downs, doesn't it?" she added lamely.

"But you and Paul – well, you're like rock. Solid, stable."

"I'm sure it's nothing that can't be sorted out," said Chris, more positively. "We've both been so busy lately. We're not spending enough time together, that's all. Things will calm down again."

"Are you sure?" said Karen doubtfully.

"Course I'm sure," said Chris with a brightness she did not feel inside. "We're fine. She scrabbled around for some diversionary tactic to get Karen's attention away from the subject. "Bernie's planning to come back in mid-July," she said, finding inspiration. "Same time as Raymond and Shona."

"Oh," said Karen, taking the bait, "that reminds me. We need to talk about their party. Now they're arriving here just after the Twelfth, on the fourteenth of July. They're staying for a few days with Mum and then they've got a house on short-term lease to move into."

"Already?"

"Yes, Raymond said he just went online and sorted it. It's amazing. You can do everything on the internet now."

"I'm not sure that was wise. He could've got one of us

to go look at it first," said Chris, slightly peeved that her brother had not called upon her for help, especially as she considered herself something of a property expert. "He should've asked us."

"Oh, I don't think there'll be a problem with the house," went on Karen, misinterpreting the cause of Chris's concern. "It's a complete renovation at Cairndale Heights. Everything's brand new and it's furnished. And it's only a stop-gap until they buy somewhere."

Just then they were interrupted by the waiter, a slim handsome guy with spiky brown hair and a rugged five-o'clock shadow, with two plates of food in his hands. Karen put her hands up to the sides of her face and mouthed "Gorgeous." She wasn't referring to the food and Chris had to work hard to stop herself bursting out laughing like a schoolgirl.

When he was gone Chris teased, "And I thought you only had eyes for Tony."

"I do," said Karen, seriously. "Sure you know I'm only kidding about. But you have to have a laugh now and again, don't you?"

"You sure do," said Chris and they ate their starters of Thai salmon fishcakes in relative silence.

"Delicious," said Karen. She laid her knife and fork on the cleared plate, and then resumed their earlier conversation. "Now about the party. Do you think we should make it a surprise?"

"Oh, I don't know about that," said Chris, doubtfully. "I'm not sure that would be fair on Shona. She doesn't know our family and it might be a bit much pulling a surprise party out of the hat when she's only just moved here and met Raymond's family. In fact she'll most likely be meeting most of them for the first time at the party."

"Agreed."

"And maybe we should call it a 'Welcome to Ballyfergus' party, rather than an engagement party."

Karen paused while the waiter cleared their plates. "Why's that?"

"It'll only be our side of the family that's invited, not Shona's. She might feel a bit put out that her family's not there."

"We could invite them."

"We don't know them. They'd have to come over from Scotland. We'd have to get them somewhere to stay. The whole thing would be getting a bit out of hand then, don't you think?"

"Yeah," said Karen with a heavy sigh. "I guess you're right."

"There's something else, Karen. I know you said you wanted to host it at your house but that's only four weeks after your operation. I think you might be taking on a bit much. Why don't you let me do it at ours?"

"I hadn't thought, but you're probably right, Chris. You wouldn't mind?"

"No at all."

"That's settled then."

"Right," said Karen, fumbling in her handbag, "Let's have a look at dates." She pulled out a slim volume. It was predominantly pink and covered in drawings of handbags and glamorous high-heeled shoes.

Chris pulled out her diary – a solid little plain black book made by Moleskine, exactly the same as last year's and the year before that. She smiled. The diaries said much about the difference in their personalities.

"How about the end of July?" Karen proposed. "That would give them a couple of weeks to get settled."

"Sounds good."

"How about the last Sunday in the month? Round 'bout three in the afternoon?"

"Okay. We've nothing on then. And it's far enough away that if we issue the invitations now, most people should be free. Apart from those away on holiday."

"Right. I'll get the invitations printed up at the nursery," said Karen. "Daphne'll do it – she's great at that sort of stuff. I'll get her to put little pictures on them – you know the sort of thing. Little cartoon drawings you can download from the internet."

"Sounds great," said Chris. "Now what about guests? Shall we make a list so we don't forget anyone?"

"Good idea," said Karen and Chris turned to a blank page at the back of her diary. "Let's start with Mum and you and me, obviously," Karen went on, "and our families . . ."

They spent a few minutes brainstorming the list and then the waiter came with the main courses.

"Who's having the oven-roast smoked Cassler bacon chop with honey and mustard-crushed potatoes and chutney?"

Karen peered suspiciously at the plate in his hand and then her face brightened. "Oh, you mean the pork chop and mash? Yes, that's me," she said, unintentionally crushing the restaurant's pretensions.

Chris hid a smile thinking that it was such fun to go places with Karen.

"And you're having the baked goat's cheese tart, Madam?" said the waiter and Chris nodded.

"Bon appetite!" said Chris and lifted up her knife and fork. She was about to eat and then abruptly hesitated, with the cutlery poised in mid-air. "There's just one more thing, Karen."

"What's that?"

"About the guest list. Bernie's going to be on it."

Twelve

It was midday when Paul left the surgery to undertake his rounds for the day, pleased to be released from the stuffy atmosphere of the surgery. He held the worn handle of his black leather doctor's case firmly in his hand. The traditional doctor's bag had been a gift from Chris nearly fifteen years ago – hand-crafted from top-of-the-range Italian leather with solid brass fittings. It was the only outwardly visible symbol of his profession and he had always carried it with pride.

He opened the door of the car, tossed the bag in the passenger seat and wondered if, a year from now, he would still be a doctor in this practice. Would he still be practising as a doctor at all? Would he still be living in Ballyfergus? He got in the driver's seat and closed the door, then sat in the car park and contemplated his future.

If, only a few weeks ago, someone had suggested to Paul that he would walk out of his marriage and home he would have laughed in their face. But he had fallen in love and love, as the famous song says, changes everything. And he found this to be no exaggeration.

He saw his existence and the wider world around him in an entirely different light. Instead of viewing his future as sliding inexorably towards a comfortable middle age and predictable retirement, he found himself at the precipice of a new life. An exciting and unknown future lay ahead of him, full of possibilities and potential for self-fulfilment. He would shed his old life like a chrysalis and enter this new one, hand-in-hand with the woman he now regarded as his soul mate. He felt, for the first time in many years, that his life had a purpose above the mundane and that Bernie would help him discover it.

Death had nipped her heels and she had the scars to prove it. She had survived both breast and ovarian cancer and his heart ached for the suffering she had endured and the legacy of the illness. She would not let him see her scars even though he had assured her that they would not repulse him. And her resultant infertility was so unfair – he thought it a tragedy that a woman as loving as she would never be a mother. He wanted to take care of her and give her the best life he could. And he pushed from his mind the possibility that the cancer might come back. She had had no reoccurrence in over four years and that was definitely a very good sign, but with cancer you just never knew. He would get her registered at the practice as soon as possible and make sure she was referred to the best cancer specialist in Northern Ireland.

He wondered if this brush with death explained Bernie's enormous zest for life, her wonder at everyday miracles that the rest of the world took for granted, and her lack of cynicism. Her enthusiasm for life and her energy could be mistaken as naivety but she wasn't naive. She had seen as much of life as the rest of us to be jaded and sceptical – she simply chose not to be. She chose to see the good, look on the bright side, she saw the glass half-full.

And that approach was refreshing.

What he loved most about her was her open-mindedness, her receptiveness to the new and unconventional. He admired her willingness to challenge convention and her positive outlook on life. She often said that life was not a rehearsal and, coming from her, it did not sound like a worn cliché, but wisdom of the ages. She had made him realise that money wasn't everything and that a life without love was a travesty. She encouraged his passion for wine – not dismissing or belittling it as he felt Chris did – even to the point where he had seriously toyed with the idea of making a career out of it. He even loved her fondness for making love in the near-darkness so retaining an element of mystery and elusiveness. She knew how to make him want her.

Bernie had been in Australia for nearly a month now, clearing out her flat, selling her possessions and making arrangements to move her business over here. He missed her desperately. He missed the feeling of her fragile body in his arms and the simple joy of looking upon her face. He yearned to make love to her, but his desire transcended the mere physical. She had worried that their being apart would make him forget her, make him love her less. In fact, as he told her on the phone last night during a middle-of-the night phone call made while Chris was fast asleep upstairs, the very opposite had happened.

In her absence he had learned to overcome the reservations that had held him back before – duty to Chris and concern for the children. He was ready now to make the commitment that she asked of him. He was ready to leave his wife. But he was not ready to do that without Bernie. They agreed that he would break the news to his family on her return to Northern Ireland. And the reason for this, though he did not admit it to Bernie, was that he was scared.

He was terrified of Chris's wrath and afraid of the disappointment on the children's faces when he told them. He dreaded the scandal that would follow his actions and the fact that he, an upright pillar of the community, would become fodder for office gossip across Ballyfergus. Though he knew it to be the inevitable fall-out of what he was about to do, Paul feared the loss of contact and friendship with Karen and Tony and even his mother-in-law, of whom he was fond.

But most of all he was afraid of afterwards, of being alone. Of opening the door to an empty dismal flat or hotel room, devoid of the warmth of human companionship. He needed Bernie's reassurance and support to go through with this. He needed to know that, when it was all over, she would be there, waiting for him with open arms and a welcome heart. He needed someone to tell him that, in following his heart, he had done the right thing.

His visit to the solicitor's office in Belfast the week before before had been a bit of a reality check, but he tried not to let that dampen his enthusiasm.

In seeking out a solicitor to advise him on his forthcoming divorce, he had had to avoid the firms in Ballyfergus (naturally), and all firms with which Chris had a connection. He was also unable to ask friends and colleagues for advice as no-one yet knew of his dark secret. That left him at the mercy of the Law Society for Northern Ireland's website.

A search had thrown up seventy-three firms in Belfast alone practising family law. In the end, he chose McCartney and Mann because it was one of the oldest (established

1823), one of the biggest and it had its own professional, and impressive sounding, website. On the phone he had explained his requirements to the receptionist and was directed to the unlikely sounding Heidi Rice, senior partner specialising in family law. They spoke briefly on the phone, and an appointment was made.

The offices of McCartney and Mann on Bridge Street in Belfast city centre were sleek and professional. Housed in modern purpose-built premises over three floors they made a good first impression, reassuring him that he had made a wise choice.

Heidi Rice was a handsome, immaculately dressed lady in her late fifties of medium height with steel-coloured hair and piercing blue eyes. She wore discreet diamond earrings and a handsome Rolex on her wrist. She was also plain-speaking and to the point.

"So, Dr Quinn," she said over the top of her silver-rimmed spectacles, her black-suited elbows resting on the mahogany table, "I understand you are here to consult me today because you wish to petition for divorce."

"That's right."

"Now first of all, may I ask who's representing your wife?" she said, looking down at the Montblanc fountain pen in her hand which was poised over a sheet of clean unlined paper. A small diamond pendant dangled on a fine chain from her neck, between the folds of her white silk blouse. He paused and she added encouragingly, without looking up, "We must make sure there is no conflict of interest."

"My wife doesn't know yet."

She looked at him over the top of her spectacles and said, "She doesn't know what yet?"

"That I'm here. That I want a divorce. She doesn't know any of it."

Heidi frowned. "Are you separated?"

"No. We live in a house we own jointly with our two teenage children."

Heidi Rice put the lid on her pen with great deliberation and laid the pen down on the writing pad carefully so that the nib was pointing at her, the little Montblanc symbol of a snowy mountain at Paul. It was the first time in his adult life that he felt intimidated.

"I see, Dr Quinn," she said slowly, framing her hands, joined at the fingertips, into an arch. "I wonder if your visit here today isn't a bit premature." He blinked and opened his mouth to speak but she went on, "Divorce is an extremely unpleasant, very expensive, frustrating and heartbreaking process, especially when children are involved. And, like marriage," she continued, sounding more like a priest or minister than a lawyer, "Divorce is not a state into which one should enter lightly." She paused to allow her words to sink in. "Divorce should be a last resort when all other avenues to save a marriage have been exhausted."

"There is no hope of saving this marriage. I've met someone else," he said firmly.

"I see," she said and paused, regarding him critically all the time. "Nonetheless, I would urge you to share your intentions with your wife as soon as possible. Apart from the fact that there may be hope of a reconciliation –"

He shook his head but she ignored him.

"– it is crucial that we find out if she will agree to the divorce. If she does, and you admit to adultery, then matters should progress speedily. If she does not agree, then things will prove much more difficult."

He frowned and rubbed his chin.

"You see," she continued. "The court will only grant a divorce if it can be proved that the marriage has irretrievably broken down. As you are still living together, you must prove one of two things: that adultery has taken place and that because of it, your wife can no longer bear to live with you."

"I don't know how she'll react."

"Exactly. Alternatively you may prove that your partner has behaved unreasonably. Am I right in assuming that this doesn't apply in your case?"

He nodded grimly and she moved on quickly.

"So you see, your wife's view on this matter is critical. If she absolutely refuses to agree, you may have to live apart for two years before a court will grant you a divorce."

"That long!"

"I'm afraid so."

"My wife's a reasonable woman. I can't see her refusing just out of spite."

"You might be surprised, Dr Quinn. Divorce can bring out the very worst in people."

"I intend to tell her," he said. "I plan on telling her just as soon as Bernie returns from Australia."

"Bernie?"

He felt his face redden with embarrassment and was annoyed that he was unable to stop it. "The other party," he said euphemistically, not knowing what else to call her. His lover? His mistress?

"I see. Now, that aspect aside, there are many matters to be considered. What age are your children?"

He told her and she said, "Legally then they're adults."

"I intend to fulfil my responsibilities towards them," said

Paul quickly. "My daughter's been accepted at Edinburgh university to study medicine so she's going to need financial support for several years to come. And my son, though he's working, will need help to get on his feet."

She nodded and said, "And then there's the matter of financial assets, including the family home . . ."

He had left Heidi Rice's office forty minutes later with a black cloud hanging over him. He couldn't fault her professionalism, knowledge or experience as she guided him thorough the various miserable stages of the divorce process. And, though he had not wanted to hear it, he knew that her advice to seek a reconciliation, stemming from long and bitter experience working in the field, was sound.

Her advice to remain in the family home at all costs was particularly unwelcome. This he could not do, even if it jeopardised his position. He had promised Bernie and he could not go back on that promise. More than that, he had promised himself that he would find the courage to go through with this. Staying in the house with Chris, after he had told her, just wasn't an option.

* * *

Paul started up the car engine and set off on his rounds. By the time he finished, it was late afternoon and, wearied by his overwrought emotions, he phoned the office to say he was making a late call on Derek Beattie. This was a lie of course, but like all good lies it was based on a grain of truth. He had already visited Derek that morning and left him weak but comfortable in the care of his sweet, uncomplaining wife. They had been married for nearly forty years and still doted on each other. He worried how

Doris would cope without her husband.

Back at the house, no-one was at home apart from Murphy who started yelping with excitement as soon as he heard the front door open. Paul went through to the utility room where the dog was effectively caged and let him out. Murphy leapt up on Paul, his little front paws only reaching as high as his knees, his entire back end wiggling with excitement.

"No," said Paul firmly and pushed the dog to the floor.

Then he let him out into the garden and watched him frolic on the back lawn for a few moments. Murphy went over to the pond and tried to catch the fish with his paw, his latest trick. It was only a matter of time, thought Paul, before the dog would fall in; if no-one was around to rescue him the silly mutt might drown.

Chris would have Murphy of course, not that he minded. The puppy, cute as he was, was nearly as much work, at this stage anyway, as a small child. He required feeding, walking, cleaning up after, chewed everything in sight and demanded constant attention. Yappy and over-excited all the time, Paul found him irritating and refused point blank to clean up his messes. So far Chris had done all of the work associated with having a puppy in the house and it was she who had signed him up for training classes.

He filled a glass with water from the tap and drank it standing at the sink. He looked at his watch – it was one o'clock in the morning in Melbourne just now and he imagined Bernie asleep in her bed. How he wished he was with her.

He turned the television in the family room on and sat down and flicked through the channels. All he could find was the usual anodyne afternoon fare of chat shows, game shows, cookery programmes, a re-run of the seventies detective series, Colombo, and old black-and-white movies.

Unable to settle, he went upstairs to the bedroom where he began to clear out his wardrobe. Unbeknownst to Chris he had been reviewing every corner of their home with a critical eye – it gave him something to do while Bernie was away, while he was waiting for his new life to begin. And he had been stashing away in a box in the attic the essential papers that he would need to take with him – his passport, birth certificate, medical school certificates and photographs.

He had no great attachment to anything in the house, apart from the pieces he had inherited from his parents and the contents of his cellar. The apartment he and Bernie would be living in, in the short-tem at least, had no storage space for wine. He could take some of the younger, drink-me-now bottles with him and stack them in the kitchen of the new flat but, if he tried to take it all, he was in danger of ruining good wine by exposing it to unsuitable storage conditions. He would have to leave the bulk of it here and trust that Chris would be fair about it when it came to dividing up their assets – the wine was worth several thousand pounds. He couldn't imagine her doing anything malicious like smashing it all up. Still, it might be wise to put a lock on the cellar, just in case . . .

He was still in the bedroom when he heard her come in, late again. Sam McIlwaine was working the staff to the bone although Chris didn't seem to mind. In fact she seemed happier than she'd been for some time – then again she always did like a challenge. She positively thrived on hard work. It was funny, he thought to himself, how only a few weeks ago he might have resented her working these long hours. And now he couldn't care less.

He heard her steps on the stairs and busied himself in the wardrobe. On the floor by his feet were two black bin bags, nearly full of his cast-offs. He took a well-worn cashmere-blend jacket off a wooden hanger, folded it roughly and placed it in one of the bags. Chris came into the bedroom, said hello and dropped her handbag on the floor. Then she came over to him and kissed him chastely on the cheek. He did not return the gesture.

"Did you have a good day?" he said.

"Yes, fine. And you?"

"The usual."

"What are you up to? Clearing out again, are we?" said Chris and there was something unpleasant, critical even, in her tone that immediately got his back up. He chose to ignore her comment.

"Did you get home early?" she said, as she peeled off her jacket, skirt and blouse. Stripped to her underwear, her fine body on display, he was surprised to find he was not aroused. He no longer had any interest in Chris, sexually, or otherwise. All he could think about was Bernie. It was like a fever eating him up. He longed to make love to her.

"Yes, I'd had enough for one day," he replied, focusing on the clothes inside the wardrobe.

"Tough day?"

"No more so than usual. I just decided to come home and do this. I've lost a bit of weight," he said. "A lot of these clothes don't fit me any more." Paul had not realised before how emotional angst could make the pounds literally fall off.

"Last week it was the garage, the week before the study, now it's the wardrobe. What's got into you?" she said.

"Don't you think it's time we had a good clear-out?"

"Well, yes," she said, and he was pleased that his reply seemed to, temporarily at least, have stumped her. "It's just you're not usually so – so house proud," she observed. "It's usually me that has to initiate these things. Still, it makes a nice change. It's nice to know you can still surprise me after all these years of marriage."

She sounded almost happy. He felt a lump in his throat, a sadness not for what he was about to lose, but for what was already lost – the love he had once shared with Chris.

He realised that she was waiting for a reply.

"Well, there you go," he said lamely, unable to think of a witty retort. All he could think about was that the next time he surprised her, her reaction would not be so calm.

"Paul," she said, "There's something I've been meaning to talk to you about."

"What's that?" he said, arranging on one side of the wardrobe all the essential clothes he intended to take with him when he left. The others would have to wait until later.

"Has Hannah said anything to you about having doubts about doing medicine?"

"What?" he said, spinning round to face her, his attention now fully captured. She was dressed in casual red linen cut-off trousers and a white linen sleeveless shirt. Chris always wore elegant clothes.

"You heard me."

"No, she hasn't said anything to me," he said, and his heart sank. Hannah was such a bright girl, so suited to medicine. Surely she wasn't going to follow in her brother's footsteps and fail to fulfil her potential? "Why?" he demanded fearfully. "Has she said something to you?"

"No, but Karen told me the other day, when we were

up in Belfast, that Hannah had expressed some doubts to her."

"Karen!" he said dismissively, "Sometimes that sister of yours has some funny ideas. What's she doing sticking her nose into Hannah's business anyway?"

"She wasn't sticking her nose in, she was taking an interest," said Chris loyally. "All the same, like you, I think it unlikely that Hannah said she was having second thoughts. But I wonder if we should talk to her?"

"Of course. Let's do that," said Paul, relieved that the source of the rumour was unreliable. He was very fond of Karen but she was a bit too emotional and apt to extrapolate unintended meanings from the most banal of conversations.

Chris went downstairs and later, when Hannah came in, they both confronted her in the kitchen.

"What's this nonsense your Aunt Karen's been telling your mother about you not wanting to do medicine?" said Paul.

Hannah looked at her feet, encased in chunky biker boots and leaned with both hands behind her back against the island unit. "I never said that."

"There, what did I tell you?" said Paul triumphantly to Chris, but her brow remained furrowed.

"Are you worried that you might not get the grades you need?" said Chris gently. Hannah stared at them with her black-rimmed eyes, her gaze moving quickly from one to the other. She bit her bottom lip, the way she used to do when she was a little girl, worried about something, and nodded.

"Oh darling, you don't need to worry about that," said Paul, cross with himself for doubting Hannah's commitment to a career in medicine, even for a second. He put his arm across her shoulders and squeezed her awkwardly. "I am absolutely confident that you have done brilliantly."

She gave him a brave smile.

"And even if you haven't – not that you will have – but even if you did, it's too late to do anything about it," said Chris brightly. "So worrying really is a complete waste of time."

"Yeah, I guess you're right," said Hannah and, apparently dropping the subject from her thoughts, she knelt down and tickled Murphy's tummy. Immediately he went into a state of ecstasy, stretching and snapping the air with his sharp, jagged teeth, soaking up the attention like a sponge.

And thus reassured, Paul put the entire incident out of his mind.

Thirteen

Four days and three hours before Bernie was due back, Paul left work, got in the car, drove to Karen's house and parked outside on the street. She would not be expecting him but he viewed the call as a pseudo-professional one, even though she wasn't one of his patients. It was just over a week since her operation and though Paul did not approve of what she had done, he knew that major surgery like this was never a pleasant experience and rarely completely straightforward. He did not support cosmetic surgery except in exceptional cases where an obvious disfigurement was affecting a patient's quality of life. He did not approve of major surgery on women, like Karen, who were too lazy or weak-willed to do what was necessary to regain their figures after childbirth. Or women who simply could not accept that childbirth would change forever the shape of their bodies.

It was a bit of a lottery, he would admit to that; some women were genetically blessed and regained their figures effortlessly. Others were not. But they all expected to look like Kate Moss even after two, three, even four children.

He also wanted to make sure that Karen was all right. He did not know, either, when he might see her again. His bags were all but packed. He was ready to leave Chris. He did not doubt Karen's loyalty to her sister – he was certain that she would never speak to him again once she knew about Bernie. He remembered many happy informal evenings spent drinking in the cosy kitchen at Castlerock and knew that he would miss her.

He rang the doorbell and waited. It seemed a long time until she answered the door, wearing loose grey jersey clothing and stooping slightly like an old woman. Her hair, normally so carefully groomed, was untidy but she wore full make-up and a brave smile.

"Come in, Paul," she said, when she saw him. "I wasn't expecting you to call."

"Well," he said, glancing down at his doctor's bag, "someone has to make sure you're being looked after properly." He followed her inside and, realising that the house was unnaturally quiet, asked, "Where's Tony and the kids?"

"He dropped the kids off at the nursery for a bit so that he could do the shopping in peace," said Karen, leading him into the lounge. "Thank God for the nursery, that's all I can say. It's been a godsend this last week. And so have Chris and you, having the kids over for tea three times."

"That was Chris's doing. And you know we loved having them. Hannah and Finn really enjoyed playing with them. One of Finn's friends was round and the two of them played rough and tumble with Jack until he was exhausted and begging them to stop."

Karen laughed and immediately winced with pain. "Ow, I must stop doing that."

"Are you in a lot of pain?"

"It's pretty bad," she admitted. "You think you're

prepared. You listen to everything they tell you but it still doesn't sink in, does it? Especially when it's something you want so badly you think you'll put up with anything to achieve it. You don't mind if I lie down like this?" she said, arranging herself in a supine position on the sofa with her legs on the armrest, elevated above her body. "Keeping my legs up above my head's supposed to help with the swelling. It hurts if I sit up normally and, if I stand for any length of time, the pressure builds up and I feel as if the wound will burst."

"Do you think it's been worth it then?"

"I honestly can't answer that, Paul. If you'd asked me that question three days ago I'd have said no way. But things are settling down now and the pain's not so bad. And I can see that my tummy is much, much flatter and that horrible flap of skin has gone."

He sat opposite her in an armchair and said, "The pain will pass."

"Oh, I hope so. It's not nearly as bad as it was, though. The first few days were terrible. At the hospital they made me get up and walk every hour."

"That's to prevent blood clots."

"I know, but it was just agony. And I was crying all the time. I felt so guilty when I realised what I had done. I missed Tony and the children," she said, her eyes filling up with tears. "I realised I could've died and that I had spent all this money on myself. I feel so selfish."

Paul, used to listening, shifted in his seat. "Those feelings are only natural after major surgery, Karen. Your body's undergone a severe trauma. You've got to give yourself time to recover properly. And don't be so hard on yourself."

She sniffed, holding back the tears. "It's still unbelievably sore. The corset they gave me to wear feels so incredibly uncomfortable. It's hard to breathe and my stomach feels all tight and distended as though it's filling up with fluid or blood."

"Have the drains been taken out?" he asked, masking his concern at her comment.

"Yesterday. I can't believe what they pulled out of me. You should've seen them, Paul. There was one on each side and there must've been two foot of perforated tube inside me on either side. The pain was excruciating."

Even Paul, used to gruesome sights in the surgery, winced at her graphic description. He thought how silly she was to have subjected herself to this. He hoped for her sake that it was a success. The problem with so many of these cosmetic surgeries was that people were often disappointed with the results.

"Do you mind if I take a look?"

"Not at all – you're a doctor, aren't you? And to be honest, Paul, I could use some reassurance that everything's okay." He came over to her and knelt on the floor and she rolled up her T-shirt to reveal a stomach rounded like that of a heavily pregnant woman. It was sheathed in a tight beige-coloured corset, spotted with dark blood from the drainholes.

"Do you mind if I peel this back a bit?" he said, anxious to check for himself that nothing was amiss.

"Go ahead," she said and sucked in her breath when he peeled back the corset.

The injury was gruesome. Her belly was swollen and yellow with bruising and, underneath the bandages, her reconfigured belly button bristled with blue stitches. Across her lower abdomen was a jagged, brutal-looking, bright pink scar, nearly sixteen inches long that stretched from one hipbone to the other. The stitches had started to dissolve and the wound was held together by a thin line of surgical tape. He wondered if she realised what a large and unsightly scar she would be left with.

He checked carefully for early signs of skin necrosis, looking for discolouration or blistering of the skin. He worked hard to keep the distaste from showing in his face. His revulsion stemmed not from the actual wounds – he had seen worse – but from then fact that they had been so unnecessarily inflicted.

But thankfully the flesh around the wounds looked pink and healthy. He touched her stomach, checking for patches of redness and heat, signs of possible infection, and looked for indications of haematoma – bleeding under the abdominal tissue – and seromas or pockets of fluid collection. But there was nothing that he could see to cause concern.

"Well," she said anxiously, "what do you think? Does it look all right?"

"I'm no expert on surgical procedures, Karen, but everything looks absolutely fine to me. I think he's done a fairly neat job too," he said, examining more closely the stitching round her bellybutton.

He was impressed with the surgeon's handiwork. As a student doctor he had shown flair with a scalpel himself, having the necessary combination of a steady hand and even steadier nerve. He wondered where his career would have taken him if he had opted to become a surgeon rather than a general practitioner. He could've become a cosmetic surgeon like Dr Mezz, he thought wryly, and made himself a small fortune operating on vulnerable women like Karen.

"Oh, thank God," she said and visibly relaxed. "I can't tell you what a weight that is off my mind."

"The level of bruising and swelling is consistent with an injury on this scale," he continued. "The swelling should start to come down in the next few weeks and then you'll notice a big difference. It's just going to take your body time to recover, Karen."

He put the bandages and corset back in place gingerly so as not to inflict unnecessary pain.

"Well, I'd better be going," he said and stood up. "I've got my rounds to do."

"Come here, Paul," she said and held his right hand in hers. "Thanks for coming round. You are such a honey. You've really put my mind at rest, you know."

"I'm glad," he said and he gave her hand a squeeze. "You know you are my favourite sister-in-law."

"I'm your only sister-in-law, Paul," she said with a big smile. She started to laugh, and then checked herself with a hand on her belly. "Better not!"

"You're still the best," he said, but the words did not come out in the light-hearted tone he'd aimed for. He felt a lump in his throat.

"Are you all right?" she said, looking at him quizzically.

"Fine. Absolutely fine," he said brightly. "I'll see you later, Karen."

At the doorway into the hall he stopped and looked back. She had picked up the remote for the TV and was about to switch it on.

"Karen?" he said and she looked at him with the control still pointed at the TV.

"You and Tony mean a lot to me. Over the years, well . . . let's just say that I regard you as my friends. I hope you never forget that. And it's been my privilege to know you."

Her hand fell to her side, the TV suddenly forgotten.

She stared at him in disbelief, the corners of her mouth twitching like she had a nervous tic. He knew from her character that she would be torn between the urge to laugh (was he teasing her?) and the desire not to offend him (don't tell me he's serious!). She would at the very least be wondering what on earth had got in to him. Fond of Karen and Tony as he was, he never spoke to them on an emotional level like this.

"Are you pulling my leg, Paul Quinn? For if you're not, you've got me worried. That's the sort of thing you'd say to someone you didn't think you'd ever see again. Someone who was about to die!"

"I'm not pulling your leg, Karen," he said with a sad smile. "And you're not going to die." Then he walked out of the house and pulled the door firmly shut behind him.

Fourteen

It was ten o'clock on Friday morning – time for coffee break. Declan handed Chris a mug of steaming tea.

"Oh, thanks very much. You're a star," she said.

Today Declan's hair was so heavily gelled that it stood up in dark spikes all over his head like a hedgehog. The girls in the office loved him to bits – he joined in their talk about hairdressers and clothes and he was funny and kind too. He was also a bright kid who could have done better at school – if he'd not been so badly bullied because of his overt femininity. He left school as soon as he could with eight GCSEs under his belt, four of them grade A. It was a shame, thought Chris, for he was intelligent and certainly capable of higher level study.

Chris made a point of joining the staff for a fifteen-minute coffee break every morning. Mostly they just lazily scanned the papers and swapped idle gossip. But it was an important ritual and one that Chris valued in keeping the staff motivated as a team. It also made for a pleasant and friendly place to work. And happy workers were productive workers as she'd pointed out firmly to Sam McIlwaine when he'd queried the custom.

She turned her attention to *The Ballyfergus Courier* and

said, to no-one in particular, "It looks like we're getting another chance."

"What did you say, Chris?" said Rose, wiping the flaky remains of a croissant from her lap onto the floor.

"It says in *The Courier* that, because of the number of objections, the planning authorities are going to call a public meeting about Tesda. We still might stop them yet!" she answered, the fire of opposition reigniting in her breast. Based on events in other towns across the United Kingdom, she suspected that the campaign to stop Tesda was ultimately doomed. But she wasn't going to give in without a fight.

"What's that?" said Sam, coming up unexpectedly behind Chris's desk, and peering over her shoulder. He wasn't wearing his suit jacket and she was unsettled by both his proximity (so close she could smell his aftershave and feel the heat radiating from his body) and his presence in the room.

In spite of his genuine efforts to integrate, Chris knew he still felt like an outsider. And she sensed that the staff were not as relaxed with him in the room as they were before he entered. Which was a shame and a bit unfair really because he was trying very hard to get along with everyone.

She pointed to the relevant article and said, "It's brilliant news. There's been a big campaign locally –"

"Spearheaded by Chris," interjected Rose.

"And others," said Chris, glaring at Rose. "Anyway, there's a campaign against Tesda building a supermarket in Ballyfergus. The main objection is the effect it'll have on local businesses by drawing money away from the independent shops and potentially turning Ballyfergus

Main Street into a ghost town. And there's the environmental impact too. They want to build a four-storey car park. Can you imagine? In Ballyfergus?"

Sam leaned on the table to read the article, his big hand spread-eagled right beside Chris's. She had a sudden urge to touch him and quickly removed her hands, stowing them safely under the desk, out of harm's way.

"I couldn't agree with you more," said Sam. "The big chains have too much power over both suppliers and customers. Let me know if there's anything I can do to help."

"You mean that?" said Chris, surprised.

He looked her in the eye and nodded.

The phone rang and Mandy answered. She held the phone to her chest and said "It's for you, Chris. Karen. I'll just transfer it."

Chris put her hand on the phone waiting for it to ring. Sam straightened up, slid his hands into his suit trouser pockets, and said, "Can I have a minute when you're ready?" Then he went back into his office and Chris put the phone to her ear.

"What's the plan for tomorrow then?" said Chris, referring to Raymond and Shona's scheduled arrival in Ballyfergus the following day.

"I'm not sure yet," said Karen. "They arrive in London at seven-fifteen in the morning and then they're hoping to catch an eleven o'clock flight to Belfast International."

"That could be cutting it fine," said Chris.

"Well, hopefully everything will go to plan."

"So they'll be here about lunchtime?"

"All being well, though I imagine they'll be absolutely shattered. Mum suggested that we pop round for a quick sandwich at lunchtime and then give them the rest of the day in peace."

"Does she mean all of us, Paul and Tony as well and the kids?"

"I suppose so, if they're around. But I think so long as you and I are there, they can always meet the others another time."

"Wait a minute," said Chris. "Who's picking them up from the airport?"

"Raymond says he'll pick up a hire car."

"Oh, that doesn't seem right. I can go and collect them or I'm sure Paul would."

"It's okay," said Karen. "Raymond's cool about it. I volunteered Tony's services as a chauffeur but Raymond said he'd need the car here anyway – until he gets round to buying one."

"If you're sure," said Chris doubtfully.

"Honestly, he's very happy to drive."

"Oh, I'm so excited," said Chris, and her stomach did a few somersaults in anticipation of seeing her brother. "It's been over two years since I last saw Raymond and I keep trying to imagine what this Shona's going to be like. He never did send a photo of her, did he?"

"You know Raymond. He said he would send pictures, but they never materialised."

"Never mind. We get to see her in the flesh tomorrow. I wonder if she's pretty."

"We'll have to wait and see," said Karen and she cleared her throat with a raspy little cough, a technique she had perfected since the operation. Proper guttural coughing, and sneezing for that matter, was agony for her.

"Are you sure you're up for it, Karen?" said Chris,

suddenly realising that it was less than a fortnight since her sister's surgery. "You mustn't push yourself, now."

"Oh, I feel much better today," she said brightly. "I'm still getting some pain now and again and a weird burning sensation round my abdominal muscles, but nothing like it was before and nothing that can't be managed with painkillers. The worst is having to wear this horrible corset, but that's only for another two to three weeks."

It was great to hear Karen talking positively after being so depressed and emotional in the early days after the operation. More than once Chris had to bite her tongue when she'd seen the pitiful state her sister was in immediately after the operation. And she was surprised at how angry she had felt with Karen. But those feelings had passed and now she was just grateful that her sister had come through it unscathed and that, though it was still early days, she seemed happy with the result.

"Dr Mezz said it was okay for me to start moving about a bit more – so I'm sure I can manage an hour or so over at Mum's. Anyway, you know yourself what you're capable of, don't you?"

"If you're tired I can take you straight home. Anyway, I don't suppose we'll stay too long. They'll be wanting a hot bath and bed, I should imagine, after that long journey. I'll pick you up round about one, shall I?"

"If that suits Mum, it sounds great to me," said Karen. "See you then!"

Chris replaced the handset and smiled to herself. Raymond was finally coming home to settle, making the family complete again. That would've pleased Dad – he had been proud of Raymond and his success, they all were, but he had missed him dreadfully when he went to work overseas. And she had a new sister-in-law to get to know and a wedding to look forward to. Maybe even, in time, new nieces and nephews. Chris's heart swelled with happiness at the thought.

The children were happy and doing well. Hannah appeared to have survived her exams unscathed and Chris believed firmly that, in spite of her daughter's fears, she had done well. Come September she would be off building a new life in Edinburgh. Chris knew she would miss her dreadfully, but there was also a wonderful sense of satisfaction in seeing her take her first real steps to independence and adulthood. And Finn, when his father wasn't nagging him about his career choice, seemed happy and well-adjusted. What more could a mother ask?

Karen was going to be fine after that horrible operation - it was only now that it was over, that Chris realised how worried she had been about her sister. And already she could detect a difference in Karen's attitude to her body — she was happy to show off her visibly flatter tummy (under clothes) whereas before she had spent all her time trying to conceal it. Chris was genuinely pleased for her.

And Chris's relationship with Paul seemed to have improved slightly. True, they weren't sharing any more time together than before (in spite of her resolution to address this) but he seemed contentedly busy, both at home and work. As was she.

In fact, she was enjoying work more than ever before. Now that the stress and worry of the buy-out was behind them, she was starting to enjoy working with Sam McIlwaine. He treated her like an equal and sought her opinion on every matter of consequence in the office. With his sharp mind and mesmerising energy he was stimulating to be around. She found herself looking forward to the days he was in the office and disappointed when he was not.

She no longer denied to herself that she fancied him, but the attraction was primarily mental, rather than physical. Right now there was no-one in the world she preferred to converse with than him. And she found that she wanted to learn more about him as a person and his private life, not that the opportunity to discuss such matters ever arose in the office environment. Perhaps it was the element of the unknown about him that made him so intriguing to her.

It had crossed her mind that she was being unfaithful to Paul in thought, if not in deed. But, she assured herself, so long as she kept it that way no harm could come of it. Perhaps that was why she and Paul were rubbing along better these days – with Sam she enjoyed the intellectual meeting of minds that for some reason now eluded her and Paul. And she did not, therefore, expect so much from her marriage.

At home they were polite to each other, and much kinder than before, but increasingly distant. And neither, it seemed to Chris, had any great desire to resolve matters. Before this would have bothered her a great deal, now she accepted it as part of the ebb and flow of a long marriage. She could honestly say that she was, if not exactly happy, then content in her marriage. And that, she reasoned, was as much as anyone could expect after twenty long years together.

The only cloud on the horizon was Bernie. She had not forgotten that Bernie was due to return to Ballyfergus tomorrow. In fact she found it hard to put the thought out of her mind. It was possible that she was arriving on the same plane from London as Raymond and Shona. She wondered who might be picking her up from the airport. Her brother perhaps?

Bernie had not been in contact to let Chris know her plans, nor had she asked for a lift. But perhaps, Chris thought guiltily, she should've offered. It would've been the kind thing to do. She was surprised that Paul had not suggested it. Mind you, he had probably forgotten all about Bernie.

Chris's feelings towards Bernie were complex and confused. On the face of it she had no reason to dislike her, yet she felt uneasy about her coming back to Ballyfergus. She wished, rather unkindly, that she would go back to Australia and stay there.

"Chris?" It was Lynette's voice, wakening her from her thoughts.

"Sam was wanting a word, remember?"

"Oh, thanks for reminding me. It had gone straight out of my head," said Chris. She got up and went to his office and knocked on the open door. His silver head was bent over his desk. He looked up and, when he saw it was her, he smiled broadly. "Come on in, Chris, You don't need to knock."

She sat down on the chair opposite him. She crossed her legs, then uncrossed them again and smoothed her skirt over her knee.

"Everything all right?" said Sam.

"Yes, of course," she said with a shrug, wondering what he was alluding to.

"The phone call?"

"Oh, that," she said with a sort of relieved grin. "It was just my sister Karen making arrangements for my brother and his fiancée's homecoming tomorrow."

"Have they been away somewhere?"

"Raymond's been living abroad – he's worked in the Far East for years. He visits every couple of years or so. But the big excitement is his intended. We've never met her before, you see. And they're moving back here to settle for good. So it's all very exciting. Anyway," she said, suddenly realising she was gabbling. "I'm sure you don't want to hear about that."

"I do. Really," he said, managing to convey what appeared to be genuine interest.

Chris smiled at his politeness. "So, what can I do for you?"

"Good news, Chris! We've appointed contractors and work on the new premises will start next week."

"That's great. Who's got the contract?"

"Bobby McAllistair and Sons."

"They're very good. They did the attic conversion on our house. When will the work be completed?"

"All being well, early autumn. Thirtieth of September to be exact."

"If they're on time."

"Yes, these things often run over, don't they? But let's hope everything goes to plan." He made a show of very deliberately closing the file on his desk and placing it to one side. Then he rested both shirt-sleeved arms on the table. His blue enamelled cufflinks matched exactly the small royal blue stripe in his otherwise plain white shirt.

"Chris," he said and paused.

"Yes?" She waited, noticing that his hands were nicely groomed, the nails pale pink and lightly buffed.

"I just want you to know that I really appreciate everything you've done to make the transition of the firm run smoothly. I know that you've taken on a lot of responsibility, including a lot of extra work to do with the new office. And it hasn't gone unnoticed."

"Thank you," said Chris coolly, but inside she positively glowed in the warmth of his praise. She was slightly annoyed with herself that his opinion should matter to her as much as it did.

"I've been impressed by your intellect and technical ability but also by your management skills. With the planned expansion of the business down here in Ballyfergus, Chris, the firm is looking for a new partner. Would you be interested in that role?"

It was more than she had hoped for, even imagined. She had been happy in her old job as second fiddle to Bob McMillan, but the truth was that she had always known she was capable of a lot more. Opportunities in Ballyfergus were, however, limited and she had been content to sacrifice career advancement for the quality of life offered by a small town and proximity to home, especially when the children were younger. To have the chance of becoming a partner without having to uproot was fantastic. But almost immediately her thoughts turned to Sam.

"I'm very flattered," she said, annoyed that she couldn't think of something less hackneyed to say, something that conveyed her genuine delight. "But would that mean I was in sole charge of the Ballyfergus office? Or would you still be based here? I mean, would you be staying on?"

"As you know I plan to make Ballyfergus my permanent base, both professionally and personally."

"Good. I mean it's good to know – what the set-up will be. So I know exactly what's involved. I mean, you need to know, don't you? Before you agree to take something like this on."

He waited for her to stop rambling and said, with a half-smile that made her suspect he was laughing at her, "Yes of course. I will, however, continue to monitor our other offices so I would work from them occasionally. In terms of day-to-day running of this office, though, you would be in charge."

She nodded.

"So, that's settled then? I can tell Charlie Stevenson that you'll accept?"

"Haven't you forgotten something?" said Chris with a wry smile.

He shrugged his athletic shoulders and shook his head. "What?"

"The small matter of remuneration," said Chris boldly and Sam put his hand to his mouth, partly covering it, to hide the smile that sprang to his lips.

"That will be addressed in due course," he said, removing his fist, his expression unreadable again. "And I don't think you'll be disappointed."

"Can't we talk figures now?" said Chris, mindful of the financial drain Hannah's university education would put on the household budget. And she knew that when they moved office premises, the staff complement would increase; Sam had talked about employing another lawyer and more office staff to cope with the projected increase in business. And that meant more responsibility for Chris. Well, if Stevenson and McIlwaine valued her as much as Sam said they did, then they should put their money where their mouth was, so to speak.

"I need to have a talk with Charlie and the other senior partners first and then I'll be in a position to have that conversation."

"Okay," she said, but reluctantly, just to let him know that she expected him to deliver on his promise.

There were a few moments of awkward silence and then Chris stood up.

"Right then," she said brightly, "I'd better get back to it."

He paused and his brow furrowed, bringing his eyebrows low over his deep-set eyes, like overhanging cliffs. It was an expression he invoked when troubled – or perplexed.

"Chris?" he said.

"What?"

"Why did you ask if I'd be staying on?"

"As I said, I like to know what I'm getting into."

"So do I," he said enigmatically, and she looked away, unable to bear his unflinching gaze.

What did he mean by that? Was he hinting at something – some possibility between them? Or was she looking for meaning in his words and actions that simply didn't exist, except in her imagination? Was she going totally insane and blurring the line between reality and her ridiculous, schoolgirl notions?

Her fantasies surrounding Sam were very vague and almost wholly unformed. She only knew that she wanted sometimes to touch him and she wondered what he would do if she did. She just wanted to feel his arms around her, nothing more. No, that wasn't entirely true . . . Get a grip, Chris, she told herself crossly. Keep it professional.

Thankfully, someone rapped on the door and Chris turned eagerly to greet them, and, more importantly, to hide her flushed face.

"Mr and Mrs Loughlin are here to see you, Chris," said Declan and when she failed to register any comprehension in her expression, he added, "About the sale of their house in Ballygally."

"Great!" said Chris with more enthusiasm than a routine client appointment merited. She strode the few short steps to the door. Then she turned and, as calmly as she could manage, she said, "Perhaps we could finish this conversation later?"

Then she exited Sam's office just as quickly as her shaking legs would carry her.

★ ★ ★

"I'm home!" shouted Chris as soon as she got through the door, fairly dancing her way across the tiled floor in her low-heeled leather court shoes. For the first time in years she felt properly excited for herself – rather than vicariously through the achievements and milestones of others, like the children.

Her head was full of the possibilities opening up before her with Stevenson and McIlwaine. It was only on the way home in the car, with time for reflection, that she had realised just how timely this promotion was – and not just in terms of finances. She had been dreading Hannah going off to university and knew that it was only a matter of time before Finn too would fly the nest. A new challenge at work would keep her busy. It would cushion the blow of the children leaving home and disguise the distance between her and Paul. There was nothing like hard work for avoiding uncomfortable issues one didn't want to face. And the money, of course, would be very welcome. It was perfect.

"In here," came Paul's voice from the drawing room and Chris popped her head across the threshold to find him standing in front of the unlit fireplace. He stood on the balls of his feet, his heels resting on the hearth. His hands were clasped behind his back and, peculiarly, he still wore his work jacket. Normally it was one of the first things Paul discarded as soon as he crossed the threshold.

"Isn't it a gorgeous night?" she said, glancing out the window where the late afternoon sun, still strong and hot, cast shadows across the gravel turning circle in front of the house. Dappled patches of dark green danced beneath the foliage of the silver birches they had planted to replace the rotten elms all those years ago. It was lovely to see them now matured into fine tall specimens.

"Why don't we go out to Carnfunock?" she went on, referring to a pretty parkland on the coast, a few miles outside Ballyfergus. She longed to explore the shady forest trails and stride out along the coastline. "It'd be lovely to take a walk out there. Murphy would love it. It'd give him a chance to burn off some energy."

He did not answer her but said instead, rather solemnly. "Come in and have a seat, Chris."

She walked into the room and stood behind the sofa. She shed her navy linen jacket and threw it over the back of the sofa, suddenly anxious to be free of her uncomfortable work clothes. She loosened the pussybow tie on her cream silk blouse and kicked off her shoes. She wondered if she would have time for a quick shower.

"Oh, do let's go out, Paul!" she said, feeling reckless.

Full of energy, she wanted to do something to make her feel alive. They rarely did things together in the evenings, unless it was to socialise with other people. Paul sometimes played a round of golf but, more often than not, he would retire to the conservatory and lose himself in medical or wine magazines. And she busied herself with running the home, work, PINBAT or keeping fit.

"Are the children about?" she asked.

"Finn's in his room. I don't know where Hannah is."

"Well, maybe they can come with us. We could stop at Linden Heights for a bite to eat on the way home. Or maybe The Mill. The kids might like that better," she mused and then turning her attention to Paul she added, unable to suppress a wide grin, "We have something to celebrate."

With the sudden, self-conscious realisation that she rarely smiled at Paul in that genuine, unrestrained way, the grin faded from her face as quickly as it had taken root.

He looked at her as though seeing her properly for the first time and said, "What?"

"I'm going to be promoted," she said and couldn't help fluffing herself up with a little bit of (well-deserved) pride. "Sam McIlwaine called me into his office today and offered me a partnership. We haven't talked figures yet but it'll mean a substantial increase in salary. And responsibility."

"Oh," he said, and the interest in his eyes faded.

He was acting as though what she had just told him wasn't of the slightest importance. She recalled the fuss she always made when Paul did well at work and felt aggrieved. Her shoulders sagged a little with disappointment – but then she resolved not to let his lack of enthusiasm dampen her spirits.

"You know promotion never crossed my mind," she went on. "And then, when Sam offered it to me I realised that I did really want it."

He stared at her blankly and a little shiver ran up her spine. It was only then that she realised he had not cracked a smile since she had come into the room. He seemed pre-occupied, distracted

"Well?" she said, raising her eyebrows encouragingly,

and forcing herself to smile brightly. "What do you say to going out? Why don't we? It'll make a nice change."

And then, when he did not reply, she let the smile slip from her face and said, "Paul, aren't you pleased for me?"

There had always been a little bit of career rivalry between them, especially in the early days before they had kids. Chris suddenly realised that it had been a long time since Paul had made any significant advancement in his career. The new GP's contract negotiated a couple of years ago had meant a material increase in salary but in terms of advancement, Paul was pretty much doing what he had been doing for the last twelve years. Was it possible that he was jealous of her success?

"Of course," said Paul in a flat, monotone voice she had never heard him use before. "I always said you were very capable, Chris. You deserve your success. And I'm sure you'll do well." He spoke as though every syllable required great effort. He sounded as though he did not mean a single word of it.

"Paul, what on earth is the matter with you?"

"Nothing. Everything." he paused and let out a long, weary sigh. "Look, we need to talk, Chris." He averted his gaze to stare out the window, as though he could not bear to look upon her. "Please, Chris, will you take a seat?"

She found herself propelled forward as a sense of foreboding rolled across her happiness, like a sea fog obliterating the sun. She sat obediently on the edge of the sofa her hands folded primly in her lap. Nervously she twirled her wedding band and engagement ring with the index finger and thumb of her right hand. She held her breath. And waited.

Paul sat down heavily on the sofa opposite and clasped

his hands together so hard that his knuckles went white and the tips of his fingers pink.

"I hardly know how to tell you this," he said, shaking his head slowly, and looking down, between his legs, at the hand-knotted Kilim rug they had bought on holiday in Turkey.

Chris watched with horrible fascination as his face became suddenly flushed and dewy beads of sweat formed on his brow. His face, so expressionless before, was now a window on his anguish. Had he lost his job? Was he sick? Had something happened to the children?

"Hannah! Finn!" she cried out at once and stood up, turning already towards the door. "Are they all right?"

He frowned and shook his head. "There's nothing wrong with the children, Chris. They're absolutely fine."

"Who then? Has something happened to Mum? Karen?"

He shook his head vehemently and raised a hand to quieten her. "No, Chris. No-one's ill. Or hurt. Everybody's absolutely fine."

Her greatest fears allayed, she sat down again, feeling drained. Whatever was wrong, and something certainly was – that much she could tell from his demeanour – it must be something to do with Paul, and Paul alone. She thought of that feared and stealthy killer, cancer. She let out a little gasp and put her hand to her mouth.

Paul paused for a moment, as though composing what he wanted to say next, the way she imagined he would when delivering such terrible news to patients. She waited patiently, forcing herself to think of less horrific alternatives to cancer – like gallstones. Something that was curable with surgery or medication. Something that wasn't life-threatening.

"Do you remember when we got married," he said at last, still not looking at her, "and we used to scoff at the way people stayed together, even though it was obvious that they hated each other and had nothing in common?"

"Yes," she said, so quietly she could hardly hear herself speak.

"Take my parents, for example. My father had affairs all through his married life and yet he would never leave. And my mother would never leave him, no matter how much humiliation he heaped on her. They were trapped in a marriage that was meaningless."

Chris cocked her head to one side, trying to make sense of what he was saying – or, rather, why he was saying it.

"But I thought, in spite of it all, that they were happy?" she said warily.

He shook his head. "They put on a good show, Chris. Especially for you. But they fought all the time. I think they rather hated each other."

"So why did they stay together?" she said, forcing the idea that he was drawing some sort of analogy between his parents' marriage and theirs out of her mind.

"Too much invested in the marriage. The house, us," he said referring to himself and his younger brother, Tommy. "And of course there was terrible pressure from society to stay married. Thank God that doesn't exist, at least not to the same degree, today."

She sat in silence and stared at him, all the horrible fears she had so recently suppressed rushing back.

"We always said we never wanted to be like that, didn't we, Chris? We always said that if one of us felt like that, we would end it."

A cold chill ran up Chris's spine and, in spite of the

oppressive heat of the summer's evening, she began to shiver. Suddenly it was crystal clear what he was talking about and she found that she could not bear to hear it. She clasped her hands together and, hunched over, wedged her elbows between her shaking thighs in an attempt to gain some control over her body.

"I believe that it's time for us to go our separate ways," he went on, making eye contact with her at last. The whites of his eyes were yellow and bloodshot. He looked like he hadn't slept in days. How come she hadn't noticed before?

She exhaled slowly and took a deep, steadying breath. But the blood rushed to her brain regardless. Her heart pounded in her chest and something inside felt like it was falling, spiralling downwards at a speed that made her feel nauseous. She closed her eyes and she was floating above where they sat, looking down, observing. Watching with detachment as she, and her life, fell apart.

Now that her marriage was under threat, she realised how much she needed it. How much she wanted to be part of a couple – this couple. She and Paul were bound together by their shared past, the children, the house. Almost everything by which she defined herself, apart from work, was linked in some way to Paul. She looked at his familiar face and saw in it something of the man she had fallen in love with. In spite of her nit-picking and fault-finding she still felt something for him – she still, on some level, thought that she loved him.

"Chris?"

She opened her eyes. She touched her cheeks where they were cold and realised that she was crying. No histrionics, no keening, just salty tears that slid from the corners of her eyes, marked tracks through her make up, like skis on fresh snow, and rolled coldly into the neck of her blouse.

"I don't believe that I have made you happy these last few years, Chris. And I certainly haven't been happy. Not lately anyway. I want you to understand that it's not anything you've done — it's just that we've grown apart."

She put her arms around her body and hugged herself, protectively. "I . . ." she began and trailed off. "I thought you were sick . . . ill . . . how stupid of me . . ."

The expression on his face was one of sympathy. She could bear anything, but not his pity. She wiped the tears from her cheeks and willed them to stop flowing. She unclenched her hands and sat up straight-backed.

"Are you telling me that you're leaving me?" she demanded, her innate instinct for absolute clarity coming to the fore. "Is that what you're telling me, Paul?"

He nodded grimly. "I am."

"But why?" she said, her brain selecting happy flashbacks of their marriage to parade before her eyes; holidays and parties and time spent with the children. Images that defied his claim that they had not been happy.

"I've told you why."

"But that's — that's not fair, Paul. You never said anything before. And we did have happy times."

"Of course we did, Chris. And I'll never forget them. But not lately. In the last few years, I feel as though you've come to dislike, even hate, me."

She blushed and looked at the floor, recalling her many uncharitable thoughts towards Paul, thoughts that she had not shared with another living soul. By keeping her treacherous views to herself, she had imagined them harmless. But clearly they had not been.

"I'm sorry, Paul," she said, with genuine regret. "I had no idea I made you feel like that."

"Well, it's water under the bridge now," he said with a finality that terrified Chris. "I did try, Chris. I really did try to reach you, to make things better. Do you remember I suggested that trip to Venice? But you just didn't want to know."

"That's not true," she said, jumping to her defence. "I would've gone but we had things on, social obligations to fulfil. I was happy to do it, just not then."

"You make it sound like a chore," he said, and she looked at the floor, because his analysis had been accurate – she hadn't wanted to go. "Anyway, I think it was too late by then, Chris. I'd put up with so much over the years – your snide comments and –"

"I thought you said that it wasn't my fault. That we'd just grown apart."

"Okay, okay!" he said, raising his hands in the air, palms facing her. "I don't want to apportion blame, Chris. It's not constructive."

"How very noble of you!"

"That's exactly the sort of pointless comment I'm trying to avoid, Chris. I'm trying to be grown-up about this. I never wanted this to happen. You know how much I value family life. It just seems to me that you and I . . . well, we're living separate lives, aren't we? We share the same house but we don't share our lives."

Swallowing her anger she replied, "But it's not too late, Paul. It's not too late to save our marriage."

He shook his head. "I'm afraid it is."

"Don't say that, Paul. Please. We can go for counselling. I'll change. I promise." She hated herself for pleading with him. But the prospect of her life, as she knew it, coming to an end was absolutely terrifying. "We've been married for so long that I can't see myself as anything other than half of this marriage. I can't imagine a life on my own, Paul. Without you, well I don't know what I'd do."

"You're going to have to get used to it, Chris."

"But Paul, how can you throw away everything that we've built, and worked for, without even trying to save it? I'm willing. Why aren't you?"

He stood up. "I'm sorry, Chris. I'm sorry that it's come to this. But it's over. I'm leaving tonight."

"But where to, Paul? A friend's sofa? Or some grotty bed-sit? Look, you don't have to do this. Please reconsider. I appreciate everything you said and I accept I've been partly," she swallowed, "maybe even largely, to blame. But we can work this out. I'm sure of it. I'll sleep in the spare room, if you like. Just please don't go tonight."

The back door opened and Chris heard the sound of Hannah coming in, the squeak of her rubber-soled trainers on the tiled floor, the thud of her bag on the island unit, the sound of the fridge opening as she grabbed the carton of organic apple juice and drank greedily, straight from the box. Sounds so familiar it couldn't be anyone else.

"If you won't reconsider for me, then do it for Hannah and Finn. Think of them, Paul. Think of the effect it'll have on them. They'll be devastated. And all our family and friends."

Paul stared at her for a few moments. He looked very tired but there was a determination in the set of his weak jaw and the way he bit his full bottom lip.

"You've given me lots of reasons why I shouldn't go, Chris. And do you know what?"

She shook her head.

"Not once did you say that you wanted me to stay because you loved me," he said sadly. He walked to the door that led into the hall.

"Where are you going?" she said.

"To get Hannah and Finn. We need to tell them."

"Don't you think we should talk about this properly, Paul? Before you tell the children?"

"No. There's nothing more to say, Chris. If you don't want to be there when I tell them, I'll do it alone."

She followed him into the kitchen trying to work out how she could minimise the harm he was about to do.

Hannah, immediately sensing that something was wrong, said, "What's up?"

"Your father wants to talk to you," said Chris, with a heavy heart.

"Take a seat at the table, Hannah. I'll be there in a minute," said Paul and he stepped into the hall and hollered up the stairs for Finn.

"Is something wrong, Mum?" said Hannah, her big eyes wide with apprehension.

Chris could only shake her head, unable to speak. She folded her arms across her chest and looked away. She walked over to the sink and turned on the cold tap. By the time she had filled a glass with water Finn was in the room, seated opposite Hannah, with their father between them at the head of the table.

Chris leaned against the unit that housed the sink unable, in her distress, to approach the table. She took long sips of the water, trying to calm herself. She knew that the children, Hannah especially, adored their father. She would be devastated. And Finn, always her protector since babyhood, would side with her and make himself hate his father.

It was so unfair on both of them. Chris could not in her heart honestly say that she blamed Paul for the way he felt about her – a lot of what he said had been entirely justified. But she could not forgive him for what he was about to do to the children. He had not even tried to avert this domestic disaster. He had not given her the chance to fix things and for that she did not think she could forgive him.

"Hannah. Finn," began Paul and he paused dramatically.

The brother and sister looked at each other across the table, their eyes wary and full of unease.

Paul stared at his hands splayed out on the oak surface, as if inspecting them.

"Your mother and I have decided to separate," he said and Chris, having agreed to no such thing, couldn't help but snort in derision. Paul shot her an angry glance.

Finn looked frightened and confused, like a small trapped animal.

Hannah turned to Chris, her arm over the back of the chair and simply said, "Mum?" It was a habit from childhood when she had often sought confirmation from Chris, as though she did not quite believe what other adults, including Paul, told her. At the time, it had greatly grieved Paul.

"Your father just told me, all of five minutes ago, that he's decided to leave us."

"I'm leaving your mother, not you two," said Paul quietly, but his head was ducked down, as if in shame.

Hannah and Finn were both now staring at him in astonishment.

"He's leaving tonight," said Chris and then she realised

how little Paul had told her of his plans. Had he for example, got a place to stay tonight? Had he perhaps booked a room at The Marine? Had he packed his bags already? If so, where were they?

"But where are you going?" said Hannah, asking one of the questions Chris was thinking. Her voice was plaintive, the voice of a little girl Chris had not heard in years. It cut her like a knife.

"I have a place . . ." said Paul, and his voice trailed off. "I have a place to stay."

"But where?" persisted Hannah.

"It's a rented flat. In Ballyfergus."

"You have a flat already?" said Chris incredulously. "You had this all planned?" She felt her anger grow with him for not giving her the opportunity to redeem herself, for not giving their marriage a chance. She suddenly realised that tonight had been carefully planned and orchestrated. It had been premeditated, like a crime. Paul did not answer, so Chris went on, "Why didn't you say something before now, Paul? You've obviously been planning this for some time. Weeks, months even, and you never said a word."

"I had my reasons," he said, jerking his chin up defiantly. "And one of them was that I wanted to wait until Hannah had finished her exams."

"You needn't have bothered," said Hannah, her voice breaking down. She put her hands to her face and started to cry.

"Oh, darling," said Paul and he reached out and put his hand on her right shoulder. "It's okay. It doesn't change anything between us."

"Don't touch me!" said Hannah through her tears and Paul removed his hand as though he'd touched hot coals.

"Don't touch me!" she repeated, this time her voice growing more hysterical. She pushed the chair back quickly, the wooden legs screeching on the floor, and stood up. "This changes everything. Everything. I can't believe you're so stupid you can't see that, Dad!" she cried and ran out of the room.

"Oh, Hannah," said Paul with a sigh.

Chris, her legs suddenly feeling like they were about to give way, came over and sat at the far end of the table, as far away from Paul as possible.

"Happy now?" she said and he ignored her.

Finn's gaze darted back and forth between his mother and father. His eyes were narrowed slightly, an indication that he was thinking hard. Although he appeared outwardly calm, Chris could see the sinews standing out on his neck. He drummed the table with his fingertips, the tempo growing ever more agitated.

"Where's this flat exactly, then, Dad?" he said.

"It doesn't matter," said Paul.

"But what if I want to come visit you, Dad?" said Finn, a dangerous edge to his voice. "I'll need to know where you live, won't I?"

"I can't remember the exact address right now," said Paul dismissively. "I'll text you or phone you tomorrow."

"No, tell me now."

"I told you, I can't remember . . ."

Finn stopped the drumming action with his fingers immediately. "It's her, isn't it?" he said with a vicious sneer as he leaned across the table.

The hairs stood up on the back of Chris's neck.

"I think I'd better go," said Paul and he stood up. He patted the pockets of his jacket until he located his car keys.

"What are you talking about, Finn?" said Chris.

Finn stood up, his lithe young body tense with rage. He squared up to his father, taller than him by two inches, barring the way to the back door, and said again, "It's her, isn't it?"

"This has got nothing to do with you. It's between your mother and me."

"But I think Mum has the right to know, don't you?" persisted Finn. "What do you think, Mum?"

"Know what?" said Chris.

"That the reason Dad's walking out on you is so that he can shack up with his little whore."

"Finn!" cried Chris in horror. "Don't say such things . . ." but her voice trailed off when she saw the defiant expression on Paul's face. "No," she said, under her breath.

Paul looked uncomfortably from his son to his wife, backed figuratively into a corner. "I suppose you might as well know now, Chris," he said, as though he was volunteering the information, not having it dragged out of him. "It'll not be a secret for long. It's true, I've met somebody."

"You? You've met someone?" said Chris incredulously. The idea of Paul, never the greatest womaniser in the world, having an affair was almost absurd. Chris had been certain, wrongly so it appeared, that Paul had never looked at another woman but her. If he hadn't looked so deadly serious and Finn so angry, she might have laughed out loud at the notion.

"Aren't you going to tell us who it is?" said Finn, his voice full of loathing and Chris wished he would stop.

"I don't care to know," she said, deeply troubled by something in the tone of Finn's voice.

"Well, if you won't tell her, I will," said Finn. "It's Bernie Sweeney, isn't it, Dad?" he said without taking his eyes off his father.

"Bernie?" whispered Chris. "No, it can't be." Not the woman who had stayed in her house, under her roof, for nearly a month? The woman she had called a friend? The woman she had trusted like a sister?

"I saw your car round at her new flat the week after she moved out of here," went on Finn, his voice both accusatory and self-satisfied. "We were doing a job down Bay Road all that week. You didn't know that, did you? Your car was there almost every day – at lunchtime, or just after knock-off time. I did think it a bit strange at the time . . . but I never put two and two together until now . . . well, I couldn't believe the most obvious explanation . . ."

"Tell me it isn't true," said Chris to Paul.

Paul cocked his head to one side and looked at the floor. His expression betrayed him. He looked guilty.

"Not in my house?" she whispered and his head dropped a few degrees more, confirming her worst fears.

Chris looked about her, imagining every surface that Bernie had touched. She raised her eyes to the ceiling, boring through the floors above to the top of the house. She visualised the bed Bernie had slept in and imagined them together in it. Or worse, in her own bed. She was repelled by the thought.

"Did you . . ." she began but could not bring herself to vocalise the awful deed. "In my house?"

"Don't torture yourself, Chris," said Paul and she knew then that they had made love in the home that was almost sacred to her. The house was contaminated. It would never be the same again.

Finn began to swear at his father then, an angry jumble of the worst expletives. But beneath the outburst, his terrible hurt was obvious and Chris could see he was on the verge of tears. She put a restraining hand on Finn's arm and said, "Hush, now." He was quiet then, but she could feel the muscles in his arm quivering like taut strings.

Then she turned to Paul, and said, "Yes, you go now."

Only moments before she had been begging him to stay, now she could not tolerate his presence in the house. He had betrayed her and the offence was unforgivable.

"Okay," said Paul, without once raising his eyes to look at Finn or Chris. He went out the back door, they heard the sound of Murphy greeting him with yelps and barks, the low grumble of Paul's voice in response, his feet on the gravel as he walked round the side of the house. Then the rumble of the car engine firing up, the crunch of the big tyres on the gravel and the sound of the car driving away.

Chris collapsed, exhausted, into the chair Finn had recently vacated at the table. It was still warm from his body heat. Now that Paul was gone, she did not have to be brave any more. She folded her arms on the table, rested her head on them, and wept.

She cried so hard that her chest ached and she gasped for breath and when she opened her eyes she could not see for the tears. She had not cried in this gut-wrenching, sobbing way since her father's death five years before. She thought of how happy she had been only an hour before and wept afresh. It was hard to believe that a day that had started out with such promise could end like this.

Finn knelt down beside her and put his arm around her shoulders. He pressed his stubbly face against her cheek and she could feel it was wet with tears.

"Don't worry, Mum," he said. "You're going to be all right. You just wait and see. I'm going to look after you. And we'll be just fine. We don't need that bastard or his money."

Chris raised her head from the table and smiled weakly at him. He was still just a boy and he didn't understand at all.

Although it had never been her area of interest, Chris knew enough about family law to know how it would ultimately work. With both children now independent (Finn had turned seventeen on his last birthday), Paul was under no obligation to contribute to a family home. He would provide for the children she imagined (and no doubt generously) but without Paul's income, Chris could never pay for the mortgage or the upkeep of the house on her own. The house would have to be sold.

She covered her face with her hands and cried some more. She told herself it was only a house but it meant so much to her. It was the pinnacle of everything she had worked for and dreamed of. It was the place where the children had been raised – it was the place they called home.

"I'm sorry for going on like this, Finn," she said when her weeping had eased. "It came as such a shock. I had absolutely no idea."

She found a hankie and wiped her eyes, blew her nose and tried to compose herself. This had come as a complete shock to her, but it was a bolt from the blue for Finn and Hannah as well. And no matter that they were nearly adults, they would still be deeply traumatised.

"That Bernie Sweeney's a sneaky bitch," said Finn.

Chris put a hand on his arm and shook her head. "Don't say that, Finn."

"Why not? It's true isn't it?"

"It – it diminishes you. It makes you as bad as him. And her."

"But she stole him from you! From us."

"You can't make someone love you unless they want to, Finn – unless they're looking for love," she said, and she looked into his blue eyes that were a mirror for his father's. It was the very first time that she had ever alluded to the rocky state of her marriage in his presence.

"Stop making excuses for her. And him," said Finn crossly and he stood up, clearly unwilling to take on board the concept that his parents' marriage had not been the idyll he'd imagined. "I don't know why you're standing up for them."

Chris understood that it was easier for him to put the blame squarely on his father but, even in her shock and disbelief, she could not apportion all the blame to Paul. He may have put the final nail in the coffin, but their marriage had been failing for a long time.

"Are you going to be all right, Finn?"

"Yeah. Yeah. I just need to get my head round this, that's all," he said, digging his hands deep into the pockets of his over-sized jeans. "I feel a bit sick, to be honest," he said, impressing Chris with his maturity and composure now that his initial fury had abated.

"I know. Me too." And then she added, "Will you let Murphy in, Finn? He's been scratching at that door for the last ten minutes."

A wave of fear came over her then as the puppy loped across the floor towards her and she automatically cracked a smile, said a few words of endearment and patted his little back. Life did not stop. They would wake up in the morning with jobs to go to and things to be done. How was she to cope with everything on her own? The dog still needed to be walked and fed, laundry would still need to be done, the house maintained. She would still have to put a meal on the table every night, hold down a job, sort out the finances, never mind the arrangements that would have to be made with Paul. How would it all be paid for? And all their friends and family would have to be told. Suddenly it all seemed utterly overwhelming.

"Do you mind if I have a beer, Mum?" said Finn and she forced herself to twist her mouth into an approximation of a smile. The strength of her maternal instinct surprised her, even in the face of complete disaster. Her priority, she realised with utter clarity, was and would always be, the children – long before herself.

"Darling," said Chris, attempting humour as a way of reassuring Finn she had not gone completely off the rails, "after what you've just been through you can have whatever you like."

She was rewarded with a grim smile.

"I'd better go and see Hannah," she said. Wearily, she went into the drawing room, pulled on her jacket (she was suddenly freezing cold) and padded barefoot up the stairs.

She found Hannah in her room, lying on her back on the bed, with her hands laced together on her stomach, staring at the ceiling. Her eyes were puffy and red-rimmed but at least the tears had ceased. Chris sat down on the foot of the bed and put her hand on Hannah's ankles. She waited for her daughter to speak.

"I'm sorry, Mum. I wasn't much use to you, was I? Bursting into tears like that."

"You got a terrible shock, Hannah. We all did. I think

your reaction was entirely understandable under the circumstances." Part of her wanted to comfort her daughter and make sure she was all right. Another part of her wanted to curl up into a ball and die. The shock of it was just too much.

"So what happens next, Mum? I mean, how do these things work? Will we have to move? Cat had to move house when her parents divorced."

"I honestly don't know, Hannah. I guess the house will probably have to be sold, in the end," said Chris gloomily. "But I can't think that far ahead just now. As for your father, you can see him anytime you want to."

"I don't want to."

Chris shrugged, not able right now to say the things she ought, like that this had nothing to do with Hannah's relationship with her father. Anyway, that was a lie. Everything had shifted, changed. Nothing would ever be the same again.

"Did you know, Mum? Before tonight, I mean."

"I had no idea, Hannah."

"But why did Dad leave like that – in such a rush?"

"Because," said Chris and she took a deep breath, steeling herself so that she would not cry, "because he wanted to get away from here – and from me – as fast as possible."

"But why?" asked Hannah and Chris stared at her, wishing she could spare her this pain. Hannah's heavy eye make-up was smudged with tears – she looked so terribly young and vulnerable.

"Your father's met someone, Hannah," Chris said, as bravely and matter-of-factly as she could.

Hannah raised herself up on her elbows and stared at her mother, disbelieving. "He's what?" she said, her face and voice suddenly full of anger.

"I know. I find it hard to believe too. But it's true. He's been having an affair and now he's left me for her."

"Left you? Who for?"

Chris swallowed, remembering the easy friendship that Bernie had struck up with Hannah. She hated her for it now – for winning Hannah's trust and betraying it.

"Who, Mum? Who is it?" said Hannah, her cracked voice betraying the fact that she was close to tears.

"It's Bernie Sweeney, Hannah."

"What? Bernie? Your best friend?" cried Hannah, her emotions swinging in an instant from sorrow to violent rage. Chris nodded and Hannah punched one of the cushions that lay on the bed. "Bernie! She did this to you? I don't bloody believe it!"

"I wish it wasn't true," said Chris quietly.

"If Cat did that to me, I swear I'd kill her. I'd tear her bodily limb from limb. I really would," shouted Hannah in fury. "And after you treated her like royalty! The scheming cow, I hate her!"

"You can't place all the blame on Bernie, Hannah," said Chris carefully, trying to be reasonable, though she too hated Bernie with a vengeance and would have spat in her face had she been present tonight. But she acknowledged, to herself at least, that she had in fact been unhappy for a long time. "Your father's responsible for his own actions. We don't know what happened between them. And I don't want to know."

"It's obvious. She seduced him. And the stupid old fool fell for it."

"She may have, but the point is your father chose to respond. No-one made him."

"Maybe he'll come back," said Hannah, with hope in her voice and a wary eye on her mother to gauge her reaction to this statement. "Maybe it's all just a mistake and he'll come back and we'll all carry on the way we were before. Do you think that might happen?"

"Maybe," said Chris, considering this possibility. If Paul came back would it be possible to erase what had happened tonight? Would it be possible to reconstruct their lives? She didn't know. She wished that it could be so. But she wished most of all, that tonight had never happened.

"I still don't understand what Dad sees in Bernie. She's a funny-looking little troll of a thing. And she's got weird ideas about things. She's nothing like you."

"Perhaps," said Chris with a tired sigh, "that's the very reason he's leaving me for her."

Hannah frowned and looked at her mother. "But I thought you and Dad were happy."

"So did I," said Chris, staring unseeing at the bedroom wall, her eyes misting with tears. "But it turns out I was wrong."

Much later, when the kids were in their rooms, no doubt as exhausted by the events of the evening as Chris was, she came down to the kitchen and looked at the old school wall clock she'd bought at auction the year they moved into the house.

When she saw that it was nearly midnight her heart sank. Suddenly she was desperate to speak to Karen. She had talked to Hannah and Finn over a very late supper of pizza and salad that nobody ate, answering their questions, addressing their concerns, pretending that she was okay. Now all she wanted was to hear a sympathetic voice on the end of the phone.

But it was far too late to phone Karen without alarming her – she would almost certainly be fast asleep in her bed. And much as Chris was desperate to talk to her sister, Karen was recovering from a major operation and had to take strong painkillers at night-time. It just wouldn't be fair to burden her with this tonight. Karen needed to rest for she was so looking forward to seeing Raymond and Shona.

They were arriving tomorrow! Chris put her head in her hands and dragged them down her face, taking deep breaths to steady her racing pulse. She was supposed to be meeting them for lunch tomorrow and hosting a party for them in two weeks' time – the invitations had been issued, the caterers booked, the drink bought. It would be too much for Karen to cope with in her current condition – she would have to cancel.

Then she imagined how disappointed everyone would be, not least Raymond and Shona, and she hated Paul for putting her in this terrible predicament. No, she wouldn't cancel the party. She wouldn't let him spoil Raymond's moment of happiness. Why should she? She had nothing to be ashamed off – Paul and Bernie had shamed themselves by their actions. She had done nothing wrong.

She had never thought of Paul as a coward but he had, by his actions, proved himself to be one. He had only told her about Bernie because Finn had forced him to. Then, once his devastating news had been delivered, he'd bolted, leaving her to cope with the children. He had not even properly explained what was happening or what he wanted from her. A separation? A divorce?

And he hadn't had the guts to walk out before now because he had been waiting for Bernie to return. Waiting until she was there to hold his hand and wipe his brow and no doubt tell him how wonderful he was and what a lucky escape he had made from his harridan of a wife. Yes, he would be all nicely settled into the Bay Road apartment just in time for Bernie's return from Australia tomorrow.

Chris tried to banish these bitter thoughts from her mind – she did not want to become poisoned by them. She turned her thoughts instead to Karen and resolved that she would not burden her, or anyone else, with her sorrow tonight. There would be time enough tomorrow to involve them in her misery. Tonight, she would bear it alone. She would take comfort in a bottle of wine and, my God, she had never felt more in need of a glass of wine as she did now.

But when she got to the cellar she found a padlock, big and shiny new, on the door. She jumped back in horror. Paul had secured the cellar! Against whom? Her? What did he think she was going to do – drink all his precious wine? Give it away? Smash it up?

She shook the chrome padlock angrily. Did he think so little of her that he no longer trusted her? He'd barred her from a room in her own house. And he had no right to do that. She stumbled back into the kitchen, Murphy padding faithfully behind her, and for the first time in her life she felt truly alone.

And it was this action – this unnecessary act of meanness and cruelty – that made Chris realise, more than anything Paul had said earlier that evening, that he was never coming back.

In the drawing room she found a bottle of Gordon's gin and, in the fridge, tonic water, ice cubes in the freezer tray and half a wizened lemon. She sliced the lemon, put everything on a tray along with a crystal glass and went through to the drawing room. She put on a Bach CD and, first removing the coil of fairy lights from the grate, lit the fire. Going to bed was pointless. She would not sleep tonight.

She watched the flames lick round the logs, pulled a rug around her shoulders and knocked back the first drink quickly, then another, relishing the numbness that came with it. She closed her eyes and tried to lose herself in the music but her brain refused to co-operate.

It replayed the events of the evening again and again, until she was sick of it and still she could not stop. And then she remembered everything that had been good about being married to Paul, and the tears came again. She thought of the life she had foreseen for herself. Fifteen more years of rewarding work, then a comfortable, active retirement with Paul as her companion. The fear of being alone had been one of the reasons why she had stayed married. Now she would be forced to face that fear and build a new life for herself.

Her thoughts turned to Bernie and her cheeks burned with anger and embarrassment at her own stupidity. The affair must've been going on right beneath her nose and she had not noticed a thing. She felt like such an idiot – they had made a fool of her. Paul's betrayal hurt, but somehow Bernie's betrayal hurt even more.

Marriages fell apart every day, husbands and wives had affairs, but to be deceived by a childhood friend, a person you thought you could trust . . . it left Chris's faith in the world in tatters. And life as she knew it, finished.

Fifteen

On Saturday morning, in spite of the tenderness in her stomach which was still yellow and bruised, Karen was truly happy for the first time since the operation. For the past two weeks she had been consumed by guilt and doubts about what she had done – and suffered terrible mood swings, insomnia and extreme discomfort.

She had been comforted by Dr Mezz's reassurances that these feelings were entirely normal but, still, it was great to wake up and find that the depression, for that was what it most certainly was, had lifted. She had expected, and been prepared for, considerable pain, but the last fortnight had been an unexpected emotional rollercoaster. She was glad that part of her recovery was over.

She waited until she was sure Tony was downstairs with the children before getting up and locking the bedroom door from the inside. It would be some weeks yet before she would allow Tony to see her naked or even semi-clothed. To his credit, if he found her behaviour odd, he never said a word.

In the en-suite shower, she washed with care as instructed by the surgeon, singing along to pop songs on the radio at the top of her voice. Then she dried herself and went through to the bedroom again where the hideous girdle she had to wear, made from strong elasticated material in a horrible shade of beige, was laid out on the bed. She lay down on it, face upwards, and wrapped one side across her stomach. Then applying tension she pulled the other round until it felt snug and secured the thick Velcro strip down the side. Then she put on her underwear.

She hated wearing the ugly girdle thing – it was like an instrument of torture – and yet, without it, her stomach throbbed and she felt dangerously unsupported. Still, only one more week to go and she would not have to wear it at night; another month and she would be able to discard it altogether. She decided to burn it ceremoniously when its purpose was fulfilled.

Karen was sure she was over the worst now and every day she could see an improvement in the contour of her stomach – but only if she managed to overlook the bruises, and the gruesome vivid red scars across her abdomen and around her belly-button.

But, she told herself, those disfigurements were temporary. The bruises would fade and the wounds would heal and no matter how bad the scars were, they would never be as horrific as her stomach had once been. The flap of skin that had hung over her pubic area was gone, her tummy was almost flat and the fold of skin below her breasts had disappeared.

Karen did her hair and make-up, then selected a new wrap-over day dress in turquoise and teal from her wardrobe. She put it on and beamed with pleasure at her reflection in the mirror. In spite of the bulky under-garment, her bulging stomach had clearly disappeared.

Instead she had a gently rounded womanly contour, which she was certain would further diminish as the swelling subsided. She smiled at herself and, for the first time in years, was truly pleased with what she saw.

From the far corner of the wardrobe, wedged between two tent-like black linen dresses, she lifted out the designer dress she had bought online for Raymond and Shona's party, exactly a fortnight from now. She hung it on a hook inside the wardrobe door and clasped her hands together as a little shiver of excitement rippled through her body. She'd tried the dress on last night, in the privacy of the en-suite, and it was perfect.

It was a fuchsia knee-length jersey dress by Alberta Ferratti, with three-quarter length sleeves and a deep v-neckline, perfect for showing off her cleavage, even if there was a bit more of it than Karen would have liked. But what had attracted her to the dress was the waist. It was clinched in with a wide elasticated belt, secured at the front with a large silver hook and eye. Karen would never have been able to wear something like that before. She imagined herself at the party wearing the dress, and the silver strappy sandals she'd bought to go with it; wafting elegantly round the sunny garden at Chris's house, drawing admiring glances and comments from family and friends.

She ran her hand down the fluid fabric and traced her fingertips over the silver clasp on the belt. Even in the sale the dress had cost over two hundred pounds and there was no doubt it was an indulgence. But the party was a special occasion – a celebration, not just of Raymond and Shona's homecoming and engagement, but, a month after her operation, a celebration of Karen as a new woman. A woman who was no longer defined by disfigurement.

She'd kept the dress a secret, even from Tony and Chris. She imagined the surprise on Tony's face when he saw her in the bright pink outfit – she couldn't remember when she'd last worn something so figure-hugging or attention-grabbing. Most of her clothes were black or dark in colour, designed to deflect attention away from her physical failings. She couldn't wait until she was well enough to go shopping again. She returned the dress to its hiding place in the wardrobe and closed the door.

It was just as well she was up and about early, for when she came downstairs in her slippers, still taking the stairs gingerly, Tony had some puzzling news for her.

"You look lovely, darling," he said as soon as she walked into the kitchen where he was wiping crumbs off the table.

He was wearing navy shorts and a white sports T-shirt, his uniform of choice for the long summer holidays, and already his skin was lightly tanned. He looked terribly handsome and Karen thought how lucky she was that he loved her. The children were nowhere to be seen, presumably engaged in their favourite activity – watching TV.

"Thank you," said Karen, for once feeling that the compliment was deserved. She smiled awkwardly at Tony, embarrassed by his attention in a different way than before the operation. Then she would have cringed, feeling unworthy of his flattery. Now her embarrassment stemmed from her lack of experience in how to handle justified praise.

And there was the guilt of course – guilt that her new-found svelte figure had been achieved at the hand of a surgeon and not by the traditional route of exercise and self-denial. She felt that she had failed in some way, that she had taken the easy option. She had to remind herself, very firmly, that diet and exercise alone would never have solved her particular problem.

"Chris was on the phone just ten minutes ago," said Tony, giving the work surface a cursory wipe and throwing the dishcloth in the sink.

"Was she? I never heard the phone ringing. I must've been drying my hair."

"She said she wanted to talk to you, but not on the phone. I offered to go and get you but she was quite insistent. She said she'd come over at eleven-thirty so that you'd have time to talk before going on to your mum's."

"Did she say what she wanted to talk about?" said Karen, perplexed.

"No and I didn't like to ask. To tell you the truth she was a bit – well, a bit short with me."

"That's not like Chris."

"I know, that's what I thought. Anyway, it was clear she didn't want to tell me anything, so I didn't push it," he said and paused, standing in the middle of the kitchen with both hands on his slim hips. He was wearing flip-flops on his feet.

"Do you think I should call her back?" said Karen, worried.

"No, I wouldn't," said Tony, carefully. "I think you should wait until she comes over. But whatever it is, I don't think it's good news."

"Oh God, I hope everyone's all right."

"I'm sure they are," said Tony. "If there was anything seriously wrong, we'd have heard about it by now."

"Yes, of course. You're right," said Karen and she lifted a breakfast bowl out of the cupboard, wincing just a little as she raised her arms. She lowered them to her sides again and the pain went away. But the feeling of foreboding was not so easily despatched – it did not lift for the rest of the morning.

After breakfast, she lay on the sofa in the lounge and watched the second half of *The Simpsons Movie* with the children. Having seen it at least eight times – it was currently the kids' favourite film – her mind wandered constantly, dwelling on what could be up with Chris. Her main worry, which she tried to put out of her mind, was that her sister might be seriously ill.

At eleven o'clock, Tony got the kids ready to go to the park.

"Are you sure you don't want to come over to Mum's, even for a little while?" said Karen. "Raymond would love to see you and you must be curious to meet Shona."

"Your mum doesn't have the room for us all," said Tony, "and you and Chris will have a lot of catching up to do with Raymond. We'd just be in the way. Anyway, there's plenty of time for the rest of us to meet them."

"But –" began Karen.

"And you know what the kids are like," he said with a rueful grin, contorting his handsome features. "Let's just say I think you'll have a more relaxing time without us."

"Still, it would be nice –" began Karen, but Tony was already propelling Chloe out the front door. "Have you remembered sun screen?" she called after him, as he and the kids walked down the sun-bathed drive and climbed in the car. "Sunhats?"

"Yes. And yes," said Tony with slight exasperation and then he added, good-naturedly, "Now will you go inside and stop fussing!"

"Okay, okay," said Karen. She plodded along the path to the car still wearing her slippers, opened the car doors and kissed both children. Then, when they had all shouted their goodbyes, she stood in the drive waving manically until she could no longer see Chloe or Jack's face.

Inside the house, Karen put on her going-out shoes, touched up her make-up, left her handbag by the front door and lay down on the sofa again to wait for Chris. When the doorbell rang at eleven thirty-five precisely she hauled herself up and answered it as fast as she could, given the current restraints on her mobility.

Chris was dressed in jeans and a black T-shirt, a lightweight cream raincoat and flat cream suede loafers. Her appearance surprised Karen. She looked well – she always did - but very casual. Chris would normally dress smartly for an occasion such as today. Perhaps she had decided not to go to Mum's after all . . . perhaps she and Raymond had fallen out. Maybe that was what she'd come to tell her.

After exchanging the briefest of greetings on the doorstep, Karen ushered Chris into the lounge where she stood in the middle of the floor, feet close together, swaying slightly as though she might topple over at any moment, like a ten-pin. Karen came and stood before her and it was only then, when Chris raised her head to make eye contact, that Karen saw her face properly for the first time.

The well-applied foundation could not conceal the bags under her eyes, nor the paleness of her complexion. And the three harmonious colours of eye-shadow so expertly blended across her eyelids, could not disguise the fact that the tender skin around her eyes was red and swollen. Indeed her whole face was a little puffy, giving her the well-fed look of someone on steroids.

But more than her appearance, there was something slightly crushed about the way Chris carried herself. Her shoulders were slumped and gone was the self-assuredness, the unshakable confidence Karen had always associated with her younger sister. And there was something unsettling about Chris's dry-eyed composure, when from her appearance it looked as though she had spent most of last night weeping. What could have reduced her sister to such a state?

"What on earth has happened?"

Chris's shoulders appeared to sag even lower, if that were possible, and she said, cutting straight to the point in her lawyer's fashion, "Paul's walked out."

"Oh my God," said Karen, and she felt suddenly disorientated, as the familiar contours of her extended family life started to crumble.

Chris nodded her head like one of those toy bulldogs people put on the back shelf of their cars – the ones who's head bobs up and down independently of the body – as though confirming to herself, as much as Karen, the truth of this statement.

But it was incomprehensible that Paul had left Chris. It was like saying the Glens of Antrim were no longer green or that the deep waters of Ballyfergus Lough had dried up. If Karen had heard this from any other source, anyone other than Chris, she would never have believed it. But everything about Chris's demeanour confirmed it. Karen's immediate instinct was to embrace her sister.

She stepped forward, took her in her arms – her high heels equalising the height difference between them – and hugged her. She buried her face in Chris's neck, surprised to smell fresh perfume there. And it was this – Chris's attempt to keep up appearances in the face of this domestic car crash

– more than anything, which made her start to cry.

"I'm so sorry, Chris. I'm so sorry, darling," said Karen into Chris's neck. Then she released her from her embrace, sniffed and tried to hold back the tears.

"I know. I can't believe it either," said Chris, dry-eyed, but extremely agitated. She blinked her pink-rimmed eyes rapidly and said, "Can't believe he's gone. After nineteen years of marriage – never suspected a thing – he had it all planned, you know –"

"Come and sit down," said Karen, realising that Chris was in shock. She gently led her by the hand to the sofa and they both sat down. "You've had a terrible shock, Chris. Did you sleep at all last night?"

"No."

"But why didn't you call me? Was anyone with you?"

"Finn and Hannah."

"You should've called me."

"I can't believe he's left me," said Chris, as though she had not heard Karen. "Without any warning at all. It makes me feel sick. You were right. I feel like such a fool."

"Have you had anything to eat today?" said Karen, ignoring her confused ramblings.

Chris shook her head.

"You need to eat, Chris. You're going to faint if you don't."

"All right. I'll have a cup of tea, please, but nothing to eat. Maybe later."

"Right, you stay here. I'll be back in a minute."

Karen came back into the room a few minutes later with two large mugs of tea and handed one to Chris. She'd taken the liberty of putting sugar in it, which normally Chris abhorred. Chris took a sip and said nothing – she did not even notice.

Karen allowed her a few moments of silence and then said, "Are you sure Hannah and Finn are okay? You left them at the house?"

"Yes, yes, they're fine," said Chris distractedly, as though the question irritated her. "Well, as fine as they can be given what he's just done to them. He told me, you know, and then straightaway told them. They were both terribly upset."

"I can imagine," said Karen, shaking her head. Hannah, especially, adored her father. That was why, Karen believed, she'd applied to do medicine – to please him and win his approval.

"You know he tried to put all the blame on me. Can you believe that?"

"Chris," said Karen and she put a hand on Chris's shoulder, so frail and thin, "do you think you could tell me exactly what happened? From the beginning."

"Okay," said Chris. She paused, took a deep breath, and said, in a voice quavering with emotion, "When I came home from work he was waiting for me, in the drawing room with his work jacket on. He started to talk about his parents' marriage and how they had stayed together even though they didn't love each other. I knew then, Karen, I knew then what was coming." Chris blinked rapidly, her dry eyes pink and sore-looking. "He said that our marriage was over, that he didn't love me any more. And that he was leaving."

"Oh, Chris," said Karen, now crying silent tears on her sister's behalf. She touched Chris's cheek, then her shoulder, wishing she could ease her sister's distress. Wishing she could take some of the pain away. "What did you say?"

"I asked him not to go. I begged him to give us another chance, if not for me, then for the children."

"And?" prompted Karen hopefully, still convinced that this was all some horrible mistake. Some sort of misunderstanding that could be sorted out and harmony restored.

"He said his mind was made up. And then he insisted on telling the children there and then."

Karen shook her head at Paul's callousness. Chris was so clearly in shock. How could he have been so insensitive? Why couldn't he, at the very least, have given her some time to come to terms with his decision before foisting it upon the children?

"Oh, he's such a coward, Karen," said Chris, a note of bitterness creeping into her voice. "He was going to leave without telling me about her."

"Her?" said Karen, sharply.

"It's Bernie, Karen. You were right all along. They've been having an affair."

"Oh, my God," said Karen and she put her hands over her face, her emotions torn between horror and rage.

"It was Finn who guessed and forced Paul to admit it. He wasn't going to tell me you know. He was trying to make out like we'd just drifted apart and he was going to walk out without telling me."

"The bastard!"

"It's because of her, you know. We had our problems like any couple, but we were doing all right until she came along. And now she's destroyed everything!" Chris put her face in her hands and, to Karen's relief, finally broke down and cried.

Karen put her arms around her sister's shoulder, and rocked her gently while stroking her hair rhythmically. But inside she was seething. The rage against Paul and Bernie swelled up until Karen felt that she would burst. Sitting upright like this was not good for her wounds and her belly had started to ache terribly. As soon as Chris was composed again, Karen stood up and paced the room.

"How could she do that to you? How could she?" she shouted. "I knew Bernie Sweeney was up to no good. I just knew it. But I have to tell you I never expected something as mean and low as this. She's absolute scum. She's not fit to walk the same earth as you."

"Karen," said Chris is a defeated voice, "I know you're angry but this isn't helping."

Karen sighed. "I know. I know. But just let me get it off my chest." She took a deep breath, exhaled and with a great deal of willpower said, "Okay. I'll try to stay calm. What about Paul? Have you heard from him today?"

"No."

The phone in the hall rang and Karen said, "Ignore it. It'll just be Mum ringing to say Raymond's arrived." The phone tripped to the answering machine and Karen could hear her mother's voice leaving a message. "Yep, it's Mum," she confirmed, and then, returning to the previous topic said, "Chris, do you think there's any possibility Paul will come back?"

"From the way he was talking last night, I don't think so."

"Would you take him back if he did?"

"I don't know," said Chris, looking bewildered. "I just want things to be the way they were. For this never to have happened."

"It wouldn't have, if it hadn't been for Bernie," said Karen, convinced that the blame lay squarely with her.

Chris said nothing and looked at the floor.

"God, it's just occurred to me!" said Karen. "The flat in Bay Road. That's how Bernie was able to afford it."

"No – I already know how," said Chris. "The money came from Bernie's brothers. It was her share of her father's inheritance money."

"And you believe that?"

"I've no reason not to," said Chris and shrugged her shoulders despondently.

"Paul's paying for the house, Chris. There is no inheritance money. That was just a lie Bernie made up."

Chris frowned doubtfully, then opened her eyes wide in astonishment, and said, "Wait a minute. Do you remember that day I saw them coming out of Hunter Campbell? The day we met for lunch at The Mill. Paul wasn't looking for a holiday home. They were looking for a place together. Oh, Karen that was weeks and weeks ago. He was planning to leave me even then. I can't believe he's been so – so clinical about all this. All the lies he must have told and carrying on with her in my house!"

Chris put her hands over her face and the sobs came again. Although it was upsetting, at least Chris was expressing her emotion in a healthy way. Bottling it all up couldn't be good in the long run.

Karen went over and knelt down on the floor beside Chris. She patted her on the shoulder and said, "You have a good cry, love."

Chris wept quietly for some moments, and Karen simply stayed where she was, with her hand on her sister's back. She recalled the last time she'd seen Paul, when he'd visited her at home soon after the operation. She remembered the odd things he'd said; how much she and Tony meant to him, how he considered them his friends and how it had been a privilege to know them. That had been his way of saying goodbye, she thought bitterly, for he must have known that, after this, she would never speak to him again.

Eventually Karen got up, the kneeling position at last proving too taxing for her traumatised stomach muscles. She found a box of tissues and handed them to Chris. She took the empty mugs into the kitchen while Chris blew her nose and wiped away her tears. At the sink she paused and took deep breaths to steady her nerves.

The truth was, she was devastated by this news. When something you consider as solid as rock comes undone, it has a knock-on effect on everything that you take for granted. Karen thought of Tony and the children and the possible harm that could come to them – illness, an accident, injury (or worse) at the hands of some stranger. She felt suddenly anxious for them and wished they were safe at home where she could watch over them. She took her happiness too much for granted. For if Chris and Paul's marriage could fall apart, then anything was possible.

She went into the hall and listened to the message on the answering machine. It was her mum, telling her that Raymond had arrived at the airport on time and would be in Ballyfergus for lunch. When she came back into the lounge, Chris was composed again.

"I don't know what to say," said Karen. "I really don't, Chris. This is the last thing in the world I expected. I love you and Paul. I've known him longer than I've known Tony, for God's sake. He's like a big brother to me. And I know it's maybe a bit early to say this, and probably the last thing on your mind at the moment, but my wish would be to see you back together if that's at all possible."

"I don't think that's going to happen," said Chris sadly, shaking her head. "He's in love with Bernie Sweeney."

"Now hold on a minute. Just because he's shacked up with that scheming cow it doesn't mean he's in love with her."

"No," said Chris quietly, shaking her head. "He is in love with her. Don't you remember the way they were together, at that dinner party you gave here at your house? The way they talked almost exclusively to each other all night. That wasn't the first time. They were falling in love right under my eyes and I choose to ignore it."

"You mustn't give up on your marriage so easily, Chris," said Karen, unwilling to entertain Chris's version of events.

"I'm not giving up, Karen," said Chris sadly. "I'm just being realistic. I honestly don't think the future of my marriage is in my hands. Where we go from here is very much up to Paul."

"Well, one thing's for certain."

"What's that?"

"You and he need to sit down and talk about this. Properly. If he hasn't phoned you by tonight, promise me you'll phone him tomorrow."

"I don't want to talk to him."

"That's understandable. But you must. At the very least, you need to sort out practical arrangements like paying the bills. The last thing you need is to end up in debt. And, if Paul isn't coming back, then the sooner you start talking about these things, the better. You must act to protect your interests, Chris."

"I suppose you're right," said Chris unenthusiastically. "If Paul is paying for the rent of the Bay Road flat –"

"You bet your bottom dollar he is," interrupted Karen.

"Then he'll have to start dipping into savings to pay for

it. We earn a lot of money, Karen, but we spend it too."

"That's why you need to address these things sooner rather than later," said Karen, who had an ulterior motive. If she could just get Paul and Chris talking, then maybe there was some way to sort out this whole mess. Maybe they could find a way to make their marriage work. "Now," she said, glancing at her watch. "It's nearly one. Why don't you go home and get some rest and I'll tell everyone that you're not feeling well. Unless, that is, you want me to tell them the truth."

"But I'm taking you to Mum's. You shouldn't be driving."

"It's okay, really, Chris. I'm perfectly capable of driving myself. Anyway, I'm not so sure you should be behind the wheel of a car."

"But I want to come. I want to see Raymond," protested Chris.

"But Chris, you're in no state!"

Chris, sounding more like her old self, said angrily, "I'll be damned if he's going to spoil Raymond's homecoming for me or anybody else. Mum's expecting me for lunch and I'm not going to let her down or allow my problems to spoil this for everyone."

"Okay," said Karen, glad to see signs of Chris's spirit returning. "But you have to promise me one thing."

"What's that?"

"That you have something to eat when we get there."

Chris tried to raise a smile but it died before it reached maturity. "You're worse than Mum. But I'll do my best."

They went outside and got in Chris's car.

"Are you planning on telling them about Paul?" said Karen.

"Not today," said Chris, firmly, as she eased the car onto the road and drove off. "This afternoon is about Raymond and Shona, not me. I'll tell them tomorrow."

"Okay," said Karen.

"And about their party —" began Chris.

"Yes, we need to sort that out. Look, I can have it at my house. It'll be a bit of a squeeze but we'll manage. Or I suppose we can always cancel — I mean postpone it. People will understand."

"Thanks. But no," said Chris, pausing at a deserted junction to raise her sunglasses and turn her steely gaze on Karen. "The party goes on as planned in our house. As I said before, I'm not about to let Paul and Bernie Sweeney ruin this for Raymond and Shona. Or the rest of the family — Mum's been looking forward to the party for months."

"Are you sure, Chris? Are you sure you're really up for it?"

"It's a fortnight away. I'll be fine by then. No, that's not true — I won't be fine. But I'll be able to cope." She replaced her shades and turned the car into the main road. "And if Paul's not coming home then I need to face up to that. I can't go round sticking my head in the sand any more. That's what got me into this trouble in the first place."

"You mean ignoring what Bernie was up to?"

"I mean, Karen," said Chris, and her voice dropped so low it was barely audible, "that my marriage has been in trouble for some time. We've been living more or less separate lives. Perhaps if I'd faced up to that, instead of pretending nothing was wrong, this never would've happened."

Karen did not press for details and was quiet for the rest of the short journey. It was unsettling that she had been so blind to the reality of Chris's marriage. She thought she knew Chris and Paul, and yet it seemed she had not known them at all. It was amazing what people could keep hidden from those closest to them. Things were not at all the way Karen had imagined them to be – and she couldn't help but wonder what other unpleasant surprises life had yet to offer.

Her earlier euphoria was gone. She thought of the pink dress hidden in the wardrobe and how her excited anticipation about the party had turned to anxiety. Now all she could think about was how awful it would be for Chris and Hannah and Finn. Because by then everyone would be aware that Paul had left Chris and was living with Bernie Sweeney.

Sixteen

So far Tony had managed to evade a meeting with Shona but, as the day of the big party approached, he knew there was no avoiding it. For one thing Karen was starting to become suspicious. He'd even feigned illness to avoid going out for lunch with Raymond and Shona last Sunday.

He would have to meet Shona eventually – he couldn't hide from her forever – and a busy party might be a better option than most. He told himself he would've phoned her, but he couldn't get her phone number without raising suspicions. He could, of course, have called at her rented home in Cairndale Heights, in the hope of catching her at home alone. But what if Raymond, or someone else, had been there? The truth was, he was a coward. He had put the inevitable off until it could no longer be avoided.

On Saturday morning he got up (after lying awake for hours) and went for an early morning jog. The air was mild, the sky was blue; it was going to be a beautiful day, but the realisation bought him no joy. All he could think of was Shona and how he could minimise the risks to his marriage.

As he pounded the pavements, he planned his strategy. His objective was to blend in with the crowd and ensure the introduction to Shona was as brief as possible. He would need to talk to her properly at some stage, but it was important to get that initial meeting over with as quickly as possible, whilst making it clear that he was going to pretend he did not know her. Shona would not be expecting to meet him, let alone find out they were to be related by marriage. But she was, or had been, a very level-headed person. It was in her interests as much as his, he imagined, to keep their shared past a secret. His priority was to protect Karen from ever finding out about it. And everyone else for that matter.

Timing too was crucial. He didn't want to arrive at the party too early – that awkward stage when the focus is on new arrivals – and he didn't want to arrive too late, which would attract unwanted attention. Half a mile from the house, overwhelmed with mental fatigue, he stopped running and walked home. But his heart still pounded in his chest with anxiety rather than physical exertion. What if Shona betrayed him? Intentionally or not, it might happen. He tried to prepare himself for the eventuality but the outcome was so awful he could not seriously contemplate it.

After a shower and a late breakfast he took the children swimming and, after lunch, Karen ushered them upstairs to get ready for the party. When she brought them downstairs fifteen minutes later they looked adorable – Jack in a smart pair of beige linen trousers and a white shirt and Chloe in a yellow sundress. She sat them down in the playroom in front of a DVD and went upstairs to get ready herself.

When she came down again nearly an hour later, dressed in a tight-fitting pink dress, she took his breath away. She looked absolutely amazing, with her flowing blonde hair and silver high heels. She wore a pretty silver necklace around her neck and her nails were painted a glamorous pink to match the dress. He had never seen her look so sexy. And it wasn't only her appearance. She exuded confidence and sex appeal in the way she moved her hips, tossed her hair and shimmied up the hall. She was, once again, like the woman he had married and had feared, for a while, would never return. He had not entirely approved of her surgery but, if this was the result – restoring his wife's confidence as much as changing her physical appearance – then it had been worth every penny.

He let out a long low whistle. "You look absolutely stunning, Karen."

She put her hands on her hips, tilted her head back like a nineteen- fifties screen goddess, and gave a throaty laugh. She smiled properly for the first time since that terrible business of Paul Quinn and Bernie Sweeney.

Tony thought Paul a complete fool and would have told him so had he had the chance. But Paul seemed to have disappeared off the face of the social world. He had, for example, stopped frequenting the golf club, formerly one of his favourite haunts. Tony knew he should call Paul. Had they not been brothers-in-law they would never have been friends but, still, they had known each other for over ten years. But right now Tony had much more important things to worry about; he put Paul and his problems out of his mind.

"Will you look at the time?" said Karen and tutted. "You'd better hurry up and get dressed. I promised I'd be over nice and early to help welcome the guests. Chris needs the moral support and I can't let her down."

"Of course not – but I'll need a shower first."

"You had one after you came in from your jog this morning."

"But I went swimming."

"Didn't you shower at the pool?"

"No."

"You don't need one. You'll be fine. Just get dressed and we can go."

"Chlorine," said Tony, bringing his forearm up to his nose. "It stinks. I need a shower to get rid of the smell."

"Oh, Tony," she cried, sounding exasperated with him, "the party's supposed to start at three. We're going to be late!"

"Look, why don't you go on ahead with the kids and I'll be over just as soon as I've had my shower."

"But I wanted us to go together, as a family!"

In the end, after a short but not acrimonious debate, he won. Karen bundled the kids into the car, her pretty smile now replaced with a temporary scorn and Paul watched them drive away. He went upstairs, had a leisurely shower, got dressed slowly and sat down on the bed to put on his shoes. He put on some aftershave, combed his hair and, when he had procrastinated as long as possible, he finally got in the car, put on his sunglasses and drove slowly over to Chris's house. The air conditioning in the car was on, but beads of sweat formed on his brow and his stomach churned uncontrollably. In an effort to quell his nerves, he rehearsed what he planned to say to Shona in his head.

When he got to Castlerock, a row of cars was parked on the normally quiet street. He drove up the lane and found an assortment of vehicles littering the forecourt in front of the house. That was a good sign - there must be lots of people here already. He squeezed the car in a gap between the hedge and a big BMW he didn't recognise, and turned off the engine. He sat for some minutes fighting his instincts to turn the car around and drive away. But he knew that this moment could be delayed no longer. He told himself, as he often told his pupils, that worrying about something was always much worse than actually doing it. He closed his eyes and prayed that this would be the case. Then he took a deep breath, stepped out of the car into the glorious sunshine and walked into the house.

After the brightness of outside, the interior was dark and relatively quiet. He removed his sunglasses and waited for his eyes to adjust to the gloom. He could hear women's voices from the kitchen, and the squeals of children at play in the garden. He walked to the door at the end of the hall that lead directly into the garden, put on his shades, opened the door and stood on the threshold.

He quickly scanned the garden for Shona, his heart pounding in his chest. There were perhaps fifty or sixty people in the garden, standing in small groups on the red brick patio, on the grass lawn to his left, and sitting on chairs in the sun. A dozen or so children, amongst whom he immediately spotted Jack, ran wildly around the grassed area playing with the puppy. Karen, looking lovely, was with Chloe over by the rose patch, attending to some small crisis and had not yet noticed him. She had a half-full wine glass in her hand.

But Shona was nowhere to be seen. He breathed a sigh of relief.

The south-facing garden of Casterock was large and walled and always reminded him of *Tom's Midnight Garden*, his favourite book as a child. The garden wasn't as big as the one in the story but it had a magical, entrancing quality to it that had always appealed to Tony. In the house's previous incarnation as a dental practice, the garden had been neglected. But, over the years, Chris and Paul had restored many of the original features and returned the garden to its former glory.

Beyond the patio was a pond with water lilies floating on the surface and a weathered fountain in the centre, from which a gentle trickle of water cascaded into the pool beneath. To the right lay Paul's vegetable patch, greenhouse and fruit canes, burgeoning with unpicked raspberries. Up the east wall, by the lawn, grew trained pear and apple trees that produced the most delicious fruit Tony had ever tasted. He wondered briefly who would look after the fruits and vegetables, now that Paul was gone. And it occurred to him how foolish Paul was to throw all this away.

"There you are!" cried Chris and she hurried over to meet him. She was elegantly dressed in wide-legged cream trousers and a cream silk top, draped around her thin figure. She wore discreet gold jewellery and gold-coloured pumps on her feet.

She kissed him on each cheek and he said, quietly, "How are you, Chris?"

"Bearing up," she said brightly, but the smile on her face was strained and she looked more haggard than he had ever seen her, even when her father died.

He patted her on the arm. "You know we're always here for you," he said and he meant it. "Whatever you need."

"I know. And thank you, Tony," she said softly and then, in her hostess voice, "Now you must come and meet Raymond and Shona. Raymond's been asking after you all afternoon."

She led him by the arm towards a small group he had not noticed behind a bank of flowering azaleas, covered in large pink blooms. As they approached, he recognised Karen's mum, Phyllis, a little pudding of a woman with a head of tightly permed brown curls and happy disposition. There was an aunt and uncle of Karen's from Antrim, Raymond and, to his right, Shona Johnston.

She was immediately recognisable by her high forehead and almond-shaped eyes, her too wide mouth and slightly large nose. She was older and thinner than when he'd last seen her, but still very attractive. She wore a long flowing summer dress, her dark hair was pulled back in a ponytail and she was smiling; she looked happy. His heart sank for he knew the horrible memories his presence was about to inflict upon her. He wished he could turn and run and if it hadn't been for Chris's guiding hand upon his arm he might have done just that.

His heart pounded in his breast and he felt wet patches of sweat underneath his arms. He wiped his damp brow with the back of his hand and steeled himself, going over and over in his head what he must say.

"Hello, everybody," said Chris, leading him into the centre of the small crowd. "Look who's here!"

He smiled a greeting at everyone, taking care not to look at Shona. Raymond stepped forward, a little heavier than Tony remembered him, and with less hair. He pumped Tony's hand between both of his in that friendly, exuberant ex-pat style of his.

"Great to see you, Tony," he said. "Great to see you." And he slapped Tony on the arm.

"You too, Raymond. You too," said Tony, blushing with embarrassment and wondering how Raymond would feel if he knew the truth about him and Shona.

"Tony," said Chris, "this is Shona Johnston, Raymond's

fiancée. Shona, this is Tony Magill, Karen's husband."

He forced himself to look at her then but did not remove his sunglasses, which he had always considered the height of rudeness when meeting someone for the first time. He could not bear for her to see into his soul. He did not want her to see the shame in his eyes for what he had done and what he was about to do. He wanted to keep his emotional distance.

"How do you do? Lovely to meet you, Shona. I've heard a lot about you," he said and took her limp hand in his and squeezed it firmly. She squinted at him in the sunshine, there was a flicker of recognition in her eyes and her features froze.

"I understand we were at Coleraine round about the same time," he said quickly, almost babbling, "but I don't think we ever met."

There, it was done. He dropped her hand like it was a hot coal, closed his mouth and hated himself. He watched as the smile faded slowly from her face, like the setting sun.

"Well, I think you've met all of the Mullvenna clan now," said Chris good-naturedly and everybody laughed.

"Now all you have to do is remember everyone's name," said Karen's aunt – he could not recall her name – and they all laughed again.

Suddenly there was a splash and a cry went up on the other side of the garden. Everyone but Tony and Shona turned to look.

She stared at Tony, ashen-faced, her expression one of painful confusion.

"Mum! Mum! Murphy's fallen in the pond!" cried Chloe.

"Quick!" screamed Hannah, her voice very close to Tony. "Get him out."

Shona tilted her head to one side and her eyes filled with tears. She swallowed and shook her head slowly, disbelieving. Sadness and then hurt settled on her face. Tony could look upon her no longer. He turned away.

"I'll get him," shouted Finn's voice and Tony ran over to the pond, grateful for the timely diversion. He was ashamed of himself for snubbing Shona but what else could he do? He would talk to her later, explain that this way was best for both of them. Fate had thrown them into each other's path once more, but he would not allow the past to dictate their future.

Finn was leaning on the stone flags at the edge of the pool, reaching out over the water as far as his long arms would allow. Murphy was just out of reach, almost completely submerged in the bright green algae-covered water save for his little black snout. His front legs were working frantically under the water to keep him afloat. Finn stretched his fingers a few centimetres more and managed to grab the dog's collar and haul him to the edge. He set the sodden little body on the grass and he stumbled, then almost immediately regained his footing. Everyone cheered and clapped. The puppy shook the water from his fur, soaking Finn and Tony and, entirely undaunted by his swim, ran off, tail wagging, to chase the smaller children who had already lost interest in the drama.

"Well done, Finn," said Tony and the youth gave him a wide grin and stood up.

"I thought he was a goner, the stupid little bugger," he said, his voice full of affection.

"Oh, thank you, Finn," said Chris, running over to them and giving Finn a big hug.

"Muuum!" he said, in the whiney voice that all children

have perfected by about the age of six and continue to use well into adulthood to indicate embarrassment with their parents.

"Sorry," said Chris, with a sniff. "It's just if anything happened to him . . . " Her voice trailed off and she put her hands to her face.

Finn, his embarrassment suddenly evaporated, put his arm round his mother and guided her towards the house. Tony guessed that he sensed, like he did, that her overreaction to this minor incident, had more to do with the current state of her marriage than Murphy's welfare.

Karen, who had been watching, clapped her hands loudly to draw everyone's attention to herself (and away from Chris) and said, "Okay, everybody. It's time to eat! There's a buffet in the kitchen, through these double doors here. You can eat inside or out, wherever you like."

People started to gravitate towards the house and Karen came over to Tony and kissed him on the cheek.

"Is Chris okay?" she said anxiously. "I knew this was too much for her."

"She's fine. Look, she's over there now chatting away to your cousin."

Karen frowned and watched Chris for a few seconds. Then, apparently satisfied, she turned to Tony and said, "I thought for a minute you were going to jump in there!"

"I didn't get a chance. Finn beat me to it. Anyway it would've ruined my shoes." He lifted one foot off the ground and showed her his brown suede loafer.

"Well, you're still my hero," said Karen and, smiling happily, she linked arms with him and led him towards the house.

"Are you having a good time?" said Tony, keeping one

eye on Shona who was holding onto Raymond's arm and looking at the ground. Raymond said something to her and patted her arm.

"Yeah, brilliant. And we've been so lucky with the weather. Oh, have you met Shona yet? She's just over there," said Karen, starting to steer him in Shona's direction.

He pulled her back. "We've met already."

"She's lovely, isn't she? I really like her."

"The only woman I'm interested is right beside me," said Tony and Karen laughed and cast him a coy glance through a veil of blonde hair.

"You know, everyone's been complimenting my dress and my figure," she said, and Tony smiled. This uncharacteristic, but harmless, display of vanity made him suspect that she might be a little worse for drink.

"And so they should, so they should. Because you, Karen, are the most beautiful woman here."

Seventeen

"Do you think everybody's finished?" said Chris, standing in the middle of the kitchen and surveying the table which was covered in the remains of the buffet.

"Yeah, I think so," said Karen, with a loud but happy exhalation of breath. "By the time we get this cleared up, it'll be time to go home. Come on, it'll not take long."

She picked up some dirty plates and began stacking them. The party had been fun but it had taken a lot out of her and she felt suddenly fatigued. She was feeling much, much better than a fortnight ago, but still experienced a little bit of swelling and discomfort. Dr Mezz had said it could take months for things to finally settle down. But a little bit of pain couldn't eclipse her joy for Raymond and Shona. Shona had turned out to be just great. A lovely person whom she was sure would soon become her, and Chris's, friend.

Some of the other female relatives leant a hand and soon the food was all decanted into plastic containers and the serving dishes washed and neatly stacked for the caterers to collect in the morning.

"There's loads left over," said their mum. "Enough to feed you for a week!"

"Here," said Chris, "why don't you take some, Mum? And Karen. And you too, Auntie Gladys. And Tracy." Tracy was their first cousin on Dad's side. There were murmurs of dissent, everyone too polite to accept and Chris urged, "Please take some. Go on, it'll only be wasted and it'll save you having to cook tomorrow. There's rice salad and potato salad and some of that nice ham."

"Mmm, the ham was particularly delicious," said Auntie Gladys, Mum's lovely bird-like sister, who had never married. At seventy-six she was eight years older than Phyllis and she looked so insubstantial with her thin little legs, and skinny arms. But her appearance was deceptive for she had the constitution of an ox. She lived alone in a terraced house on The Old Glenarm Road and walked to Drain's Bay and back almost every single day of her life, a round trip of over five miles. Karen had never known her to be ill.

"Is there any beef left over?" said Phyllis, peering into the plastic containers on the table.

"Loads," Chris said. "Go on, help yourself. There's some disposable foil trays in that cupboard over there you can use."

"Thanks," said Karen. "The food was delicious. You gave them a wonderful party."

"Do you really think so?" said Chris, as the women descended on the table like locusts.

"Absolutely fabulous, darling!" said Karen, doing a Joanna Lumley impression and Chris laughed and then became serious again.

"I never got the chance to tell you earlier, Karen, but you look fantastic. Not just your tummy – it looks great – but your hair and your dress and everything. You just look amazing. You're ... you're," said Chris, searching for the right word, "radiant."

"That's because I'm happy," said Karen and she beamed with pleasure.

"You know, I had great reservations about your operation. Not just because of the risks but because I thought that it was unnecessary, that you were obsessing about your stomach. But now that I see the difference it's made – that flap of skin that used to hang down is completely gone. And I think I understand now how diet and exercise would never have shifted that."

"I really, really appreciate you saying that, Chris," said Karen, ecstatic to have her sister's approval. It meant more to her than Chris could possible realise.

Someone called "Chris, we're just leaving!" from the hall. She rushed off and Karen noticed Hannah lurking in the doorway.

"Han!" she called and waved her over to her.

Hannah loped across the kitchen with her hands in her pockets, and Karen noticed a fresh piercing in the top of her right ear, the flesh around the bright gold stud red and throbbing.

"Ouch! That looks sore!"

Hannah shrugged. "It isn't," she said nonchalantly and Karen suppressed a smile, quite sure she was fibbing.

"I bet your mum went ape when she saw that," she said. Having an older niece and nephew gave her an insight into what her own children would be like as teenagers one day. There was no doubt it was a challenging stage, but she hoped she would be more tolerant than Chris and Paul. While they were great and loving parents, they demanded a level of conformity from their children that Tony and she found too restricting. The result was Hannah's multiple body-piercings and Finn dropping out of school. But both kids had good hearts and Karen loved them very much.

Hannah smiled coyly, revealing white teeth between nearly black lips and said, "You could say that. But I guess she's got more important things on her mind at the moment."

"And your dad? What did he say?"

"I'm sure he doesn't give a shit," she said, the smile falling from her face like curtain going down.

"When did you last see him?" said Karen, ignoring the profanity which she considered understandable under the circumstances. Hannah had always confided in her and she did not want to break that trust now by acting like a parent.

"Not since he left us."

"He hasn't left you, Hannah," said Karen, hiding her concern that Hannah had not seen her father for a fortnight. "He's left your Mum. And with any luck that might only be a temporary state of affairs."

"I doubt it," said Hannah gloomily.

"Have you spoken to him on the phone then?"

"Yeah. He keeps calling me on my mobile trying to talk me into coming round to see him. And her."

Karen sighed and said, "And what about Finn? Has he seen him?"

"Nope."

"Doesn't he want to?"

"He's too busy going out and getting pissed all the time to care."

"Does your mum know about this?"

"I don't know. I guess so," said Hannah with another shrug and Karen made a mental note to address this with

Chris as soon as possible. Finn was still below the legal drinking age and while Karen had a pretty relaxed attitude to nearly-legal drinking, it sounded like a cry for help.

Karen stared at her niece, long and hard, disappointed by the cynicism that she detected in her and which, she was quite sure, had not been there before. She hated Bernie Sweeney even more because of it.

"Listen Hannah," she said urgently and leaned closer. "Paul is still your Dad and always will be. And no matter what's happened between your mum and him, it's important that you keep your relationship with him. Why don't you arrange to meet him somewhere neutral, like Zanzibar?" she said, referring to a trendy local coffee shop. "All you have to do is have a coffee with him. Will you do that? For me?"

"I'll think about it," said Hannah, kicking the floor with the toe of her chunky black boots.

"Thanks," said Karen.

The conversation at an end, as far as Hannah was concerned, she grabbed a handful of crisps from a bowl on the island unit and slunk out of the kitchen.

Karen watched her go and sighed. Then she collected up all the wet tea towels and went into the utility room to throw them into the washing machine, navigating her way round Murphy's furry little body on the floor. He was flat out asleep, exhausted after the day's excitement, cuddled up to a tatty old stuffed toy – too mangled to discern what it might once have been.

She bent over to load the machine, and thought of how much she liked Shona and what a great day it had been, apart from the sad business between Chris and Paul – and the knock-on effect on their kids. Something would have to be done. She shook her head sadly and tried to put their problems out of her mind for the moment.

She added some powder to the machine, switched it on and straightened up. She ran her hand over her belly and thought that the sheer pleasure of that feeling would never cease – a taut, smooth surface instead of the grotesque apron of flab that had once existed. She knew it sounded farfetched, but the operation had changed her life. She felt sexy and attractive again. Her joviality, which she had used partly as a way of covering up her inadequacies, now sprang naturally from genuine contentment. And although it was early days, she was slowly becoming less self-obsessed and genuinely focussing on others rather than thinking constantly about herself.

The operation had also helped her put her fears in perspective. She knew that she had become paranoid about Tony, imagining that every attractive female within ten miles was a threat to her marriage. This had been very unfair to him, she now realised, because her fears were based on the assumption that, faced with temptation, he would be unfaithful. And he had never, in all their years of marriage, given her any cause to doubt him. She had so much to be grateful for she thought happily as she closed the door and left the utility room.

Just as she emerged, she happened to glance into the conservatory, which was attached to the east gable end of the house and not directly visible from the kitchen. She saw a man step inside it from the garden, and a few seconds later he was followed by a woman. Curious, she drew closer. She stopped a few paces from the half-glazed door that led into the conservatory, surprised to see that it was Tony and Shona, standing facing each other.

But her surprise quickly turned to confusion. Tony said something to Shona, put his hand on her arm and it was brusquely shaken off. Karen could not hear what they were saying, but from their body language and expressions – she could see them both side on – it was clear that this was not the ordinary, social conversation one would expect from two people who had just met.

Karen held her breath and watched with increasing anxiety as an emotional exchange took place between Tony and Shona Johnston. Shona appeared angry, upset and at one point Tony put his hand over his face as if overwrought with emotion. Then Shona stormed out and, a few moments later, Tony followed her. The conversation had lasted less than two minutes.

She let out her breath very slowly, battling to keep the sobs from coming. Very quietly, she retraced her steps to the utility room and closed the door. She sat down on a small stool in the corner, which Chris kept for reaching high places, and felt the blood drain from her face. She folded her arm across her body, suddenly chilled. The tears came then but she told herself to calm down, think rationally. She brushed them away crossly and tried to think clearly.

What had she actually witnessed? Nothing more than a conversation. But not a conversation between two strangers. A conversation between two people who knew each other, and who had deliberately sought out the privacy of the conservatory where they thought no-one would see them. What were they talking about and why was Shona angry with Tony? Had he said something to her, offended her in some way? If so, why the secrecy? No, it wasn't that. It wasn't in Tony's nature to go around insulting complete strangers and anyway, any slight or insult would've been dealt with in public with Raymond as Shona's defender.

Had Tony met Shona at some point in the last fortnight? If so, when and where? And why would he have kept it a secret from her? Was it possible Tony had known her in a previous life? It wasn't impossible, but it seemed unlikely. Anyway, why would he keep a former acquaintance, even a former lover, a secret?

She had a feeling about this and it was a very bad one. No matter how she tried to rationalise and come up with scenarios to explain what she had seen, there was only one explanation that made any sense to Karen. They had something to hide. And that, in Karen's book, could only mean romantic involvement of some kind.

Her head swam and she steadied herself by holding on to the adjacent unit. She worried she was going to faint and damage her still tender wounds. How could she have been so stupid to think that an operation could overnight turn her into some sort of siren? She was still plain old Karen, with her dyed hair, big hips and boobs, sagging eyelids and a face that had never been pretty enough. Tony did not love her – he probably only stayed with her for the kids' sake. And why should she be surprised that he had fallen for Shona Johnston? She was gorgeous – slim and pretty, everything Karen wasn't. And if Paul could leave Chris, what made her think her marriage was safe?

But, there was hope. Karen was sure she detected genuine affection, love even, in Shona's feelings towards Raymond. She was engaged to marry him. She was not a free agent, unlike that scheming Bernie Sweeney.

So maybe, just maybe, whatever had transpired between Tony and Shona, it was over. She had to believe it. She could not believe otherwise for she could not countenance the thought of losing Tony. And she would do anything, put up with anything, if only he did not leave her.

★ ★ ★

Out on the lawn, once the excitement of Murphy's near-death swim was over, Tony waited for the opportunity to speak to Shona alone. He watched her like a hawk, never once taking his eyes off her. Towards the end of the party, when people were starting to talk about making tracks for home, his chance came. He happened to notice that Shona was momentarily standing alone by the conservatory, looking lost, with a wine glass in each hand.

Seeing his opportunity he quickly excused himself from the company he was with – some cousins of Karen's and their spouses – and went over to her.

"We need to talk," he said.

"I'm sorry?" she said imperiously.

"Can we go somewhere where we can talk?" he said, though he was quite convinced she'd heard him the first time.

"Oh, so you want to talk to me now," she said, her voice dripping with sarcasm.

"Please, Shona," said Tony, glancing over his shoulder, "we have to talk. Look, come in here a minute," he said, spying the deserted conservatory, much too hot on a sunny day like this to be in use.

He walked over and tried the door. "It's open," he said over his shoulder and put his hand on the brass handle. She hesitated, looked at the glasses in her hands, then back at him.

"Please," he said. "Just two minutes."

And, casting a parting glance at the people in the garden, she walked towards him across the lawn.

Inside the Victorian-style conservatory it was stifling hot, like the stove wing of the Palm House at the Botanic Garden in Belfast. The glasshouse had been added to the house ten years ago and it was tall and large, about the size of Tony's lounge at home. It was bursting with lush, green foliage and grapes vines groaning with the weight of heavy clusters of dusky black grapes, which Paul had tried and failed to make into palatable wine over the years. The air was thick and still and humid – you could've cut it with a knife. Shona stood just inside the doorway still holding the wine glasses, one empty, one half-full, in her hands. Tony glanced behind her to make sure no-one had followed them, the sweat already starting to drip from his brow.

"Shona," he said, acutely aware that they only had a few minutes before someone would come looking for them. Instinctively he put his hand on her arm. "I'm very, very sorry about earlier. I've known who you were for some weeks and I didn't know what to do. I didn't know if you would find out from Raymond who I was. If you would put two and two together, like I did."

"I didn't," she said flatly. And shook his hand from her arm.

"Well, I'm sorry it came as such a shock. I didn't mean to snub you."

"Well, what did you mean to do then?"

"I meant to protect us. Both of us. From our past."

She stared at him impassively. "Since when have you given a fig about me? Or anyone else, other than yourself?"

376

He sighed, and decided to ignore this comment because deep down he thought she had a point – the Anthony Magill she knew had been extraordinarily selfish. He liked to think he was a different man today. He hoped he would get the chance to show her.

But right now he needed to secure her agreement to keep their shared past a secret. "The thing is," he said, "everyone thinks we don't know each other."

"Thanks to you!"

"I'm assuming," he went on, ignoring this barbed comment, "that Raymond doesn't know about us? About what happened?"

She shook her head. "Why should he? I never expected to see you again."

"Same here," said Tony. "But the thing is, well . . . my wife Karen can be very possessive. I can't ever tell her. And I'm sure you'd rather Raymond didn't find out either."

"But you didn't have to pretend we'd never met before," she said crossly. "Why couldn't you just have said you recognised me from Uni and we'd been out socially in the same company a few times? That was all you had to say and leave it at that. A half-truth is better than a complete lie."

"I don't know. I guess I panicked. I'm sorry."

"You're sorry about a lot of things," said Shona bitterly.

"More than you know," said Tony and he felt his voice choke up with emotion. He put his hand over his eyes, suddenly faint with the heat. "I think about – about what we did almost every day . . ."

"What *I* did," snapped Shona and her eyes were ablaze with fury. "What *I* did, Anthony Magill. It's my story, not yours. It happened to me, not you, and I have the right to keep that a secret."

He closed his eyes with relief when she said this, and opened them again when she added, "Or not."

But he knew that was an empty threat. He had seen the way she looked at Raymond. She loved him and would not do anything to risk losing him. She said this, he was sure, because she was still angry at him.

She turned and walked out the door into the garden before he had the chance to say another word. Seconds later he stumbled after her, almost sick with the heat. He found a chair and collapsed into it and a relative sense of peace began to descend upon him.

Meeting Shona again had been extremely unpleasant and he'd felt like a cad all over again – just as he had done all those years ago. But he'd done it, and the old maxim had been proven right – thinking about something was always worse than doing it. He'd averted disaster and hopefully secured happy futures for them both. He wished Shona all the luck and happiness in the world, he really did, because she deserved it.

"Are you all right, Uncle Tony?" said Hannah, dressed from head to toe in black and plastered in dramatic make-up, which failed to completely hide her good nature and pretty face.

"Just too much sun," he said, and gave her a weak smile, squinting into the early evening sunshine.

"Daddy, Daddy!" cried Chloe. She bolted across the lawn and threw herself into Tony's arms. Her mouth was smeared with chocolate, her tidy ponytail all askew and the front of her little dress splattered with food stains. Tony imagined what Karen would have to say when she saw the state of her and smiled.

"What's wrong, Chloe?" he said.

Chloe grinned, her perfect little teeth even and white. "Nothink."

"I love you, Chloe."

"I love you, Daddy." She put her arms around his neck and kissed him on the lips with her soft little mouth all puckered up and her eyes squeezed shut. He had never seen or experienced anything so adorable.

"How cute is that?" said Hannah.

Tony hugged Chloe to him, his eyes full of tears – he loved her so much – and his heart soared. It had been months since he'd had a decent night's sleep. He'd endured weeks of worry, imagining the worst, ever since he'd first heard Shona's name at that dinner party they'd hosted. And now he had faced her, and his own demons and, if not quite put them to rest, then at least subdued them for the time being. But there was still work to be done.

He had minimised the risk, as much as possible, of Shona exposing their shameful secret. Now he would have to rebuild a relationship with her – as a sister-in-law this time – with their past put firmly behind them, where it belonged. But, with good will on both sides, there was no reason why a harmonious state of affairs couldn't be reached. And everyone could live happily together.

★ ★ ★

The sun had lowered in the sky casting long shadows on the grass beyond the conservatory and Karen realised she had been sitting there for some time. She checked her watch. Nearly half an hour had passed. It was surprising that nobody had come looking for her.

She composed herself as best she could and hauled

herself to her feet. She walked through the house looking for the children, her glamorous heels digging into her feet like instruments of torture. Every movement required great effort and she felt ugly and foolish in her fashionable dress and strappy shoes, more suited to a girl Hannah's age than a forty-two-year-old woman. She just wanted to take the children and go home.

She met Phyllis in the hall who said anxiously, "Is Chris all right, do you think? I saw her in the garden earlier and she seemed a bit upset. What was all that about?"

"The dog falling in the pond."

Mum tutted and said, "She's far too attached to that animal. It's only a dog. It's not as if a child nearly drowned."

"I don't think," said Karen, wearied by sadness and her mother's insensitivity, "that it was entirely to do with Murphy. Chris is under a lot of stress, Mum. Murphy falling in the pond was just the trigger that set her off. She wasn't crying over him. She was crying about Paul."

"I see," said Phyllis, thoughtfully, and she narrowed her eyes. "I liked Paul Quinn, you know. Loved him even, like a son. And now that he's gone and run off with that harlot, I think I really hate him. I don't know what he sees in her."

"Me neither," said Karen truthfully.

"Do you think there's any chance of them getting back together?"

"I don't know. Would you want them to? After what Paul's done? Do you think she should take him back?"

"If he wants to come back, yes."

"She should just forgive and forget?" said Karen, thinking of herself, rather than Chris.

"I think that, if she loves him, she should do everything within her power to save the marriage."

"That's what I thought," said Karen and, suddenly faint, she sat down on the bottom step.

"Are you all right?"

"I . . . I . . .," she said. "I think I might have overdone it. I need to go home. Mum, can you get the kids for me, please?"

"Is this because of that stupid operation? Or have you had too much to drink?"

"Please, Mum," said Karen, her eyes filling with tears, unable to bear her mother's criticism.

"All right, I'm going!" she said and disappeared into the garden shouting, "Tony! Jack! Chloe!"

Chris came out of the drawing room and, as soon as she caught sight of Karen, said, "What's wrong?"

"Oh, I just feel a bit unwell," said Karen, hauling herself to her feet. "I think I've maybe overdone it. Had too much to drink, knowing me! And I don't think standing about all afternoon in these heels has helped. I think they put a bit of a strain on my stomach muscles."

"Is your tummy sore?"

"A little," lied Karen, for the pain in her heart far eclipsed the minor discomfort in her belly.

"Well, then, we'd better get you home," said Chris and she sprang into action and disappeared after Mum. A few moments later both women arrived back in the hall with Chloe, Jack and Tony in tow.

"What's wrong, darling?" said Tony, his face etched with concern and he came over and put his arm across her shoulders.

She could hardly bear the touch of him. "Oh, it's nothing really. I just feel a bit unwell. I'd like to go home now."

"Of course, sweetheart," said Tony, his arm still around her shoulder and he kissed her on the side of the head. "Chris, thanks for a wonderful party. Goodbye, Phyllis."

The children said their goodbyes and everyone exchanged kisses.

"Aren't you going to say goodbye to everyone, Karen?" said Phyllis. "I think most of them are still in the garden."

"No, you say it for me," said Karen quickly, terrified that she would come face to face with Shona. She would have to confront her again soon – there was no avoiding it – but she wasn't sure she was up to it right now.

Phyllis frowned, always a stickler for protocol and Chris stepped in with, "Karen's not feeling well, Mum. She needs to go home."

Karen gave her sister a grateful smile and Chris said, "You're not driving, are you?"

"If it's okay, I'll leave my car here and collect it tomorrow."

"Or I might take a walk down tonight and get it," said Tony.

"Whatever. Either's absolutely fine by me. Now you go on home," said Chris, and Karen suddenly noticed how exhausted her sister looked. She was putting on a brave face but today had taken a lot out of her. Not least, she imagined, having to cope with the well-intentioned, but intrusive enquiries about Paul from everyone at the party. But she had been determined to host the party and Karen, who only now felt she truly understood what Chris was going through, was full of admiration.

Karen longed to unburden her heart to her, to break down and share her fears with a sympathetic and loving listener. But she knew that would be unspeakably selfish.

Chris had more than enough on her plate at the moment and the last thing she needed to hear about were Karen's problems. She would worry herself sick. So Karen forced herself to smile as best she could and left.

In the car on the way home Karen kept her eyes trained on the view out the passenger window and said, "Are you sure you've never met Shona before?"

Tony laughed. "Of course not. When would I have had the opportunity? She's only been in the country less than two weeks."

"I don't mean in the last fortnight. I mean before. When you were at Uni, maybe?"

"It's possible. But if I did, I don't remember her. You know what it's like when you're a student. All those drunken parties – you're meeting new people all the time." He paused and then said, the tone of his voice betraying him, for she could hear the anxiety underneath the attempt at light heartedness, "Why, did she say something to you?"

Karen paused and felt the tension in the air. She was sure Tony was holding his breath.

"No," said Karen and she was just as certain she could feel his relief. She let a few moments pass and added, "I thought I saw you talking to her in the conservatory."

"I was. She was looking for the way to the loo."

"Mum," came Chloe's quiet little voice from the back seat, "I think I'm going to be sick."

"Too much ice cream," said Tony calmly, without giving any indication that he was going to stop the car.

"Quick! You'd better pull over!" cried Karen and the car came to a dignified halt.

Karen was out of the car before Tony had even undone his seatbelt, tore open the back door and hauled Chloe onto the grass verge, just in time for her to spew the contents of her belly onto the road. Karen could never understand how Tony responded with such composure to domestic crises such as this, albeit a minor one. It wouldn't be so minor, she thought dryly, if Chloe had puked up inside his car.

The pale pink milky vomit splattered on the tarmac and over Karen's sandaled feet, which seemed a fitting way to end the day. She held her daughter's hair above her head, to save it from being soiled, and whispered words of comfort while Chloe retched again. And Karen's heart felt like it would break, because she believed that Tony had never lied to her before.

★ ★ ★

On Monday morning Chris did something she had not done in her entire career. She called in sick when she knew she was capable, physically at least, of going to work. But emotionally, she simply could not face it.

After the last of the guests at Raymond and Shona's party had left at nine o'clock last night she had literally crawled into bed, absolutely exhausted by the strain of the day. She had put on a nightdress but not taken off her make-up: another first. And she woke up late – she must've forgotten to set the alarm – feeling as exhausted as when she'd gone to bed the night before.

She pulled on her dressing gown (peach silk to match her nightdress) and made the call to work hoping Rose, who was always first in, would answer it. She was in luck. And when she said she wasn't feeling well and would not be in work today, Rose, who knew what was going on at home, did not press for details.

Downstairs, Finn and Hannah had already left for work, as evidenced by the remains of their breakfast still on the table. It irritated her that they had not cleaned up after themselves and then she remembered that was her fault. She had spoiled them. Now that she was on her own she realised that they would have to pull their weight around the house more. She could not do everything herself. Until they left home, that was, and she would be entirely on her own.

She looked around the kitchen at the mess still to be cleared away from yesterday and put her head in her hands Her aunts and cousins and other female guests had done much to tidy up but there was always a limit to what strangers could do in someone else's house. Hence the pile of dishes on the island unit still to be put away (because no-one knew where they went), the garden chairs strewn about the garden to be folded and stored in the shed. There was a stack of drink people had brought on the floor by the sink to be dealt with and a cardboard box of cans and bottles to be sorted for recycling. Two black bin bags full of rubbish sat by the back door and the floor was filthy with dirt from the garden, spilt drink and food crumbs.

Before Paul left she would never have gone to bed and left these things undone, even if it meant staying up 'til the small hours to do it. Yesterday had been hard work – too hard – and she realised that she would, as people kept telling her, have to drop her standards. But she was a perfectionist and it did not come easily. She despised Paul for placing her in a position where she would have to compromise her standards.

She opened the door to the utility room, and Murphy came bounding out. She petted him and went over to the patio door to let him into the garden.

"Sit!" she commanded and the dog ignored her. She

repeated the command but he continued to stand, sniffing at the bottom of the door. In the end she had to physically force his bottom to the floor with her hand before he would obey. That was another thing that had gone to pot; the dog's training. And if she didn't get on top of it soon, she would have an unmanageable dog on her hands. She opened the door and let him out.

When the doorbell rang she decided not to answer it. She stood completely still in the centre of the kitchen, listening, and her heart started to pound in her breast when she heard the sound of the handle being turned and the door opening. She thought for one terrifying moment that someone was breaking in and she glanced around for a suitable weapon. Then she realised that whoever it was, they had a key. She thought of the children first, but deemed it unlikely to be them. It must be Paul.

She listened to the sound of the door closing and the soft tread of his footsteps on the stairs. She realised that he thought the house was empty. He had only been back to the house twice, as far as she knew, to collect the rest of his clothes and some of his wine, but it occurred to her that, with a key, he could come and go as he pleased. She followed him upstairs to the study where, through the open door, she saw him take medical books off the shelves and place them in a sturdy cardboard box he must have bought for the purpose. He was dressed for work in blue slacks, white shirt, blue tie and a tweed jacket.

She looked at the gaps on the shelves, like teeth knocked out in a fight, and there was something so final about this action that it galvanised her. She realised that if she did not act decisively, and soon, there would be no hope whatsoever of saving the marriage.

And when all was said and done, she realised that she had been hard on Paul. He wasn't a bad man, just a bit of a bore and she had plenty of faults herself. She had been cold and unloving – no wonder he had sought comfort in Bernie's arms. But she had loved him once and she felt that, with help, she could learn to love him again. She realised that she did not like to be without a partner. She had missed him these last couple of weeks.

She stepped into the room and he jumped with fright and dropped a book on the floor.

"Jesus, Chris," he said and placed his hand over his heart. "You scared the living daylights out of me."

"Well, it is my house, Paul. Who did you expect to find here?"

"I thought you'd be at work," he said, bending down to retrieve the tome.

"Of course," she said and refrained from making some other sarcastic comment. She went and sat on the sofa underneath the window and watched him.

He glanced up at her and frowned and she remembered that she must look a fright with last night's smeared make-up still on and greasy hair plastered to her head. "Are you not well?"

"No. I'm off sick."

"I'm sorry to hear that." He finished placing the last of the books in the box and closed the lid.

"Paul," she said.

"Chris," he said, at the same time.

"You first," he said.

She swallowed. "I've missed you, Paul." She paused but he did not say anything. He stood with his hands in his pockets, looking at the floor.

"Would you consider going for marriage counselling, Paul? In the hope that we could save our marriage. I'm willing. I'd go on my own too if that would help. I know I'm very controlling and a bit anal and maybe I need some help to change."

He sat down heavily on the office chair that sat in front of the computer. He let out a long sigh and put his hands together between his knees. He looked at the floor for some moments before raising his eyes to meet hers. There was something superior about the way he looked at her. Worse, she detected pity in his gaze.

"I think we're past that stage, Chris," he said calmly and paused for his words to sink in. "I'm happy, really happy, for the first time in, oh, I don't know, years probably. And I'm sorry about how that happened and I appreciate that you must feel very hurt and betrayed, but believe me I would never have fallen in love with Bernie if I had still been in love with you."

She stared at him, undecided if she should respect him for his honesty or despise him for it.

"Maybe marriage guidance could have made a difference a few years back but I feel it would be too late now," he went on. "I just don't care any more. No, that's not true, I do care. I care about you, Chris, and I'd like to see you happy but I don't, and can't, love you."

"I see," said Chris slowly, regretting her earlier candidness.

"Chris," he said and paused. "I've been to see a solicitor. I'm quite keen to get things sorted out properly. I'll fulfil all my obligations financially and I promise I'll take care of the kids. But we need to start thinking about our future. Our separate futures."

"Oh," she said and felt like she'd been winded. Involving a solicitor was such a decisive, serious step.

"Have you . . ." he said gently, "have you spoken to a solicitor yet?"

"No, why would I have?"

"Well, I think maybe it's time you did."

"Are you telling me that you want a divorce, Paul?"

"Eventually, yes. Meantime we need to come to some sort of arrangements regarding household expenses and the like. In a few months' time Hannah will have left home and, well, things will change once again."

She knew what he was hinting at. Once Hannah left home there would only be her and Finn rattling around in this big house, their main asset. One of the grandest houses in Ballyfergus, it had to be worth nearly a million pounds. No doubt he would want to liquidate his share of it – and Bernie would want to get her hands on the money. Chris didn't have the resources to buy him out and he knew it. Eventually it would have to be sold.

"Forget everything I said," said Chris and she stood up. "You're going to have to give me the key to the house back."

"Pardon?"

"You heard what I said. The key to the house, Paul," she said, her voice like sharpened steel.

"I don't think so," he said with a half-laugh, "It's my house too."

"Half of it may legally belong to you Paul but it is no longer your home. And I can't have you coming in here and snooping around when I'm not here. How would you like it if I did that in your flat? How would Bernie like it?"

"But I need to collect my stuff. I've loads of things in the garage to go through."

"You'll get your stuff. I certainly don't want it. But you'll need to make proper arrangements to come and collect it when I'm here."

He looked at her warily, undecided if she was serious or not.

To help him make up her mind, she added, "I'll get the locks changed if you don't, Paul, and I'll charge it to your credit card. And that would be a silly waste of money, wouldn't it? And at a time when you have so much extra — expense."

"Okay," he said defeated, took the key from his fob and set it on the desk. "I hope we can do things amicably, Chris. You're a reasonable woman. I'm sure if we use mediation and a collaborative arrangement, it would be easier on us both. It would be crazy to involve all the expense of going to court."

"Collaborative arrangements. Mediation," she said sarcastically. "You've obviously done your homework. But don't worry about me, Paul. I'm perfectly capable of looking out for my own interests and, believe me, I will."

He picked up the box and without another word walked down the stairs and out to the car. She followed him barefoot onto the forecourt where the sharp shingle cut into the soles of her feet. He put the box in the boot of the car.

"And another thing, before you go," she said, pulling the flowing dressing gown across her chest. "Have you forgotten that you're a father?"

"Don't be facetious, Chris. Of course I haven't forgotten."

"Oh, good. Because you haven't seen either of your children in a fortnight."

"That's not for want of trying," said Paul, and he

slammed the lid of the boot down. "I've spoken to both of them several times on the phone. But they don't want to come to the flat."

"And why do you think that is?"

"How should I know?"

"It's because they hate Bernie."

"They don't hate Bernie. You hate Bernie. You just wish they did too."

"I don't hate Bernie," said Chris, seething with anger and lying through her teeth because she wanted to appear superior. "I feel sorry for her, pinning her hopes of happiness on you, Paul Quinn. Because in the end you'll let her down."

"Yeah, yeah, yeah," he said in a bored tone and she truly hated him then. He got in the car, turned on the engine and pulled away from the house.

She picked up a stone and threw it at the car. But her aim was poor and the stone fell far short of its intended target. As the car disappeared down the drive, she put her hands over her face and burst into tears.

She wanted to hurt him the way he had hurt her. And she knew exactly how to do that. She ran into the house, went out into the back garden and across the grass, still wet with dew, and opened the door of the shed. She found the rusty felling axe that Paul used to chop wood in the winter for the fire. She carried it in both arms back to the house, the hem of her wet dressing gown slapping against her bare legs.

She walked through the kitchen, past the utility room, and set the axe down, head first, on the floor in front of the wine cellar. The padlock was still there, glinting at her menacingly in the morning sun that streamed through the window in the back door.

She lifted the axe, both hands on the haft, and swung it. Her first attempt was a poor one. The blade went into the doorframe and stuck there. She pulled it out, breathing heavily. There was a vertical gash in the wood. She took careful aim and tried again. This time she struck home but the axe simply bounced off the metal. She examined the padlock. It was dented but still very much intact. She realised she would have to try a lot harder if the padlock was to give.

She stood still for a few moments, collecting her thoughts and concentrating her energy on the glinting metal lock. Then she picked up the axe, placed the blade on her target, breathed in, swung it back and hit home with vicious vengeance. The padlock rattled against the door but did not give way. She did the same over and over, each blow becoming more expert than the last. She did not stop until the shackle was hanging from the padlock. Then she set the axe on the floor, let out a long, hot breath and fell to her knees. She felt terrible and she felt elated. And most of all she felt justified.

After she'd recovered from her exertions, Chris got up, pulled the shattered remains of the padlock from the door and opened the cellar. Inside she could see that Paul had already taken some of the cheaper wines from the section nearest the door. The finer ones were all still there, probably because he did not have suitable storage for them and feared they would deteriorate in the wrong conditions. She wondered what his long-term plan was for the wine. He probably hoped to force an early sale of the house, get his share of the proceeds and buy a house with a cellar – or somewhere with the potential to create one.

It wasn't difficult to find what she was looking for. In

addition to storing wines by type, Burgundy, Bordeaux etc., for some reason Paul liked to put the very finest wines on the bottom row of his shelving system. She knelt down, pulled out a few bottles to read the labels and soon found what she was looking for.

She stood up with a bottle in each hand, weighing them. Two dusty bottles of red Bordeaux, not her usual choice but tonight was special occasion. She was celebrating the fact that she was, to all intents and purposes, now a single woman. It would be some time before the marriage was legally dissolved but, after today, she knew that it was effectively over. And, in spite of her anger and grief and sorrow, there was something to be said for knowing where she stood.

She took the bottles through to the kitchen, wiped the dust carefully, almost lovingly, from the bottles. She remembered buying these for Paul on their twentieth wedding anniversary last year. They were 1961 Margaux, the labels badly soiled but legible. Each bottle had cost over five hundred pounds and they were the pride of Paul's cellar. She set the bottles snugly in a corner of the kitchen work surface away from direct sun. By tonight they would be the perfect temperature for drinking.

She picked up the phone and dialled Karen and two of her closest friends, Julie and Clare. She left a message asking them round for a carry-out supper. Then she busied herself cleaning up the kitchen and when she was finished she ran a hot bubble bath in the en-suite bathroom.

She lay in the hot suds and eased her wedding band and three-stone diamond engagement ring from her finger. She had some difficulty getting them over her knuckles, but they came off in the end. And though she had always been able to twirl them round her ring finger, she was surprised to see that they had left indentations at the base of her digit. She set them on the side of the bath and realised that, in amongst her mix of torturous emotions, there was an element of relief. She no longer wanted to be married to Paul. But still she cried all the same – for what had been and what might have been, had they been able to love one another.

That night she poured the wine for herself and her three guests and took a glass through for Hannah and Finn to try. After all it wasn't every day she opened a bottle of vintage wine.

"What happened to the label on the wine bottle?" said Julie, a Pilates teacher Chris had known for fifteen years. They had met when their children were small.

"Oh, it must've got damp at some point and deteriorated."

"Is the wine okay?" said Karen, examining the ruby-coloured liquid in her glass with suspicion. She sniffed it, wrinkling up her nose and said, "It's not been in the cellar too long, has it?"

"Oh, no. The wine itself is absolutely fine," said Chris. "Do you like it?"

"What is it?"

"Oh, just some old bottles of Bordeaux I found lying around."

"It's okay," said Karen, "but you know me, I'm a Chardonnay girl at heart."

"And you, Julie and Clare, what do you think of it? Be honest now."

They both nodded politely and Clare said, "I prefer Pinot Noir. But it's very, very nice."

Chris put the glass to her lips and took a small sip of the wine. Lovely though it was, a price tag of five hundred pound was ludicrous. And she smiled at the delicious irony of it all. If Paul could see them he would weep. And he deserved to.

She woke up the next morning with a raging hangover (so much for the theory that you didn't get one with fine wines), her euphoria of the previous evening gone. Her little act of revenge, so sweet and delectable at the time, now tasted stale. Paul would be genuinely upset when he discovered the wine gone and there was no way of replacing it. She deeply regretted what she had done and, more than anything, she was disappointed in herself. She resolved not to let herself sink that low again.

And with the hangover came despair. Yesterday she had felt an element of relief, today all was blackness. Her marriage was over and everything that she had worked for, strived for, all these years seemed pointless. Her beloved home which she had so lovingly restored and furnished would in the end be lost to her. Her children too would soon be gone, embarking on their own independent lives. She hoped they did not make the same mistakes as she. She hoped that they would find true and enduring love. All she had to look forward to was a lonely middle age and growing old alone.

But she still had her career – the one thing that, along with her children's and Karen's love, was constant. At work she was competent and successful. At work she could try and forget what a mess her life was in and she could pretend, for a little while at least, that she was someone else.

So she showered and dressed and went into the office and tried to act as though her world wasn't falling apart.

She found it hard to concentrate. Rose had to tell her things twice before they sunk in, three times she picked up the phone and dialled a number only to forget who she was calling and why. Quickly she slammed the receiver back in the cradle, her heart pounding, before she made a complete fool of herself.

At coffee break she sat quietly at her desk, a mug of tea cradled in her hand until it went cold. She stared out the window at the busy street completely unable to engage in the usual office chitchat. She felt that she was moving through a thick fog, everything muffled by grief. And she was surprised when, checking the missives for a client who was buying a house, a spot of water landed on the documents. She touched her cheek and realised that she was crying.

"Chris," said a voice she recognised, but it was much softer, much gentler than she had heard it before.

She looked up, the rims of her eyes stinging with tiredness.

It was Sam, standing over her with his suit jacket on. "Come on," he said, quietly. "I'm taking you for an early lunch."

She looked at the papers on her desk, and tried to form the words to decline but no sound came out. He eased her gently to her feet, thrust her handbag into her arms and led her out the door, the office staff watching in complete silence.

In the car Chris tried to collect her thoughts. She felt like her head was in a vice, pressure building up, pressing in on both sides of her head until she thought that she would scream. She thought of asking Sam to take her home but realised that she didn't want to be alone. She felt safe with him.

At the restaurant Chris rummaged in her bag for paracetamol while Sam ordered.

"Shall we have the soup?" he said. "And perhaps a ciabatta roll with mozzarella, tomatoes and basil?"

She nodded, and washed the pills down with water. He understood, without the need for her to say anything, that she was incapable, at this moment, of making any decisions for herself.

When the waiter had gone and they were alone, Sam said, "Do you want to tell me what's going on, Chris?"

She fiddled with the soup spoon and said, "No, not really."

"It's affecting your work."

"Is that all you care about?" she snapped and immediately regretted it. "I'm sorry. I've got this terrible headache," she said by way of apology.

"I heard that you were having some – marital problems," he said tactfully.

"That's Ballyfergus for you! No chance of keeping anything a secret in this town, is there?"

"Doesn't look like it."

There was a long silence which she broke at last. "Paul left me two weeks ago. He's gone to live in a rented apartment in Bay Road with a woman whom I thought was my best friend." A little sob escaped her and she composed herself before going on. "This woman, Bernie, she'd been staying in our house as a guest. She was on an extended trip from Australia."

The telling of the sorry tale seemed to sap all her energy.

"So that's how Paul met her?"

"Yes," she said with a long sigh. "I had no idea it was going on, Sam. None at all. I feel that Bernie deceived me. I feel like they made a fool out of me."

"They both betrayed your trust," said Sam, "but no-one's made a fool out of you."

"Well, that's what it feels like. They were having an affair right under my nose and I never noticed. And I thought there was a chance we might be able to save our marriage but it seems, well, it seems there's no chance of that now. Paul's consulted a lawyer and he's told me to do the same."

"And have you."

"No."

"Well, we'll get onto that right away. Pamela Craig is one of the best family lawyers practising in the province."

Chris was familiar with the name. Pamela worked for Stevenson and McIlwaine and she'd met her briefly on a visit to the Belfast office where Pamela worked. She was in her early thirties, attractive with slicked back dark hair and blood red lipstick. She looked like a woman you would want on your side.

"There'll be no charge," he said.

"I can't accept that. The bill could run into thousands."

"Consider it a perk of the job."

"No, really I can't . . ."

"Nonsense, Of course you can. I insist."

She did not have the energy to argue with him.

"So you accept?" he said.

She nodded and said, defeated, "Yes. Thank you."

Their soup came and they ate quietly.

When it was finished he said, "You've taken your rings off." He took her hand and touched the place on her finger where the rings had once been. There was still an indentation there. "Why did you do that?"

"I don't really know. To make it real," she said and gently pulled her hand from his grasp. She looked at the empty place on her finger and started to cry. "I feel like my life is over. I don't know what to do or how I can go on."

"Oh, Chris, please don't cry." He handed her his napkin – hers had slid to the floor – and she dabbed her eyes. "I've been through a divorce, Chris, and yes, it's painful. Don't believe anyone who tells you otherwise. But you'll get through it. And though it might seem impossible now, you will one day be happy again."

"I can't ever imagine that. The pain is unbearable. I can't go on."

"You can and you will," he said firmly. "Believe me, there are a lot worse things than divorce, Chris."

The waiter came, giving Chris the chance to compose herself. The soup plates were cleared away and filled rolls appeared on the table. Neither of them touched them.

Sniffing back tears she said, "Why did you get divorced, Sam?"

He took a deep breath. "We lost our only son, Chris. And I guess neither of us ever got over it."

"Oh my God!" she cried out and put her hand on her heart. "What age was he?"

"Twenty-one months old," he said. His face contorted momentarily and his eyes misted with tears.

"Please don't tell me if it's too painful," she said, her own problems temporarily forgotten, her eyes filling on account of his grief, not her own.

He cleared his throat and said, matter-of-factly, "No, no I want to. Maybe, it'll help put things in perspective for you." He paused, rearranged the cutlery on the table and went on. "Deirdre, my wife, was a lawyer with Nicolson and Dudgeon. She'd taken maternity leave to have Conor and she'd always planned to go back to work eventually, when he started school. She had a great pregnancy, and a natural birth, but Conor was a difficult baby. He was under six pounds when he was born, he cried a lot, had difficulty feeding and went on to become a poor eater and very clingy to his mother. He was always underweight and he remained slight for his age. We were exhausted most of the time from lack of sleep and Deirdre was desperate to go back to work. It always makes me sad to think back to that time. We were so blessed with our little boy and we were too stressed to appreciate him. We were always saying things like 'It'll be easier when he can walk', 'It'll be easier when he's at nursery', 'It'll be easier when he's at school'. The truth is that it's never easier, is it? It's just different, and we were too young and foolish to understand that. If only I could have that time with him again . . ."

His voice trailed off. He took a drink of water. Chris said nothing, gripped by his narrative.

"Anyway, we agreed that she would go back three days a week and Conor would go to a childminder. One Monday morning at the beginning of June she took him into the office, which had by this time relocated to new premises on Great Victoria Street, to discuss the terms of her contract. I never blamed Nicolson and Dudgeon – they were only renting the premises after all. And the building had passed all the necessary building regulations. It was shared with several other businesses. There was a tall atrium as you came in with a reception desk and a flight of stairs that led up to the first floor where the firm had their suite of offices. It was all very modern with lots of chrome and glass. There were frosted glass panels on the side of the staircase instead of traditional balusters; you know the vertical bits that hold up the handrail."

She nodded and he went on.

"The meeting was over and they were coming out of the meeting room and Conor ran ahead. Deirdre never thought anything of it. She guessed he would head for Moira's desk, one of the secretaries, because she had talked to him and given him sweets earlier. But Moira was on her coffee break when Conor came out and he kept on going. He got to the top of the stairs, somehow squeezed through the gap between the glass panel and the metal newel post, and fell twenty-eight feet onto the stone floor below."

Chris and put her fist in her mouth, speechless with horror.

"He died instantly. Multiple internal injuries. Broken bones all over his body, fracture to the skull, massive internal bleeding. The doctors said that, had he survived, he would've been severely brain-damaged so maybe it was a blessing that he died."

Chris bit the back of her hand. Sam sighed heavily and stared forlornly at a place on the wall as though he could see an image of his little son etched there on the plaster.

"Because it was summer he was only wearing a wee pair of shorts and a T-shirt. Deirdre's mum had bought them for him. They had pictures of Winnie the Pooh on them. He loved Winnie the Pooh. Maybe if it had been winter and he'd had on a big padded jacket . . . Maybe if he hadn't been so slight for his age . . . Who knows? But the moment his little head smashed on that floor, that was the end of our marriage. It just took us six and a half years to realise it."

"Jesus, Sam. I'm so sorry. I don't know what to say. I had no idea."

"Not many people do," he said sadly, looking at her once more. "It happened a long time ago, Chris. Conor would've been nineteen in September, had he lived."

"Oh, Sam."

"Of course, Deirdre blamed herself. For wanting to go back to work in the first place, for allowing him to run ahead of her as they came out of that room. And for a while I blamed her too, which was totally unfair. Somehow we co-existed miserably until Deirdre met someone who made her happy and, do you know what? I was glad. Heart-broken but relieved. I knew I couldn't make her happy – I think we reminded each other too much of Conor. We couldn't even bring ourselves to try for another child. It was too painful. Anyway we weren't living, we were simply existing, surviving from day to day. I heard that Deirdre got married to the man she left me for and went on to have three kids."

"And you never married again?"

"No. I never met the right person."

"Oh, Sam," said Chris and she fought very hard to hold back the tears, "how did you go on living?"

"You take each day as it comes. You find something every day to be grateful for and you focus on that. It can be something as simple as birdsong, or the sun rising or a smile from a stranger. And you never close your heart to the possibility that good things will happen again. That's how I survived, Chris. And that's how you will survive your divorce. You will go on and one day you'll be ready to love again."

She nodded, trusting in what he said. Believing that, if he could survive the worst tragedy imaginable, then she would get through the trials that lay ahead.

"Why are you telling me all this, Sam? It must be very painful for you."

"Because when that day comes, Chris," he said, leaving her speechless for the second time, "I will be waiting for you."

Eighteen

It was Saturday afternoon and Bernie was unpacking her art materials in the spare bedroom which was to become her studio. She was keen to get working again because, of all the insults she imagined being heaped upon her at the moment, she didn't want gold-digger to be one of them. It felt uncomfortably close to the bone and she was doing a rather a good job of convincing herself that love, rather than money, had been her primary motivation in her relationship with Paul.

She had managed to hold onto some of her clients but she didn't know how long that would last. In the end people liked the personal touch, they liked to hold original drawings and have meetings face-to-face, which would prove impossible if she was here and her clients in Australia.

It was essential therefore that she built up a new client base here in the United Kingdom and Ireland. From the preliminary research she had done, no-one was producing anything quite like her work, so she hoped she would find a niche somewhere. If she could just get one client, more would follow. She would never earn the kind of money Paul did, but it was important that she had her own source of income; income that was hers and hers alone that she did not have to account to Paul for. If he covered day-to-day living expenses, then she could spend her own money as she wished without it having to go under his scrutiny. And Paul had financial commitments, like putting Hannah through medical school, that would make serious inroads into his income. So every little helped.

Paul had wanted the bedroom as his study but eventually they'd compromised with her taking the room and he a corner of the lounge downstairs. It was a bit of a squeeze in the apartment because Paul, unlike Bernie, was not used to living in a confined space. He'd already brought over all his clothes, medical journals and books, golf clubs, quite a lot of young, drink-now wine (stacked against the lounge wall) and there was more to come – items of furniture and objects d'art that he had inherited from his side of the family. Along with her belongings, many still in cardboard boxes, the little flat was bursting at the seams.

They would buy a bigger place, he promised, when Castlerock was sold but Bernie wasn't holding her breath. She couldn't imagine Chris giving the house up without a fight and who could blame her.

Paul reckoned they'd have enough for a decent four- or five-bedroomed house; Bernie just didn't want it in Ballyfergus. She knew she was being branded a harlot and had already been snubbed, on separate occasions, by Finn and by Chris's mum on Main Street.

The problem with Ballyfergus was that it was far too small – meeting people was unavoidable and she had the feeling that strangers were pointing at her and talking about her in the shops and places she frequented. She knew that much of this was paranoia but still she longed for the anonymity of a new place – where no-one knew them and they could start afresh.

But convincing Paul of this was another matter.

"I told you before, Bernie, I can't leave Hannah and Finn. Maybe in a couple of years, I might have a clearer idea of where they are going to settle and we can make a decision then. I'd be surprised if Hannah comes back to Ballyfergus after she qualifies but Finn could very well stay here."

"Paul," she'd reasoned, "if he won't even speak to you, does it matter where you're living?"

"He'll come round," he said confidently. "He's just angry with me at the moment."

So, much as she loved him, living with Paul wasn't quite the romantic idyll she'd imagined. Now they were actually sharing a home, the passion inspired by the illicit nature of their relationship had waned a little and the pressures of routine life took their toll. She was learning, for example, that Paul did very little around the house. Chris of course had had help – cleaners and gardeners and what not. But with the current financial strain of maintaining two homes, that option wasn't open to them. She would either have to tackle him about it, or put up and shut up. She chose the latter.

And then there was the guilt. Guilt that she had stolen another woman's husband, guilt that she had broken up a home, even though the children involved were nearly adults. Guilt that she had inflicted misery on others, especially Chris who had shown her such kindness and generosity. She had to remind herself frequently that she had not stolen anything. She had not set out to ensnare Paul. She could not be held responsible for him falling in love with her.

She took a small metal tin from a cardboard box, opened it and glanced inside. Everything was as it should be. She smiled to herself, closed the lid and hid it on a shelf behind a stack of art books – somewhere Paul would never look. She glanced at her watch. Paul was due back any minute. He'd arranged to collect his pushbike and ski equipment from the house (though God knows where they were going to put it) and then take Hannah to a coffee shop, the first time he'd seen her since he'd moved out three weeks ago. She hoped it had gone well, for she did not want to be responsible for him losing contact with his children.

She heard him come in and slam the door and a little ripple of fear made her shiver. Sometimes, his temper reminded her of her father. She had not witnessed it while living at Castlerock and wondered if he regretted what he'd done. More likely, she told herself, it was the effect of stress. Once things had been sorted out with Chris and the kids had accepted the new status quo, things would calm down and so would he.

When she came downstairs he was wrestling the cork out of a bottle of red wine.

"Well, darling," she said, "how did it go?"

The cork came out with a pop and he said, vehemently, "That Philistine!"

"What? Hannah?" she cried.

"No, Chris. She broke open the padlock on the cellar and she and her pals drank my 1961 Bordeaux."

"I told you that lock was a bad idea!"

"Of all the wine in that cellar, why'd she drink those two bottles? She said she didn't realise what they were but I don't believe her. It was her, after all, who bought them for me in the first place."

She followed him into the kitchen where he found two stemmed wineglasses and filled them almost to the brim. His hand was shaking.

"It's only a couple of bottles of wine, Paul. Let it go."

"It wasn't 'only wine'," he said paraphrasing her and there was a nasty, mocking tone to his voice. "They were worth over five hundred pounds each."

"Oh," said Bernie, understanding his anger and understanding too that Chris must have been very, very annoyed indeed to have pulled off a stunt like this. Indeed she couldn't help but admire her spirit just a little. It proved that she wasn't going to go down without a fight. But it was bad news for her and Paul. Instead of the amicable settlement Paul and she had hoped for, it looked like Paul's divorce was likely to become nasty – and that meant protracted and costly. Already she was sick of hearing about Chris.

"What about Hannah, Paul? How did that go?" she said, changing the subject in an attempt to alter his mood.

"Very well, if I'm not mistaken," he said, took a drink of wine and visibly relaxed. "She was reticent at first but we had a very worthwhile conversation in the end."

"What did you talk about?"

"Mostly about her going to Edinburgh and whether she should go into halls or a flat. And we speculated about what she might eventually specialise in, although that's rather premature. I think she'd make an excellent GP."

"Will she see you again?"

"We've agreed to meet for coffee once a week."

"That's great, Paul. Now you just need to work on Finn. Come here," she said and put her arms round him and gave him a big hug. "I don't like to see you so upset."

"Forgive me. I don't mean to take it out on you." He

kissed her on the top of the head.

The doorbell went and he sighed loudly and said, "What now?"

"I'll get it," said Bernie, wondering who it could be for, since they'd moved in, they'd had precious few visitors.

It was Karen.

"I'm looking for Paul," she said coldly and looked past Bernie into the hall.

"You'd better come in," said Bernie and she walked into the kitchen.

Karen stayed where she was, on the doorstep.

"It's Karen. She's asking for you."

"What does she want?" hissed Paul.

"How should I know?" said Bernie, hurt at being ignored yet again. She was sick of being made out to be the evil husband-stealer. Paul did after all have a free will. It was his choice to be here.

Paul went out to the front door and she heard Karen say, "No, I'll not come in."

"It's all right," said Bernie, grabbing a cardigan from the sofa. "I'm just going out." She brushed past Karen and was sure she detected a smirk on her face.

As soon as she'd left the house, Karen went inside.

Bernie walked down Bay Road, past the public swimming pool, with its wonderful sea views, on down to the seashore, hugging the thin cardigan round her small frame. It was one of those summer days made chilly by the white haar that blew landward off the sea. The hulk of a passing P&O ferry loomed large in the eerie mist and the tall Baird memorial tower, built to commemorate some prominent townsman from a time long forgotten, was almost invisible.

There were no pedestrians on the wide concreted promenade today. She hobbled over the shingle beach, picked pebbles up and hurled them inexpertly at the ocean. The smell of seaweed was, as she remembered it, overpowering. She used to come here with Chris to swim in the over-chlorinated indoor pool. It had been remodelled since then and the building was almost unrecognisable. A training pool for young children had been added, the reception area and changing facilities completely transformed and the centre extended to include squash courts, an indoor sports hall, a theatre, health suite, weights and fitness rooms. She remembered the decrepit concrete changing rooms and the grumpy old female attendant, who safeguarded your clothes while you were swimming, with grim fondness.

The café, where they used to buy post-swim greasy chips and Refreshers, a chewy treat in the shape of flat bars with a fizzy centre down the middle, was gone. It had been replaced by soulless self-serve automated machines whose contents were no healthier than the fare offered in the café nearly thirty years ago. Afterwards, they used to walk out to the tower, along a raised walkway. She had a picture somewhere of both of them sitting on the steps at the bottom of it.

She had given up a lot to be with Paul, not least her friendship with Chris. But she believed that the sacrifices were worth it. She believed that their love was strong enough to prevail over all the obstacles placed in their way, even though, like today, it was sometimes hard going. They had already overcome much and Paul, who had given up far more than she, had stood by her, steadfast in his love.

In spite of all the difficulties, she was sure that they

could make a happy life together, especially when it was cushioned by a comfortable income. This was their most challenging time when, faced with hostility and resentment like she had experienced from Karen today, it would be easy to give up, to say it wasn't worth the fight. Paul had never once expressed any doubts. But maybe that was partly because he wasn't being painted as the villain of the piece. That particular honour had been reserved for her. Bernie sighed, picked her way back across the shingle beach and started to walk home.

Back at the house, Karen was gone. Paul was sitting on the sofa, with a glass of wine in his hand, watching cricket on the television.

"What did she want?" said Bernie as soon as she came in, rubbing her chilled hands together.

"Are you cold?" he said.

"Mmm," she replied, sat down beside him and he took her hands between his and rubbed them together briskly.

"Better?" he said, lifted her hands to his lips and kissed them.

"Much," she said and smiled. And then she asked again, "What did she want?"

He let out a long sigh, picked up the remote for the television and switched it off. "She came here to try and persuade me into giving my marriage to Chris another go."

"Really? Do you think Chris put her up to it?"

He shook his head. "I don't think so. I think she just wants to turn the clock back. To restore the status quo. She wants to see Chris happy again. But I can't make her happy. I haven't made her happy in a long time."

"So. What did you tell her?"

"I told her that I didn't love Chris any more and there

was absolutely no hope of reconciliation. She was quite upset. We used to be good friends, Karen and I," he said sadly. "I'll miss her."

"Did you tell her that you loved me?" said Bernie, testing him and hating the neediness in her voice.

"My relationship with you is none of Karen's business," he said and it was a good reply but not the one she wanted to hear.

"She might not see it like that."

"Well, it isn't anyone's business but ours and I think the sooner I make that clear to people the better. I may have left Chris for you, Bernie, but our marriage was over a long time ago."

Bernie laid her head on his chest and laced her hands in his. She was weary of all this angst, of people interfering in their relationship, of Hannah and Finn and Chris and Karen. Sick of them all. What they needed was to get away.

"Look," she said, brightening, "that fog's supposed to lift in the morning. Why don't we take a run up the coast, Paul? We can make a real day out of it. We could be in Portrush for lunch, and walk along Portstewart strand in the afternoon. I'd love to visit Castlerock. And I could call in and see my Auntie Jean. It wouldn't take more than half an hour."

"Who's your Auntie Jean?" he said with an amused laugh. "You never mentioned her before."

"My mother's sister. With everything that's been going on with us, I haven't had a chance to go and see her yet."

"Where does she live?"

"In a nursing home in Portstewart."

"Are you sure she's not senile? She might not even know who you are."

"Oh, Auntie Jean has all her wits about her. Last time Michael went to see her anyway."

"I don't know. I'm so tired." And he yawned as though to prove his exhaustion to her.

"You're tired because of all the emotional stress you're under, Paul. It's taking its toll on me too. It would do us both good to get out of Ballyfergus for a day, clear away the cobwebs, get a blast of that North coast air. I'd do the driving," she added. Although she did not hold a UK license she was permitted to drive for up to twelve months on her Australian licence. "So all you would have to do is sit back and relax. Go on," she said, sensing that he needed further encouragement. "What do you say?"

"What do I say?" he repeated and put his hands behind his head, regarding her playfully. "I say, what are you going to do to persuade me?"

She laughed and throwing her legs over his, sat astride him and kissed him long and hard on the lips.

"How about that?" she said, when she pulled away.

"How about this?" he said, taking her buttocks in his hands and she started to giggle. And suddenly she had a strong sense that, in spite of all the difficulties, everything was going to turn out just fine.

★ ★ ★

The next morning Bernie was up early, doing what had to be done - packing a flask of filtered coffee with hot milk, just the way Paul liked it, and a picnic. The sun was up and it looked like it was going to be a bright, sunny day.

"What are you doing that for?" he said sleepily, as he came into the kitchen wearing nothing but boxer shorts.

"Sure we can eat out."

"I know, but a picnic's much more fun," she said, folding napkins and placing them in the top of the picnic basket. She didn't tell him what she was really doing in case he thought her foolish. She was trying to recreate some of the magic that a 'day up the coast' had inspired in her as a child. And a home-made picnic was an essential part of the package. As was eating an ice cream from Morelli's on Portstewart promenade, and salty *dulse* (dried red seaweed) from the greengrocers.

Australians raved about the health-promoting properties of Japanese seaweed, hailed as the latest superfood, which amused Bernie. It had been eaten in Ireland since the dawn of time. She closed the lid, secured the wicker toggles and said, "You'd better get a move on or you'll be left behind!"

"You won't leave me behind. You can't bear to be away from me."

She laughed and went over to him and put her arms around his neck. "You are absolutely right, Paul Quinn," she said and felt a wave of affection for him wash over her. "I love you, Paul, and I will never go anywhere without you."

She took a hanky from her sleeve and wiped her nose.

"Are you feeling okay?"

"Yeah, fine. It's just a touch of hayfever."

"You should take some tablets."

"Maybe I will."

It was late afternoon by the time they got to the nursing home in Portstewart, a double story building on Strand Road with panoramic views of the sea. It looked like it had been a hotel in a former life, though any grandeur it might have had was long gone and replaced with utilitarianism, the scourge of such places.

"It's getting fairly late," said Paul when they pulled up outside the white-harled building. "Do you still want to go in? After all, she doesn't know you're coming."

"True."

"You could always come another day," he suggested.

"It seems a shame to have come all this way and not pop in and see her, if only for a few minutes."

"Go on then," he said and swung the car into a visitor's space near the entrance.

She got out but he did not follow.

"Aren't you coming?" she said.

He pulled a face. "Malodorous nursing homes aren't really my thing."

"Oh, come on, Paul! Don't be like that. It's only for a few minutes. Anyway, she's the only aunt I have left and I want her to meet you."

He gave her a crooked smile, and then got out of the car. "I can't say 'no' to you, you do know that, don't you?"

"Just as it should be," she replied primly and gave him a flirtatious look.

The home, unimaginatively named Seabreezes, was average. Pleasantly, though not richly, decorated there was no smell of stale urine or unwashed bodies, just a rather over-powering smell of Jeyes fluid and other cleaning agents.

"These places go from one extreme to the other," said Paul wryly, as they walked down the corridor towards the sitting room. "They either smell like a sewer or the inside of a hospital. Why can't they smell like a normal home?"

The sitting room was unlike any other Bernie had seen, for the chairs were all arranged round the perimeter of the room, facing inwards. There was no furniture in the large central space in the middle, not even a lonely coffee table. It was as though the residents were arranged thus, waiting for a troupe of performers to come in and entertain them for the afternoon. But the only entertainment on offer was the background hum of a small television in the corner. Most of them weren't even looking at it. Half of them, Bernie realised, were gaga. A few of the more alert inmates who were busy knitting or reading, looked up with interest when Paul and Bernie came in.

The reason for this bizarre layout soon became clear. Almost all the residents required a walking aid of some sort, from a simple cane to a Zimmer frame. The absence of furniture facilitated their freedom to move about. A conventional arrangement of coffee tables surrounded by chairs would've made traversing the room impossible.

Bernie searched for her aunt's face along the rows of pensioners and soon found her sharp features turned in her direction, bright eyes squinting behind thick glasses.

Bernie approached and said, "It's me, Aunt Jean. Bernie."

"I know who you are, you daft girl! Now will you wheel me down to the privacy of my room where we can talk."

Bernie glanced over her shoulder at Paul, raised her eyebrows and pulled a face. Aunt Jean had always been a bit abrupt – but old age had clearly exacerbated her irritability. Bernie noticed that her aunt had put on a considerable amount of weight and her knees, just visible below her skirt, were badly swollen and marked with old scars, the results of operations to replace her knee joints. She had a hearing aid in her right ear. Every thirty seconds or so she put her hand to her ear and fiddled with the contraption.

Her room, the last at the end of the hall, was a single

one, spacious and well furnished with antique pieces Bernie remembered from the three-storied terraced house in Ballyfergus that her aunt had lived in when Bernie was a child. Her husband, who worked for Northern Ireland Electricity, had been posted to Coleraine when Bernie was seven and the family had moved away. But Aunt Jean, in spite of her testy nature, had stayed in touch and, in her own way, had been good to Bernie. She always remembered her birthday and, every summer, Bernie went to stay with her for a week in her bungalow on the banks of the River Bann. Though her aunt was strict, Bernie had loved being in a home with a mother and used to pretend, for the duration of her stay, that her cousins Rachel, Amanda and Derek were her siblings.

Bernie positioned her aunt by the window and sat in the winged chair opposite.

"I'd like you to meet Paul," said Bernie.

Paul stepped forward and extended his hand but Aunt Jean ignored him. Giving her the benefit of the doubt, Bernie supposed she had not heard her make the introduction. Or perhaps her eyesight was failing.

"Michael said you'd come home," said Aunt Jean to Bernie. "I wondered when you were going to get round to visiting me."

Paul shrugged and went and sat in a rocking chair in the corner of the room.

"I'm here now," Bernie said. "I've been busy. I had to go back to Australia to sort out my things. You know that I've moved back here for good?"

"Michael told me."

"So I'll be able to come and see you more often."

"He also told me that you'd taken up with a married

man," she said, and her face clouded. She narrowed her eyes and lowered her voice and Bernie realised that she was well aware that Paul was in the room. "I don't know what you're thinking of, my girl, taking up with him!" she hissed. "Breaking up a home! I'm ashamed of you."

Bernie glanced at Paul and blushed, her aunt's censure cutting deep. She had expected, if not a warm welcome from her aunt, at least a pleasant one. And certainly not a lecture on morality. She felt guilty enough already. She did not need the knife pushed in any further.

"So this is him, is it?" said Aunt Jean, satisfied that she'd said her piece. "Aren't you going to introduce me?"

Bernie sighed with exasperation.

Paul came and stood beside Aunt Jean's wheelchair again and Bernie repeated the introduction. They shook hands, rather limply, and her aunt addressed him.

"My nephew Michael tells me you're a doctor."

"That's right," said Paul.

"What do you think of these knees?" she said, hoisting her skirt up just enough to expose her swollen and painful-looking joints. "I've had the joints replaced twice and now they say they can't do any more. The nerves are damaged. What do you think of that?"

"Orthopaedics isn't my specialism, I'm afraid."

"What is then?"

"I'm a GP."

"In Ballyfergus?"

"That's right."

She stared at him then with a frown on her face and said, "You look familiar to me. Have we met before?"

Paul shook his head and said, with an amused glance at Bernie, "I don't think so."

"What's your family name?" she demanded.

"Quinn."

A strange look passed over her face and she said, "Bernie can you fetch me a glass of water from the sink over there."

When Bernie handed it to her aunt she noticed that her hands were shaking. Aunt Jean took a few sips, then handed the glass back to Bernie who placed it on the windowsill, within her aunt's reach.

"Are you okay, Aunt Jean?" said Bernie. "Do you need me to get the nurse?"

"A Doctor Quinn was our doctor when we lived in Ballyfergus," said Aunt Jean, addressing Paul now and doing her ignoring act again. "He looked after all my children until we moved to Coleraine. And he was Ellie's doctor too," she said, referring to Bernie's dead mother. "As far as I remember he had two sons."

"Yes, that's right. I'm the eldest," said Paul, perking up at the mention of his father's name and Bernie hoped that this tenuous connection would make Jean warm to Paul.

But her aunt's expression could not have been more murderous when she said to Bernie, "Are you sleeping with him?"

"Aunt Jean!" cried Bernie, truly mortified by her aunt's frankness.

"Oh, don't come over all coy with me. I've seen it all. Are you or aren't you living together?"

"I really don't think," said Paul, calmly, "that this is any concern of yours." But Bernie could tell by the way his corner of his mouth twitched on the right-hand side that he was really getting a bit annoyed with Aunt Jean now – and so was she. What right did she have to delve into a personal matter such as this? Maybe she wasn't as sound of mind as she appeared. Maybe she was going senile. She certainly seemed to have lost all concept of what was acceptable in polite conversation. And what was sad about that was, like Bernie's mum, she had always been very prim and proper.

A look of fury crossed her aunt's face and she pursed her wizened lips into an angry pout. "Bernie is my niece, my sister's only daughter, and I'll make it my damn business if I want to!" she spat out and Bernie was certain that was the first time she had ever heard her aunt swear.

"Calm down, Aunt Jean," said Bernie, concerned for her aunt's constitution. She had gone red in the face and appeared to be having difficulty breathing. She jumped up, went over to her and put a hand on her shoulder. "Are you all right, Aunt Jean?"

But Jean wheezed on and did not answer.

"Maybe we should go. We're upsetting her," said Bernie to Paul, disappointed that the pleasant interview she'd envisaged had, for some unfathomable reason, deteriorated into an undignified squabble.

But her aunt grabbed her by the arm, dug her surprisingly strong fingers into her flesh, and said, "No, don't go just yet. Just give me a few moments." She took a few deep breaths, composed herself, and asked, much more calmly, "Do you plan to marry?"

Bernie looked at Paul and blushed. They had never talked about marriage, but it had been her secret hope that one day, when Paul was finally divorced, that they would. Already sick of slander and sniggers behind her back, she wanted their relationship to be legitimised.

Paul stared at her aunt long and hard for few moments with his arms folded defensively across his chest. And then, apparently deciding to be perfectly transparent with her, said, "We have no plans to marry. Not at the moment. I am not yet divorced. But I hope that one day Bernie will become my wife. If she will accept me."

Bernie looked at him and her eyes filled with tears. She thought of her mum's simple wedding and engagement rings nestling in the felt box at home. They would be her rings when the time came. And when she was married, she would be safe, protected. Paul would not be able to say no to her then, no matter what she asked of him. Paul had just made her the happiest woman alive.

Aunt Jean stared in horror from Bernie to Paul and back again, and then a look of grim realisation settled on her face. She nodded slowly to herself as though accepting very reluctantly something she didn't want to.

Bernie found herself suddenly angry with the old woman. Why couldn't she be happy for them? Paul was an honourable man and he had more or less promised to marry her when his divorce came through. Wasn't that good enough? Was Aunt Jean so old-fashioned that she expected them to live apart and refrain from sex until that day?

"What's wrong, Aunt Jean?" said Bernie. "Why do you look so miserable? Why can't you be happy for us?"

Her aunt let out a long sigh and Bernie was astonished to see a lone tear slip from the creased corner of her eye and make its way down the crevices of her face, in a zigzag, the way a skier descends a slope. She had never seen her aunt cry before. She looked at Paul and shook her head, completely perplexed.

"Maybe I should wait outside," said Paul quietly, sensitive to her aunt's distress. He walked softly towards the door.

"Yes. And it's time you went too, Bernie," said Aunt Jean very quietly and, despite a softness in her voice which Bernie had never heard before, she was hurt.

Bernie did not move and Aunt Jean pulled a monogrammed lace handkerchief from her sleeve and dabbed at her cheek. Then she placed a liver-spotted hand, the thin skin on the back of it as delicate as tissue paper, on Bernie's bare arm.

"Please," she said. "Leave me now. I'll write to you. Leave me your address."

Bernie pulled a notebook from her bag, scribbled down her address, ripped the sheet from the book and placed it on the table in front of her aunt. She did not look at it.

"Go on. Go!" urged Aunt Jean and Bernie did as she was asked because her aunt was not someone to be gainsaid.

* * *

They drove home in silence, Paul at the wheel this time for Bernie was too distressed to drive.

"I don't understand it," she said. "Asking us if we were sleeping together, swearing, crying. I've never seen her like that before. It was totally out of character."

"Try not to let it upset you," said Paul. "It's quite normal for elderly people to become irascible, even with those they love. It's possible she's had some sort of mini-stroke or suffered neurological impairment that's affected part of her brain. It can make people say, and do, things that are completely out of character. You mustn't take the things she said too much to heart."

But Bernie did take them to heart, for Paul had never known Aunt Jean in her prime. And, while she wished that she could take comfort in his assurances, she knew that there was nothing wrong with Aunt Jean's brain. Had she been able to put her aunt's obvious dislike of Paul and odd behaviour down to feeble-mindedness, she might have been reassured. But her aunt was as sharp and perceptive as ever and that was what bothered Bernie.

Bernie's intuition had never failed her, except in the glaring case of Gavin and she attributed that particular failure to being blinded by love. No, she just knew that something was wrong.

Nineteen

One Thursday evening a week or so into August, when Tony got home from football coaching (he had volunteered to help run a two-week-long course for primary school children), he found Karen in the kitchen with her mum. His mother-in-law's presence was no surprise for she usually came round once a week to join them for tea.

The kids loved having her there and Tony enjoyed seeing them interacting with their grandmother. After tea she invariably stayed to put them to bed and read them their bedtime stories, giving him and Karen a welcome break.

She was a loving granny and it was a ritual that he was sure the children would always remember with fondness. It reminded Tony of his granny when he was a boy – though she had lived with them and was therefore available every night for bedtime duties. Until, that was, she got Alzheimer's when he was twelve and her personality changed. He used to think she had been possessed by the devil then. Poor soul – her last few years had been tortured. But those early days, cocooned in the warmth of his granny's love, were very precious memories. He just wished his own mum was there to see Jack and Chloe grow up.

He said hello to both women, kissed them on the cheek and briefly exchanged small-talk about their respective days. Then Chloe came in and dragged her grandmother away to read a story to her.

"So, how are you, love?" he said to Karen and she gave him a strained smile.

"I'm great," she said but there was something incongruous about her words and her body language. They simply didn't match. Her expression was sullen, her shoulders hunched and did not look at him when she spoke.

"Are you sure?" he said doubtfully.

"Of course I'm sure," she replied rather sharply and he wondered if she was suffering from pre-menstrual tension. Or perhaps her bad temper was related to the operation – another cycle of hormonal imbalances, perhaps, that affected her mood. She had gone from being very depressed after the surgery to euphoric (he couldn't get the image of her, flirtatious and sexy, in that fabulous dress at the party out of his mind) back to depressed again. She had stopped talking about her flat tummy and new silhouette. The pink dress had been confined to the back of the wardrobe and, to his despair, the woman who'd worn it that day at Chris's house appeared to have disappeared.

"What's for tea?" he said.

"Spaghetti bolognese."

"Great," he said, wondering why he felt he was treading on eggshells. "I'll just pop upstairs to change," he added and, when Karen didn't answer, he went up to their room and changed out of his sports gear into light cotton trousers and a polo shirt.

Maybe she was worried about Chris and Paul. He knew

she had, against his advice, gone round to the flat in Bay Road to try and persuade Paul to go back to Chris. He'd refused of course and she had come home very upset. Maybe she was anxious about work – she was back full-time now. Maybe it was too pressurised or maybe, after spending time at home recuperating, she was missing the kids. Whatever it was she wouldn't discuss it with him. He had tried to talk to her twice in the previous week but she'd insisted nothing was wrong.

But lurking in the back of his mind was the possibility that she had found out about Shona and him. But how? He was quite sure Shona wouldn't have told anyone. No, that couldn't be it. And anyway, if Karen had found out, he was quite sure she would have confronted him. His guilt was making him paranoid. He wished that she would let him help her. He wished that the old happy Karen would come back. He sighed and thought that women were very complex creatures. He would just have to give her time. He would have to wait.

"So, when are you all off on your holidays?" said Phyllis brightly as they sat round the table in the kitchen, eating spaghetti bolognese, slices of baguette and salad. It was simple, but one of Tony's favourite meals.

"The twenty-first," said Karen and Tony hoped that by then she would have cheered up a bit.

"Oh, that's not long, is it, children?" said Phyllis happily, playing the role of granny with great gusto.

"How many sleeps, Nana? How many sleeps?" cried Chloe, her face fairly plastered in tomato sauce.

"Here, love, let me get something to wipe your face," said Karen and she got up, found a wet flannel and wiped Chloe's face clean. Karen was such a good mum.

"Eleven sleeps," said Phyllis, counting in her head. "Is that right, Karen?"

"That's too long!" Jack moaned. Chloe copied him.

"Twelve actually," said Karen, with an apologetic smile for her little boy and girl.

Even more moans, louder this time, playing up to the audience. The adults all laughed and Tony was pleased to see genuine joy on Karen's face for the first time in over a week.

"It's not long really," said Phyllis. "And it'll pass quickly because there's lots of exciting things happening before then."

"Like what?" said Jack.

"Well, do you remember I promised I would take you to the zoo during the holidays?"

"Yes!" shouted Chloe and Jack nodded.

"Well, I thought we could go next week," said Phyllis and the children cheered. "Maybe next Tuesday?" she went on, directing her question at Karen and Tony. They looked at each other and shrugged their shoulders in agreement.

"Sounds great to me," said Tony, thinking that he could meet Karen for lunch. Maybe take her somewhere nice to cheer her up.

"What else, Nana? What else?" cried Jack.

"How about a sleepover?" said Phyllis. "At my house."

Even better, thought Tony. He and Karen could go out for a romantic meal, or better still, a romantic night in. He couldn't remember the last time they'd had a bath together or shared a bottle of champagne, just the two of them. And maybe they could make love, something that Karen hadn't, understandably, been up to since the operation.

"Brilliant!" cried Jack. "Can we stay up late and watch a DVD?"

"Of course."

"Can we bring our cuddlies?" said Chloe doubtfully, referring to her soft toys.

"You can bring whatever you like, darling," said Phyllis gently, patting Chloe's grubby little hand, which was resting on the table.

"What else, Nana? What else?" said Jack and everybody laughed.

"We'll see," said Phyllis, refusing to be drawn further before she had committed herself to a week's worth of activities. "I'm sure we can think of lots more exciting things to do together."

"Will you play Shopping List with me?" said Chloe, referring to her favourite board game.

"Yes, after tea," said Phyllis.

"I'm full up," said Jack.

"Me too," said Chloe.

Karen looked doubtfully at their half-full plates and said, "What do you think, Mum?"

"Oh, I think they've done very well, don't you? After all, they have to leave room for their Curly Wurlies!" said Phyllis, referring to the chocolate-covered caramel bars Tony could see sticking out of her handbag, which was hanging on the back of her chair.

"You bought us a Curly Wurly!" said Jack in astonishment and Chloe giggled with nervous excitement.

"Okay, you two," said Karen. "You can leave the table."

The children vacated their seats at the speed of light.

"Can we watch TV in the playroom?" said Jack.

"Yes," said Karen.

Chloe shouted, "Yeah!" and ran round the table.

"Can we have our Curly Wurlies now, please Nana?"

said Jack and the two of them stood in front of her quivering with excitement, holding out both hands to receive the treasured treat.

"When you ask like that, Jack Magill, you can have almost anything," said Phyllis and she placed a chocolate bar in the hands of each child.

"Thanks, Nana!" they shouted in unison and ran out of the room.

"Don't get chocolate on the carpet. Or the sofa," Karen called half-heartedly after them, probably well aware that her pleas fell on deaf ears.

Phyllis sighed. "They're adorable, aren't they?" She rubbed the back of her neck with her hand, took a sip of red wine, lifted her plate to one side, and said, "That was delicious, Karen. Thank you."

"Yes, it was," said Tony. "As always," and Karen looked slightly uncomfortable with his praise.

"Jack reminds me a bit of Raymond when he was that age," said Phyllis thoughtfully. "He had the same blond hair and they've both got your dad's nose."

"Yes, I see it too," said Karen and then she asked, "Have you seen Raymond this week?"

"Just the once. He's started his new job so he's very busy. Shona's been left to do all the unpacking on her own. I stopped by for a coffee with her on Tuesday. And I think Chris was planning to call in today."

"I've just been so busy," said Karen quickly. "I haven't had the chance to call by the house. I'll send some flowers."

"That would be nice. I'm sure she'd appreciate them," said Phyllis. "Maybe you and Chris could take her out sometime, for a meal or something. She hasn't got any friends here you know. Wouldn't that be a nice thing to do, Tony?"

This was Phyllis' way of having a not-so-subtle dig at Karen for not, in her view, being proactive enough in engineering a friendship with Shona. It did cross Tony's mind that it was unlike Karen, she was normally so friendly and sociable and had talked a lot about making friends with Shona.

However, in her defence he said, "Karen's back working full-time, Phyllis. Between that and two kids to look after, there's not much time left for anything else. And I'm not sure she's fully recovered from the operation yet."

"I'm fine," said Karen a little irritably, and he was annoyed that his attempt to defend her had been rebuffed.

Letting the matter drop, Phyllis said, "Raymond did pop in on Wednesday night for a short while." She let out a long sigh and added, "I'm afraid I had a bit of a go at him."

"What about?" cried Karen.

"Setting a date for the wedding. He and Shona don't seem to be in any hurry at all. But I don't like them living in sin. It's not right."

Tony had to suppress a smile at her traditionalism but he respected Phyllis too much to openly mock her values. He wiped the smile from his face.

"You know what people in Ballyfergus are like," she went on. "Tongues are wagging already. Everybody at the party was asking when the wedding was going to be. And they all know they're living together in the same house."

"Oh, Mum. You're imagining it. No-one cares about that sort of thing nowadays," said Karen, expressing sentiments Tony shared but, as Phyllis' son-in-law, would not articulate for fear of offending her.

"Your generation might not. But mine does. Hilary Carson," said Phyllis, referring to her second cousin, "acted all horrified when I told her at the party that they were moving in together. I could've hit her." She let out an exasperated sigh and added, rather sadly, "There's something else."

Karen looked at Tony, raised her eyebrows and said, "What, Mum?"

"You have to promise you won't tell anybody. Not even Chris."

"Tell her what, Mum?"

"Promise. Both of you."

Tony and Karen exchanged sceptical glances but mumbled the necessary guarantees of secrecy all the same.

"I don't think they would want this commonly known," said Phyllis, "but Shona can't have children."

Tony felt like he had been stabbed in the stomach. Poor Shona! How could this be?

"That is sad," said Karen. "Poor Shona!"

"I guess there won't be any more grandchildren, then," said Phyllis. "I feel so sorry for them. Raymond would've made a fine father. It's a hard cross to bear."

"Did Raymond say how they found this out?" said Tony. "I mean, do they know what caused it?"

"He never went into that level of detail, Tony. And I'm not sure I want to know. There are dozens of causes of infertility. I suppose they must've had some tests done to establish that it was her, rather than him."

"Maybe there's some treatment for it," said Tony, thinking of the exquisite joy his children gave him, a feeling unmatched by anything he had ever experienced. It wasn't right that Shona should be denied the chance to have children. Not after what she had been through. Not after what he had put her through.

"I don't think so," said Phyllis, shaking her head. "Not from the way Raymond was talking. He sounded like it was something they had accepted. Something they just have to learn to live with."

"Was he upset?" said Karen.

"Not terribly. I was going on about how any children Shona had out of wedlock would be illegitimate and that's when told me. To shut me up as much as anything, I suppose."

"I should ring him," said Karen suddenly, standing up.

"You're not supposed to know," said Phyllis.

"Oh, I forgot," said Karen.

"Anyway he's working late tonight. He said he wouldn't be home until well after nine. He's only started with the company and they're getting their pound of flesh out of him already."

Tony got up and started clearing away the dishes.

Karen said, "Come on, Mum, and we'll get these the kids to bed."

Phyllis paused and stared at her daughter thoughtfully. "No, Karen. You look tired. Why don't you sit down and have a rest and I'll put them to bed tonight? You know I love to do it."

"Are you sure, Mum?"

"Absolutely."

"Okay, then. That'd be great."

She went into the lounge and Tony heard her switch on the TV. He heard Phyllis talking to the children and then their giggles, like the sound of tinkling bells, as she chased them up the stairs.

Was this God's punishment for what he and Shona had done? He had thought in his arrogance that God had spared them, that apart from a guilty conscience, they had escaped his wrath. And he had. But not Shona. Shona had been punished in the most cruel, ironic way possible. Oh, God, he thought, sometimes I hate you.

The number was easy to find because Raymond and Shona had by now been assigned an index card in Karen's filing system, with their address, phone and e-mail numbers on it. Tony fished out their card from the filing cabinet in the small study upstairs and thanked the Lord he had such an organised wife.

Shona picked up the phone within a few rings.

"It's Tony," he said and without giving her time to reply, went on, "I'm coming round to see you. It's very important that I see you tonight. I need to ask you something."

"Tony, what is this about?"

"I can't talk on the phone," he whispered, lowering his voice at the sound of the children on the landing outside. "I'll be round in five minutes."

"But Raymond could come home at any minute."

"Phyllis told me he wasn't due back until after nine. It's only seven-thirty. I'll be long gone by then."

He replaced the receiver, put the index card back in its place and closed the filing cabinet. Downstairs, Karen was still on the sofa.

"Who was that on the phone?" she said.

"No-one," he replied, too dull-witted to think of a plausible explanation.

"Oh, it's just I thought I heard you talking on the phone. You know how sound travels in this house."

"Not me," he said with a casual shrug, shaking his head. "Must've been the TV."

"Must've been," she replied and turned her attention back to the box.

He breathed a sigh of relief. "I'm just taking this register round to Scott," he said, waving a red folder at her from the doorway. "I forgot I won't be at the football tomorrow. He needs it for the morning. I'll not be long."

"Okay, love," she said, not taking her eyes off the screen.

He drove as fast as he could round to Scott's house and delivered the folder (having learnt from his previous error with Shona that a half-lie, or a half-truth depending on your point of view, was always better than a complete fib). Unfortunately for him, Scott, a garrulous chap with a beer belly and a passion for football, was in. He stood on the doorstep in the warm evening sun, kids playing in the street outside and talked for ten minutes about the mini-tournament that would round off the following week's football camp.

Once he'd managed to peel himself away from Scott, Tony raced round to Cairndale Heights, slowing his speed as he entered the street so as not to attract undue attention.

The houses in Cairndale Heights, as the small cul-de-sac was called, were large and all individually designed. He and Karen had once looked at a house for sale here but it was way out of their budget. He crawled along looking for number eight and soon found it, a large house set well back from the road behind a hedge. He drove up the sweeping tarmac drive which led to an imposing entrance, parked the car and got out. The house looked far too big for just Raymond and Shona. He rang the doorbell and Shona answered almost immediately, looking anxious.

He stepped inside without being asked and she scanned the street before quickly shutting the door behind him. She was wearing jeans and a faded T-shirt and her hair was tied back with a red silk scarf that looked Far Eastern in origin.

She looked even handsomer than she had done at the party and still relatively young; it made his heart ache to think that he might have denied her the joy of being a mother.

"Well," she said, without inviting him in any further than the hall where they stood, "what is it, Tony? You'd better be quick."

Superfluous conversation with Shona was clearly not needed nor welcomed. He took a deep breath and said, "I just heard today that you can't have children. Is it true?"

"Who told you that?"

"It's irrelevant. Is it true?"

"Tony Magill, you have a bloody cheek coming in here and asking me personal questions like that. It's none of your damn business."

"Is it true or not?"

"Why do you want to know?"

"It is true, isn't it?" he said, and she looked at the floor and folded her arms.

"What if it is?" she said quietly.

"You weren't born infertile, Shona. Something happened."

"Yes," she snorted and tears filled her eyes. "I met you, Tony Magill. That's what happened."

"It was the abortion then, wasn't it?" he said, voicing at last the horrible word that sounded as brutal as the action it described.

Now it was out in the open, now it was said, he felt a mild sense of liberation. He had been unable for so long to discuss this with anyone, bottling it up inside his head and his heart. So, along with the more familiar emotions of guilt and shame, he felt a sense of relief. If her infertility was the result of the abortion then he was responsible for it. He braced himself to accept this burden.

"It wasn't the abortion," she said quietly.

"But you just implied it was. Tell me the truth, Shona. Was it a botched job? A backstreet operator? Or an infection afterwards?"

"No," she said, a defiant look on her face that he suspected hid more pain than he could ever imagine. "None of those things. It was all done properly at a very nice clinic in Glasgow. All done on the QT, paid for by Daddy. Does that make you feel better?"

He stared at her in confusion. He couldn't deny that his heart soared a little at this news. Could he be exonerated after all? From responsibility for her infertility?

"But I thought you said it had to do with me," he said.

"It does," she said, deliberately enigmatic, and he ground his teeth, starting to lose patience with her. Karen would be wondering where he was. The kids would be wanting to say goodnight to him. Oh, God, the kids! The thing that Shona could never have. Suddenly he was full of pity for her.

"Look, Shona. I don't understand what you're telling me. I'm really sorry that you can't have kids. And perhaps it is none of my business. But if it had nothing to do with the abortion, how can it be my fault?"

"Well, why don't you come in and I'll tell you a little story, Tony, and then you can make up your own mind. How about that?"

He didn't like the creepy, madwoman tone of her voice but he had no choice. He followed her into a nicely furnished lounge, though bereft of the usual personal touches. Packing boxes sat in the middle of the floor. Two of them were open, the contents – books, vases, oriental-looking carved boxes and trinkets – spilling out onto the floor.

"Sit down," she commanded and he sat uncomfortably on the edge of a chair, his hands joined loosely between his knees.

He just wanted to go home but he knew that he owed her this hearing. It was the very least he could do. And he needed to know. So he waited nervously, unsure of her now that she had taken control, wondering what on earth she was about to tell him.

She arranged herself on the sofa with her legs tucked up under her, like a student, and her face to the window so that her features were illuminated by the pink-orange glow of the evening sun. And then she began her story, staring out the window, not looking at him.

"My infertility is the result of the abortion."

He glared at her. What sort of game was she playing with him? One minute it was; the next, it wasn't.

"But," she added, "only in an indirect way."

He exhaled slowly and decided that if she didn't start making sense soon, he was going to get up and leave.

"Patience, Tony. I'll get to that in a minute. But first I'd like to start at the beginning, if I may."

He let out a long sigh. "Okay then."

"Let's go right back to the time we met. I was only seventeen, fresh from a Catholic girls' school in Ayrshire and a full year younger than most of the students at Coleraine. A year doesn't mean much to us now, does it?"

He shook his head and opened his mouth to tell her that he didn't have time to listen to her life story, but Shona beat him to it.

"Heck, a decade doesn't mean much! We prefer to forget about age once we're over forty. But back then, well, I think it made all the difference between maturity and immaturity. It meant the difference between the ability to make sound judgements – or not. It meant that one could so easily be taken advantage of."

Tony hung his head, understanding in part at least where the conversation was going. She wanted to rub his face in the fact that he had used her. Yes, he had and he was heartily ashamed of his behaviour – but, he reminded himself, she had been over the age of consent and a willing participant at the time.

"You were three years older than me, Tony, and you were so popular and glamorous. When you showed me attention I lapped it up like a puppy. I was crazy about you. I would've done anything for you."

Tony looked at her and narrowed his eyes. His subsequent behaviour might have been reprehensible – but he wasn't going to let her get away with blaming him for the fact that they had embarked upon a sexual relationship. "Don't you think you're laying it on a bit thick, Shona? Making out like you were a complete innocent? If my memory serves me correctly you were never forced, nor coerced, into doing anything. In fact, I recall there were several occasions when you took the initiative."

"Oh, don't look so glum, Tony!" She gave a twisted smile, and her eyes bored into him like daggers. He crossed his arms protectively across his chest. "I'm not saying that it was entirely your fault. You were immature yourself, though compared to my wanton silliness you seemed like a sage at the time. I had led a very sheltered life and I blame my parents for that. I had hardly tasted alcohol before I came to Coleraine and that was part of the problem, wasn't it? I went mad for it, like a camel finding a pool of water in an oasis. I was drunk all the time. It made me feel confident, grown-up, sexy. In fact, I wonder if I might have alcoholic tendencies. I'm very careful what I drink nowadays."

"I'm not responsible for the fact that your parents prepared you so ill for the world, Shona," said Tony quietly.

"No, but you were quick to take advantage of my naivety, weren't you?" she snapped viciously, her icy composure cracking under the strain of her suppressed rage.

Unsure if this charge was justified or not, Tony stared at the toes of his trainers and said nothing.

Shona inhaled loudly, placed the palms of her hands on her knees, her legs now crossed Buddhist-like under her. She closed her eyes and rotated her head slowly clockwise, then anti-clockwise, several times. Tony glanced at his watch and wished she would say what she had to say and let him go. Karen would be wondering where he was.

After a few moments of this calming ritual Shona opened her eyes and levelled her unflinching gaze on Tony. When she spoke again, her voice was once again crisp and emotionless. "When I went back home, with your encouragement, pregnant after the second term, my parents were horrified. I think I'd told you enough about them by then, Tony, so that you knew how they'd react. Mum was Catholic and so was I, but Dad wasn't. And there was no way a daughter of his was going to bring that sort of shame on the family. I think you knew that they'd make me have an abortion, didn't you?"

Tony hung his head in shame because what she said was true. "I panicked, Shona," he said in his defence. "I was out of my depth. I didn't know what to do. Neither did you. I thought your parents would know what to do for the best."

She gave a cruel little laugh. "It was a very convenient way of dealing with the problem though, wasn't it? In a way you must've felt exonerated – after all, it was my father who took control of the whole thing. You didn't have to get involved with any of the sordid details. It must've salved your conscience a little."

It was true. He had offloaded a problem of his making onto her family and the truth was he had not wanted to know, nor had he cared, what the outcome was. All he was concerned about at the time was that he had escaped premature fatherhood, and possibly marriage to someone he did not love. His actions had been unspeakably selfish.

"If I could go back ..." he began, his voice choked with emotion, but she did not allow him to go on.

"If you could go back, what, Tony?" she snorted. "What would you do differently?"

"I would've faced up to my responsibilities, whatever that meant," he said firmly. "I would've supported you no matter what you'd chosen to do."

"You might now, Tony. But you wouldn't have then. You were terrified. Petrified that I would have the baby and haunt you for the rest of your life with an unwanted little bastard in tow. I could see it written all over your face, though at the time I mistook it for concern for my welfare." She threw her head back and laughed again. "And the ironic thing is that I have haunted you, Tony, haven't I? Not only by the cruel twist of fate that's thrown us together in these circumstances over which neither of us has any control, but I can tell I've been in your mind all these years. I knew as soon as I saw your face at the party, racked with guilt. Which proves that you are not a bad man – you have a conscience."

"Of course I have a conscience, Shona," he said, heatedly. "What sort of a man do you think I am? There isn't a day goes by that I don't regret what I did."

She stared at him, her face full of bitterness, and cocked her head slightly to one side, like a bird. "You know, I think I might have found it easier to forgive you, Tony, if I'd thought you loved me. If I'd thought that you were motivated by concern for my welfare. But you didn't love me and you didn't care, did you?"

"No, I didn't love you, Shona," he said with a sad sigh. He felt exhausted, emotionally wrung out. He rubbed his face, the stubble rough against the palms of his hands, and pressed his index finger between his brows.

"That explains why you were so keen to get rid of the baby – that particular baby. I saw you with your children at the party and I must confess I was jealous – but I saw that you are a good dad and, from what I've heard, a good man."

Tony closed his eyes. He could not contest her analysis. Her ability to get inside his head, or rather to understand what was going on inside it twenty years ago, was uncanny. She must have spent much of the last two decades thinking about it. As he had done.

"So," she said, in a calm voice that chilled him to the bone, "you must feel terribly guilty about what happened."

He nodded his head and a single tear fell onto the back of his hand. He had never cried about Shona, or his dead baby before. He had felt guilt and shame and lived with the fear of discovery, but he had never grieved. Maybe that was why it had tortured him all these years. Suddenly desperate to escape Shona and the house, he wiped his tired eyes, and said, "What connection is there between the abortion and your inability to have children, Shona?"

She took a big breath and went on in that scary, matter-of-fact voice. "When it was over, well, I went off the rails. I had a breakdown and spent four months in a psychiatric unit. I was self-harming, you see."

"Oh my God," he said, completely shocked. "I'm so sorry, Shona. I had no idea."

"Of course you didn't," she said briskly. "You'd stopped communicating with me by then." She paused momentarily to gauge the effect of these words on him but he was too ashamed to hold her gaze. "They put me on suicide watch but I wasn't trying to kill myself. I just hated myself for killing my baby. Because I always thought of the foetus as a baby and I still do to this day. And I think you do too, don't you, Tony?"

He put his head in his hands and wished that she would stop. He couldn't bear to hear any more. What agonies she had gone through – and he had been responsible. Had he handled the situation differently and supported her, she might never have had the breakdown.

"I came back to Coleraine to complete my degree the following year – I had to repeat the first year of course. But by then you had graduated and were long gone. I'm sure you prayed you would never see me again. But I looked for you every day because I was still under the romantic illusion that we were doomed lovers, torn apart by my cruel parents. I wrote to you constantly at your parents' address but you never replied."

"I burned the letters," he said, addressing a patch of the parquet floor. "I never read them."

"Hear no evil, see no evil? I wonder if that applies to the written word too, Tony. By ignoring the letters did you think you could divest yourself of any responsibility?"

"I just thought it was best for both of us to end the relationship."

"No, you didn't," she said with a sneer. "You thought it was best for *you*. Anyway, it took me quite a long time to accept the real version of events. So, that leads us onto the big question. How did I become infertile?"

Tony sat upright in the chair, rested his palms on his thighs and waited for what he sensed might be the worst part of this terrible story.

"Once I came to my senses and realised that you'd never loved me and had only used me, well, I went off the rails for a second time. But this time I used sex to harm myself. I had so little self-respect; I cared nothing for my body or what happened to it. I knew, you see, that I was a murderess. I debased myself, I degraded myself. I slept with any man who would have me from middle-aged lecturers to first year students, just out of school and green behind the ears. And – once we started practical training at Altnagelvin Hospital – doctors, porters, orderlies, anyone and everyone."

Tony put his hands over his ears but he could still hear her. By his actions he had driven her to insanity. He couldn't bear it. "Stop!" he cried, standing up suddenly. "What happened to you is horrific, Shona. And God knows I'm sorry for my part in it. But I don't want to hear any more!"

"Oh but you *will* hear it!" she said defiantly and raised the volume of her voice. "When I became ill, I ignored the symptoms because I wanted something bad to happen. I wanted to be punished for what I'd done."

He started to walk towards the door with his hands pressed against his ears, but her voice was too loud and persistent to block out.

"And then one day I collapsed with such severe

abdominal pain that I had to be rushed to hospital. But by then it was too late. The chlamydia infection had travelled up the uterus into my fallopian tubes and ovaries and developed into full-blown pelvic inflammatory disease. And that is what made me infertile."

He stopped at the door and his arms fell to his side. He turned to face her. "Oh, Jesus, Shona, I am so sorry." He stood, staring at her, his eyes full of tears.

"I believe you are but I don't want your pity," she said with a benign smile. "I love Raymond and he loves me. We're pinning our hopes of happiness on each other, not on children. You asked me if you were responsible for my infertility. I can't answer that question for you. Maybe we were both too young and naïve to understand the implications of what we were doing. Maybe we should have. But we have to live with the consequences and I would have to say, Tony, that you got off a damn sight more lightly than I."

Tony thought of his family and thanked God for his good fortune. Right now, he wanted nothing more than to be with them.

"I think I'd better go now," he said.

"Do you know what?" said Shona, staring at him with a satisfied glint in her eye. "I've waited twenty years to say all that. And I feel better for it." She got up suddenly from the sofa and said briskly. "Yes, it's time for you to leave now."

Drained of all energy, he allowed her to lead him meekly to the front door.

There she stopped and said into his face, quite impassively, "You want me to blame you, accuse you, berate you and ultimately forgive you. You want me to say it was your fault – and then absolve you. But I won't do any of those things, Tony. Because you blame yourself enough already, and only you know if you deserve to be forgiven. I can't forgive you because the forgiveness that you seek can only come from yourself. But there is one thing I want you to do for me."

"Anything," he said, his heart heavy with remorse. Would he ever be able to forgive himself?

"I never want you to talk to me about this ever again. Do you understand? I want you to act as though I am your new sister-in-law, and act convincingly. And if you ever so much as put a foot over this door uninvited again, so help me God, I'll tell Karen in a heartbeat."

Stunned, Tony walked out of the house without a word and got into his car without looking back. The woman was demented. Had he made her so? Or had she always been unstable?

He drove quickly away from the house and got as far as the Old Glenarm Road where he pulled into the locked entrance of the old GEC factory and killed the engine. Then put his hands over his face and wept like a child for the first time in over thirty years. And when he was done a sense of peace came over him.

Poor Shona had been driven to the brink of madness and back again. He wasn't sure she was completely normal even now. He'd had no idea about the breakdown, the self-harming, the psychiatric unit and what she'd done to herself after that. Of course not, because as soon as he'd persuaded her to get on that ferry back to Scotland, he'd wiped his hands of her.

It had suited him to picture her in a nice clean hospital somewhere under the care of kind nurses. A simple, straightforward procedure, chicken soup recovery in the loving embrace of her family and then on with her life. Because that was what he wanted to believe. He had always beaten himself up about the abortion itself, the taking of a sacred life. He had never considered how it might've affected Shona. And that omission was possibly a greater sin that the abortion itself. What he had done was wrong, callous, selfish. But he refused to condemn himself for it. He would not, could not, let that one terrible mistake ruin the rest of his life.

God knows, Shona had suffered, but he had paid his penance too. He'd tortured himself these last twenty years. He had lived a good life since then and, if not quite given his life to God, he had tried to live by His commandments. He was a good husband and father. He was more than that – he was a good person. He gave of himself to others – the community, the church, charities. He could do no more. He would stop judging himself.

He looked at his watch and sighed. It was nearly nine o'clock. He'd missed the kids going to bed and Karen would be wondering where he was. He would have to tell her that Scott had invited him in, that they'd spent the last hour and a half discussing the arrangements for the mini-tournament. That was good – convincing and close to the truth.

Then he turned on the engine, pulled onto the road and made a promise to God and to himself. After tonight, he would never tell Karen another lie so long as they both lived.

Twenty

When the letter eventually came, on a Friday at the end of September, Bernie hid it on the mantelpiece behind a large clock that Paul had brought from the drawing room in Castlerock. There was nothing on the thin cream manila envelope to indicate from whence it had come. No return address and an indecipherable postmark. Nor did Bernie recognise the spidery handwriting, but she knew instinctively that it was from Aunt Jean.

It sat there for two days, her sense of foreboding growing stronger by the hour until, on Monday morning, when Paul had left for work, she finally plucked up the courage to open it. She sat at the small table in the kitchen and tore open the envelope with the sharp blade of a paring knife. Inside was a single sheet of cream paper, to match the envelope, folded in three. She opened it and read:

Dear Bernie,

I hope this finds you well. I have put pen to paper many times to write you and find that what I want to say, what I am __compelled__ to say, out of conscience and duty to my sister, Ellie, does not come easily. How can you know that you are making a terrible mistake – a mistake that would make your mother grieve – unless someone tells you? There is a secret that you must know and I believe I am

446

*the only one alive that knows it. And so, though I do not wish it
to be thus, the burden of telling you falls to me.*

*So I must ask you to make the journey north once again and
come and see me. You __must__ come, Bernie, as soon as you can, and
come alone.*

*I hope with all my heart that you find someone more worthy
of you – and the happiness you so richly deserve.*

Yours, Aunt Jean

The blood in Bernie's veins suddenly ran cold and she
dropped the letter on the kitchen table and stared at it. '*I
hope . . . that you find someone more worthy of you.*' What an
odd thing to say! Bernie folded her arms and frowned. She
didn't like the tone of the letter; she didn't like it at all.

What was this secret that her aunt had to tell her?
Maybe it had something to do with her dad. Maybe Aunt
Jean knew why her father did not love her. Could that be
it? But what could that possibly have to do with Paul? For
Aunt Jean clearly did not like him one little bit. And what
was this 'mistake' she was on about – did she mean her
relationship with Paul? Did she know of some reason that
she and Paul could not be together and if so, what could it
possibly be?

She re-read the letter several times but was unable to
make much sense of it. She toyed with the idea of showing
it to Paul and decided against it. She might not like what
her aunt had to tell her. It might be something, though she
could not for the life of her imagine what, that she might
wish to keep to herself. A family secret best kept as one.

Bernie folded the letter and put it back in the envelope
and went upstairs and hid it amongst paperwork in her
study. She would go tomorrow, she decided.

"I was wondering if I could borrow the car tomorrow?"

she said over a dinner of vegetarian egg-fried rice she had made.

"If you like," said Paul, with a shrug. "I don't think I'll be needing it. Just so long as you can drop me off at the surgery in the morning."

"No problem," she said and chewed for a few moments on a mouthful of rice. Then she pushed the half-eaten meal away, her appetite suddenly gone. "I was thinking of taking a drive up to see Aunt Jean in Portstewart."

"Oh darling, are you worried about her?" She nodded and he patted the back of her hand and said, "I think that's a great idea. I'm sure she'll be in better form. It'll put your mind at rest to see her again."

There was a silence while they ate, Paul took a swig of wine and said, "I thought you had to get some samples mocked up for that advertising agency in Belfast?"

"I do. But they can wait. I've done two drawings already. I can do the other one on Friday. And finish it over the weekend if I need to."

He nodded, wiped his mouth with a napkin and said, "You know, I've been thinking about what you said about starting a wine business. Do you really think I could do it?"

"Oh yes, Paul, I do. You have so much knowledge about wine and you're so passionate about it."

But Bernie knew enough about business start-ups to know that they were rarely profitable in the first few years. They could not survive on any less income than now – by the time all life's little essentials had been taken care of, there was precious little left. Thankfully, Paul was not particularly money-wise (he must've left all that up to Chris) and he handed the running of the house over to Bernie. So long as the bank account didn't go overdrawn he did not seem to notice how much she was spending or what she was spending it on. He did not notice how economically she shopped – she served a lot of pasta and bread and very little meat. Not that she had much interest in food these days – her appetite seemed to have dwindled. She must make more of an effort to eat, she thought, for she couldn't afford to lose any more weight. But so long as Paul had a decent bottle of wine to open of an evening he was happy. And that was how she wanted to keep things.

"The only thing is," she said, sounding a note of caution so that he didn't get too carried away, "you would need to be sure you could earn the same income from it as presently. Otherwise your standard of living would have to drop."

"Yes, fair point. I could start an online business," he mused. "That would keep costs down, to start with anyway. See how successful that is before taking the plunge. And maybe one day I could have my own premises. Upmarket, of course. We could do wine tastings and I could have my own cellar under the shop."

"I'm sorry that you don't have a wine cellar here," said Bernie, looking at the bottles which had now spread like a virus from the lounge to the kitchen floor.

"I'll have another one, once Castlerock is sold and we have a place of our own. Don't forget that this place is only temporary. You, my darling, weren't meant to live like this. And meantime, I'd still rather be here with you than in Castlerock." He shivered and shook his head. "I'd much, much rather be here with you. Now, what do you think we could call the wine business?"

★ ★ ★

She took the most direct route to Portstewart, rather than the scenic coastal route she had taken with Paul in August, anxious to get there as soon as possible. The weather had turned suddenly and though it was only September, the air had a pronounced autumnal chill. The leaves on the trees had turned brown and were just starting to fall. She drove the big Range Rover fast and it ate up the miles in no time. She was in Portstewart by half past ten.

Aunt Jean was in her room, sitting by the window where she had last seen her, as though she hadn't moved, as though she was waiting for her. The sea view was disconcertingly not much changed from last time – without deciduous trees and foliage as part of the view the passing of the seasons was not so obvious. Here, one relied on the level of human activity on the beach, the change in temperature and the changing skies to signal the change of seasons. Aunt Jean did not seem surprised to see Bernie, nor did she seem pleased.

"Have you come alone?" she said.

"Yes. Just as you asked."

"Good. Have you got a cold, Bernie? You sound a bit blocked up."

Bernie shrugged. "I think I'm allergic to a new perfume. Or maybe I'm coming down with something."

Bernie set the flowers she'd bought in the sink in the corner, put in the plug and added some cold water. She wiped her hands on the pink hand towel hanging by the sink and said, "Aunt Jean, have I done something to offend you?"

Her aunt sighed and said, "No, my dear. No, you haven't. Come here and sit with me."

Bernie sat in the winged chair she had occupied the last

time she was here. She realised that her aunt was now ready to finish the conversation they had started that day.

Aunt Jean stared at her for some moments until, uncomfortable under her scrutiny, Bernie said, "You said you had something to tell me."

She let out a long, sad sigh and said, "Yes. Will you shut the door please?"

Bernie did so and sat down again and her aunt looked out of the window, as though it was too painful to look at Bernie. "I'm sorry to have to send you that letter but I have struggled with this and decided in the end that it was best, that it was only fair, that you hear this face to face."

Bernie steeled herself, told herself that whatever it was, she would handle it. Everything would be okay.

"Your mother, my sister Ellie, was a troubled woman," Jean said and frowned. "She married your father impulsively after a whirlwind romance. They had only known each other a few months. My parents tried to caution her that she was too young, that she hadn't known him long enough. But she was so strong-headed, so wilful that she wouldn't listen. She was determined to marry Jim Sweeney – oh, he was terribly handsome when he was young – and she did. She was only nineteen."

Bernie listened patiently and started to relax. None of this was news to her.

"She had the boys quite close together and for a few years they occupied her fully but by then it was clear, to me at least, that your mother and father were having difficulties. They were just so different. He was dour and quiet; she was like a butterfly, bright and colourful. You couldn't pin her down; you couldn't contain that spirit. And she was delicate and beautiful, like you, Bernie." Her aunt smiled briefly at her and Bernie blushed and looked at the floor. "She was always wanting to go out; to the cinema, to dances and have fun. But your father didn't have the money for a lifestyle like that and anyway he was quite content to sit in of an evening and watch the TV. They just weren't suited and the age difference didn't help, though I believe he loved her very much. In fact, I know he loved her very much, for he would never have done what he did later if he hadn't."

Bernie looked up quickly but her aunt was staring out the window again, looking back in time.

"And then, when Michael was about eleven, she seemed to change. She settled down a bit and I attributed the change partly to the anti-depressants she'd been prescribed. She seemed a lot more content and happy and I thought she had, finally, accepted her lot and grown up. And then she got pregnant with you."

Bernie looked up with a half-smile on her lips, anticipating a happy telling of her birth and early years but her aunt's face was twisted with sorrow.

"She'd been having an affair," she said and looked at Bernie.

The half-formed smile fell from Bernie's lips. A sense of dread crept over her.

"And you were born of that relationship. Jim Sweeney was not your biological father."

"But how do you know that?" gasped Bernie.

"Because she told me. And she told Jim."

Bernie's initial reaction was shock. Everything she had believed about her identity came crumbling down around her. She thought of Jim, her paternal grandparents and all her other relatives on her father's side. She had no biological connection to any of them. They were nothing to her – in terms of blood anyway. And her real father was a man she knew nothing about, a man she had never met.

"Is my real father still living in Ballyfergus?" she said, hopefully.

Aunt Jean shook her head. "I'm sorry, Bernie, but he died some years ago."

"Oh," said Bernie, suddenly realising that this was a source of bitter regret. She had been robbed of the chance to know her real father. A man who might have loved her in a way Jim Sweeney could not.

"Are you all right, Bernie?" came her aunt's gentle enquiry.

Bernie nodded and sniffed back tears that had suddenly sprung to her eyes. To her surprise, the shock slowly gave way to a sense of relief. So that was the secret and it was a shock, no doubt about it, but it wasn't so terrible after all. She had always known that something wasn't quite right between her and Jim. She had always known he didn't love her and the knowledge of her true identity made her feel less guilty for not loving him. She realised that this information finally gave her the answers she had been looking for all her life.

"That explains everything," she said, as she wiped the tears from her face.

"What do you mean?" said her aunt, cautiously.

"All my life, I wondered why Dad didn't like me, why he wasn't kind to me. He never told me that he loved me you know. I sometimes thought he hated me."

Jean sighed. "He did the best he could, Bernie. It's hard for a man to love another's child, much harder than it is for a woman."

"But what about my real father?" said Bernie, imagining

herself the fruit of an epic love affair. The idea transformed her miserable childhood into something much more exotic. "Didn't Mum love him? Why didn't she leave Dad for him?"

"She said she loved him but your real father was already married, Bernie, with a family. He was well-known around Ballyfergus as a bit of a playboy. I was shocked when you mother told me she'd taken up with him. I thought she had more sense."

"Oh," said Bernie, as her aunt put a dent in the notion that she was the love-child of star-crossed lovers, cruelly separated by circumstances beyond their control,

"Jim agreed to bring you up as his child on the condition that your mum never saw her lover again. She agreed and as far as I know she kept that promise. That's how I knew your father really loved her, because he took her back – and he took you in. And there was Michael and young Jim to think about as well. It's a big decision, breaking up a family."

Bernie bowed her head and thought fleetingly of Chris and Paul and the part she had played in breaking up their marriage. As for her parents, far from a passionate love affair, the relationship sounded more like a short-lived, cheap fling. Suddenly Bernie felt dirty. She was illegitimate. The child of the local playboy.

"And I think it would've worked out all right but then your mum died and, well, your poor father was left to cope on his own."

"But what about my real father? Did he ever acknowledge me?"

"As I said, he was married, Bernie," Jean explained very gently. "As far as the world was concerned you were Jim

Sweeney's daughter. And Jim promised your mum before she died. He promised her that he would take care of you."

The tears came now and Bernie managed to ask, "But my real father . . . he did know about me?"

Aunt Jean nodded. "He knew all right but he didn't want to know. Apart from him, only your mother, Jim and I knew the truth."

"My brothers?"

Aunt Jean shook her head.

"Maybe they guessed. I always thought they were mean to me."

"They may well have picked up on your father's feeling towards you. Children can be quite instinctive, and cruel, that way."

Bernie wiped the tears from her face and smiled. "Thank you, Aunt Jean. Thank you for telling me. I'm not as upset as I look, really. I'm more relieved than anything. I thought that Dad didn't like me because I was a difficult, selfish child."

"You were neither of those things, Bernie."

"It even explains the business about the will. And now that I know the truth, I forgive Dad. It must've been very hard for him. Every time he looked at me, I must've been a constant reminder of another man – and his wife's infidelity."

Suddenly she noticed that her aunt was staring at her with a strange look on her face.

"What's wrong? Why are you looking at me like that?" Telling the story must have brought back too many upsetting memories to Jean. Bernie got up, went over to her aunt and squeezed her hands as they lay clasped together in her lap. "Please don't be upset. I'm okay. Really. It's all in the past now. It doesn't matter."

"Oh, but it does," said Aunt Jean. "You haven't yet asked me who your father was."

"Oh, no, I haven't." Bernie sat down abruptly. She realised that she wasn't particularly curious to know. Whoever he was, he was gone and he'd never taken the slightest bit of interest in her. And she couldn't very well foist herself on his surviving relations. What was the point of finding out now?

"I'm not sure I want to know," she said.

"You have to know," said Aunt Jean.

Bernie gave a little nervous laugh, spooked by her aunt's deathly pallor and deadpan delivery.

"Your father was Charles Quinn."

"Charles Quinn?" repeated Bernie.

"That's right."

"Not a relation of Paul's?"

"I'm afraid so."

Bernie stared at her aunt as a sickening feeling took hold.

"How close a relation, Aunt Jean?"

"Can you get me a glass of water?"

Bernie hesitated. She felt like shouting 'Damn you and your bloody glasses of water!' But she did as she was bade, got the water, sat down opposite her aunt again and watched her take a long, slow drink.

Her aunt always took her time about sharing gossip and revealing secrets – she always had. Bernie thought it had something to do with being in control. She liked being the centre of attention, all eyes focused on her, waiting for the release of whatever nugget of information she withheld. And Bernie had no choice but to be patient, though the suspense was killing her, for she knew from experience that her aunt would not be hurried.

She and Paul were related. But the big question was: how closely related? What if they were *too* closely related? Like first cousins, or, even worse . . . half-siblings? No, that would just be too awful to contemplate. She tried to remember if Paul had ever mentioned his father's first name but, if he had, she couldn't remember it. Oh, she couldn't bear it! She balled her fists in her lap and willed her aunt to speak, to release her from this torment.

Aunt Jean coughed, adjusted the cushion behind her back and said, "Charles Quinn was a well-known businessman in Ballyfergus."

"Not a doctor then?"

"No."

Bernie breathed a sigh of relief.

"You're not his half-sister if that's what you thought," said her aunt, reading her mind.

"Thank God. We're related, but not closely enough for it to be a problem. Is that right?"

"It depends how you look at it, Bernie," said her aunt with a scowl. "In my book being related in any way to a Quinn is a problem."

"I don't see how."

"Perhaps when you hear how Charles Quinn and his rotten family ill-used your mother, you'll change your mind," said Jean sharply.

Bernie frowned. "Go on then. You'd better tell me."

"Charles Quinn ran the undertakers at the top of the Main Street as well as an adjacent garage. He was successful and had a bit of money to throw about in the days when most people didn't have much. He was also quite good-looking and he had that self-assured way about him that all those Quinns have. I saw it in Paul when he was here. I didn't like it."

"Well, I like a man who's confident," said Bernie defensively.

"It's not confidence. They're vain, cocky, full of themselves. They think they can take whatever they want. Charles Quinn did anyway. I never liked him." She paused, shook her head and went on, "Anyway, both Michael and Jim were at school and your mother had too much time on her hands. I thought a part-time job would do her good because I could see that she wasn't content, that there was a restlessness about her. I thought it would keep her occupied and that some money of her own – a bit of pin money for going to the cinema and the like – would make her happy. She'd been a bookkeeper before she married and a good one. So, when the advert came out in the paper for a part-time bookkeeper at Quinn's garage, I encouraged her to go for it. She was offered the job straight away at the interview. Now I know why – the old letch!"

"Was he older than her?" said Bernie, displeased by the disparaging term Jean used to describe her father. She put it down to her aunt's abhorrence of adultery, rather than a slight on Charles Quinn's character.

"By about twenty years. His family, a boy and two girls, were grown up. I still feel guilty about what happened, Bernie. If I hadn't encouraged her to go for that job, she wouldn't have applied. I'm quite sure of it. And all this heartbreak would've been avoided."

"You mustn't blame yourself, Aunt Jean."

"Well, I do," she said and let out a long sigh. "They started an affair. I'm quite sure he forced himself on her but she always denied that. She always stood up for him, the silly fool."

"She must've loved him," said Bernie, losing herself in a romantic fantasy about her parents' love affair.

"She thought she did. But he didn't love her."

"How do you know that?" said Bernie irritably, not wanting the bubble to burst.

"Because when his wife found out about the affair, he sacked your mother. Just like that. She'd just told him that she was pregnant with his baby. And do you know what he did? He and his family spread a rumour that she'd been caught taking money from the till."

"He did not!" cried Bernie in horror. What kind of a monster would do such a thing?

"He did," confirmed Jean grimly. "He made out that he didn't call in the police because he felt sorry for her, because she had a husband and two young sons with a baby on the way. Made himself out to be the big-hearted hero."

"But why? Why would he do something so cruel and mean?" said Bernie, her romantic illusions in tatters.

"Because he didn't want people to find out that he was the father of her baby. By accusing her first of theft, it meant that anything she said subsequently could be discredited. If Ellie had accused him of being the father, he would've said it was just vindictiveness – that she was trying to get back at him."

Bernie sat back and stared at her aunt in horror. She had been unwanted then, by her real father, by Jim, and maybe even her mother as well. And poor Ellie had been a victim of this man's vicious spite.

"Poor Mum," she said softly.

"Now what do you think of Charles Quinn? Blackening her name to protect his reputation."

"I almost can't believe it, Aunt Jean. I can't believe that he could've been so cruel."

"He was a selfish, heartless man. Like I said, it beggars

belief that Ellie ever got involved with him."

"I'm glad he's dead," said Bernie, her heart suddenly bursting with anger. "And I'm sorry that he's my father. I'd rather have Jim Sweeney any day."

Jean sighed loudly. "Jim was a good man, Bernie. In spite of what you think of him. He really did try and do his best by you and Ellie."

Bernie looked at the floor and nodded, forced to reconsider her opinion of Jim in light of these revelations. He had, unlike her real father, acted with honour and dignity.

"But those Quinns," said Aunt Jean, shaking her head, so full of bitterness for the injustice to her sister. "Those Quinns are evil, Bernie. And they're all tarnished with the same brush."

"But what was the relationship between Charles Quinn and Paul's father?" said Bernie, anxious to satisfy herself as to the degree of kinship between her and Paul.

"They were first cousins once removed. That makes you and Paul Quinn second cousins once removed."

Bernie paused to consider this information. She was relieved to hear that the relationship was a distant one. But, even so, there was something disturbing about the idea that her lover was kin. It made her feel uneasy, it made her wonder if it had something to do with the instant attraction between them. There had been recent cases in the news of siblings and half-siblings falling in love, having children and unwittingly marrying each other. And she had found the whole concept utterly gross. But, she told herself, there was no impediment in the eyes of the law or the Church, to their relationship. There was no reason why they couldn't be together. Just a vague sense that it wasn't right somehow.

And then there was the issue of Charles Quinn himself. The idea that Paul was related to such a monster was disturbing. She almost disliked him for it, though she knew this feeling to be irrational. It wasn't Paul's fault that he was related to Charles Quinn, any more than it was her fault that she was his illegitimate offspring. She must not allow this issue to come between them.

"But that's okay, isn't it?" said Bernie. "There's no law against falling in love with, or marrying, your second cousin once removed, is there?"

"Are you telling me that you're considering going ahead with this relationship?"

"I know what happened to Mum was awful, Aunt Jean. It's heartbreaking. But it isn't Paul's fault."

"He's a Quinn, Bernie! They destroyed your mother. She was never the same after Charles Quinn did that to her. She thought that he loved her. It destroyed her faith in people. And she had to live with that accusation, that smear against her name, until she died. I sometimes think . . ."

"You think what?"

"That it was partly responsible for her death."

"But she died of cancer!"

"I know. But they say your state of mind can affect your physical health. And I believe that. Charles Quinn may not have killed your mother, Bernie, but I believe he helped her on her way."

"That's a very grave accusation to make, Aunt Jean."

"I know it is and I don't make it lightly." She narrowed her eyes and leaned forward in her wheelchair, as far as she was able, and said, "That's why I will never condone your marriage to that man. And I never want to see him, or you, again so long as you are together!"

Outside the nursing home, Bernie sat in the car and her heart filled up with sadness. Aunt Jean was the only person in her family whom she felt truly loved her. And now she was refusing to see her anymore so long as she was connected to Paul. But Bernie depended on Paul now. She could not do without him. She understood her aunt's hurt and anger about what had happened to her sister, but it wasn't fair to project that hate onto Charles Quinn's descendents. And there was Quinn blood in Bernie's veins. Did that mean her aunt hated her too? She closed her eyes and tried to calm her brain, over-stimulated by far too much information.

Finding out that Jim Sweeney was not her father was traumatic, but in a curious way it helped resolve many of the riddles of her childhood that had for so long puzzled her. And she was almost pleased, because it explained why he did not like her. It provided a legitimate reason for his inability to love her, rather than the fact that she was intrinsically unlovable. Her father hadn't hated her; he just couldn't love her and now she understood why.

Given time, she was sure she would adjust to this new reality, come to terms with it, and forgive her father, even, for his many shortcomings in raising her. Even now, Bernie warmed to him when she thought of the pain her mother's affair must've caused him, the promise he'd made her (and kept) and the sacrifices he'd made on Bernie's behalf.

She did not blame him for leaving her out of his will. In providing a home for her perhaps he felt he had fulfilled his promise. He had done his best but he could not take her into his heart. And who could blame him? Her face must have been a daily reminder of Charles Quinn and the injustice he had done to him and to his dead wife. And without a dependent little girl in tow, perhaps he might have met someone and remarried. And not lived out the rest of his life as a lonely widower.

No, all the hate she felt was directed towards Charles Quinn and she wished him in hell for what he had done to her mother. But it was a futile, unsatisfactory hatred because there was no-one alive on whom to project these feelings. Because of what he and her mother had done (she was not entirely blameless in spite of what Aunt Jean thought), Bernie had been denied the chance of a normal loving childhood. Her mother might still have died but, had she not been illegitimate, she would have been raised by a loving father rather than a man who, despite his best intentions, could not love her. And that made her heart ache. Life had been so unfair. She wondered sometimes how, in the face of it all, she managed to keep going.

She switched on the car engine, and sat and looked at the façade of the nursing home, wondering if she would ever see her aunt again. And suddenly she was filled with a desperate need to get back to the flat; to close the door on the world and its cruel ironies, and cocoon herself in the privacy of her own home. She tried not to think too much about the familial relationship between her and Paul because it was, well, it was a bit too creepy. And she would have to overcome this uneasiness as she had no alternative now but to cling to Paul.

She drove back to Ballyfergus and the flat in Bay Road as fast as she could. She felt dazed, aware of little but a dull pain in her chest. In spite of her hatred of him, she was grieving for a father she had never met – and a mother she had barely known.

It had been a taxing morning and, by the time she got

home, her body ached as though she had a fever; the slightest movement sent jags of pain shooting up the back of her skull. And she felt cold, so very, very cold. She shivered and pulled her cardigan closer, perspiration forming on her upper lip. She knew what she had to do.

* * *

Chris was in Hannah's bedroom helping her to pack for university. The room had pale lemon walls and a pink bedspread and, on the bed, Hannah's favourite soft toy from when she was a child – a well-worn rabbit called Bunny Hop. Bizarrely, in spite of her intimidating appearance, Hannah was emotionally attached to the room and, despite repeated offers, had not allowed her parents to restyle it.

It would not be redecorated now, thought Chris sadly; the house would be sold as it was. And maybe it would become someone else's little girl's room and she would grow up within these four walls as Hannah had done.

Chris held a folded cardigan against her chest and fought back the tears, grieving for the little daughter she once had. Aching for the closeness they had shared when she was little. She told herself that she was being selfish, that her sadness had as much to do with the break-up of her marriage, as Hannah leaving home. She knew that to be the case because she was emotional about almost everything these days. And it wasn't fair on Hannah; she had to love her less, she had to let her daughter go.

So she smiled brightly and said, "Do you think you have enough jumpers? It'll be freezing over in Edinburgh. Much colder than here." She pushed from her mind an image of Hannah pounding the pavements in the shadow of

Edinburgh Castle, shivering in the cold. Suddenly Edinburgh seemed so far away.

"Oh, Mum, stop fussing," said Hannah and she closed the lid on the suitcase.

"What about towels? Will you get towels provided in Halls?"

"How should I know?"

"Don't you think you should find out?" said Chris, slightly irritated with Hannah's distinct lack of enthusiasm.

She knew the cause of it. Hannah hadn't been the same since the day Paul left home. She saw him once a week but the bounce in her had gone. She was more reserved and cautious, as though she expected to be disappointed by life. Chris hated to see such cynicism in one so young.

"Why don't you pack a couple just in case?" she said, softening her tone.

"Whatever," said Hannah and Chris had to bite her lip to stop herself from chastising her. They were due to take the early morning car ferry to Troon (on account of the amount of stuff Hannah had to take with her) and she did not want them to fall out on this, Hannah's last night at home.

Chris went and got two each of her best hand and bath towels from the airing cupboard and squeezed them in the suitcase, then zipped it up.

"There!" she said, brightly. "I think that's everything."

Hannah was over by the dressing table, disinterested, looking in a little box of trinkets she held in her left hand. She pulled out a ski school badge from some long-ago holiday and looked at it.

"What will you do with my stuff when you move?" she said, staring at the enamelled brooch.

"I'll pack up everything and take it with me."

"Everything?"

"Yes."

"Good."

"And wherever I move to, Hannah. I'll make sure it has a bedroom for you."

Hannah nodded, replaced the badge in the box, closed it and set it down again. She seemed sad. And she shouldn't be. Going to university should be one of the happiest and most exciting experiences of her life. She shouldn't be worrying about what she was leaving behind (that was Chris's job); she should be looking to the future with joy and anticipation.

"It's great that Emma Dobbin's going to Edinburgh too, isn't it?" said Chris brightly, in a desperate effort to cheer her up.

"She's doing languages. I don't suppose I'll see that much of her," said Hannah, flatly.

"But still, it's good to know that a friend is close by. If you need them."

"I suppose so."

"And you know that I am always here for you, Hannah. No matter what. And I will always love you." The words sounded so hackneyed, like they had been borrowed from a toddler's picture book; she hoped Hannah understood that she meant every one of them.

But Hannah turned to the window, folded her arms across her chest and did not say a thing.

★ ★ ★

The next morning on the, rather unseasonably, rough ferry

journey, Hannah spent the entire time vomiting into thoughtfully provided sick bags. Chris felt nauseous but managed to refrain from actually throwing up. She and Hannah were to stay two nights in a Bed and Breakfast near the university and, once Hannah was settled into Halls in time for the start of Fresher's Week, Chris would return alone. Paul was due to fly over the following weekend to visit Hannah – it wasn't ideal, but it was the best the estranged parents could do.

They had fun that weekend, visiting the castle, browsing in the shops on the Royal Mile, going to the cinema, shopping on Princes Street. But already Chris could see that she was losing her daughter – Hannah was distracted much of the time. And it was understandable. No doubt part of her was itching for her mother to be gone so that she could start her newly independent life. Chris couldn't blame her; at that age her eye had been firmly on the future. She remembered the desperate urge to leave home and the cruel necessity of leaving your family behind you, both physically and emotionally, because, until you did that, you could not be truly independent.

On Sunday afternoon she helped Hannah move into a room at the sprawling Pollock Halls – a huge utilitarian complex of nine houses that provided accommodation for nearly two thousand students. The en-suite room was functional; clean and comfortable, with a single bed, small chest of drawers, a desk and chair. It was also soulless and, compared to the relative luxury in which Hannah lived at home, very basic. But Hannah didn't seem to mind; in fact, she didn't seem to notice. The first thing she did was walk over to the window and stare out at the view of a hill – Arthur's Seat, a well-known local landmark – in adjacent Holyrood Park.

But at least here she was provided with meals and, Chris was pleased to discover, a pleasant girl from County Fermanagh was in the room next door to Hannah. She wished Hannah would show more enthusiasm but she put it down to nerves – or perhaps the desire to appear cool and unimpressed. And so she said her goodbyes to Hannah without embarrassing her with a display of tears and left her to it, returning to the chirpy landlady in the Bed and Breakfast whose window boxes and lavishly furnished hall and breakfast room belied the grimness of the bedrooms. Gone were the days of staying in posh hotels: Chris had to watch her pennies nowadays. At least until the house was sold, she'd bought her own place and she knew she could manage comfortably. Meantime, she could not afford to be extravagant.

She lay in the narrow bed that night under a lumpy duvet and thought of Hannah and smiled. She was probably right now making friends over coffee, or something stronger, with other equally lost and nervous souls from all around the country and beyond. And Chris was glad that Hannah was in Halls, basic as they were, because it meant she was surrounded by people in the same boat as her. Her father would be visiting her next weekend. She would be fine. All Chris had to do now was let her go.

She tried to distract herself with other thoughts lest she become too depressed thinking of Hannah alone in that little room, instead of in her bed at home where Chris still felt she rightly belonged. Where she could protect her and keep her safe – ludicrous notions, she acknowledged, when the child in question was big strapping lass of eighteen.

So she thought of Sam and what he had said to her that day in the restaurant – his sweet words of promise as yet unfulfilled. Since then he had treated her with nothing but kindness and professional courtesy although he always took the opportunity when they were alone to say, "How are you today, Chris?" in a tone that suggested he really wanted to know. She would reply honestly and briefly, commenting on how she felt that particular day – hurt, angry, grieved. And he would listen intently and offer her some words of advice and support. Often he would say, "It will pass," and she had come to believe him. She was grateful for his gentle friendship.

She did not know if they might have a future together – her feelings were much too raw, and her focus was still very much on her car-crashed marriage, for her to think clearly about tomorrow, never mind beyond – but she hoped that one day they might. It was morale-boosting, if nothing else, to know that he was there watching over her like her guardian angel. And if that was fanciful, she did not care. She had learned to take her joys and pleasures where she could find them. And to welcome friendship from whatever quarter it came.

Her feelings towards Paul were complex and violent. She hated him so much that every time she thought of him she tasted a metallic bitterness in her mouth. And whilst they had decided to go down the non-confrontational route of a collaborative divorce, which she agreed was best for them and the children, she found it very hard to sit in meetings with him and be civil. Pamela Craig had been brilliant; intelligent, tactful, and sympathetic. She veered Chris away from dwelling on the things that were wrong and encouraged her to look constructively to the future.

Paul had appeared stressed at the last meeting they'd attended together with their solicitors, where it was agreed that the house would go on the market. And he had cancelled the meeting scheduled for the middle of this month due to ill health. So maybe he was finding it all a strain as well. Maybe, with straightened circumstances, life with Bernie wasn't all a bed of roses. She hoped so.

As for Bernie, she tried not to think of her at all for she thought that she hated her even more than Paul. There was something so very calculating about what she had done, and the secrecy with which it had been conducted, that was so deeply hurtful. She realised – and she was not proud of herself – that she expected more of Bernie simply because she was a woman.

But she was trying to be good; trying not to let the hate and rage and bitterness destroy her and her life. Most recently she had even begun to look forward, albeit cautiously, to moving on, getting the house sold and starting a new life. The house had played such an important role in their marriage – the pinnacle of all their shared hopes and dreams – that it had to go, for both their sakes. It would be easier to start over as a single woman if she wasn't still living in Castlerock surrounded by things that reminded her daily of her failed marriage. And the fact that she was able to view the house sale as a vaguely positive step, rather than an unmitigated disaster, was huge progress.

She sighed and reminded herself that she had an early start in the morning. The ferry left Troon on the west coast just after ten o'clock and she had to cross Scotland to get there in time. It meant leaving Edinburgh before seven. She must get some sleep. She punched the hard foam pillow with her fists and dreamed of her comfortable bed at home. And Sam McIlwaine and what it would be like to kiss him . . .

* * *

Thankfully, the next two weeks at work were hectic, due to the imminent move into the new premises which, miraculously, looked like it was going to be on schedule. Chris had little time to think of Hannah and, when she did, she forced herself to think happy thoughts, imagining the parties, the new friends, a boyfriend even. Hannah phoned or texted every other day, to reassure Chris that she was okay. She wasn't very forthcoming about what she was doing or who her new friends were but then she had a right to privacy, thought Chris. She was eighteen after all.

Chris and Paul had met at university and, in spite of the way she felt about him now, she remembered those days as the happiest of her life. She made a mental note to treasure her memories always and not allow them to be tarnished by what had come later. She had spent such a long time with Paul and most of that time had been happy. She would not disown her past, presenting it as somehow less than it had been, washing over it in retrospect with the distemper of her disappointment. For many of those memories were the children's too and she would not diminish them.

Finn, she hardly saw. He spent most of his time in his room after work and went out at weekends with his pals. They still came round to the house from time to time to watch football or rugby matches but not as much as they used to, and she wondered if they sensed the same sadness about the place as she did. She had given up insisting that she and Finn eat together – it was just too depressing to sit at the kitchen table trying to keep a conversation going while ignoring the spaces where Paul and Hannah used to be.

She was well aware that Finn came home the odd time a bit worse for drink, though he liked to think he hid it from her. The young men he ran about with were a couple of years older than him and Finn, with his broad shoulders and imposing height, could easily pass for eighteen. She knew he went to pubs and bars but was forced to take a lenient view, so long as it was done in moderation. After all, how could she stop him?

Only last week, she had asked Paul to have a word with Finn but Paul had looked at her as though she had two horns and said, "I have more important things to worry about than Finn having the odd drink." Which struck Chris as very odd because, before Bernie, he had been very firm about underage drinking, except for the occasional glass of wine or beer taken at home under the supervision of responsible parents. In the end he promised to have a word with Finn, but it seemed to have little effect. Finn's behaviour did not change; he only went to more ingenious lengths to hide it from her. And without Paul's support, what could she do?

At the end of September, on the day she was due to move office premises, she came downstairs to find a letter from Hunter Campbell, the estate agents, and one from Hannah on the doormat. She ripped open the envelope from Hunter Campbell, addressed to both her and Paul. Inside was a letter from Keith Chalmers with a valuation and suggested marketing price for the house. Keith's letter said that he would expect the house to sell for in excess of a million pounds. She sat down on the bottom stair in surprise, clutching the paper to her breast.

Of course she had known roughly what Castlerock was worth; her work as a conveyancing solicitor meant that she had a good handle on property prices. But it was a little more than she had thought and seeing it in print, confirmed by an independent professional, well it was a shock. After paying off the mortgage, and setting up trust funds for Hannah and Finn, that would leave her and Paul with three hundred thousand pounds each; more than enough to buy outright a very nice home for herself with plenty of room for Hannah and Finn. And with her imminent elevation to partnership status at Stevenson and McIlwaine, and the commensurate increase in salary (negotiations with the firm on this subject now happily resolved), she would be very comfortably well off. She thanked God that she had kept her independence and remained a working mother.

With so much invested in Castlerock, both financially and emotionally, she had, at one time, thought it beyond price. She thought she could never sell it. Now it was reduced to pounds and pence, she tried to think of it as just a commodity; a springboard to a new life. But it was a life she was being forced to embark upon, not one of her choosing. And selling the house, much as she tried to rationalise it, was a huge emotional wrench. She could hardly bear to think of leaving it, and yet she must. She hated Paul as much for this as for his other crimes.

She picked up the letter from Hannah and let the pleasure of seeing it addressed in her neat, little girl handwriting, displace her sadness. She ran her finger over the writing, feeling where Hannah's pen had dug deep into the paper; a habit from childhood which she had not yet broken, and perhaps never would. She held it in her hand weighing it, appreciating it; the very first letter Hannah had ever written to her.

Hannah e-mailed, texted and phoned but she had never put pen to paper to communicate with her mother. She had never had the need. Chris smiled. Maybe Hannah had suddenly come to realise what an expensive toy a mobile phone was. For the cost of a stamp she could write realms. Still, it was a little odd, considering she had a computer of her own which Paul had bought her before she went away to Uni. Why did she not just e-mail?

The grandfather clock in the hall struck eight and she frowned. She couldn't be late for work today of all days. Yet she wanted to savour the letter, in peace and privacy, curled up on her favourite armchair in the kitchen with Murphy sprawled across her lap. She heard Finn in the kitchen and decided that the letter would have to wait. She propped it up on the top of the carriage clock that sat on the hall table. It was a delicious treat she would look forward to all day. She kissed the pad of her forefinger and pressed it lightly to the front of the envelope. Then she smiled and went into the kitchen to snatch a few precious minutes with her son before he left for work.

A removal company had been employed to transfer the contents of the filing cabinets from the old office to the new. The last few days at work had been spent sorting and shredding old documents and files so that no unnecessary paperwork was transferred to the new office. None of the furniture was going. And once the old place was cleared of paperwork, personal possessions and the files, it did look rather shabby. No-one would want the chipped furniture or anything else they left behind – lamps, old computers and printers, the leaky coffee machine and the knackered photocopier that only Mandy could get to work by kicking it in exactly the right spot with the toe of her shoe. It was all consigned to the skip.

At the new office, less than a hundred yards down the road, it was pandemonium. The public would have to manage without the services of Stevenson and McIlwaine for the next two days because it was going to take that long, and more, to get this place sorted.

A telecom engineer was still trying to get the telephones to work, two IT specialists were working on the computer network, the electricity was off, temporarily they were told, and a plumber was doing something to the toilet in the loo. The wallpaper paste was not yet dry and the place stank of fresh paint. Under Lynette's hesitant direction, Declan, Mandy and Rose were attempting to bring some order to the boxes of files flooding the office and pretty much obscuring the plush new carpet.

In the midst of this chaos, Chris sat in the main office at the only desk that wasn't covered in files, trying to conduct essential business by mobile phone – two clients were completing on house purchases today. Round about eleven o'clock Sam came out of his new office, jacketless and shirtsleeves rolled up. He looked like he was enjoying himself. He went outside onto the street and came back some ten minutes later with a tray of coffees in polystyrene cups and a big bag from the bakery which he deposited in front of her.

Chris finished her call and he whispered, "Who says you can't teach an old dog new tricks?" and winked.

She felt herself blush and smiled. He was truly an inspiration to her. For in spite of the unimaginable tragedy that had touched him, he remained positive and enthusiastic about life. She hoped that she too would one day be able to put her misfortunes behind her and move on.

Sam clapped his hands and hollered loudly, "Coffee

break everyone!" Declan, Rose, Mandy and Lynette looked up from what they were doing in surprise. For Sam McIlwaine had never initiated a coffee break before.

Then they descended on the coffees and Paris buns – deep-fissured conical cones of soft cake, topped with sugar crystals the size of small hailstones – like they hadn't seen food in days, although it was only a matter of hours since breakfast. There was enough for the engineers and workmen too which they accepted with bemused expressions.

Then the staff stood around Chris's desk talking about the merits of the new office and its drawbacks: the tall glass windows made you feel as if you were in a goldfish bowl with the world and its mother looking in at you. Everyone was excited; the atmosphere was fun, playful. Like on a high day or holiday, as Chris's mum would say.

"You'll have to keep your desk tidy from now on, Rose. Now that everyone can see you from the street," said Declan, with a cheeky grin.

"And you'll have to stop combing your hair every five minutes," retorted Rose, good-naturedly.

"No empty crisp packets on the floor behind your desk, Lynette," warned Mandy.

"I don't do that," she protested and everyone laughed, because she was notorious for it. "Well," she conceded with a red face, "maybe I have done it once or twice."

More friendly banter followed until Sam coughed and said, "I have some news that I'd like to share with you all." He looked even more pleased with himself than before; in fact he was positively beaming. "I'd like you to meet Stevenson and McIlwaine's new partner, Christine Quinn."

Though not exactly a surprise, Chris hadn't been

expecting the announcement right here and now so she was a little taken aback.

"Oh, Chris, well done, you!" cried Rose, kissing her on the cheek.

"Congratulations!" said Mandy, giving her a hug.

"That is so cool, Chris!" said Declan.

Sam extended his hand formally, Chris took it and he encircled her digits with his firm grip.

"Welcome aboard, Chris," he said. "We'll celebrate with the other partners next week at the monthly meeting."

"Well, you deserve it," said Lynette. "I've learnt so much from you, Chris."

Chris smiled and thanked them all and felt truly happy for the first time in over two months. "I'll tell you what – that is, if it's okay with you, Sam – lunch is on me!"

Declan punched the air and said, "Wicked!" and everyone laughed.

And Chris remembered what Sam had said about finding something to celebrate in each and every day. She caught his eye and he smiled at her and nodded his head slowly. She returned the smile and realised that today was the first day since Paul had left that her focus was on the future, rather than the past. Today was a turning point; it was the start of the rest of her life.

★ ★ ★

When she got home that evening she was still on a high.

"Finn!" she called as soon as she came through the door, discarding her bag and jacket at the bottom of the stairs.

"In here," came his voice from the kitchen, talking with his mouth full.

She found him standing up by the sink, hungrily devouring a slice of buttered bread. Slices of brown bread spilled out of the plastic bag onto the work surface and a buttery knife lay amongst the crumbs that littered the counter. Murphy came bounding over in welcome and she ruffled the fur behind his ears. He flopped over onto his back, belly up and panted eagerly, waiting to be tickled on the tummy. She obliged and he writhed in ecstasy, slobbering at the mouth and covering her hand in wet kisses.

"Daft dog," said Finn affectionately.

"Yeah, isn't he?" said Chris and she smiled. "Who's a good boy then? Who's a clever boy?" undulating the pitch and tone of her voice the way she used to when the children were babies. After a few moments of this she turned her attention to Finn. "Guess what? I've been promoted to partner."

"Aw, Mum," he said. "That's cool. It really is. Well done, you!" He came over and gave her a hug and said, "I'm proud of you, Mum."

"And I'm proud of you, son. Tell you what, why don't I take us both out for a slap-up meal to celebrate?"

"Oh, Mum," he said, reddening, "Mikey's picking me up in half an hour. We're going up to Glenarm to look at a car."

"For you?"

"Yeah. Dad said he would buy me it. A late birthday present, he said."

"Did he?" said Chris coldly, not because she opposed the idea in principle, or begrudged Finn a car. But because Paul had not consulted her. And there was the financial aspect to consider too – at one of their recent meetings they had both agreed to reign in the spending until things were sorted out. But Paul had gone out and bought Hannah a brand new computer and now this. He was trying to buy his children's affections – and their acceptance of Bernie.

"But what about insurance? It'll be astronomical to insure you," she said doubtfully, aware of how little he earned. She did not want him to make the assumption that she or his father would subsidise the luxury, although in reality of course, that was exactly what would happen.

"Dad said he'd cover that too. I'll only have petrol to pay for and I should be able to manage that myself."

"Fair enough," said Chris.

Two pieces of lightly charred bread popped out of the toaster, startling her.

"I'm just making some beans on toast," said Paul, following her gaze. He paused, and said, looking sheepish, "Maybe we can do it another night?"

"Of course we can, Finn. It was just a thought," she said brightly, but it was a bitter lesson. She had no right to expect Finn to change his plans to please his mother. He had his own life to lead. "You have a good time, Finn. And give that car a good going over. Don't be buying a lemon now."

"That's what I'm taking Mikey for," said Finn confidently, tipping a can of beans into a small saucepan. "He knows everything there is to know about cars."

Upstairs she changed out of her work clothes into jeans and a shirt and phoned Karen from the bedroom, hoping that she might be available to join her for a celebratory supper.

There was no answer. She glanced at the clock. That was

odd. Then she remembered it was Swim Club night for Jack. He didn't finish 'til seven o'clock and Karen had to then collect him, take him home and feed him and Chloe before putting both kids to bed. And she'd forgotten that Tony was out at football on a Monday night. Then she phoned her mum – she was in, but going out to her art class at seven thirty. Raymond would be working late – he was always working late. She didn't feel she knew Shona well enough to call her.

She put the phone down, picked it up, then put it down again. She could phone other friends but who wanted to go out at short notice on a Monday night when they had husbands and partners and families of their own? If one of them did agree to join her, it would only be because they felt sorry for her – a chore rather than a pleasure.

This, then, was what it meant to be alone. It wasn't the everyday companionship she missed so much because she was quite good at keeping herself busy. It was times like this, when she realised she had no-one with whom to share the highs (and lows) of her life. No-one to spontaneously pop open a bottle of champagne and celebrate her success with. She no longer came first in anyone's life, apart from Murphy. She didn't want to become an eccentric middle-aged woman with only a dog for company. She wasn't sure she could endure the loneliness of it.

She heard a car pull up outside, the slam of the front door and Finn's voice. Then a car door slammed shut and the car drove off, the engine revving madly. She was completely alone now and just falling into a state of self-indulgent melancholy, when she remembered Hannah's letter. She would read it and then phone Hannah with her wonderful news.

Chris jumped up from the bed and skipped down the stairs two at a time, retrieved the letter from its temporary home on the clock, and took it through to the kitchen. She poured herself a glass of white wine from a stash she kept in the fridge. She hadn't gone near the wine cellar since that embarrassing day when she'd smashed the padlock and drunk the best of Paul's wine – a silly act of revenge which she now deeply regretted. Now, if she wanted wine, she bought it herself and kept it in the kitchen, well away from Paul's precious store.

She slit the envelope open with a sharp kitchen knife, pleased to see several sheets of paper inside. Then she eased Murphy off the battered armchair by the window and took his place – the seat was warm from his little body. Ousted from his throne, he looked at her sorrowfully, then padded happily over to his basket on the floor and collapsed into it. That was one of the many nice things about dogs – unlike humans, they immediately forgot wrongs. Chris put on her reading glasses restored, if not to happiness, then to equanimity, took a sip of wine and read the letter.

It was a long letter, handwritten on lined A4 paper, but the content was straight to the point.

Hannah was pregnant.

Chris put the glass of wine down on the deep windowsill because suddenly her hand was shaking so much she doubted her ability to hold it any longer. She gripped the first page of the letter with both hands to steady it enough to read it; the remaining pages fell to the floor like autumn leaves. She blinked rapidly to restore her suddenly blurred eyesight and held the page further away from her face to focus on the words. Hannah had known before she went away to university. She was two months

pregnant, she reckoned. The father was a one-night stand –
someone's cousin from Crumlin she'd met at a house party
in July. He didn't know about the baby; she thought he
wouldn't want to know.

Chris turned the page over and continued to read, every
neatly scribed word twisting like a knife. Hannah had done
a pregnancy test, twice, just to be sure. Of all the things that
had happened in her life, thought Chris, this was the worst.
The one thing she had prayed would never happen to her
daughter. It was her worst nightmare.

"Oh, Hannah! How could you?"

Hannah said she hadn't known what to do. She was
sorry she hadn't told Chris before now but she hadn't
wanted to worry her – she had enough on her plate as it
was. Chris was suddenly angry with herself – her daughter
was in the midst of the worst crisis of her life and she felt
she couldn't tell her own mother. Chris had been so
wrapped up in her own selfish concerns, wallowing in self-
pity, that she had not noticed what was happening right
under her nose. Looking back, the signs that something was
wrong were all there – the jaded approach to packing for
Edinburgh, the vomiting on the ferry, the complete lack of
interest once she'd got there. How could she not have
noticed?

Chris scrambled on the floor to retrieve the remaining
two pages of the letter and read them where she was,
kneeling on the cold slate.

*I know that you and Dad will be very disappointed in me and
Dad especially will feel let down. He so wanted me to be a doctor,
Mum, but I'm not sure I can do it. It's not the work, you know,
it's just that I don't think in my heart that I really want to be one.
I can't think of anything more disgusting than looking at sick*

people, with their infections and warts and God knows what else, all day long. But I can't tell him that because he doesn't want to hear it. As far as he's concerned no other job is worth doing, which is a bit funny given you're a solicitor.

Chris remembered Karen's perceptiveness on this particular point, and her own obtuseness, and cringed with horror at her stupidity. By confiding in her aunt, Hannah had tried to tell her parents (knowing full well that the conversation would be relayed to Chris) but they hadn't listened.

I can't say these things to you and Dad – not to your face anyway - because you've always expected so much of me. You never allowed me to fail. I feel that you've always wanted me to be Miss Perfect and I can't be. I can't go on doing the things that you want me to do.

Had they been pushy parents? Was this Hannah's way of rebelling after years of pressure from them to perform? Of course they had always encouraged her to do her best and, yes, Paul had probably influenced Hannah's decision to do medicine. But had he coerced her? Had Chris allowed it to happen? Should she have stood up for Hannah's right to make independent choices?

I know that I've been very stupid. I don't know why I did this apart from the fact that I was drunk. I have had sex before – are you shocked? – but I've always been careful. I just want things to be all right. I want things to be back the way they were. And they can't be. I know that. But it doesn't stop me wanting it.

I'm not asking for help, Mum, from you or Dad. You have your own problems and I can't expect you to take this one on board as well. I'm an adult after all. I haven't decided what to do about the baby yet. But don't worry about me. I'll be all right. I know that you'd be ashamed of me if I came back to Ballyfergus so I won't.

*I can get benefits here and help with the baby from the state. I'd
like to do a different course but I don't know if I'll be able to stay
on at university. I'll have to see.*

The poor misguided girl, thought Chris, and now she
wept. Hannah had no idea what living off the state meant,
she had no conception of poverty. She had no
understanding of what it cost to run a home and raise a
child, nor how difficult it was for happy couples, never
mind immature single teenagers. She would never finish
university, never fulfil her potential. Saddled with a baby,
her life would be a struggle for survival. And an abortion,
even if Chris approved (which she didn't), wasn't the easy
solution it appeared.

If she had one, Hannah would be scarred for life by the
emotional trauma of aborting her baby. Chris and Paul
were not great churchgoers and, while nominally
Catholics, the children had been brought up very loosely
with regard to the teachings of the Church. But the
fundamentals had somehow stuck: like the rest of her
family, Hannah regarded abortion as murder.

When she had managed to stem the tears, Chris folded
the letter and placed it carefully back inside the envelope.
Hannah was two months gone. If her dates were accurate,
that meant she had fallen pregnant round about the time
Paul had left to go and live with Bernie. That was more
than coincidence.

Chris remembered how distraught Hannah had been at
her parent's break-up and the subtle change in her
behaviour after it. She had become withdrawn and secretive
and Chris, though she had at one level noticed, had been
too preoccupied on another to take the time to talk to
Hannah about her feelings. She imagined Hannah, angry

and confused, getting drunk and throwing herself at some stranger. Allowing some creep to maul her body.

She went through to the hall where a cream Bakelite phone from the nineteen fifties stood on the table. She replaced the letter carefully on top of the clock, wishing she could turn time back to when she'd first placed it there, unopened, and then freeze it forever . . .

The phone wasn't entirely decorative; it did work but it was only ever used to receive calls. Dialling out using the old-fashioned dial was slow and tedious; dialling each number with the tip of your index finger inserted in the metal holes, waiting for the dial to return after each number, listening to the reassuring tick-tick-tick as it went round. But for this call, today, it somehow seemed appropriate. Chris put her finger in the round hole for the number zero and began, slowly and deliberately, to dial Paul's mobile number.

When he answered she said coldly, "Would you be able to come over to the house, Paul? Now. It's about Hannah and it's very important." Then she hung up and sat on the bottom stair and waited.

When she opened the door to Paul he was cross and tired-looking.

"Don't do that to me again, Chris," he said, marching past her into the hall. "Telling me there's something wrong with Hannah and then hanging up like that."

"I'm sorry."

His anger deflated a little and he said, "So, what's wrong?"

In answer Chris went over to the clock, picked up the letter and handed it to him. "You'd better read this."

"Can't you just . . ." he began, but something in her

expression silenced him. She went into the kitchen and, taking her time, made tea. Much as she hated Paul she couldn't help but empathise with what he must be feeling right now. He would be absolutely horrified and shocked as she was.

When she came into the drawing room some ten minutes later he was sitting on the sofa with his head in his hands. The pages of the letter were strewn across the coffee table. And though she wasn't proud of herself, vindictively she was pleased. He should be hurting; he was responsible for this. If he hadn't run off with Bernie, she was quite convinced this calamity would never have happened.

She set a cup of tea down in front of him with a biscuit on the saucer and he looked up at her, his face streaked with tears. His eyes were bloodshot, his cheeks hollow and his skin had a deathly pallor. She sat down opposite and pushed the cup of tea towards him.

"Here," she said gently, in spite of herself, "drink this. And have something to eat. You look like – you look like you could use it."

He lifted the cup to his lips with both hands shaking and took a few sips. He looked absolutely traumatised, as though someone had died.

"It's not the end of the world, Paul," she heard herself saying, sensing that something needed to be said to pull him back from the brink of despair.

"It's the end of her life," he replied. "Oh, God! My little darling Hannah!" And he put his hands over his face and wept.

Chris, silent, looked at the table.

"Why did she do this, Chris?"

"Didn't you read the letter, Paul?" said Chris, all

compassion now evaporated. "It's because she was upset about you walking out and because she felt she was being pushed into doing medicine."

"But I thought she wanted to be a doctor. She's always wanted to be a doctor. Ever since she was a child."

"Maybe you wanted her to be a doctor, Paul. It's not the same thing. Maybe all along she was just trying to please you. Trying to win your approval." Approval that Hannah was well aware might be withdrawn if she failed to live up to his expectations; witness Finn. "And," she said, bowing her head, and remembering her proud boast, to anyone that would listen, that Hannah was going to be a doctor. "Maybe I was as much to blame for pushing her in that direction as you."

He shook his head more in disbelief than denial and said, "What are we going to do, Chris? What are we going to do?"

Suddenly nothing had been clearer to Chris in her entire life. She knew exactly what they were going to do.

"We're going to bring her home, Paul."

"Are we?" he said, the despair in his voice turning to something like hope.

"Yes. And if she wants to keep that baby then we're going to help her do it."

Twenty-one

Karen placed a bowl of salad in the middle of the big table in Chris's house and checked the number of place settings – Mum, Chris, herself and Tony, Hannah, Finn, Chloe and Jack and, of course, Raymond and Shona. Her stomach churned at the thought of Shona's name, but she stilled her nerves. The meal was to celebrate her mum's birthday but also to celebrate the fact that Raymond and Shona had named the day – they were to be married next August. And that, in Karen's book, had to be very good news indeed.

"Lovely looking salad, Karen," said Chris cheerily and Karen, lost in her thoughts, gave her a distracted smile.

She had never challenged Tony about the phone call. But she remembered that balmy August night as though it were yesterday. Mum was putting the kids to bed and she was in the lounge on the sofa watching TV. When he came downstairs, Tony denied making the call, but he'd forgotten one vital thing. When one phone in the house was picked up all the others gave a high-pitched 'tring'. It was a simple matter of hitting the 'last number dialled' button on the phone he'd used and she had the evidence – Shona and Raymond's home number.

She had sat on the office chair in the study, weighing the

handset in her hand, and staring out the window at kids, older than her own, playing kerbie in the street, in the fading evening sunshine. The neighbour's nine-year-old daughter threw the football at the right-angled edge of the curb, on the side of the street bathed in the glow of a slowly setting sun, and it bounced back into her waiting arms. The rest of the kids cheered. Karen checked the number and checked it again. Why was Tony phoning Raymond and Shona? And, more significantly, why had he tried to keep it a secret?

There was only one way to find out. She cleared her throat, dialled and, when Shona answered said, after the preliminaries, "Can I have a word with Raymond?"

And somehow she wasn't surprised when the reply came. "He's not in at the minute. I'm not expecting him 'til after nine, Karen. Can I get him to ring you then?"

"It's okay. He'll be tired after a day's work. It wasn't anything important. I'll call another time."

She hung up the phone and sat there for a full fifteen minutes thinking. She tried to think of a rational explanation why Tony would've phoned Shona. Was he trying to arrange a surprise party or something like that? But there were no big celebrations on the horizon and anyway his natural port of call for something of that nature would be Chris – not a newly acquired sister-in-law she hardly knew.

Karen told herself to focus on the facts. Tony had phoned Shona and denied it. That much she knew, and she suspected the worst, but it wasn't much to go on. In the end she decided that she must know for certain. She told Phyllis that she was nipping out for milk from the garage, got in her car and drove round to Cairndale Heights, her heart pounding like a drum, the sweat pouring down the back of her neck. And when she saw Tony's car in the driveway of number eight, she crept past like a thief in the night, praying to God that there was some innocent explanation. Giving Tony one last chance.

At home she arranged herself on the sofa and waited for his return. There was every possibility that he would come in and explain where he'd been and all would be well. But when he came in and breezily announced that he'd been round at Scott's for well over an hour, her fears were confirmed. Tony was having an affair with Shona.

Nearly ten weeks had passed since then and in a peculiar kind of way, it was almost a relief to know. At least she knew where she stood. What she was up against. What her choices were. She had thought long and hard about it and decided that she would do anything, put up with anything, to keep Tony and her little family together.

She told herself that the affair might be a short-lived fling that was over already. She'd watched Tony like a hawk these last ten weeks and every movement, outside of work, was accounted for. And if she blew Tony and Shona's cover now, she would jeopardise her brother's happiness, and perhaps force the lovers into each other's arms. Left alone, the affair might just peter out.

Shona was, after all, pressing ahead with arrangements for marriage to Raymond. And she did seem genuinely to love him. Surely she wouldn't want to enter into the sacred state of matrimony while conducting an affair? No, if they'd wanted to make the affair public they'd have done it by now.

And she had witnessed first hand the devastation Paul had wrecked by breaking up his marriage to Chris – and his kids were much older than Chloe and Jack. She couldn't imagine the damage that a separation or divorce would have on them. And she took comfort in the fact that she wasn't alone. There were thousands of women all across the country who lived with their husband's infidelity, weren't there? She just had to be strong, sit tight and ride the storm – and hope and pray that Tony never left her.

The holiday to Donegal in August, with so much time spent in close proximity to Tony, had been a test. She kept imagining Tony with Shona, touching her hair, kissing her, telling her that he loved her. It was almost unbearable - she couldn't bring herself to sleep with him, making up all sorts of lies about pain in her stomach. If it hadn't been for the distraction of the children, she might not have been able to keep the knowledge to herself. But she had done – and she was proud of herself. She would get through this.

She thought of what she had put herself through with the surgery, and involuntarily touched her smooth stomach underneath a beige satin shirt and flowing wide-legged trousers. She did not entirely regret having the operation but she had been a fool to think that it could make Tony fancy her. That it could make him love her. There was too much wrong with the rest of her.

"This might be the last family get-together we have in this house," said Chris, and Karen followed the direction of her gaze. She was staring at the red and green 'for sale' sign secured to the gatepost at the end of the drive. The brisk October wind churned up a sea of copper beech leaves on the lawn and threatened to wrest the sign from its moorings.

"There's always Christmas," said Karen, mindful of the many wonderful family Christmases Chris and Paul had hosted here.

"No," said Chris, firmly with a shake of the head. "I don't think I'll do a big family Christmas here. Not this year. I think it would be too – too upsetting."

"I understand," said Karen quickly. "We can always do it at mine. Anyway the house might be sold by then."

"Yes, it might be," said Chris and a look of such sorrow crossed over her face that it made Karen's heart ache for her.

If only she could tell Chris about Tony and Shona, she thought, glancing at her sister's worn face. If only she could share the burden of this terrible secret. But Chris had returned to her task of slicing bread and was attacking the chore with such a look of concentrated vengeance on her face it was frightening. Chris had her own burdens to shoulder – the break-up of her marriage and now Hannah. There were lines on her face in places where there had been none before. Karen could not possibly add to her woes.

She walked over to the island unit where she had discarded her bag and pulled out a bunch of small white cards. She returned to the table and laid them, one at a time, in the middle of the place settings.

"What are you doing?" said Chris, from behind her right shoulder.

"Putting out place settings," she said casually. "I thought it might give lunch a bit of a sense of occasion."

"What a lovely idea! Mum'll love it," said Chris with genuine delight. "Why didn't I think of that?" and Karen couldn't tell her, of course, that her objective in setting out place cards was simply to keep Shona Johnston as far away from Tony, and her, as possible.

"Is the food nearly ready, Mum?" said Hannah coming

into the room and Karen's gaze was drawn involuntarily to her niece's stomach. It still looked as flat as a pancake. She lowered her eyes because she couldn't bring herself to look Hannah in the eye – not just yet anyway. The girl had no concept of the grief she had brought upon her mother – upon the whole family.

It wasn't that Karen was ashamed of her or cared what people thought. She couldn't give a damn. It was that Hannah had no idea what having a baby really meant and therefore could not foresee the possible complications and dangers. She did not see that her whole future was compromised – the possibility of a successful career, true independence and a happy and advantageous marriage. These were, after all, the things every parent wished for their daughter.

Hannah seemed to be drifting blithely along under the impression that – well, Karen didn't know what. But she certainly didn't appear to be aware of the seriousness of her situation. Yet no-one wanted to enlighten her to the reality of her plight because her naivety was somehow preferable. And so all the adults in the family worried on her behalf.

"Five minutes," said Chris. "In fact, why don't you ask everyone to come through, Hannah?"

"Sure," said Hannah, pinching a piece of cucumber from the salad bowl, and disappearing. In the drawing room Karen could hear her rounding up everyone for lunch and a few minutes later they all came through.

Shona was first, wearing an innocent smile on her face and a pretty jewelled sleeveless polo top in burnt orange. Karen could never wear anything like that. Her chest was too big and her neck too short. She hated Shona for the way she looked as well as what she had done.

"No," she said rather sharply, as Shona approached a chair and put her hand on the back of it. "I mean, you're up here, Shona." And she smiled beatifically, thinking that her only objective from today was to further seal the contract between Raymond and Shona. She must focus on that and put aside all thoughts of Shona and Tony together.

"Will you put Murphy in the utility room, Finn?" said Chris as soon as her son appeared, with his hands stuffed deep into the pockets of his oversized jeans. He had on a sports T-shirt, his hair was carefully gelled and his trainers virginal white. This casual look was so studied it made Karen smile.

Jack, coming into the room just in time to hear Chris's request, cried, "Does he have to, Auntie Chris? Can't he stay? I promise I won't feed him. And he'll be very good, won't you, Murphy?" He dropped to the floor and flung his arms round the little furry body.

And Chris, relenting in a way that Karen had never before witnessed, stared at the puppy, his cute little face upturned as though he understood and was pleading his case. "Oh, all right then, So long as you don't feed him."

"Yes!" cried Jack and then, more softly, he coaxed the dog, "Come on, Murphy. There's a good boy." He led him over to the table and got him to sit on the floor by his seat.

Once everyone was seated, Raymond, being the head of the Mulvenna family now, toasted Phyllis's health and everyone wished her a Happy Birthday. Karen tried to put Shona and Tony – they were all she thought about these days – out of her mind and concentrate on her mum.

Phyllis said a few words of thanks to Chris and Karen for the lovely lunch (a joint effort). Then she lifted her glass and said, "I'd like to propose a toast to Raymond and Shona who, as you all know, have announced a date for their wedding. And made me very, very happy indeed."

"Here, here!" said Tony, clinking his glass with hers.

"Congratulations," said Chris.

"Yeah, great," said Hannah and Finn mumbled something similar.

Jack and Chloe, who were looking under the table at Murphy, giggled.

Karen raised her glass but couldn't quite bring herself to say anything – the words died in her throat. Luckily no-one noticed and everyone set about the cold starter of Italian ham, rocket and shaved Parmesan.

"Can you pass the dressing, please, Karen?" said Shona.

"Sure," she said. It was so unfair. Was one man not enough? Why did Shona have to have Tony as well as Raymond? And what about her brother? Was she going to be unfaithful to him with someone else? Was she going to destroy Raymond's life the way she had destroyed hers?

"What's in it?" asked Phyllis.

"Balsamic vinegar and olive oil," said Chris.

Karen picked the bottle up and considered, just for a moment, chucking the contents over Shona's face and clothes. That would take the stupid smile off her face. That would teach her a lesson.

But she didn't, of course. She passed the container meekly to Finn who passed it along to his aunt-in-waiting. Karen looked at the food on her plate and felt like she was going to be sick.

"So how's life in the new Stevenson and McIlwaine premises?" said Raymond to Chris. He leaned his elbow on the table, took a swig of wine and waited for her reply, a contented smile on his face.

"Great. I've finally got a lovely new office. It's so big there's room for a sofa and a coffee table as well as my desk!"

"You could have a party in there," said Karen, trying to enter into the spirit of the conversation.

"Makes a big change from the last one," said Phyllis. "You could hardly swing a cat in it."

"I thought you two were told not to feed the dog," interjected Karen, talking to Jack and Chloe. They looked up guiltily. She raised her eyebrows in warning and looked away.

"I haven't seen your new office," said Shona. "I'll need to think up an excuse to come and see you."

"You don't need an excuse, Shona. Call in any time. Better still, let me know you're coming and we can go for lunch or something. How about one day next week?"

"That'd be great!" said Shona. "Let's do that."

"What about Wednesday?" said Chris.

"Sounds good."

Karen was suddenly jealous for her sister's affections. Not content with trying to steal her husband, was Shona to take Chris from her too? Friendship between Karen and Shona was now completely out of the question and she resented Shona getting close to Chris.

"Why don't you join us, Karen?" said Shona.

Karen, taken aback, mumbled, "Oh. I'll have to see. I might be busy."

Chris looked at her in puzzlement and Karen blushed and gazed at the table.

There was a pause and Tony said, "How's the new car then, Finn? Running okay?"

"Good, now. It needed a bit of work doing – the timing

belt and front brake discs need to be changed and I had to replace a couple of tyres, but I used remoulds that Mikey got for me so it wasn't too bad."

Tony sucked in air through his teeth and said, "It all adds up though doesn't it? It's the labour costs more than the parts. They really cream you."

"You're right there, Tony. Luckily I only had to pay for the parts and they came to next to nothing. Mikey wouldn't take any money off me for the labour."

"Is he a mechanic?"

"Yeah."

"Sounds like a good mate."

"He is. The best."

"You don't fancy a spoiler and flashy hub caps, then?" said Tony, teasing.

"Maybe, when I've a bit of spare cash," said Finn, his cheeky grin with boyish dimples on show, betraying the fact that he too was joking. And then changing subject he said, "What about you, Tony? That old banger of yours must be due for an update."

"Hey, you!" said Tony, pretending to be offended. "That old banger as you call it is a quality piece of metal. There's years left in her yet!"

Finn laughed and the conversation revolved around cars for some minutes. Then Shona helped Chris clear away the plates and serve the main course of chicken chasseur, baby potatoes and vegetables. They talked about arrangements for the wedding and, over a dessert of Chris's home-made Key Lime Pie, Raymond told them about houses he and Shona had been looking at with a view to buying a permanent home.

"You could buy this house," said Chris, seriously. "It

would be nice to keep it in the family."

"I wish I could, Sis," said Raymond sincerely, "but I'm afraid our budget doesn't stretch to a mansion like this."

"That's a shame," said Chris and she stared out the window.

Coffee was served and Chloe and Jack were released into the garden to play with Murphy. They took turns throwing a yellow tennis ball for the dog to retrieve. But he preferred to run off with it in his mouth, so setting up an exciting chase round the garden.

And inside, Raymond, emboldened by wine perhaps, tackled the subject that no-one else dared mention. "So, are you glad to be home, Hannah? It's been what, three weeks now?"

"Mmm," she murmured and looked at her half-empty plate. Evidently she too was having difficulty eating, but for an entirely different reason from Karen.

"What are you going to do with yourself until . . . you know," said Raymond.

Hannah's gaze flitted from Chris to Raymond and back again. "I dunno. Hang out, I suppose."

"She's been offered a job at the day centre," said Chris, smiling bravely.

"Yeah," said Hannah as though she'd only just remembered. "I was going to do that for a while."

"Job in the day centre," muttered Phyllis bitterly, and then more clearly, "And to think she could've been studying to be a doctor."

"Mum," said Karen, indignant on Hannah's behalf, "you're not helping."

"It's all right," said Hannah. "Gran's entitled to her opinion." But she shot her grandmother an evil look.

Raymond stared long and hard at Hannah and said,

"Have you decided to have the baby then?"

Phyllis inhaled sharply and Chris said quickly, "Of course she's having the baby."

"Chris," said Raymond softly, "I didn't ask you. I asked Hannah."

There was a silence then and everyone's gaze turned on poor Hannah, who was seated beside Karen. She blushed furiously, her eyes darted back and forth not knowing where to look, and she twisted her hands together in her lap. Karen, moved by her distress, reached out and patted Hannah's restless hands.

"Well, Hannah?" said Raymond.

Shona put a hand on his arm and said, "Raymond, I don't think . . . "

"It's okay, Shona," he said, and touched her arm reassuringly. "I just want to be sure that Hannah's doing the right thing for her. What she wants to do. Not what other people think is right," he said, throwing a shooting glance at Phyllis and Chris.

The tennis ball hit the patio door with a thud but everyone ignored it. The tension in the room, while everyone waited for Hannah to speak, was palpable.

"Maybe," said Hannah at last. "I don't know."

"What do you mean you don't know? Look, of course she's having the baby," said Phyllis. "Whether she keeps it or not is another matter."

"You don't have to, Hannah," said Raymond gently, ignoring his mother. "You're eighteen, old enough to make your own decisions. You can have the baby and keep it. Or have it and give it up for adoption," he paused momentarily, glanced at his mother and added, "or not have it."

"You mean an abortion?" whispered Shona and she put

her hand to her throat. Her face went suddenly pale.

"She's not having an abortion," said Phyllis.

"Raymond, will you stop this!" hissed Chris evenly, through gritted teeth.

"No, Chris. Not until I've heard from Hannah what she wants."

"Oh for God's sake, why are you all so set against an abortion?" blurted out Finn. "It obvious that no-one wants the baby. All you keep going on about is how it's going to ruin Hannah's life. Well, isn't an abortion the obvious solution?"

"Finn!" growled Chris, the muscles on her jaw taut with anger. "Will you please keep quiet?"

"What?" he said, innocently. "What did I say?"

"You don't know what you're talking about," said Chris.

"All I said was . . ." he began but Hannah interrupted.

"You stupid idiot!" she cried. "What do you know about anything?" And she jumped up from the table, fled into the hall and pounded up the stairs.

"Now look what you've done," said Chris. She let out a defeated sigh.

"I'm just being honest," said Finn. "More honest than the rest of you. You don't want her to have the baby but you don't want her to have an abortion either. Why bring another unwanted child into a world where there are so many already?"

"It's not as simple as that, Finn," said Chris with a weary sigh. "Apart from the ethical issue of whether an abortion's right or wrong, it may not be the best thing for Hannah either emotionally or physically."

"But maybe Finn has a point," said Raymond, his features creased in concentration. "Just bear with me for a minute. I'm not proposing it as the only solution. It's just an option, but perhaps one we shouldn't dismiss out of hand. It depends very much on what Hannah wants and her state of mind. Having the baby could be as detrimental to her health and well-being as not having it."

Karen frowned, considering this persuasive point of view.

"Has she," Raymond went on, "had any professional counselling?"

"Of course not," snapped Phyllis. "She doesn't need some over-paid psychoanalyst to tell her that abortion's wrong."

Karen looked at the table. She had always believed that abortion was immoral but, then again, she had never been placed in a situation where someone so close to her was affected in this way.

"All Catholics who procure or participate in an abortion are automatically excommunicated from the Church, Raymond," said Phyllis darkly. "That may not matter to you, but it matters to me."

Raymond looked at the faces round the table and said, "And I respect that point of view, Mum. But none of the rest of us are practising Catholics. I know it's a very difficult issue, but perhaps there are some circumstances under which it might be justified."

Karen was torn. Raymond was alluding to a recent case of a very young rape victim in the South falling pregnant and having to travel to Britain to procure an abortion. Hannah hardly fell into that category (the sex having been consensual) and yet, if her young niece's life could be saved from ruin . . . Karen didn't know what to think. She rubbed her brow with her right hand.

"If it's what Hannah wants," Raymond went on, "it could be the right thing for her. I'm not suggesting it's right for everyone in this situation, but for some girls, especially bright ones like Hannah, maybe an abortion is okay. Afterwards, she could go back to university and get on with her . . ."

Suddenly Shona stood up and the movement was so abrupt that Raymond's words died on his lips. Her face had gone from white to red and she was shaking so much that Karen thought she might be having some kind of fit or seizure. Karen watched in morbid fascination. It was like watching a volcano about to explode.

"So you think an abortion's the answer then, do you?" Shona demanded. Her question seemed to be aimed generally at the company rather than just at Raymond.

But it was he who answered, rather hesitantly, "I'm just saying it's an option, Shona."

"And you think that's the answer, do you? Have you considered for one moment the damage it would do to *her*?"

"Possibly less physical damage than going ahead with a pregnancy, I would've thought," said Raymond.

"I'm not talking about physical damage. I'm talking about what it'll do to her in here. In her head," said Shona and he stabbed at her skull, hard, with her index finger to illustrate her point. "You think that getting rid of the baby's the easy way out. You think it's so simple just to flush it out and everything can go on as before." She was crying now, great sobs of anguish, tears flowing freely down her cheeks.

Raymond stood up and attempted to put his arm around her shoulder. "You've had too much to drink," he said, but instinctively Karen knew that this outburst had nothing to do with alcohol.

Shona shook him off. "What will she think of herself if she kills her own baby? You don't forget, you know. You never forget. It's all you think about day and night until you go mad with it!"

"Shona, dear," said Phyllis, "calm yourself. We're only having a discussion."

But there was no stopping her now.

"You see, getting rid of it is so convenient, isn't it? Oh, yes, I know. It avoids all the shame and humiliation. All those neighbours talking and pointing fingers at you. It's not a pleasant thought, is it?"

"Shona – please!" said Raymond, his expression now one of shock. "I don't care what people think. My concern is only for Hannah's welfare."

She ignored him. "No doubt Daddy will arrange it all. A nice clean clinic somewhere, over the water perhaps, where no-one knows you. A few weeks for her to recover and then pack her off back to university. But that won't be the end of it, not by a long shot. Because she'll never be free of it. It'll completely screw up her head. It's her that has to live with the guilt, not any of you. And then one day she'll find out that she can't have children because of it!"

"No-one said Hannah's having an abortion," said Chris firmly but Shona was too far gone to hear her.

"And that's the cruellest thing of all. The hardest thing to bear. And it's so unfair because I was only a child, just like Hannah!"

The room went suddenly quiet, apart from Shona's sobs, as the penny dropped. That then was why Shona couldn't have children. She was sterile because of a botched abortion she'd had when she was just a teenager. In spite of her hatred for Shona, Karen felt an instinctive rush of sympathy.

"And I'll be damned," said Shona, attempting and failing to pull herself together – she slammed one closed fist into the open palm of the other, "I'll be damned if I'll stand by and let you do that to her! I swear to God if you –"

"Shona. That's enough."

It was Tony. He stood, facing her diagonally across the rectangular table, where Karen had seated him at the opposite end to Shona.

Amazingly, Tony succeeded where the others had failed. Shona stopped crying immediately and stared at him with a look of such grief it was painful to watch. Raymond sank down slowly into his chair, like a balloon deflating.

Tony walked to the other end of the table and put his arm across Shona's shoulder. She buried her face in his chest, like a child seeking comfort from a parent, and was still. Tony held her for a few moments and then, very gently, eased her back onto the chair where she sat with a glazed expression on her face, staring at the wall.

Karen closed her eyes and started to cry cold, silent tears. There was nothing she could do now. It was over. The thing she had tried with all her heart and soul to avert had happened. It would be clear to everyone now that Shona and Tony were having an affair. Raymond would want nothing to do with Shona. Tony would run off with Shona and her marriage would be over.

"What is going on here, Tony?" demanded Raymond, suddenly galvanised and then angry. "Can you tell me just what the hell is going on between you and my fiancée?"

"It's simple, Raymond. They're having an affair!" said Karen between sobs.

"No!" cried Chris in disbelief.

"Yes," said Karen. "It's been going on since before the party at your house at the end of July."

"Jesus, Karen," said Tony, "what in the name of God are you talking about?"

"I saw you. I saw you, Tony. Don't even try to deny it."

"You saw what?"

"I saw you sneaking into the conservatory to talk with her when you thought no-one was watching!"

"Yes, but –"

"And you pretended that the party was the first time you'd met. But it wasn't, was it?"

Tony's shoulders slumped, he shook his head and said very quietly, "No."

This admission brought fresh tears forth but Karen fought to control herself, determined to have her say after her long anguished silence.

"I thought so. At least you're man enough to admit it. I followed you, you know. That night in August when you pretended you were going round to Scott's house, I followed you. And I saw where you went. You went to see Shona and you lied about it. You lied to my face."

"I –" began Tony.

"I can't believe this," Raymond interrupted, his face ashen and Karen's heart ached for him as well as herself. He was utterly crestfallen, all the confidence knocked out of him. He sat on the chair like a rag-doll.

There was a stunned silence.

Phyllis broke it with, "I think maybe you should leave now, Tony."

"But you've got it all wrong, Karen," he cried, as though his mother-in-law had not spoken.

"I don't see how," said Karen. "God knows, I've closed

my eyes to what's been going on between you two. I thought if I ignored it, the affair would peter out, and I could keep our marriage intact. I loved you so much, Tony, I would've done anything to keep you. I tried to be strong, I tried to carry on as though everything was normal. Even though it broke my heart." She broke off to sob uncontrollably for a few moments.

"Tony —" began Phyllis.

But Karen raised her hand, contained her weeping and said, "No, Mum, I haven't finished."

"But, Karen, let me explain!" Tony pleaded.

"I hoped that Shona's marriage to Raymond would put an end to it," Karen continued, ignoring him. "That's why I was so pleased when they set a date for the wedding. And, Raymond," she turned her gaze on her shell-shocked brother, "I'm sorry for keeping this from you — but I could see how much you loved her and, foolishly, I thought I was protecting you. I didn't want to see your happiness destroyed, as well as mine."

"Will you give me a chance to explain!" Tony shouted and he hit the table with his closed fist. "There is no affair going on. There never was. At least not the way you think."

"I'm going now," said Karen. She got up and threw her napkin on the table. "I don't want to hear any more of your lies."

"Karen, please!" he cried.

But she was deaf to his pleas. How much of a fool did he take her for? She still had some dignity left — and she intended to leave with it intact. She walked to the patio doors, and was about to throw them open and call to the children when Shona spoke.

"He's telling the truth, Karen," she said softly.

506

Karen froze where she was, with her hand on the doorknob, her heart thumping. Her head felt like it was about to explode and suddenly it was hard to breathe. She turned slowly and stared at Shona. Her expression was blank, her head was cocked slightly to one side and she rocked ever so gently, back and forth, her arms wrapped tightly round herself.

"Karen," said Phyllis firmly, a voice of authority in the midst of so much confusion, "why don't you sit down a minute? Chris, Finn – I think we should leave the room now."

"No," said Tony and he shook his head as though resigning himself to something. His eyes were full of tears and he looked at Karen with such sorrow etched on his handsome face she had to look away. "Stay where you are. I want you – I want all of you – to hear this. That is, if you've no objection, Shona?"

Shona shook her head but said nothing.

"Will you please come and sit down, Karen?" he said.

She stared at the children playing happily in the autumn sunshine and thought that, for them if nothing else, she owed him this audience. Reluctantly, she took her place at the table and he took his place beside her.

"Thank you," he said, and attempted to take her hand in his but she snatched it away. "I would never, ever do anything to hurt you," he began. "I love you, Karen."

Unable to bear hearing those words, she snapped, "Shona said you were telling the truth! If you and she aren't, and weren't, having an affair then I think you'd better tell me what exactly has been going on."

"Yes," he said with a heavy sigh and glanced at Shona, "so do I. And I think it's an explanation that's long overdue.

You see, Shona and I have known each other a very long time although, until the party here in July, we hadn't set eyes on each other in over twenty years."

"But you said you'd never met before," said Chris.

"I know. I lied."

There was a murmur of shock from Phyllis. Karen's mind was racing . . . twenty years ago Shona would have been very young . . . as young as Hannah was now . . .

She had been right all along, thought Karen bitterly. So Tony and Shona had known each other, they had probably been lovers once. They must have reignited their affair after the party. She closed her eyes.

Tony sighed heavily. "Shona and I met at university. She was seventeen, I was twenty. We had a brief relationship, the upshot of which was that Shona fell pregnant."

Karen's eyes snapped open in shock. But Shona had an abortion . . . which left her infertile . . . oh, God, no . . . let it not be Tony . . .

"Shona," interrupted Raymond, his face wretched with anguish, "is this true?"

She said nothing and looked at the floor.

"Let me finish, Raymond, please," said Tony.

Raymond gave Tony a hateful look but said no more.

"I didn't know what to do," Tony went on. "I was afraid of being saddled with a baby and a girl I hardly knew. I panicked. I persuaded Shona to go back to her parents in Scotland, knowing full well they would persuade her to have an abortion."

He paused and the room was deathly silent.

Karen looked at Shona who had covered her face with her hands and Chris voiced the words Karen could not utter.

"And did they?" she said, her voice barely more than a whisper.

Tony looked at Chris and then at Karen, his eyes red-rimmed and his face full of fear. Shona let out a soft whimper and Tony simply nodded in reply to Chris's question. Raymond put his arm around Shona and she turned her face into his broad chest.

Karen put her hand to her breast, her feelings in complete tumult. Poor Shona had clearly gone through the most terrible, traumatic experience. And her heart ached for Tony. He looked so wretched and broken. Suddenly she wanted to take him in her arms and tell him that no matter what he'd done, she still loved him.

"I washed my hands of her," said Tony. "I broke off communication with her as soon as she went back to Scotland. I thought that was the end of it. I thought we would never see each other again."

"How could you be so cruel? How could you be so callous?" said Raymond, his voice full of rage, and he hugged Shona to him in a strong embrace, as if she were a child.

Tony hung his head and looked at the floor between his feet. "You're right to be angry. I am ashamed of what I did. And believe me, Raymond," his voice choked with emotion, "if I could go back and change things I would. If I could save her from what she went through . . ." He sniffed and went on, looking round the shocked faces at the table, "I've tried to live a good life to make up for what I did. Because every day I regret it. I regret my stupidity in ever getting myself and Shona into that situation, I regret the immature way I handled it and the fact that, because I washed my hands of her, I was responsible for an abortion. The taking of an innocent life. I knew then, as I know now, that although we created that life, we didn't have the right to destroy it."

Karen looked at Chris who had bowed her head and she thought briefly of poor Hannah's predicament. Her heart ached for her sister and her niece.

"But I learned to live with my guilt," Tony went on, "or at least I thought I had. And then of all the bizarre coincidences I find out that you, Raymond, are to marry Shona Johnston and bring her back to Ballyfergus to live. Again, I panicked. I didn't know how you would react, Karen, if you found out."

Karen blushed and looked at her hands. She would probably have been jealous, envious of a prior relationship even though it was long dead and buried under the most tragic of circumstances.

"I thought that it would be best for everyone if it remained a secret and I made that decision without consulting Shona. That day at the party, I approached her and pretended we were strangers. And later on, I cornered her, desperate to secure her agreement to keep quiet."

That explained the clandestine meeting in the conservatory, thought Karen. She stared at Tony dumbfounded, torn between elation and sadness. She had been completely mistaken. There had been no affair, only a sad, sordid tale from Tony's past that he had foolishly tried to conceal. And yet it unsettled her that he was capable of such deception. He wasn't quite the man she thought he was. He wasn't quite so flawless – and she loved him more because of it.

"But why didn't you tell me, Tony?" she said. "Did you think I would hold you accountable for something you did in your past? Did you think I would judge you?"

"Yes, and I didn't want you to be disappointed in me. But the main reason was that I knew how jealous you can be, Karen. I worried that you would see Shona as some sort of threat, that you would resent the fact that we had once been lovers."

Karen hung her head. He was right of course. Had her stupidity – her unfounded suspicions – been partly responsible for forcing him down this route?

"Oh, Shona baby," said Raymond "why didn't you tell me?"

Shona looked up into his face, hers now streaked with tears. "I couldn't. I was ashamed. I thought you would think less of me. I thought you might not love me."

"But why would this affect my love for you? It's in the past and you were only a child. Oh, Shona, darling! How could you be so mistaken? If anything, it makes me love you even more."

"But it's not just the abortion, Raymond. There's more." She swallowed, her face went red and she said quietly, staring at the table, "After it, I was so distraught I went through a period when I was sexually promiscuous. I contracted an infection that went untreated until it was too late. It was this that made me infertile, not the abortion itself."

"You weren't responsible for your actions then, Shona," said Tony, quietly. "You went through some sort of breakdown."

Karen found herself nodding in agreement and the faces of Phyllis and Chris were full of sympathy.

"None of it is your fault, Shona," said Raymond and he held her tighter still, rocking her gently back and forth.

"But it means we can't have a family," she persisted.

"I don't want to marry you because I want you to have my babies. It would've been nice," he said with a smile, "but it's you I want. No more and no less. You, Shona Johnston, exactly the way you are regardless of anything that's happened before." He embraced her fiercely, nestled his face in her hair and whispered softly, "Come here, my baby. Oh, my baby!"

Karen wiped the tears from her face – tears shed for Shona and for Raymond. For the sorrow Shona had endured and the fact that she and Raymond would never have a family. Tears also of shame – for assuming that Shona was capable of having an affair behind Raymond's back. It was so clear to her now how much they loved each other – why couldn't she see it before? And tears of relief – that Tony wasn't having an affair. That he still loved her.

"Let's go," said Raymond and, without paying the slightest attention to anyone else in the room, he led Shona into the hall. The front door opened and shut, car doors slammed and they drove away.

Everyone was silent for a long time. Then Phyllis got up and walked out of the room. Without a word passing between them, Chris, and then Finn, got up and followed her, leaving Tony and Karen alone at the table.

"Do you believe me now?" he said.

"Yes."

He put his hand to her face and pushed back a strand of unruly hair.

"But what about that time in August when you went to see Shona?" she said. "What was that about?"

"I needed to find out why Shona couldn't have children. Do you remember? Phyllis told us over tea earlier that night."

She nodded.

"I needed to know if it was because of the abortion."

"And it was," said Karen glumly.

"Indirectly, yes," he said and sighed. "And now I have to live with that too."

"Oh, Tony! You've beaten yourself up over this for the past twenty years. It's time to let go. You are not the man you were then. In fact, you were just a boy."

"Do you forgive me?"

"There's nothing to forgive, Tony. You made a mistake and you, and Shona, have paid the price for it. She, God help her, can't have children and you have tortured yourself for the last twenty years."

"And nearly lost you over it."

"That's why you must let go."

"I'm not sure I can," he said and put his head in his hands, ruffling his thick black hair with his fingers.

"I know, Tony. Because the absolution you need can only come from in here." She pressed her hand to her left breast. "The forgiveness you want has to come from yourself."

He was crying softly. "That's what Shona said."

"And she was right. Don't you think it's time you forgave yourself, Tony? Don't you think you've done enough penance? I do."

He looked into her face and there was hope there. He nodded. "Okay."

"Say it."

"What?"

"Say that you forgive yourself."

"I …" he began hesitantly, "I forgive myself."

"For what?"

"For being a party to an abortion. For the taking of an innocent life."

"And?"

"And for Shona becoming infertile because of it."

"Good," she said nodding. "Better?"

He sniffed and said, "Yeah. It does feel better."

She leaned over and kissed him full on the lips. "Can I ask you to do one thing for me?"

"Anything."

"Promise me that you will never keep another secret from me again."

"I promise."

The patio doors burst open and Chloe came running in, squealing with delight, her dress all dirty, followed by Jack and a very muddy Murphy. Karen smiled brightly, the way a mother, even if her heart is breaking, will do to protect her children from fear.

Chloe stopped in her tracks.

"Why are you crying, Mummy?"

"Because I'm happy," she said.

Jack put his hands on his hips and said, humorously, "Now that is really weird, Mum. Most people cry when they're sad, but you're crying because you're happy!"

"Oh, come here, you two!" she said, suddenly overcome with elation. The children came close and she hugged them both, nestling her face in, first, Chloe's soft head of blonde hair, then Jack's.

"Family hug! Family hug!" chanted Jack.

And Karen felt Tony's arms around all of them, encircling them in his strong embrace. And she knew that everything was going to be all right.

Twenty-two

It was Friday lunchtime. Paul sat at his desk in work doing the interminable paperwork and cursed under his breath. He had not become a doctor to sit at a desk pushing a pen (or typing on a computer keyboard) but that is what he seemed to spend a lot of his time doing. He threw down the pen and rubbed his eyes.

But, that aside, it was still the most rewarding job. It was a bit like being a detective, collecting the evidence in the form of symptoms from the patient, analysing them in the context of the patient's clinical history and solving the mystery. Only today he'd seen an eight-year-old boy presenting with what seemed like appendicitis but a urine test had shown him to have, very unusually in a boy of his age, a urinary tract infection. Left untreated it could have spread to his kidneys. Now he was on appropriate antibiotics and would be back on his feet in a matter of days. That was what made his job so rewarding.

Hannah would've made a great doctor. He sighed. Every time he thought of her, his heart ached. Her life was ruined in his opinion. She had decided to have the baby and she said that she was going to keep it. She had no idea what was ahead of her. No idea how a baby would limit her opportunities and destroy her chances of a successful career and a good marriage. He had such high hopes for her (was that a crime?) and now they had been dashed. Maybe he had been too proud.

He could only admire Chris's fortitude and pragmatic handling of the situation. In the short term, she had persuaded Hannah to take a job at the day centre (to stop her sitting around moping all day, getting depressed) and had encouraged her to think of applying for a university course next year. Chris said she would take time out from her job to help with the baby. Paul tried to be as supportive but his heart wasn't in it. He was just so disappointed in Hannah. But he would, taking his cue from Chris, try to do his best by her. And he would make sure Hannah, and the baby, wanted for nothing financially.

He frowned when he thought of his finances. For some reason money was becoming a bit of a problem. He and Bernie were going through it like there was no tomorrow and he couldn't see much to show for it. True he had splashed out on a car for Finn but that had come from savings, not income, as had the first year's insurance.

He and Bernie were spending up to the limit every month and sometimes the bank account even went overdrawn. He didn't understand it. When he and Chris were together they never had money problems, even though there were four of them in the house and Castlerock was expensive to heat and maintain. But then they had two healthy incomes coming in. He must have underestimated the difference it would make living on one income, for Bernie earned next to nothing. She wasn't making much headway in promoting herself and Paul wondered, disloyally, if she was trying hard enough. He wondered too if she might be a bit depressed about her work situation. She suffered from insomnia sometimes and other times she could sleep for Ireland.

If she wanted to have a nice lifestyle, she would have to get the finger out soon. Clearly, his income alone wasn't enough. Or else Chris had been a very good housekeeper and Bernie a very bad one. But Paul was a firm believer that every problem had a solution. He wasn't very good with figures or money, having always relied on Chris to manage finances. But every time he tried to raise the subject with Bernie she somehow managed to distract him and they ended up talking about something else. But this time he would be firm. They would sit down and go through their outgoings with a finetooth comb to see where savings could be made. He didn't like to deny Bernie, but a few economies here and there could make all the difference.

And the sooner Castlerock was sold the better. That would free up a huge chunk of capital to buy a house outright and save on rent. And, he told himself, once Bernie got some business under her belt, they would be much more comfortable.

He glanced at the clock on the wall, then picked up the phone and dialled home.

"Hi," said Bernie, sounding winded.

"Hi, gorgeous. You sound out of breath. What are you doing?"

He could hear another voice in the background.

"I was just running downstairs to answer the door."

"Who's there?"

"Oh, just the man to read the gas meter. Hold on a minute and I'll see him out."

She must have dropped the phone because the clunk it

made as it hit the table, or whatever, nearly deafened him. He smiled at her goofiness.

"There. That's him gone," she said, sounding a bit flustered. "So. How are you?"

"Fine. Missing you."

"Me too."

"What're you up to?" he said.

"A bit of work. And then I was going to start on dinner."

"You sound distracted."

"You know me," she said, brightly. "I'm not very good on the phone."

"Okay, then," he said laughing. "I'll not keep you any longer."

"Oh, Paul?"

"Yes."

"When will you be home?"

"The usual time."

"Have you a surgery this afternoon?"

"No. Health Board Meeting at two thirty. And I've a pile of papers to read for it beforehand. Anodyne stuff, I'm afraid. I'd much rather be at home with you."

She laughed and said, "So the usual time, then? What? Sixish."

"Thereabouts," he said, wondering why she was so keen to know. Maybe she had something special planned for dinner tonight. Or maybe she was going to treat him to something else . . .

They said their goodbyes and he hung up the phone.

He sat thinking about the things Bernie's Aunt Jean had told her. The revelations had come as a complete surprise to Paul. He had only the vaguest recollection of Charles

Quinn, a cigar-smoking, wrinkled old man, who was related in some way to his father. From what Bernie had told him he sounded like an absolute scoundrel. His treatment of her mother had been atrocious. And as a child Paul had always thought him a harmless, kindly old gent; it just went to show how easily people could be fooled. He liked to think that he wasn't so gullible. He spent all day dealing with people and he thought he was a pretty good judge of character.

But the idea of Bernie and him being related, albeit distantly, was interesting if not a little disturbing. He wasn't sure exactly how he felt about it; he just wasn't completely comfortable with it. Not that these feelings of disquiet were strong enough to make him question their relationship. It was just something that he would have to get used to.

He'd read somewhere that siblings and half-siblings, who had been raised apart, often felt a strong attraction to each other on meeting for the first time as adults. Psychologists reckoned it was because we seek out, as partners, those most like ourselves. And who could be more like you than your own flesh and blood? Normally, being raised together in a family environment had the effect of switching off this natural attraction.

Did that phenomenon partly explain the instant and strong attraction between him and Bernie? They weren't siblings of course, far from it, but they must share some common genes. Maybe on a subconscious level that was why they had clicked on that first meeting like long-lost friends. Why within weeks, days even, of meeting, they knew that they were soul mates. It was an interesting hypothesis and one he hadn't yet had the chance to discuss properly with Bernie. He would rectify that tonight.

There was a knock on the door and one of the receptionists, a young buck-toothed brunette called Wendy, popped her head round the door.

"That was Doctor Lynch on the phone, Paul. He says that Eileen Watson and Doctor O'Brien can't make the meeting this afternoon, so he's cancelled it. He said he'd be in touch next week to reschedule."

"My dear, that is the best news I've heard all week!" he said and closed the folder of papers on his desk with a flourish.

"Thought you'd say that," said Wendy with her toothy grin and left.

Paul leaned back in his chair and linked his hands behind his head. His shoulders ached from sitting at the desk for the past two hours. He yawned, tired out by a hard week's work. He looked out the window onto a fine autumn day.

"Oh, sod it! I'm going home."

He decided to walk. He could phone Bernie, who had borrowed the car for the day, and ask her to come and pick him up. But he decided not to – he would walk. He was always extolling the health benefits of exercise to his patients. A brisk walk would do him good – it was only a mile or so – and it would have the added advantage of surprising Bernie.

He put the papers in his briefcase – he could read them just as easily at home as in this stuffy, over-heated place. Then he switched off the computer, locked the filing cabinets and flicked off the light as he left the room.

"Afternoon, ladies," he called to the receptionists as he passed them, raising his right arm in the air by way of salute. "Have a good weekend."

He walked out of the building with an impish grin on his face and a spring in his step. There was something terribly wicked about knocking off early. He felt like a naughty schoolboy skipping class and he couldn't wait to see the look on Bernie's face when he surprised her. It was about time he took her out for dinner, he decided. They hadn't been out for a meal in a while – Bernie was never very keen on going out to eat. She said it was a waste of money but, hey, it was time they both had a treat. He would take her to that new up-market Italian, Osteria, that had just opened and make a special night of it. And if Bernie didn't have to worry about cooking dinner maybe they could pass the afternoon in a much more pleasant fashion.

At the flat he was surprised to see Finn's new car parked on the street outside. He wasn't expecting him today. Finn knocked off work early on a Friday but he had never called round at the flat uninvited. In fact it had been hard persuading him to come round at all, but he had, in the end, given in. Paul thought his reluctance was out of a misplaced sense of loyalty to his mother. Perhaps Finn wanted to talk to him about something – it pleased him to think of Finn calling to ask for his advice. In some ways he thought that his relationship with his son had improved since he'd moved out of Castlerock. Maybe two men living under the same roof made for too much competition. Too much testosterone kicking about.

It was only as he pushed the door open with his foot, one hand occupied with his briefcase, the other with the keys, that he remembered that Finn would not be expecting him home at two o'clock in the afternoon.

The scene that he walked in on would stay with him for the rest of his life.

A CD was playing – some sort of modern music he did not recognise. Bernie was kneeling on the floor in front of the coffee table in a long-sleeved flowing dress of blue, a patterned scarf tied round her hair, hippy fashion. Finn was lolling on the sofa, his legs splayed apart like some sort of yob, watching her. She had a white straw in her hand and, on a small round mirror on the coffee table, were two rows of white powder, laid out in what looked to him like expert lines. Beside the mirror lay a crumpled piece of foil and a razor blade.

Both of them turned to look as he came in. The door banged shut behind him. And all of them froze for what seemed like many long minutes though it could only have been for a matter of seconds. It took Paul a long time to understand what was going on.

At first he was simply stunned. It was like walking onto a film set, or bursting into someone else's living room, where the events taking place were completely disconnected from his life. Except that the players in this tableau were his lover and his son – his own flesh and blood. And one, or both of them, were about to snort what looked like cocaine.

"Paul!" cried Bernie suddenly, rousing him from his dazed state. She let out a gasp and jumped to her feet. He was so taken aback that he stumbled into the centre of the room and his briefcase fell to the floor like a dead weight. She tried to hide the mirror and its contents under a magazine, but only succeeded in knocking the powder on the floor where it dusted the dark carpet like talcum.

"Shit," she said, under her breath.

Finn stood up and moved to the back of the room against the wall, glancing over his shoulder as though looking for an escape route.

And then Bernie, who had been watching Paul with a cowed look on her face, got to her feet. She put a coquettish smile on her face, adjusted the band around her head and said, "Hello, darling. You're just in time. I've been meaning to tell you about this for a while now …"

Paul swallowed, appalled not only by what she had been about to do, but by her demeanour. Her attempt at flirtation was so wholly inappropriate that it sickened him. Clearly she was taking drugs of some sort. How long had this been going on? And what on earth was Finn doing here?

"Coke. It's coke, isn't it?" he said at last, his brain working hard now to establish the facts, trying not to let emotion come into the equation – not just yet. Of course, he had no direct experience of drug-taking, but it was an increasing problem in Ballyfergus. Although he tried to avoid taking them on, finding the whole thing utterly abhorrent, several of his patients were addicts. He had received some, but not enough, training on treating them.

"That's right," she said and glanced at Finn, who with his hands in his pockets and his head bent, was trying to make himself invisible. "It's very fashionable, Paul. All the city boys use it."

"In my home . . ." he began and found he could not complete the sentence. How could he not have noticed this going on? And, more importantly, had she involved Finn or was it the other way round?

"I wasn't sure how you'd react," Bernie was babbling. "Some people can be so ignorant about cocaine, Paul. So parochial. They think everyone who takes Candy is an addict. But it's just a recreational drug. I only use it now and again."

He stared at her, marvelling at her ingenuity, her cleverness, her deception. His training had equipped him to address the medical needs of addicts; it had not taught him how to recognise one in the heart of his own home. He realised he had been completely and utterly duped.

He remembered the conversation he had planned to have with her about finances. About how they were going through money at a speed of knots. About how, in spite of his very healthy salary, they seemed to have no money left at the end of the month. This was where the money had gone. She had been using it to buy drugs.

"The money, Bernie. Is that where all my money's gone? On financing this habit?"

"I wouldn't go as far as calling it a habit, Paul. It's more of a – a hobby." She laughed, pleased with herself at this turn of phrase, and added, "Every girl needs her little luxuries! This just happens to be mine. It's no worse than a bottle of wine every other night. Or being a shopaholic. I don't spend money on other things."

"Just on this."

"That's right." She looked pleased, as though she thought she had won him round.

He swayed, feeling slightly nauseous as his brain, slowly, began to function. The signs had been there all along; the insomnia followed by sleeping for long periods, the constant sniffling she put down to allergies of one sort or another, her skinniness and lack of appetite. How could he have been so stupid? How could he not have seen what was right in front of his eyes? He remembered how earlier he had laughably compared himself to a detective. Some detective, he thought bitterly. How could he have been taken in by her?

But he already knew the answer to that. He had been flattered, his head turned by the idea that a pretty woman found him attractive. She had made it her business to flatter his ego in a way Chris never had, to fill the role of supportive, fawning partner. And he had loved every minute of it. But how much of it had been real? Had she ever loved him?

He placed the keys very carefully on the coffee table, and noticed that his hand was shaking uncontrollably. He felt rage towards Bernie but he put his feelings for her aside for the moment. Right now his main concern was his son.

"Finn, what are you doing here?" he said calmly.

Finn looked at Bernie, then back at his father and did not say a word.

"Were you about to take some of that?" said Paul.

"God, no! He's only seventeen," declared Bernie. "I wouldn't let him do that."

"What's he doing here, then?" he said, his rage simmering, ready to explode. But he knew that displaying his temper right now would be counter-productive. By force of will he managed to contain it.

"Finn just helps me out, don't you, Finn?" she said, and put a hand to her throat.

"In what way does he help you out?"

"He makes deliveries for friends," she said in a matter-of-fact voice, as though she was talking about shopping deliveries, not the procurement of illegal drugs. "Mutual friends who can get me what I need."

"He's supplying you with cocaine," said Paul, summarising what he was hearing because his brain found it almost impossible to take in. She had involved Finn – he could be done for possession and handling of drugs. Or had he been doing worse? Had he been dealing and using? And how long had this been going on? Weeks? Months even? He might have been able to forgive her many things, but not the corruption of his son.

"It's a Class A drug, Bernie. He could get life imprisonment."

"Piffle! Nobody's going to find out. It's not like he's out dealing on the streets."

"Don't you understand the danger you've put him in? If they find out he's been selling drugs –"

"He hasn't been selling them! Just passing them on. And the police aren't interested in someone like Finn. It's the big boys they're after."

"It's the big boys I'm worried about, Bernie. Not the police. Don't you know that the paramilitaries run the drugs in this town? What do you think they'd do to him if they found out?"

Her face drained of colour and she said, "I hadn't thought . . ."

"Clearly not," he said and grabbed her firmly by the arm. He had never raised his hand to a woman in his life – he had never had cause to. But his respect for Bernie had evaporated instantly and now he had to find out the truth. He attempted to push up the sleeve of her dress but she fought him off. Grimly he hung on to the sleeve as she pulled away and suddenly it came clean away at the shoulder. And there, on her thin arm, at the crease of her elbow, were dark blue splodges on the skin. He dropped the arm and grabbed the other one; this time she did not resist. Two partially healed small needle marks were evident, close to a prominent vein.

"So you've been injecting it too. Or something worse?" he said, unable to contain his anger any longer. "Answer me!" he screamed into her face. "Are you using heroin?"

She pulled her arm roughly out of his grasp and said, "I haven't injected for four years. They're old track marks that won't go away."

In spite of her deception – the misuse of his money, the lies, the covering up – he was inclined to believe her. He had seen similar marks on one of his patients, a recovering addict.

"How long have you been taking cocaine?"

She shrugged. "Three and a half years. On and off."

"I thought you kept your upper body covered because of the mastectomy scars. But it wasn't that, was it? It was because of those!" He pointed at the inside of her arms, which she attempted to hide by folding them across her chest. She had played the sympathy card with her cancer, fooling him, using it to disguise the truth.

A sudden realisation dawned on him.

"You never had a mastectomy, did you? It was all a complete fabrication."

"No," she said defiantly. "But I did have cancer and the scars on my belly are hysterectomy scars."

"You're a junkie, a crack-head," he said in disgust. "The scum of the earth! And to think . . ." He could not finish the sentence. He had loved her, slept with her, trusted her with his money and his children. How could he have made such a misjudgement? He put his hands over his face, overcome with anger and pain.

"Don't you go calling me names," she snapped. "What do you know about me or my life?"

"Yeah, that's right," said Finn, suddenly animated.

Paul removed his hands from his face to stare in disbelief as his son took sides with Bernie.

Finn approached until he was no more than a metre or so from his father and said, "You've no right to call her those things. If she is addicted then she can't help herself."

"This – this woman," said Paul, pointing at Bernie and barely able to refrain from using an expletive, "deceived me. She used my hard-earned money to buy drugs and involved you in criminal activity!"

"Oh, you see everything in black and white, don't you, Dad?" sneered Finn unpleasantly.

"In this case, yes. What other way is there to see it?"

"There's worse things than using recreational drugs, Dad. She's not harming anyone, is she? Except perhaps herself. And who are you to judge her anyway? You, who walked out on Mum after twenty years of marriage without a thought for her or me and Hannah! And what about you and your obsession with wine? There's not a day goes by that you don't have a glass or wine and more often than not, a lot more. You're as addicted to it as she is to cocaine!"

"There's a world of difference between a few glasses of wine and an illegal drug, Finn," said Paul, and they stared at each other then, like two stags with antlers locked.

Bernie came up and took Finn's arm, claiming him as her champion.

"Why don't you ask Bernie how she got into taking drugs before you judge her?" said Finn.

"Because I don't care."

"Bernie, tell him."

Bernie scowled and folded her arms across her chest.

Finn urged, "Go on, tell him!"

"All right then. I took heroin for the first time in Australia to relieve the pain when I had cancer. You have no idea what it was like. It was excruciating and none of you so-called medical experts could give me anything that worked. And I thought I was going to die."

"I didn't know," he said, feeling genuine compassion, trying to imagine what being in that situation must have felt like. But that was the problem with drugs and addicts – everyone's story could be made to sound rational.

"So I took smack. I couldn't see how it could make things any worse than they already were. And it did help – it got me through the worst time of my life. But I don't take that shit anymore," she said proudly, as though she deserved a standing ovation. "You've no idea how it screws you up. No, I'm off that now. I'm clean."

"You're not clean, Bernie," he said, in astonishment. "I just saw you about to snort a line of cocaine!"

"That's different – it's just for fun – I'm not addicted to it," she said, with such sincerity he realised that she actually believed this. "I don't take it every day, you know."

Her self-deception was heartbreaking. He wondered if she was beyond redemption. She had involved his son in something so utterly repugnant to him that he doubted his ability to forgive her. Just as he doubted the sincerity of her feelings for him.

"You never loved me, did you?" he said, sadly.

"Of course I love you," she said, coming over to him. She attempted to embrace him but he pushed her away.

"Don't touch me," he said. He could not bear for her to lay a hand on him. God knows, she might well have AIDS, HIV, Hepatitis C. Suddenly, he feared for his health. He would have to get himself checked out at a clinic. The humiliation of it!

"You only wanted me for my money, Bernie. If I wasn't a doctor – if I was unemployed, for example – would you still have fallen in love with me?"

"Yes."

He thought back to when they'd first met. He had initiated the relationship, that day in the car on the way back from Bernie's brother's in Ballymena. Bernie had been passive, accepting but hardly passionate. Had she cared for him at all? Or had she only acquiesced because she had an ulterior motive in mind – the funding of her drug habit?

He shook his head and said sadly, "I don't think I can believe you."

"Paul, you're blowing this out of all proportion. Okay, so I take a bit of blow now and again. Big deal. It's got nothing to do with us – with the way I feel about you."

"Don't be so disingenuous, Bernie. It has everything to do with the way you feel about me." He'd treated enough addicts to know that their habit, and funding it, was the most important thing in their lives. The only thing.

"And I'm sorry I got Finn involved," she went on, trying very hard to sound penitent and rational. "It was just one day I was talking to him about how I liked to take a bit of coke now and again and I mentioned that I didn't have any contacts. He said he knew someone who could get me some. He practically offered."

"And you thought that was okay?" he said, shaking his head in disbelief. "You thought that involving my seventeen-year-old child in supplying Class A drugs was acceptable?"

She shrugged and said, "Don't try to put all the blame on me, Paul. Look at him. He's nearly an adult. He can make his own choices. He could've said no."

"But how could you think that I would forgive you for that?" he said, ignoring what she had said. "You can shoot yourself up, and snort and smoke whatever you like, but you won't do it with my money. And you have crossed the line by involving my son."

She looked frightened, then worried. Things were not going as she had hoped.

Paul imagined he understood perfectly well what was going on inside her head. She might love him (though he seriously doubted this) but her main concern right now would be how to find a way to maintain the status quo. Without him what would she do for money? How would she buy cocaine?

"Finn," he said, "can you go outside and wait in your car, please? I want to talk to you when I'm finished in here."

"Yes."

"You won't drive off, will you?" he said quite evenly. "Because you and I really need to talk, son."

"Okay."

Finn slid out of the room like a shadow. Paul, his legs suddenly weak, sat down on the sofa. Bernie knelt on the floor in front of him with her hands on her knees.

"Paul. Please. Don't leave me," she said, her eyes full of tears.

She looked so pathetic with her torn dress and the puncture marks on her arm, he had to look away. He hardened his heart.

"Because I love you, Paul."

"If you loved me you'd care about me, about my reputation as a doctor. If drugs were to be found in my flat, I'd be finished."

"Of course I care. I just think you're maybe overreacting a little, don't you?" When he did not reply she went on,

"And I do love you, Paul. I wish you would believe that."

He sighed heavily, his heart aching with grief. "Maybe you do, Bernie. Maybe you only think you do. It's irrelevant. What I've seen here today has convinced me that we have no future. I loved you, Bernie. Look what I gave up to be with you! I would have given you everything. But not for this. Not for it to be squandered on drugs. I've seen what happens to people like you. You think you're in control, but the drugs are in control of you. And sadly it invariably ends one way. I won't stand by and watch you destroy your life. And mine."

"Don't talk such nonsense, Paul!"

"I'm not talking nonsense. Until you accept that you are addicted, there is no hope for you."

"I'll give up, then!" she cried. "That's what I'll do. I'll give up and then there won't be a problem."

"Would you get professional help, Bernie? Would you go into a clinic?" Perhaps there was hope for her. If she was really committed to doing this, maybe they might – in spite of what she'd done and all he had said in the heat of the moment – have a future together.

She snorted and said derisively, "I've told you before. There's nothing wrong with me, Paul. I don't need therapy or whatever goes on in these places."

He smiled sadly. "Then I'm not sure you are capable of giving up, not in the long-term. If you won't admit you have a problem then no-one can help you."

"I'm not an addict, Paul. There is a difference between an addict and a user."

He shook his head slowly. "That's what they all say."

They stared at each other. Stalemate. Bernie's eyes darted wildly about the room, her brain searching for another angle, a way to save the situation, a way to reverse the damage.

"Okay, then," she blurted out, avoiding eye contact. "I'll check into a clinic. I'll do whatever you want." She paused, her fists curled into tight balls, and held her breath. Her expression was fearful as she waited to see the effect these words had on Paul.

He stared at her long and hard for some moments and then said, "You'd say anything to stop me leaving you, wouldn't you, Bernie?"

Her shoulders sagged, she blushed and looked away.

He sighed. He wasn't the man to save her from this addiction. He wasn't sure any man could. The desire to break free had to come from Bernie and it had to be real. And he couldn't endure the misery of living with someone in the throes of addiction. He knew what lay ahead – ongoing lies, deception, arguments, debt and the slide into physical decay. It wasn't what he had signed up for. Truthfully, had he known about Bernie's secret, he never would have got involved with her.

Suddenly it was very clear to him what he must do and a relative calmness came over him. "I can never trust you again, Bernie," he said gently, taking her hand in his "Can't you see that? I'd always be watching you, looking out for telltale signs of drug use, checking up on you, monitoring your every move. I can't live like that." He thought of Chris and his life with her. How different that was.

He released Bernie's hand, stood up and said very evenly, although his heart was breaking, "This is what's going to happen. I'm going to go online now and book you a ticket back to Melbourne as soon as possible. I'll give you money for the journey and more to help you get started back in Australia. If you choose to spend it on coke, well, that's up to you. It's got nothing to do with me."

"Paul!" She started to cry. "Don't do this! Please don't do this!"

He tried to close his ears to her pleas and focused very hard on maintaining a steady voice. "Now what I want you to do right now is go upstairs and pack. Take only what you can carry and I will arrange for the rest of your things to be sent on as soon as you send an address."

Bernie stood up. "I'm not leaving!" she spat into his face. "You can't make me!"

"Yes, you are," he said, steeling himself, forcing himself to be strong. "Nobody wants you here, Bernie. The rent is due on this place at the end of the month. And I won't be paying it. I think you'll do better in Australia. I'm sure you've friends who'll get you on your feet and you've a better chance of finding work there. Not that you tried very hard here."

"You're making a mistake!" she shouted angrily. "You do this on me, Paul Quinn, and I'll not come running back. You'll regret it. I promise you, you'll regret it."

"No, Bernie. I won't regret it. And it's far from a mistake. In fact," he said, with utter clarity, "I think it's possibly the wisest decision of my entire adult life."

Outside, Finn was sitting in his car. Paul got in beside him and wearily closed the door. He sat in silence, numbed, staring at the furry dice hanging from the rear-view mirror. He had been a fool. He had been blinded by love – was it even love? Or just passion? He had acted like a lovesick teenager. How could he have been so stupid? He had given up everything – his wife, his home and very nearly lost the affection of his children. Because of her, Finn had committed a serious crime. If he hadn't discovered what was going on, he shuddered to think where it might have led. Was it already too late? Just how involved was he in the drugs scene?

There was a silence for a long time. Paul looked at the boy – the man – in the seat beside him and did not know him at all. He sighed. He didn't know what to say, where to start. Disappointment did not go far enough. It did not even come close to describing the utter devastation he felt. Hannah was pregnant and Finn was supplying drugs to his girlfriend – former girlfriend. How had his family sunk so low?

"Be honest," said Finn, staring straight ahead. "It's what you expected of me, isn't it?"

"Don't be facile, Finn."

"No, it is. You're never done telling me what a disappointment I am."

Paul opened his mouth to retort.

"No," said Finn. "This time I want to have my say. And you can listen for a change."

The high moral ground that Paul had always stood on was swept from under his feet. Not only had he moved in with Bernie whilst still married to Chris but, by a gross misjudgement, he had shacked up with a drug addict. He had forfeited the right to tell Finn what to do.

"I've never been clever enough for you, Dad. I don't think I am stupid either but I'm not as clever as Hannah. And because I could never achieve what she could achieve, in spite of all your coaxing and pushing, I decided quite early on that it was easier not to try. You soon wrote me off, but to be honest that was better than constantly disappointing you when I did try and it wasn't good enough. I just switched off academically."

"Then I am truly sorry for that, Finn. I'm sorry that I

made you feel you weren't good enough."

"But I found something I was good at – working with my hands. Do you remember that shark I carved from a piece of wood in third year?"

"I remember. It was spectacular." It still sat, pride of place, on a shelf in Finn's room.

"I know. And that's when I realised I could do something no-one else could do. I could make things with wood, beautiful things. I couldn't wait to leave school and get started."

"But you're a joiner, not a sculptor."

"You don't know what I do at work. You've never asked. I make cupboards and units from scratch. And the things I make are beautiful. Already I'm working on all the inside jobs on site because no-one can make things from wood the way I can. And there's talk of putting me forward for apprentice of the year."

It was true – he knew nothing of Finn's job because it did not interest him in the slightest. He had despised Finn for failing to live up to his potential, for not making the most of the advantages he had been born into. But up until now he had never considered that Finn's choices and, in his eyes, his failings, might have had something to do with him. Or that they might be valid choices.

"I'll tell you what I am disappointed in, Finn. What you did in there."

Finn hung his head. "So am I."

"I can't tell you how angry I am. I don't think you've any idea how serious it is."

"I do."

"Then why did you do it? Why did you get involved?"

"I did it because she asked me. And because it was

exciting," said Finn staring at his hands. In profile, his face still had something of the boy in it. He looked terribly young and vulnerable. "You can get any kind of stuff you want out there – you name it, someone can get it for you."

Paul shivered in horror at the casualness with which Finn talked. Naively, he had assumed that his children somehow miraculously by-passed the drug scene.

"Bernie made me feel like I was important," went on Finn. "Like I was a big man. And it's easy to get hold of stuff, if you know the right people."

"Were you taking a cut? Were you dealing?"

"Hell, no. That just goes to show what you think of me, doesn't it?"

"That's not fair, Finn. I've just found out that you've been supplying Bernie. What am I supposed to think?"

"The best? Rather than the worst?"

"So you're not dealing. And you haven't supplied anyone else."

"Of course not."

"That's something then," said Paul with a sigh of relief.

"If I'm honest," said Finn, "there was something thrilling about doing it behind your back. It was a way at getting back at you for all the digs you make at me."

"Really?" said Paul, completely appalled. "You must really hate me."

"I don't hate you," said Finn and a tear rolled down his cheek. "I just want you to be proud of me. To like me."

"Finn, son," said Paul, uttering words he had never before been able to bring himself to say, "I love you. You are my son. I am proud of you. And I promise you that I will never malign you again. It is true that I haven't approved of your path in life. But I think my expectations of you have been unrealistic and unfair. I only valued academic achievement and I see now how wrong I was, how talented you are at what you do. And I promise that from now on I'll be different."

Finn sniffed and wiped the tears from his face. And Paul had to do the same. Then Finn looked at his father, gave him a half-baked smile and said, "What happens now?"

"I need to know if you take – or have taken, any drugs?"

"No. Yes, if you count marijuana. I've smoked it a few times, but that's all."

"Coke?"

"No. I just got it for Bernie."

"Where from?"

"A guy Mikey knows up in Glenarm."

"What does this guy know about you?"

"Not much. Only my first name."

"Has he seen your car?"

"Not yet. Last time we went up in Mikey's car."

"Good. Can you trust Mikey?"

"I think so."

"And there's no way anyone in Ballyfergus would know that you've been buying drugs?"

"I don't see how. Only Mikey knows and I can trust him. Why? What are you going to do?" said Finn, his voice full of wariness. "Are you going to hand me over to the cops?"

Paul looked at him in amazement. Did he think his own father would shop him?

"Of course not. I just want to be sure that you can get out of this without any repercussions."

"I don't think that'll be a problem. I only ever bought enough for myself, which I then passed onto Bernie. It's small beer to these guys. They'll not even notice I've gone off the radar."

"Good. I'll have to tell your mother, Finn. And I want you to stop hanging out with this Mikey guy. He sounds like bad news."

Finn nodded and said, surprisingly, "Okay."

Paul sensed by his ready compliance that he was almost pleased to have been caught.

"What's happening between you and Bernie?" said Finn, glancing over his shoulder at the closed door of the flat.

"There is no me and Bernie," said Paul flatly. "It's over. She's going back to Australia. Her flight leaves Belfast International in the morning."

"I'm sorry, Dad. You must've loved her to do what you did – leaving Mum and all."

"I thought I did. But you can't love someone you don't really know. And it turns out I didn't know Bernie Sweeney at all. Now, can you drive me down to the bank, please before it shuts? I have to get cash."

"For Bernie?"

"Yes. I want to get her back to Australia as soon as possible and give her enough to get her on her feet. After that, she's on her own."

"Are you going to take her to the airport? If you don't want to, I'll do it. I feel kind of sorry for her, you know."

"So do I," Paul said and stared unseeing out the window. "So do I. But I want to take her myself. I want to make sure she gets on that plane and I hope to God I never see her again as long as I live."

Epilogue

"So what do you think then?" said Chris one Saturday afternoon, almost a year later. She had just given Karen a tour of her new home on a small, exclusive estate on the edge of town, just off the Ballyboley Road. The house was modern, only three years old, with four decent-sized bedrooms, a small conservatory and a pleasant south-facing garden.

She filled the kettle and peeked out the kitchen window into the garden, bathed in late summer sunshine. She smiled at the sight of the handsome coach-built navy pram with its wide hood and big wheels parked by the fence, a cat net pulled over the aperture.

"I think it's fantastic, Chris. It looks totally different from how I remember it when we viewed it. And from how I remember it on the day you moved in. Though it was hard to see it for all the boxes lying about."

"Once you've unpacked and got your own things in place, it looks more like home."

"It's lovely," said Karen. She got two mugs out, milked them and set them on the tray Chris had just put on the table. "Castlerock took a long time to sell in the end, didn't it?"

"Nearly nine months," said Chris.

"I suppose there aren't as many buyers for a big house like that. Smaller ones sell faster."

"That's definitely true. Still, the buyers were very understanding about Hannah and the baby. When I said we couldn't move until late August they were very accommodating."

"Yes, that was nice of them. How's Hannah doing by the way?"

"Good. She's down town at the moment buying some new clothes. Her pregnancy ones are too big and she can't get into any of her old ones yet."

"It's only been four and a half months since Ruby was born. But Hannah's young – her body'll bounce back in a way ours, well, mine anyway, wouldn't. It's terrible what having babies does to your body, isn't it?"

Chris agreed, pouring hot water into a teapot. "Shall we sit in the garden? That way I can keep an ear out for Ruby."

"Sure."

They sat on teak chairs arranged around the table on the patio and drank their tea from chunky hand-made mugs. The garden, while small, was private and quiet; it was all Chris needed really. She thought of the beautiful garden at Castlerock. Lovely though it undoubtedly was, it had been a tremendous amount of work to maintain. There was a lot to be said for a low-maintenance garden like this one. And here there was room enough for a sandpit and a climbing frame, when the time came – if Hannah and Ruby were still with her of course. Hannah would have to make an independent life for herself eventually, but Chris hoped it wasn't any time soon. She couldn't see Hannah managing on her own, not yet anyway, and she would miss Ruby terribly.

Murphy came over, sniffed Karen's legs then wandered off to chew a rawhide bone lying on the grass.

"She's decided to take that place at Jordanstown," said Chris. Jordanstown was a campus of the University of Ulster on the coast road near Belfast, a half-hour drive from Ballyfergus. "They were very accommodating even though she kept changing her mind right up until the last minute."

"I'm not surprised with her grades. I'm sure they're delighted to get her. What did she decide to do in the end?"

"A BSc in Sociology with Politics."

"What does she want to do that for?" said Karen doubtfully. "What sort of a job would it lead to?"

"I don't know, Karen, and I don't really care. The main thing is that she's looking to the future and hasn't written herself off. I've given up trying to influence what the kids do. It only backfires. You have to let them make their own choices," she said, thinking not only of Hannah, but Finn. "Anyway, it's really good of you to give Ruby that place at nursery."

Once Hannah started university in a few weeks time, Ruby would go to Wee Stars three days a week and Chris would look after her for the other two days. She was looking forward to having Ruby all to herself. She couldn't wait for her to sit up and start taking notice. Work, whilst still important and enjoyable, was no longer central to her life. That position had been replaced, as it should be, by her family and the people she cared about. And she no longer gave a damn about whether or not Tesda built a supermarket in Ballyfergus. She had more important things, much closer to home, to worry about.

"Has Ruby's father been in touch?" asked Karen.

"Funny you should say that. Mrs Mulrine was on the phone last night wanting to know if they could come down next weekend to see her. I think she's far keener than her son to see Ruby. Jason is her only child, you see, and I don't think he'll be having any more children for a while. I get the impression that this experience has put him off babies for life," she said wryly and Karen smiled. Chris went on, "Hannah hasn't asked for anything from them – we don't want their money – just that he acknowledges Ruby. She doesn't want her growing up not knowing her father."

"She's a very sensible girl."

Chris couldn't help thinking that if Hannah had been sensible she never would have got herself into this mess. Still, she was proud of the way she was handling single motherhood.

There was a short silence and Karen said, "How's the three-day week working out?"

"Pretty good."

"Were the other partners okay about it?"

"They didn't have much choice. No, that's not fair. They were very supportive. And the business hasn't suffered. If anything it's better than ever. And I keep an eye on things from home even when I'm not there."

"I bet you do," said Karen, who knew her sister too well. "Old habits die hard."

"Yeah," said Chris with a smile. "They do. But do you know what? I've adjusted to a three-day week with no bother at all. To be honest I can't imagine working full-time again, though I daresay I will when I'm not needed here at home. But of course I'm only able to do it because Paul has been so generous with Hannah and the baby. Which reminds me, you have to let me pay for the nursery place. I can afford it, Karen. I've no mortgage on this house."

"No way. I won't even discuss it, Chris. You keep your

money. Use it to buy things for Ruby. She's going to need them."

Chris smiled, defeated, and said graciously. "Thank you, Karen. You're very generous."

Karen waved away the praise and said, "That is a handsome pram, even though you think it extravagant of Paul."

"It is lovely but it's impractical. You can't take it in the car or on a train. In the end I went out and bought one of those three-in-one prams as well. You know the kind – it starts off as car seat and a pram, and converts to a buggy when the baby's older. At the rate Ruby's growing she'll be out of the pram Paul bought her in no time and then I'll have to find somewhere to store the flipping thing. It cost over eight hundred pounds, you know."

Karen inhaled audibly through her teeth. "Ouch!"

"But that's Paul all over – extravagant gestures that he doesn't think through."

"His heart's in the right place, though."

"Yes, as far as the children are concerned it is," said Chris, thinking of the little Astra car he'd just bought Hannah. "And he and Finn seem to be getting on better these days. Finn spends more quality time with Paul now than he did when they were living under the same roof."

"And there's been no more bother with Finn since that incident with the drugs?"

"No. None at all. He seems to have settled down," said Chris and she recalled with horror the day Paul had told her that Bernie Sweeney had recruited Finn to source drugs. "I wonder sometimes if it wasn't a cry for help. A way of getting his father to notice him."

"Sounds like it to me," said Karen thoughtfully, looking

at the bottom of her mug. "And maybe the new girlfriend's a good influence on him."

"I think so," said Chris. Finn's girlfriend of two months, Hattie was a local girl from a decent home and she appeared to be a stabilising influence on him. Chris liked her a lot.

"Do you ever think of Bernie?" said Karen tentatively.

"More than I want to," said Chris with a sigh and she put her mug down on the table. "I don't hate her as much as I used to, you know. I mean when I found out how she was using Finn to get her drugs, I think I could've killed her with my bare hands. I really mean that. And to think she broke up my marriage in order to get her hands on Paul's money so that she could buy drugs. It's despicable." She paused and frowned. "Well, that was one of the reasons the marriage broke up, but I can't put all the blame for that on Bernie. And for all I know, maybe she did love Paul. I don't really wish her ill, you know – from what Paul told me, I think she's got enough problems of her own. Sometimes I even feel sorry for her."

"I don't," said Karen, viciously.

"I've given it a lot of thought, Karen," said Chris, toying with the sleeve of her linen shirt. "You don't become an addict without a reason. Bernie lost her mother at a very young age and she had an unhappy childhood. I'm not sure she ever got over that. And then she got cancer which is how she got into drugs in the first place. Can you imagine how awful that must've been for her?"

"I suppose," said Karen softening. "She has had a rough time of it. But it doesn't excuse her behaviour."

"Maybe not, but it does explain it. Once you're in the grip of something like that, it takes over your life. You'll do almost anything to get your next hit. And you do things you wouldn't normally entertain."

"Like steal your best friend's husband? Recruit their son as your drug dealer?"

Chris managed a wry grimace and said, "Yes, things like that."

Karen shrugged and let out a long sigh. "Perhaps you're right. I suppose if she is an addict she isn't really in control of the things she does. She'll do things to get drugs even though she knows them to be wrong."

"That's what I prefer to believe," said Chris, remembering the young Bernie she had once known, the girlfriend of her youth with a good heart whom she had loved like a sister. "None of us is without flaws. And I think she's to be pitied more than anything."

There was a pause and then Karen added, thoughtfully, "She's kept in touch with Mary Ramsey, you know."

"Really? How do you know that?"

"I met Mary on Main Street the other day – boy, that woman can talk! She made me late getting back to the office."

"What did she say about Bernie?"

"She said she'd received a long e-mail from her, telling her that she'd got this great job working for a marketing company in Melbourne and that she was living with some loaded businessman. She's says the e-mail went on at length about the wonderful house they had, their wonderful friends, all the parties they went to and the house he had on a lake somewhere. And she hinted that a wedding was in the offing."

"So she's landed on her feet," said Chris, and she couldn't help but feel that life was unfair. Everything had turned out peachy for Bernie – and she didn't deserve it. "Well, at least I can stop worrying about her now. I imagined her living in some grotty bedsit, living a hand-to-mouth existence, hooked on cocaine."

"What makes you think she's not?"

"Didn't Mary say . . . oh," said Chris, as realisation dawned. "You think it's all a fabrication?"

"Don't you think it sounds too good to be true? Bernie knows fine well what a gossip Mary is. She knows the contents of that e-mail are bound to get back to you – and Paul – eventually. It's her way of giving you the metaphorical finger and proving to Paul that he made a mistake, that she's not a useless drug addict."

Chris considered this for some moments and then said, "You know what? I think I prefer to believe it's true, Karen. After all, we've no evidence to the contrary, have we?"

"But . . ." began Karen, appeared to think better of it, and said, "Yes, you're right. It could be true."

"Well, let's leave it that way, shall we? And for all the awful things she did, try to forgive her?"

"Okay," said Karen after a long pause. "If that's what you want." And then she added softly, "And what about Paul? Do you think there's any chance that you might get back together?"

"No way," said Chris firmly. "Anyway, he's dating Elaine Robinson, the district nurse."

"He is not!"

"That's what my sources tell me."

"I thought she was married."

"She is. But she's separated, waiting on the divorce to be finalised."

"He's a brave man taking her on," said Karen. "Once

she's got her claws into him she won't let go. Elaine knows a meal ticket when she sees one."

Chris laughed. "She is a bit of a dragon, isn't she?"

"You can say that again. But it can't be that serious! It's only four months since he asked you to take him back."

"I know," said Chris, thinking back to that emotional day. Ruby was only two days old and due to come home from the hospital. Paul had called at the house unexpectedly, just as she was about to head off to the hospital with things for Hannah.

"I wanted to talk to you about something," he said. He looked thinner and the past nine months had aged him more than his years. "I wondered if you could spare me a few minutes?"

"Can't this wait until the next meeting with our solicitors, Paul? Can't you see that this is a really bad time?" she said a little snappily, because all she could think of was her daughter lying in that noisy hospital ward and the little scrap of life in a transparent cot by her side.

"It's important."

"Oh, okay," she said and led him into the drawing room. There were bare places on the walls where he'd removed family pictures inherited from his mother and taken them to his home – at that time he was still living in the rented flat on Bay Road he had shared with Bernie. "Well," she said, standing just inside the door of the room with her spring raincoat on. "What is it?"

"I um … can we sit down?"

She glanced at the clock on the wall. "I haven't got long, Paul. I need to get to the hospital."

"Please," he said and patted the seat next to him.

She sat down on the same sofa as he but as far away

from him as possible, slightly disconcerted by his meek, almost humble bearing. It wasn't like the Paul she knew.

"Chris," he said and paused before launching into what was obviously a well-rehearsed monologue, "I have something to say to you and I know it'll come as a surprise, a shock even. But I want you to hear me out. I have made a mistake. A huge mistake. I miss you and I think about you every day. I know I can't turn the clock back and make things the way they were, but I wish I could. I'm sorry for the heartache I've caused you and the children. And if my actions are in any way responsible for what's happened to Hannah I deeply regret them. And I take full responsibility for what happened to Finn. It was my gross error in judgement that led him into trouble. I know you must feel a great deal of anger towards me. That's why I don't want your answer immediately. Take some time to think it through."

"Are you asking me to forgive you, Paul?" said Chris, for in spite of his careful preparation he had not actually made that clear.

"I'm asking you to take me back, Chris."

"Oh!" she said in astonishment. Did he really think, after what he'd done, that she would even consider this? He had spoken straight from the heart, without embellishment. It deserved an equally honest and forthright reply.

"You can have my answer right now," she said, resentment simmering in her breast. Who did he think he was, waltzing in here, demanding an audience? Patronising her. He knew nothing of her feelings, and the presumption that he did angered her more than anything.

"No –" he began.

"Yes," she said. "Time isn't going to change the way I

feel, Paul. What you did is irreversible. You betrayed the trust on which our marriage was based and once that's done, there's no going back."

"Try not to see this in black and white, Chris."

"I see it the way it is, Paul. You left me for Bernie without a second thought to pursue your selfish desires. You find out Bernie's an addict and you throw her out without, I might add, a thought for what might happen to her. And then you come crawling back to me because you're lonely and you realise what you've thrown away, expecting me to take you back."

"I'm not expecting," he said quietly. "I'm asking."

"Same difference. The answer's no, Paul. Not now, not ever. You've made your bed, and mine, and now we must lie in them." And from the look of him, she reckoned that his bed was a lot less comfortable than hers.

He got up slowly, and said resignedly, "That was the answer I expected. But I told myself I had to try. Because I would've lived my life wondering if you might have given our marriage another go. But now I know."

"That's right," said Chris coldly. "Now you know. And right now I have more important things to worry about than you."

She went to the front door, her legs shaking, opened it and stood to the side for him to pass.

"I'll see you at the hospital then. At some point," he said and paused. "She's beautiful, isn't she? Our granddaughter?"

"Yes, she is," said Chris, jolting with surprise at the use of that word. It meant that she was a grandmother and Chris hadn't thought of Ruby's birth in those terms before. "She's the one wholly good and pure thing to have come out of this sorry mess."

He left without another word and Chris closed the door gently behind him. And then, and only then, did she allow the tears to fall.

Ruby's cries brought Chris back to the present. She jumped up and walked quickly over to the pram, followed closely by Karen. Murphy came over to see what all the fuss was about, lost interest quickly and started trying to dig his way out under the fence.

"I though she was never going to wake up," said Karen, clapping her hands together in delight, "and I would've hated to have missed her."

Chris peeled back the cat net and reached into the pram. At nearly five months Ruby was getting heavy now and she bent at the knees to scoop her up into her arms, careful not to strain her back.

Ruby stopped crying almost immediately. She blinked against the bright light, her head of scarce fine hairs glinting blonde in the sunlight. She had reached that chubby stage where, before a baby becomes mobile, they look so fat you think they're going to explode. Her cheeks were red from sleep, or maybe another tooth coming, and her blue eyes were wide like saucers, absorbing the world and everything in it. Chris took Ruby's tiny hand and placed it in her mouth. She made muffled noises as though she were eating it and Ruby giggled, revealing one tiny isolated tooth on the front bottom gum.

"Someone needs her nappy changed," said Chris in the singsong voice she reserved specially for Ruby. "Come on, let's go inside." And to Karen she said, "Do you fancy giving Ruby her bottle? It's all made up in the fridge; you just have to microwave it."

"I'd love to," said Karen.

"Right. I'll be down in a minute," said Chris, thinking they weren't much different from two little girls playing Mum – except they were getting to do it with a real, live baby.

Once Ruby was changed, Chris settled her on her great-aunt's lap and Karen put the bottle in the baby's mouth. She sucked greedily, her eyelids dropping and her little fists curled into balls with the pleasure of it.

"Oh, she's just gorgeous, isn't she?" said Karen. "Have a look in that bag there, will you?"

Chris opened a Dunnes Stores shopping bag that Karen had brought and laid on the table. Inside was a gorgeous set of tiny pink checked dungarees and a white blouse.

"I couldn't resist them," said Karen.

"Oh, Karen, they're lovely. You shouldn't have!"

"Oh, it's nothing. They were in the sale." And then, addressing Ruby, "Anyway, you're worth it my precious, aren't you?"

Ruby let the teat fall partially out of her milky mouth and stared at her aunt, open-mouthed. Then she gobbled it back in again and continued sucking happily, her eyes fixed like searchlights on her aunt's smiling face.

"So how are things between you and Tony?" said Chris.

"Things are great," said Karen. "Better than they've ever been. But that has as much to do with me as anything."

"What do you mean?"

"I've stopped obsessing about my body and suspecting Tony of cheating on me every time we pass a pretty girl in the street."

"And what about the breast reduction and eyelid operation? Have you decided yet whether or not you're going to go ahead with them?"

"No, I'm not going to."

"Thank God!" And Chris felt a weight of worry lift from her shoulders.

"I realise now that how I feel about myself has as much to do with confidence and my skewed self-image, as what I actually look like. And I'm not so deformed that I *need* the operations. I just have to work at developing a more positive self-image."

"Do you regret the tummy tuck?"

"God, no. That was different. That apron of flesh was never going to go anywhere without surgery."

"I have to say it was very successful. It makes a huge difference to your silhouette."

"Thank you. But even with that I only realise now how lucky I am to have come out of the surgery unscathed and with such a good result. I've been looking at forums on the web and there's all these women telling horrific tales of how their operation went wrong and they were left with worse disfigurements than when they started."

"Uh," said Chris with a distasteful grimace. "Sounds like you were fortunate."

Karen shifted the weight of the baby on her knee, shook her head and tutted. "All that business with Shona. I see how ridiculous it was and how it was largely caused by my envious nature. Tony was afraid to tell me in case I was jealous."

"And would you have been?"

"You bet. But I see now how silly my behaviour was. I'm not like that any more. I hope I've grown up a bit."

"Don't be so hard on yourself, Karen. He also didn't want people to know because he was ashamed."

"I know. He was far too hard on himself. He and Shona

were both little more than kids. But they seem to have come to some understanding now. I don't suppose they'll ever be friends – there's too much painful history there – but at least we can all be in the same room now without everyone feeling uncomfortable."

"I thought Raymond took it all quite well, considering."

"Yes, he did, didn't he? He was very mature about the whole thing. And it must've been so very painful for him to learn what Shona had gone through."

Karen lifted Ruby into a seated position on her lap and rubbed her back, while holding her chin in the cleft between her thumb and index finger of her right hand. The baby produced a loud burp and both women laughed.

"Clever girl!" said Karen and Ruby hiccupped. The women laughed again.

"Hi, it's me!" came Shona's voice, accompanied by the sound of footsteps on the narrow shingle path that ran down the side of the house. She rounded the corner, looking relaxed and happy in a long, brightly printed maxi dress and flat sandals. A lilac cropped cardigan covered her shoulders and her skin was brown from the sun. Under her arm was a plastic bag containing a large folder or book-shaped object.

"Hi, Shona!" the two women chorused. They hadn't seen her since she had gone on honeymoon.

She set the bag on the table, came over and gave Chris a kiss then did the same to Karen, her hand lingering on the latter's shoulder, a sign of the affection that had grown between them.

Ruby squealed and Shona said, "Oh, can I have her? Just for a minute?"

"Of course. She's finished with her milk, I think," said Karen.

Shona took the baby in her arms and rocked her gently for a few moments, whispering sweet nothings in her ear.

"Well, how was the honeymoon?" said Chris, when Shona was seated with Ruby on her lap.

"Fabulous!" And she went on to describe the azure seas, white sandy beaches and fantastic hotel in Barbados.

"It all sounds so romantic," said Karen with longing. "I've never been to the Caribbean. But I'd like to visit it one day."

"You will, when the children are grown," said Shona practically. "Meantime, enjoy them." And she kissed Ruby on the top of the head.

A pang of compassion clutched Chris's chest and she wondered if it would ever leave her when she watched Shona with someone else's child.

"I've got some news for you," said Shona brightly.

"What's that?" said Karen eagerly, always keen to hear the latest gossip.

"Raymond and I have decided that we're going to adopt. If we can. If the authorities will let us."

"Oh, Shona, that is wonderful news," said Chris, deeply moved, and she felt herself choke up with emotion.

"Fantastic!" chimed in Karen.

"We've had a preliminary chat with the agencies and they don't foresee any problems. Apart from the limited availability of babies. But we've said we would be happy to take older children so that increases our chances of success. After all, if we need a baby fix, we've always got you, little Ruby Tuesday, haven't we?" She buried her face in the child's fuzzy scalp.

"There's no reason why you would be turned down, is there?" said Chris, fearful lest Shona's hopes be dashed.

"Not on the face of it, although Raymond is approaching the higher end of the age bracket. So the sooner we get the process under way the better."

Chris and Karen started at each other, stunned. This news was out of the blue but it was wonderful. They talked about it at length and then Karen said, "What's in the bag?"

"The wedding photos."

"Oh, can I have a look?" said Karen.

"Go ahead. Just don't be getting them dirty now. They cost us an arm and a leg!"

Karen opened the album carefully on the table and Chris came and stood beside her, looking over her shoulder. The photos were a lovely reminder of a happy day, Shona looking beautiful in her long bead-encrusted dress and Raymond looking like the cat that had got the cream. Chris smiled.

"They're very good," she said.

"We're pleased with them," said Shona happily.

"Anybody home?" came a man's voice from somewhere at the front of the house. Chris instantly recognised it as Sam's and her heart gave a little leap.

"We're in the garden," hollered Karen and baby Ruby nearly jumped out of her skin in fright. "Oops! Sorry, Ruby!"

Sam came into the garden, casually dressed in cream chinos and a long-sleeved blue checked shirt with the sleeves rolled up looking, well, looking at home. As though he belonged here. Which in a way he did. They still maintained separate homes, and Chris would for as long as Hannah needed one, but she hoped that one day they would share their lives.

"Hi, everyone," he said. "Good to see you back, Shona.

How was the honeymoon?"

"Great," said Shona and Sam tickled Ruby under the chin. Then he came over to Chris and gave her a peck on the cheek.

"How are you, gorgeous?"

Chris blushed, still unused to his free use of endearments in public.

"Great," she said.

"Guess who I bumped into out front," he said and indicated with a nod of his head over his shoulder. It was Hannah, weighed down with shopping bags and looking flushed but happy. She immediately dropped the bags, ran over to Ruby, picked her up and held her to her breast as though they had been parted for days, not hours.

"What do you all say to a barbecue?" said Sam. "Why don't you give Tony and Raymond a ring and see if they want to come over? And the kids of course."

"Is it warm enough for a barbecue?" said Chris, pulling her cardigan tighter.

"Yeah. Let's make it the last blast of the season!" he said.

"But I haven't got any shopping in . . ." began Chris.

"That, my dear," said Sam with a grin, "is why you need me." And he went out to the car and came back with four bags filled to bursting with sausages, steaks, burgers, rolls and buns, bags of salad, beer and wine. And Chris smiled at him, loving him for his spontaneity, his pleasure in the simple things like food and the company of friends.

Sam switched on the gas barbecue and the women set about laying the table. Just then Finn appeared with Hattie in tow.

"There's plenty of food for two more!" said Sam cheerfully. "Pull up a chair."

Raymond and Tony came over with Jack and Chloe for the impromptu party and everyone squeezed around the small patio table, sitting on an assorted mishmash of chairs, four of which were outdoors, the rest raided from the house. How different from the lavish entertainment she used to do at Castlerock – and how much better! Chris looked round at the family that she loved and thought of Paul, sitting alone in his bungalow on Islandmagee – or worse, sitting there with the district nurse.

It was ironic really. He was the one who had left and yet he had gained the least. His relationship with Bernie had turned into a disaster and, whilst he saw them regularly, he no longer lived with his children. She on the other hand was just beginning to emerge from that horrible, dark place where she had been for over a year. And, when she was able to put aside the grief and sense of loss for a little while, she was surprised to find that she was actually happy in her new life.

She no longer felt a driving need to fill her time, to be busy and productive every waking hour. Sam, with his relaxed and positive attitude to life, had a lot to do with that. She had learned how to kick back and have fun. She looked at the faces round the table and thought that everything was all right with her world – and she was grateful. And she liked to think that one day she would be able to wish Paul the happiness that she had found.

She slipped her arm into Sam's, who was seated next to her wearing a black chef's apron. He squeezed her hand and winked at her.

"He's calmed down a fair bit," said Sam with a nod in Murphy's direction. The dog was lying on the grass, looking sorry for himself. "Poor soul, he's waiting for the children to finish eating and play with him."

"Yeah," said Chris, "He gets calmer the older he gets. He's seen me through a lot, our Murphy, and he's turned out all right in the end. Just like everything else."

She got down on one knee, leaned over the little dog and planted a kiss on the fur between his floppy little brown ears.

"Yes, he's turned out to be the best dog in the whole wide world."

The End

If you enjoyed *My Husband's Lover* try
Closer to Home also published by Poolbeg

Here's a sneak preview of Chapter one

Closer to Home

Chapter One

"I've decided. I'm going to do it."

Kath O'Connor paused, wondering why the words she wanted to say did not come easily. She stared out the window of the coffee shop while she summoned the courage to formulate the sentence she had thought about so often but never vocalised. Outside, on Boston's chic Newbury Street, the rush-hour traffic crawled by like a caterpillar, its progress hampered and muffled by the falling snow. Already a thick layer carpeted the sidewalk and the road. The dark grey clouds, swollen with snow, had brought with them a premature nightfall.

"Emmy," she said at last, "I'm going to ask Carl to marry me." The fingers on her right hand trembled. Quickly, she replaced the glass teacup on the saucer. The camomile tea glowed amber, like melted butter, in the yellow lights of the coffee shop.

"Oh! I see," said her best friend, sounding surprised. Then Emmy put her elbows on the table and rested her head on her hands. She regarded Kath thoughtfully from under black arched brows, her wide-open green eyes outlined in soft grey eye pencil. Her cheeks were rosy from the cold, like the bright-cheeked baby Kath had spied that very morning being carried into the nursery at the end of her street. "Well," she said finally, "that is a surprise."

"You don't think I should, do you?" said Kath and she looked at her hands, folded together on the table. The huge diamond-and-emerald-encrusted band that Carl had given her for Christmas sparkled on the ring finger of her right hand like ice – a painful reminder of the engagement ring she had hoped for but not received.

"No, no, it's not that at all," said Emmy, concern clouding her pretty face, and she gave her head a little shake.

"What is it, then? Because I sense that you don't think this is a good idea."

"I just wasn't expecting it, that's all. One minute you're dating the guy, the next you're talking about proposing to him! It just seems like a big leap to me." She smiled then and went on with more enthusiasm, "But, seriously, if it's what you want . . . well, then, go for it!"

"Right," said Kath but Emmy's half-hearted reassurance was not the reaction she'd hoped for. She watched a snowflake splatter on the window, cling for a few seconds, then slither down the glass until it melted into a miniscule rivulet. Her Celtic-pale face, reflected in the glass, was tired-looking, the freckles faded by a winter spent mostly indoors and her red-brown hair darkened by lack of sunlight. She sighed inwardly. What she needed right now was full-hearted support from Emmy, not reservations.

"I know you've never liked Carl –" she began, trying not to sound piqued.

"No," said Emmy, interrupting quickly, "that's not true. It's just I . . . it's taking a while to get to know him properly. I hardly ever see him because he's away most weekends when I usually see you. I would like to get to know him better, Kath, I really would. I'd like us to be proper friends."

There was a lull in the conversation during which Kath reflected that she was being over-sensitive. It must be nerves.

Then Emmy said tentatively, "About Carl . . ."

"Yes?"

"I didn't think you had talked to him about marriage – even in the most general terms . . ."

"Well, no, I haven't – this is why I'm thinking of asking him. I told you before – every time I try to steer the conversation towards it, something happens. The moment never seems right somehow."

"I see," said Emmy slowly. "And have you considered that maybe he's not ready for it, Kath? You've been seeing him for what? Just over a year."

"Nearly a year and a half," said Kath defensively.

"Well, whatever. It's not a long time as relationships go."

"Are you trying to stop me from doing this?"

"No, not at all. I just want you to go cautiously. I don't want to see you get hurt."

"Emmy," said Kath, suppressing the irritation that welled up unexpectedly, "*I'm* ready for it. If I wait any longer it'll be too late."

"Too late for what?" said Emmy, turning her palms upwards to indicate her incomprehension. "You could always move in together like me and Steve. Marriage is only two signatures on a bit of paper. It doesn't *mean* anything."

"It does to me," retorted Kath quickly and then she added, her voice softening as she addressed the drinks card in the middle of the table, "It's not just about marriage, Emmy. I'm going to be forty this year. And you know I want to have children."

"Ah, I see!" Emmy leaned back in her chair. "And you're sure that Carl's the man you want to have them with?"

"Of course – I love him," said Kath, meeting Emmy's gaze, "and he loves me. I want us to live together, to be a family."

"Well, in that case, I guess you should ask him," said Emmy, nodding her head sagely. Then she added, more light-heartedly, "Hey, don't look so worried!"

"But what if he says no?"

"He won't."

"How can you be sure?" asked Kath, feeling a little confused. A minute ago Emmy had been worrying about her getting hurt.

"Because he'd be absolutely stark raving mad to say no, that's why! Look at you! You've got the skin of a twenty-year-old, gorgeous chestnut hair without a hint of grey – unlike me," she said ruefully as she pulled taut a lock of her shoulder-length, unnatural Cher-black hair while her eyes strained to examine it. "And, you've got the figure of a model. Not to mention a well-paid job as a management consultant. Who wouldn't want you as their wife?"

Kath smiled then, aware that her friend was trying to boost her confidence. "You know, you're a real honey. The very best friend."

Emmy grinned and said, "I know. What would you do without me?" Then she glanced at her watch and added, "God, would you look at the time! Steve'll be wondering where I am." She peered out the window. "I suppose I'm going to have to face the Arctic out there sometime."

"Sometimes this weather gets you down, doesn't it?"

"Oh, the snow can be a pain all right – but it's magical too, isn't it? When did we ever get a white Christmas in

Ireland? I think that's one of the best bits about living in Boston. A white Christmas. Most years anyway."

Emmy slipped into the knitted black cardigan she had draped on the back of her chair and twisted a long, thin red scarf round her neck three times, before tying it in a secure knot under her chin.

"There was one in Ballyfergus when I was a child," said Kath, remembering fondly. "The trees in the garden were laden with snow and Dad could hardly get the car out of the drive."

She watched while Emmy pulled a long, tangerine-coloured, padded duvet of a coat over her neat frame.

"May I ask you something, Emmy?"

"Go ahead."

"Doesn't it bother you *at all* that you're getting older, and Steve and you aren't making plans to have children?"

Emmy paused and screwed up her face so that her eyebrows nearly met in the middle. It was some moments before she answered.

"To tell you the God's honest truth, I just don't think about it. I'm too busy doing other things, I suppose. And you know, I can't see myself changing smelly nappies and cleaning up sick all day!"

Kath laughed. "I'm sure it's not like that all the time!"

"Well, rather you than me. Now, when are you planning on asking Carl?"

"Tonight. We're going out to Piattini's – that new Italian on Columbus Avenue."

"OK," said Emmy, doing up the last button on her coat. She leaned over, kissed Kath on the cheek and hugged her. "Good luck. Now phone me first thing in the morning with the good news."

Outside, Emmy waved goodbye, her mittened hand like a paw in the dim light. With the hood of the coat pulled over her head she looked like an over-sized version of one of the orange traffic cones that accompanied the progress of the "Big Dig" through the city. Conceived on a phenomenal scale to combat Boston's horrendous traffic problems, it was the biggest construction project ever undertaken in the United States. Kath, like the other city residents, had often bemoaned the impact of the works on her life. But now it was nearing completion and everyone was both relieved and proud of their rejuvenated city. The exuberant civic pride and general optimism of Bostonians was one of the reasons Kath loved it here.

That and her friends and, of course, Carl. She gathered her things together, paid the cheque and headed for the subway station. The snow was falling steadily and she worried briefly if the bad weather would scupper her plans for tonight; after finally working herself up to ask him the "big question," that would be a complete anti-climax.

Remembering that she wanted to have a full pamper session before going out, Kath quickened her pace to the station, swiped her travel pass in the turnstile and descended on the escalator. During the journey she changed subway lines, swept along at a brisk pace by the flow of commuter traffic, like a leaf carried on the surface of a fast-flowing river.

She thought about the conversation she'd had with Emmy and how, though they came from very different parts of Ireland – Emmy was from Waterford while Kath came from Northern Ireland – they both referred to it as "home". Kath was happy with her life in Boston but home for her would always be Highfield House, where she'd grown up and where her mother and father still lived. Was that a peculiarly Irish phenomenon, she wondered, or did all emigrants feel the same?

She was sure that she would feel differently about living here when she had children and was more fully integrated into a suburban community, where she imagined she and Carl would make their home together. Moving to Ireland, she assumed, was completely out of the question. Even if Kath wanted to, she guessed there was no way Carl would consider it. He thought that the USA was the best country in the world and, peculiarly, seemed to have no desire to see other parts of the planet.

Before she entered her own apartment in a well-maintained brownstone building, Kath knocked on the dark brown door across the hall. She glanced at her watch impatiently while she waited for Mrs Eberstark, a widow who lived alone, to open the door. Kath heard the telltale scraping sound as the little metal flap over the spy-hole was pulled back – she looked at the small glass orb and smiled – then the clink-clink of the safety chain being released and the sound of the lock sliding back.

"Kath, it is you," said Mrs Eberstark, in her thickly German-accented voice, as she pulled back the creaking door. "Come in, come in!" She gestured with her right hand for Kath to enter the apartment. Her gnarled left hand gripped the marble head of an elaborately carved ebony walking-stick without which she would have fallen over. Her white hair was swept up elegantly into a tight chignon, a hangover from her days as a ballet dancer. The latter part of her career, until her retirement nearly twenty years ago, had been spent in various administration roles with the Boston Ballet.

"Oh, I can't, Mrs Eberstark," said Kath without moving. "I'm going out tonight. But I just wanted to check that you were OK."

"Ah, you will be seeing Carl, I suppose?"

"Yes. Look, can I get you anything? Milk? Bread?" said Kath, anxious, in spite of her concern for Mrs Eberstark, not to become involved in a lengthy conversation.

"He's a fine man, Kath," said Mrs Eberstark. She had a soft spot for Carl on account of his Germanic ancestry.

"I know," replied Kath, smiling in spite of herself.

"But when is he going to make you . . . what do you call it?" She mumbled to herself for some moments and then said with flair, "A trustworthy woman!"

Kath smiled and supplied, "I think you mean 'an honest woman'."

"An honest woman, that's it!" said the old lady with a wicked grin and Kath blushed like a schoolgirl. "When is he going to make you an honest woman?"

"Well, if you don't need anything . . ." said Kath, choosing to ignore the question, and took a step backwards.

"I'm perfectly fine, Kath. My daughter called over today, on account of the snow," said the old lady, a smile still playing round her lips. "But thank you for your concern."

"I'll pop over at some point over the weekend then," said Kath.

"You're a good girl. Now go and have a lovely time with your beau!" she commanded.

Mrs Eberstark was an inspiration, thought Kath, as she let herself into her pristine apartment, checked the post and, the answering machine and turned up the heating. Mrs Eberstark lived a lively and independent life in spite of her age and lack of mobility – the years of dancing at professional level had taken their toll on her body. And she was a good friend to Kath, a surrogate grandmother for the ones she'd left behind in Ireland and who were now dead.

Kath put a Norah Jones CD on and turned the volume up loud. Then she chose her clothes for the evening with care – fine wool trousers, black kitten-heeled leather boots and a crimson cashmere sweater – and laid them carefully on the quilted bedspread. She ran a hot, deep bath, poured in her most expensive bath oil, a present from Carl, and poured herself a glass of Vouvray, her favourite white wine. After replacing the bottle in the fridge, she changed her mind, retrieved it and carried it into the bathroom where she set it, along with the glass, on the corner of the white bath.

She eased herself gratefully into the fragrant, rehabilitating water, her knees emerging wet and glistening above the surface like two small islands.

Kath tried to imagine sharing her home with Carl. She'd become used to living on her own. It would be strange lying in the bath like this, knowing that Carl was pottering around outside the bathroom door. Strange but nice.

She knew very well why she was nervous about asking Carl to marry her. It wasn't that she doubted his answer, rather it was the very act of asking him that caused her disquiet. For Kath had been raised to believe that, when it came to men, a girl should retain an air of mystery and aloofness. Asking a man outright to marry you was brazen – it smacked of desperation. At least that's what her mother would have said. But, Kath reminded herself, her mother's views were moulded by the 1950s Ireland she'd grown up in. This was twenty-first century Boston and a very different place from the insular, backward-looking island her mother had known as a young woman. Nowadays women went after what they wanted as surely as men did. The nagging doubts that had held her in check until now, Kath reminded herself, were nothing more than antiquated notions from a different world and time. And she wasn't going to let her chance of happiness slip by because of them.

Emmy's less than enthusiastic support of her plan was harder to disregard. But it was only natural – she didn't want to see her dearest friend hurt. But Emmy didn't know Carl the way Kath did. She didn't know how much he adored her. She was the centre of his world, he said, and Kath knew it to be true. The only reason Carl hadn't asked her to marry him, she was certain, was that he had no biological clock ticking. He probably hadn't even thought about having children. Men simply weren't as preoccupied with these things as women.

Kath had drunk the first glass of wine more quickly than usual and now she poured herself another. She was going to need a little bit of Dutch courage. For tonight was going to be the most important night of her life.

* * *

"That's it for tonight, guys," said Carl Scholtz, throwing his Montblanc pen onto the black-and-white architectural plans on the conference table, where it landed with a slap. "I think we've done as much as we can on this for now."

He leaned back in his chair and interlocked his fingers in his thick blond hair. He felt the shirt strain across his back and, glancing down, noticed a little fold of flesh protruding slightly over the belt that encircled his slim waist. Where the hell did that come from? Carl prided himself on keeping in shape – he'd have to increase his visits to the gym. Quickly he sucked his stomach in, unfolded his hands and sat up erect in the chair. The faces round the table were tired and Carl glanced at his watch. It was after six o'clock on a Friday evening.

"I know it's been a tough week for you all," he said. "When a client changes the brief this late in a project – well, it can be infuriating. But don't forget that they are always number one. The customer gets what they want no matter how many times we have to rework the plans. That's what the reputation of this firm is built on. That and innovative design. Do you agree?"

There were weary murmurs of assent round the table.

"Good. Now, team, I want you all to go home and have a great weekend and forget all about this. You'd be surprised how great your subconscious mind is at solving problems. You just need to give it the space and time to get on with the job."

He stood up. Papers were stuffed into folders, and chairs scraped the parquet floor as people stood up from the table.

"And one last thing," said Carl.

All movement halted and a hush descended once more.

"You're doing a great job, every one of you. Thanks. I really appreciate it."

With these few words of encouragement he could see the spirits of the dejected team rise. He wasn't part-owner of Boston's biggest and best architectural practice because of his technical skills. At this level it was all about motivating other talented people to do the work for you, something at which Carl excelled.

Some of these youngsters had proven themselves to be

better architects than he. Carl was clever enough to recognise this and harness their talent to his advantage – and theirs. He could never be accused of exploiting anyone – few chose to leave the practice, because there was nowhere better to go. And those who felt they were ready to set up on their own, Carl encouraged and supported. They posed no threat to the predominant position of Scholtz & Vives Architects. The name was a misnomer really – at fifty-eight years old, Joe Vives was semi-retired to a beach-front in the Cape where he spent most of his time fishing. The firm was, in reality, entirely under the day-to-day control of Carl.

Back in his office, after everyone had gone, Carl swivelled round in his leather chair and stared at the city lights below and the gently curving black outline of the semi-frozen Charles River. Though he could have stayed in the more affordable former office premises on Commonwealth, relocating to this office suite in the Prudential Tower had been a shrewd decision. It conveyed the impression that this firm was going places – a force to be reckoned with. And that confidence had been translated into impressive business results. Who would have thought that the forty-five-year-old son of a factory worker from Wisconsin would have made it this far?

Pulling himself together, Carl realised that he couldn't put off making the phone call any longer. He checked the time and frowned – he was supposed to be meeting Kath in less than two hours. Just enough time to do what he had to, get home, changed and out again. He picked up the handset, held it against his chest for some moments while he composed himself, then speed-dialled.

"Hi, it's me," he said cheerfully into the phone. "How are you? And the girls?"

He listened for a while and then said, "Listen, honey, something's come up." A pause, then he added, "I know. I know. You think I like it? There's nothing I can do about it. We've got to get these plans right for Monday or we'll lose the job. I'll be working here till the small hours." Another pause, then he said with feeling, "Tell me about it, Lynda! But the buck stops with me and that's the way it is. Listen, I'll be down tomorrow just as soon as I can." He listened for some seconds more, then said, a little calmer now, "Yes. Yes. Don't worry. I'll be there in plenty of time for dinner at the Rawsons'. I'll see you then. Give my love to the girls. Love you. Bye."

Carl put the phone down, his mood heavy now with guilt. His mother had raised him never to tell lies, but that was all he seemed to do these days. But sometimes a white lie was better than the truth, wasn't it? If he told the truth people would get hurt, hearts would be broken. The only person suffering at the moment was himself. The rest of them were blissfully unaware and therefore happy. He was, in reality, protecting them from hurt so painful and deep they had no idea what it could do to you. But he did.

In the early days perhaps he should have walked away, before things had become so complicated. But now he was in too deep – it was too late to wish for what might have been. For how could he stop seeing Kath? He loved her. But he also loved his kids, and he cared for Lynda too. Albeit very different types of love – but each as compelling as the others.

"There's no reason things can't go on like this forever, is there?" he asked himself out loud, but he was shaking his head as he said it, an instinctive answer to his own question.

"Did you want something, Carl?" said a high-pitched

female voice and Carl nearly jumped two feet in the air.

"Mandy!" he exclaimed and looked up sharply.

The short, round frame of Mandy Cruz, his secretary-cum-personal-assistant, had appeared in the doorway of the office – he must have left it ajar. She was staring at him, her black eyes like shiny beads in her moonlike face. Her podgy feet were jammed into smart black high heels, so tight her feet must have ached.

"What are you still doing here?" he asked. "Go on home to the kids, Mandy."

"They're with their father tonight. He's taking them to the movies with Charlene."

The intonation with which Mandy delivered this sentence conveyed everything she felt about her husband and his new girlfriend, for whom he'd left her. She hated them both.

"That's nice," said Carl.

"Hmm," said Mandy, and she marched right up to the desk. "I'm sure you don't want to hear this . . ."

She was right. He didn't.

". . . but you should see the state of her. The short skirts, the low-cut tops. And," she added triumphantly, "she smokes! I don't like her around my kids. She's a bad influence."

Mandy had been with him too long, Carl decided – nearly two years. The success of his elaborate deception depended on the effectiveness of the barricade he had erected between work and his private life. If you kept a secretary like Mandy around too long she became familiar – she got to know too much about you. And she felt the need to tell you more than you wished to know about her.

But Mandy was a good, reliable worker and she desperately needed her job. Still, Carl made a mental note that he'd have to do something – perhaps he could line her up with alternative work somewhere else. He'd have to be careful how he handled it, though – he didn't want her causing trouble.

"He didn't make his last maintenance payment, you know. Spending all his money on that – that –" stumbled Mandy – she only just managed to restrain herself from uttering a profanity and finished the sentence with, "woman."

Look what telling the truth had done to the Cruz family, thought Carl. In its wake the truth had left a broken home, a bitter, angry wife and three fine-looking boys – Mandy kept a picture of them on her desk – turned overnight into single-parent latchkey kids.

"Anything exciting planned for the weekend, then?" said Mandy, suddenly cheerful, startling Carl out of his reverie.

He stood up, pulled the suit jacket off the chair and shrugged it on, both arms in the sleeves at the same time.

"Oh . . . not much. Just a quiet weekend hanging out with the kids. Dinner at a neighbour's on Saturday night. The usual."

"Hmm," said Mandy nodding slowly, without taking her eyes off him. Then she threw a glance in the direction of the window. "It's been snowing again. You'd better get on the road if you're gonna make it home tonight. You've a long drive ahead of you."

Carl put his hands in his pants pockets and said, "Yes, you're right, Mandy. Now you get off home too, will you? And have a great weekend."

* * *

Outside, the snow was still falling softly and relentlessly. On the sidewalk it was as if someone had unfurled an oversized roll of cotton wool along its length. The snow came over the top of Carl's Italian-tooled shoes and clung to the hem of his fine wool pants legs. He cursed himself for not bringing boots to work this morning, but there was nothing to be done about it now. He pulled the collar of his cashmere coat round his neck, bent his head and walked briskly.

It took only a few minutes to reach the condominium on quiet, tree-lined St Botolph Street, one of the most sought-after locations in Back Bay. Even then the cold had penetrated Carl's thick coat and he could hardly feel his feet. He fumbled for the key, inserted it in the brass lock and let himself into the classic brownstone building where he lived on the second floor. Carl's immediate neighbours were, like himself, businessmen who commuted to the suburbs at the weekends. He never saw them – an arrangement that suited him perfectly.

Inside the high-ceilinged apartment, there were fresh flowers on the mahogany table in the hall and, in the bedroom, five crisply laundered white shirts on the king-sized bed – evidence that the housekeeper had been. At once Carl felt the tensions of the day dissipate. All the rooms were tastefully decorated in shades of coffee and cream with subtle touches of gold and burgundy in the curtains, sofas and cushions. Lynda, with her keen eye for these things, had overseen the entire décor and no expense had been spared.

At the outset, the plan had been for Lynda and the kids to come to the city for the occasional weekend and during the holidays, when Carl couldn't always take time off work. But, over time, those visits had become less frequent as the impracticalities of driving two under-fives all the way from the Berkshires became all too apparent.

Lynda's life now revolved around the small, friendly community in Williamstown where they'd bought a family home. This was where horse-loving Lynda had grown up, where her parents still lived and where she insisted she wanted to raise her family. She had not set foot in this apartment for nine months. They'd not needed the three bedrooms after all.

Carl took a long hot shower, dried himself with a cream towel and wrapped it round his waist. He went into the master bedroom, selected a shirt, a round-necked navy cashmere jumper and slacks from the wardrobe. He dressed quickly, grabbed a beer from the fridge in the kitchen and went through to the study where he checked his personal emails. Then he stuffed his sodden shoes with scrunched-up newspaper and left them to dry out, propped up either side of the cast-iron radiator in the kitchen.

At eight fifteen, he called a cab, donned his coat and rode the short distance to the restaurant where he'd arranged to meet Kath.

In the cab, he remembered a newspaper article he'd read about the late President of France. For decades he'd kept the existence of his mistress and their love-child a secret from the nation and, Carl assumed, his other, legitimate family. Such arrangements, it seemed, were not unusual nor were they reviled in France. But here in the USA, Carl knew that what he was doing would attract nothing but hatred and condemnation.

And there was one vital distinction between the situations of Mitterand and Carl – a fact not lost on Carl: Kath O'Connor had absolutely no idea that she was his mistress.   THE END.

In conversation
with Erin Kaye

1. Have you always written or is it a new discovery?

I have always loved books and read avidly as a child. I read Dicken's **Great Expectations** when I was in Primary 6 (my teacher didn't believe me!) and went on to take an A-level in English literature. My interest in books stems from a desire to understand people. But, school work aside, I wrote next to no fiction until I was nearly thirty, just before packing in my banking job in 1997. Before then I had no burning desire to write – my motivation was find a different way of living and a job where I was the boss and could dictate my own working hours. And, while there is of course pressure to meet deadlines, this has come true.

2. You gave up your corporate job to become a writer – that must have been an exciting and scary step! What led you to make that decision?

With hindsight, it was extremely foolhardy to give up a well-paid and secure career to embark upon something entirely new, with absolutely no experience and such little chance of success: less than two percent of "slush-pile" novels get published. And any good agent will tell a novice writer not to give up the day job!

But I'd read somewhere that to make a success of something you have to burn all your bridges. In other words, you have to throw yourself wholeheartedly into a new venture without any safety nets (in my case, my comfortable well-paid job). I believe that had I had continued working I would not have pursued my objective with the tenacity and single-mindedness that ultimately led to getting published. It was a gamble however.

3. Tell us about your writing process: where do you write? When? Are you a planner or "ride-the-wave" writer?

I write directly onto my Dell computer (using Microsoft Word) in my study at home when the kids are at school. I take the summer and Easter and Christmas holidays off. Once I've a head of steam going and a deadline to meet, I'll work evenings and weekends over three or four months, as well as through half-term breaks when my husband Mervyn sometimes takes the kids away. These short, intense sessions over four or five days are very productive. Writing from home requires enormous discipline as the distractions are absolutely endless. I'd love a writer's retreat away from the house!

I'm definitely a planner and write detailed chapter by chapter synopses of around 15,000-20,000 words for every novel. I know what's going to happen and when, but don't always stick to it rigidly as the creative process can sometimes lead you elsewhere. But it does provide the basic structure.

4. *Since your first novel* Mothers and Daughters *was published in 2003 has your life changed much?*

My life changed dramatically in late 1997 when I decided to give up my banking career and try my hand at writing. I wrote my first novel and then fell pregnant in the autumn of 1998. By the time **Mothers and Daughters** was published I had delivered the draft for my second novel, **Choices**, and had two children, then aged 4 and 1. So by then I was used to combining writing and family life. It's easier now the children are both at school and I have more time to write – looking back I don't know how I did it when they were babies! But you do what you have to and I was highly motivated. I enjoy the publicity side of things and love doing radio and television. I'm less comfortably facing a live audience and find that nerve-wracking.

5. *Do you have a favourite character in* My Husband's Lover?

I like Tony a lot. He's a good man trying to make amends for a mistake made in his youth and I have a lot of sympathy for him. He adores his children and his wife, Karen, and is blind to the physical imperfections that absorb so much of his wife's thoughts and energy. And he's handsome, cheerful and optimistic. The perfect man really!

6. Family dynamics play a central part in your writing. Why is this, do you think?

Ultimately it is the relationships with those nearest and dearest that influence us from the day we are born. And we are all moulded by our childhood and upbringing. If we don't get on with a colleague at work, we don't have to be their friend. If a friend (or lover) lets us down we can finish the relationship. But we're all stuck with family and, whatever the conflicts within that unit, we can't get away from them – whether we try to ignore them, deny them or face up to them. And that is what makes family dynamics so interesting.

7. What character & scene was most difficult to write?

I found writing/creating Paul's character the hardest challenge. While he's a bit of an annoying idiot (with his Latin phrases and intellectual snobbery), he has some redeeming characteristics and I didn't want the reader to hate him completely. Generally, I find creating male characters harder than female ones as I don't have the same insight into how they think.

Understanding Karen's obsession with her body image – what woman doesn't have issues with her appearance? – and taking it that step further to surgery was easier. But I did find writing the scenes where she has her surgery hard, as I had to do an awful lot of research into the cosmetic surgery industry (even going so far as to pose as a potential customer). The procedure she undergoes is a pretty gruesome operation and some people are left with horrific scars, infections and ongoing problems. It made me feel a bit queasy and left me with a great deal of compassion for women who feel they have no option but to go down this route.

8. Your novels explore the idea of false appearances – the pressure to keep up an image and the idea of deception. Why does this intrigue you?

I had to think long and hard about this question and the answer, when it came, surprised me. I think it's because putting on a brave face is part of the Northern Ireland psyche, and was especially so during the era of the Troubles when I grew up. People, especially those with young children, tried to carry on a normal life in the face of intimidation and fear. It is not, after all, normal for fully-armed soldiers to patrol your street, to live under the constant threat of being bombed, or for society to grind to a complete cessation as it did for two weeks in 1974 during the Ulster Worker's Strike, when the government lost complete control of this section of the realm. Seen through the eyes of a child, I guess I saw adults trying to maintain the deception that life was normal when clearly it wasn't.

9. Who are your favourite authors and favourite novels?

I read and enjoy a wide variety of novels from the classics to crime to romance. I'll read pretty much anything, especially if it comes with a high personal recommendation (e.g. *In the Company of the Courtesan* by Sarah Dunant, or *We Need to Talk About Kevin* by Lionel Shriver, both of which were fantastic). I don't get horror or fantasy at all and never read it. If I'm looking for escapism, I enjoy a good fast-paced crime novel from someone like Harlen Coben or Tess Gerritsen. Of the Irish novels I've read over the past few years, *Star of the Sea* by Joseph O'Connor is one of my favourites.

Here are some of my favourite books:
The Mayor of Casterbridge by Thomas Hardy
The Poisonwood Bible by Barbara Kingsolver
The Blind Assassin by Margaret Atwood
Laura Blundy by Julie Myerson

I guess the thread that connects these books is that they all contain acute, painful portraits of the human condition. And, of course, the writing is beautiful. I admire and envy the talent of great writers.

10. Tell us a bit about your next book – have you started writing it yet?

I'm not quite there yet with the title, but I have written the synopsis and first eight pages! It's set in Ballyfergus and it's about the relationship between four women closely bound by a long friendship and common interests. It follows their lives over a year when their friendship is stretched to breaking point and each must overcome great obstacles to find personal happiness and fulfilment. It's a slight departure for me as I usually write about families, but the relationship between the characters is familial in the sense that they form part of the fabric of each other's lives and are intrinsically bound to each other.